STORIES T
ALL THE WAYS

"Double Solitaire" by Joyce Carol Oates tells of two sisters who are betrayed by the same man.

"Traveling to Pridesup" by Joy Williams portrays four very elderly and rich sisters who suddenly find themselves with a baby.

"Mother Love" by Candace Flynt, in the opening episode of her latest novel, shows three sisters who get together to tell "mother stories" about their dazzling and infuriating mother.

"Happy" by Ann Beattie depicts a contemporary marriage and the separation of two sisters by more than distance.

"Sisters" by Mary Robison reveals the emotional estrangement of two sisters, one of whom has chosen to become a nun.

From Sarah Orne Jewett writing in 1877 to Alice Walker writing today, these are twenty stories that render the power and complexity of the bond between sisters.

SUSAN CAHILL has edited a number of anthologies, including the three volumes of *Women & Fiction* and *Mothers: Memories, Dreams, & Reflections by Literary Daughters* (all available in Mentor editions). She is the author of the novel *Earth Angels* and co-author (with Thomas Cahill) of *A Literary Guide to Ireland* and *A Literary Calendar*, which appears yearly.

AMONG SISTERS

Short Stories by Women Writers

EDITED BY
Susan Cahill

A MENTOR BOOK
NEW AMERICAN LIBRARY
A DIVISION OF PENGUIN BOOKS USA INC., NEW YORK
PUBLISHED IN CANADA BY
PENGUIN BOOKS CANADA LIMITED, MARKHAM, ONTARIO

PUBLISHER'S NOTE

These stories are works of fiction. Names, characters, places, and incidents either are the product of the author's imagination or are used fictitiously, and any resemblance to actual persons, living or dead, events, or locales is entirely coincidental.

NAL BOOKS ARE AVAILABLE AT QUANTITY DISCOUNTS
WHEN USED TO PROMOTE PRODUCTS OR SERVICES.
FOR INFORMATION PLEASE WRITE TO PREMIUM MARKETING DIVISION,
NEW AMERICAN LIBRARY, 1633 BROADWAY,
NEW YORK, NEW YORK 10019.

ACKNOWLEDGMENTS

"A Queer Heart" by Elizabeth Bowen. Reprinted from *The Collected Stories of Elizabeth Bowen* by permission of Alfred A. Knopf, Inc. Copyright © 1941 & renewed 1969 by Elizabeth Bowen.

"Reverdy" from *The Collected Short Stories of Jessamyn West,* copyright © 1946 by Jessamyn West, renewed 1986 by Harry Maxwell McPherson, reprinted by permission of Harcourt Brace Jovanovich, Inc.

"In the Zoo" from *Bad Characters* by Jean Stafford. Copyright © 1946, 1953, 1954, 1956, 1957, 1964 by Jean Stafford. Reprinted by permission of Farrar, Straus and Giroux, Inc.

"The Springs of Affection" by Maeve Brennan, which first appeared in *The New Yorker,* is reprinted by permission of Charles Scribner's Sons from *Christmas Eve,* copyright © 1974 by Maeve Brennan.

"Like That" from *The Mortgaged Heart* by Carson McCullers. Copyright © 1940, 1941, 1942, 1945, 1948, 1949, 1953, 1956, 1959, 1963, 1967, 1971 by Floria V. Lasky, Executrix of the Estate of Carson McCullers. Reprinted by permission of Houghton Mifflin Company.

"La Vie Bohème" from *The Soft Voice of the Serpent* by Nadine Gordimer. Reprinted by permission of Russell & Volkening as agent for the author. Copyright © 1952 by Nadine Gordimer, renewed 1980 by Nadine Gordimer.

"Dingle the Fool" by Elizabeth Jolley from *Woman in a Lampshade.* Reprinted by permission of Penguin Books Australia Ltd.

(*The following page constitutes an extension of the copyright page.*)

Library of Congress Catalog Card Number: 89-60427

MENTOR TRADEMARK REG. U.S. PAT. OFF. AND FOREIGN COUNTRIES
REGISTERED TRADEMARK—MARCA REGISTRADA
HECHO EN DRESDEN, TN, U.S.A.

SIGNET, SIGNET CLASSIC, MENTOR, ONYX, PLUME, MERIDIAN
and NAL BOOKS are published *in the United States* by
New American Library, a division of Penguin Books USA Inc.,
1633 Broadway, New York, New York 10019,
in Canada by Penguin Books Canada Limited,
2801 John Street, Markham, Ontario L3R 1B4

First Printing, October, 1989

1 2 3 4 5 6 7 8 9

PRINTED IN THE UNITED STATES OF AMERICA

In memory of
Miriam Luisi Pollock

CONTENTS

INTRODUCTION

The sibling bond between sisters has always been a compelling theme in the fiction of women writers in America and England and Ireland. The many stories and novels in which pairs of sisters figure prominently reflect the experience of their writers' lives. The biographical landscape of literary women is dense with sisterhood: consider the families of Jane Austen, the Brontës, Virginia Woolf, Katherine Mansfield, Ivy Compton Burnett, Barbara Pym, Margaret Drabble, Emily Dickinson, Louisa May Alcott, M.F.K. Fisher, Alice Walker.

All these writers have worked the relationship between sisters into their long and short fiction in both major and minor keys. The ambiguity of that bonding is caught in an almost hypnotic clarity in the short stories I have chosen to include in this collection. There are stories of sisters in opposition and sisters whose solidarity, especially in adversity, is as absolute as death.

Any reader who knows the experience of growing up under the spell of her sister or sisters will recognize the familiar motifs of this relationship as re-created in the stories that follow: the affection, the taking-for-granted, the jealousy, the rivalry for a parent's (usually a father's) attention and later on for a lover's or husband's, and always the sense that one's sister is a part of one's essential self, an eternal presence of one's heart and soul and memory.

Memory in the stories that follow is as dominant and significant as character itself. In Alice Munro's superb story, "The Progress of Love," the core of feeling is the two sisters' remembering their mother's attempted suicide in completely opposite keys. One woman remembers her mother's attempt as serious and utterly desperate; she lives her own adult life in reaction to her memory of her mother's desperation. But her sister remembers the attempt as only a joke her mother was playing on her father. Her adult life has little in common with her sister's, just as their memories of this "fact" of their mother's attempted suicide do not converge.

Which sister's memory flows according to the truth of their mother's life? What was the truth of their mother's life? Neither sister can know it in its complexity and mystery. Candace Flynt, in the following episode from *Mother Love*, looks at a mother's life from the perspectives of three sisters and creates three separate but intermingling versions of one woman, three different life stories as reflections of the truth of this woman's identity and the creative and destructive force of her identity in the lives of her three daughters.

Do all sisters grow up possessed by conflicting memories of their common parents?

The memory of parents, both father and mother, is a theme of much of the literature about sisters. The widely anthologized "Daughters of the Late Colonel" by Katherine Mansfield has at its center a dead father who is still in control of his two living but paralyzed daughters. Other stories included here (by Elizabeth Bowen, Elizabeth Jolley, Joy Williams, Joyce Carol Oates, and Lee Smith) re-create old rivalries and antipathies and power struggles between two sisters (and in the splendid "Springs of Affection" by Maeve Brennan between a sister and her sister-in-law), currents of pain and loss and bitterness that can be so dominant a force in the experience of growing up as somebody's sister.

But in the stories that follow, a sister's loving memory of another sister is often as haunting a theme as dissonance. Ann Beattie's story "Happy" achieves a quick and powerful thud of feeling in one sister's sudden memory of her sister who now lives faraway, and of her own sudden recognition of having failed her distant sister when they lived together in their youth, in their parents' home.

The memory of one's sister as beloved, as a kind of muse, in the mythical days of childhood animates the stories of Jessamyn West, Nadine Gordimer, Carson McCullers, and Mary Morris. Such love suffuses the protectiveness and solidarity between sisters when the adult life of one sister turns ugly or dangerous or difficult. Nadine Gordimer and Alice Walker and Merrill Joan Gerber are contemporary voices on this theme. For each writer the sister's husband is seen as interloper, inflicting pain and sorrow.

Both Sarah Orne Jewett and Mary Wilkins Freeman tell stories about two sisters who spend their adult lives single and together. They protect each other from a common interloper who is not in their cases a husband but the lack of one: the economic security that was assumed to come with marriage in the nineteenth century meant its opposite for unmarried ladies. Both Jewett and Freeman see the poverty that diminishes the sisters in their stories as the dreary consequence of a patriarchal economy and culture. For all its cruelty and power, however, this system does not destroy the sisters in either story. Each one ends with the triumph, sounded in modest New England tones, of course, of sisterly wit and affection.

The shaping power of memory, then, and the deep springs of affection and disaffection—both thematic currents move through this collection to make its individual stories palpable incarnations of a physical and spiritual human bond, wrought by women writers of superb craft and a penetrating, luminous vision.

SARAH ORNE JEWETT was born in South Berwick, Maine—"Deephaven" in her stories—in 1849. Her father was a distinguished physician who taught obstetrics at Bowdoin College. She got her education in his library (she favored Carlyle, Lowell, and Matthew Arnold) and even more from the long rides she took with him as he made his rounds in the country districts around South Berwick. She came to know intimately the old people who were his patients, especially the aging spinsters and widows depicted in the story that follows, "The Town Poor."

Her first volume of short stories, *Deephaven* (1877), which included "The Town Poor," was an immediate success, winning her entrée to the "Boston circle" of Howells, Whittier, Lowell, and Aldrich. Her stories, those close, poetic studies of plain people (from Flaubert, she said, she learned an "almost French clarity and precision"), have been described as the best work of their sort to come out of New England. William James compared their effect to "that incommunicable cleanness of the salt air when one first leaves town." Lowell compared her to Theocritus, Kipling praised her grasp and vigor, Henry James admired her greatly. She has been criticized for being too genteel, for not writing about sex, for not feeling passion for a man in her private life. But her place in the main line of American literature is secure. F. O. Matthiessen ranks Miss Jewett with Emily Dickinson as the two foremost women writers of America. Willa Cather, who was her friend and student of a sort (she followed Jewett's advice to relinquish "the masquerade" of her male narrator and instead write from a female point of view), wrote the introduction to *The Country of the Pointed Firs* (1896), the collection of Jewett's best stories. Cather rated that volume, along with *The Scarlet Letter* and *Huckleberry Finn*, as one of the three enduring masterpieces of American literature. She wrote that the stories "melt into the land and the life of the land until they are not stories at all, but life itself."

The Town Poor

by
Sarah Orne Jewett

Mrs. William Trimble and Miss Rebecca Wright were driving along Hampden east road, one afternoon in early spring. Their progress was slow. Mrs. Trimble's sorrel horse was old and stiff, and the wheels were clogged by clay mud. The frost was not yet out of the ground, although the snow was nearly gone, except in a few places on the north side of the woods, or where it had drifted all winter against a length of fence.

"There must be a good deal o' snow to the nor'ard of us yet," said weatherwise Mrs. Trimble. "I feel it in the air; 'tis more than the ground damp. We ain't goin' to have real nice weather till the up-country snow's all gone."

"I heard say yesterday that there was good sleddin' yet, all up through Parsley," responded Miss Wright. "I shouldn't like to live up in them northern places. My cousin Ellen's husband was a Parsley man, an' he was obliged, as you may have heard, to go up north to his father's second wife's funeral; got back day before yesterday. 'Twas about twenty-one miles, an' they started on wheels; but when they'd gone nine or ten miles, they found 'twas no sort o' use, an' left their wagon an' took a sleigh. The man that owned it charged 'em four an' six, too. I shouldn't have thought he would; they told him they was goin' to a funeral; an' they had their own buffaloes an' everything."

"Well, I expect it's a good deal harder scratchin', up that way; they have to git money where they can; the farms is very poor as you go north," suggested Mrs. Trimble kindly. " 'Tain't none too rich a country where we be, but I've always been grateful I wa'n't born up to Parsley."

The old horse plodded along, and the sun, coming out from the heavy spring clouds, sent a sudden shine of light along the muddy road. Sister Wright drew her large veil forward over the high rim of her bonnet. She was not used to driving, or to being much in the open air; but Mrs. Trimble was an active business woman, and looked after her own affairs herself, in all weathers. The late Mr. Trimble had left her a good farm, but not much ready money, and it was often said that she was better off in the end than if he had lived. She regretted his loss deeply, however; it was impossible for her to speak of him, even with intimate friends, without emotion, and nobody had ever hinted that this emotion was insincere. She was most warmhearted and generous, and in her limited way played the part of Lady Bountiful in the town of Hampden.

"Why, there's where the Bray girls lives, ain't it?" she exclaimed, as, beyond a thicket of witch hazel and scrub oak, they came in sight of a weather-beaten, solitary farmhouse. The barn was too far away for thrift or comfort, and they could see long lines of light through the shrunken boards as they came nearer. The fields looked both stony and sodden. Somehow, even Parsley itself could be hardly more forlorn.

"Yes'm," said Miss Wright, "that's where they live now, poor things. I know the place, though I ain't been up here for years. You don't suppose, Mis' Trimble—I ain't seen the girls out to meetin' all winter. I've re'lly been covetin' "—

"Why, yes, Rebecca, of course we could stop," answered Mrs. Trimble heartily. "The exercises was over earlier'n I expected, an' you're goin' to remain over night long o' me, you know. There won't be no tea till we git there, so we can't be late. I'm in the habit o' sendin' a basket to the Bray girls when any o' our folks is comin' this way, but I ain't been to see 'em since they moved up here. Why, it must be a good deal over a year ago. I know 'twas in the late winter they had to make the move. 'Twas cruel hard, I must say, an' if I hadn't been down with my pleurisy fever I'd have stirred round an' done somethin' about it. There was a good deal o' sickness at the time, an' —well, 'twas kind o' rushed through, breakin' of 'em up, an' lots o' folks blamed the selec'*men;* but when 'twas done, 'twas done, an' nobody took hold to undo it. Ann an' Mandy looked same's ever when they come to meetin', 'long in the summer, —kind o' wishful, perhaps. They've always sent me word they was gittin' on pretty comfortable."

"That would be their way," said Rebecca Wright. "They never was any hand to complain, though Mandy's less cheerful than Ann. If Mandy'd been spared such poor eyesight, an' Ann hadn't got her lame wrist that wa'n't set right, they'd kep' off the town fast enough. They both shed tears when they talked to me about havin' to break up, when I went to see 'em before I went over to brother Asa's. You see we was brought up neighbors an' went to school together, the Brays an' me. 'Twas a special Providence brought us home this road, I've been so covetin' a chance to git to see 'em. My lameness hampers me."

"I'm glad we come this way, myself," said Mrs. Trimble.

"I'd like to see just how they fare," Miss Rebecca Wright continued. "They give their consent to goin' on the town because they knew they'd got to be dependent, an' so they felt 'twould come easier for all than for a few to help 'em. They acted real dignified an' right-minded, contrary to what most do in such cases, but they was dreadful anxious to see who would bid 'em off, town-meeting day; they did so hope 'twould be somebody right in the village. I just sat down an' cried good when I found Abel Janes's folks had got hold of 'em. They always had the name of bein' slack an' poor spirited, an' they did it just for what they got out o' the town. The selectmen this last year ain't what we have had. I hope they've been considerate about the Bray girls."

"I should have be'n more considerate about fetchin' of you up," apologized Mrs. Trimble. "I've got my horse, an' you're lame footed; 'tis too far for you to come. But time does slip away with busy folks, an' I forgit a good deal I ought to remember."

"There's nobody more considerate than you be," protested Miss Rebecca Wright.

Mrs. Trimble made no answer, but took out her whip and gently touched the sorrel horse, who walked considerably faster, but did not think it worth while to trot. It was a long, roundabout way to the house, farther down the road and up a lane.

"I never had any opinion of the Bray girls' father, leavin' 'em as he did," said Mrs. Trimble.

"He was much praised in his time, though there was always some said his early life hadn't been up to the mark," explained her companion. "He was a great favorite of our then preacher, the Reverend Daniel Longbrother. They did a good deal for the parish, but they did it their own way. Deacon Bray was one that did his part in the repairs without urging. You know 'twas in his time the first repairs was made, when they got out the old soundin' board an' them handsome square pews. It cost an awful sight o' money, too. They hadn't done payin' up that debt when they set to to alter it again an' git the walls frescoed. My grandmother was one that always spoke her mind right out, an' she was dreadful opposed to breakin' up the square pews where she'd always set. They was countin' up what 'twould cost in parish meetin', an' she riz right up an' said 'twouldn't cost nothin' to let 'em stay, an' there wa'n't a house carpenter left in the parish that could do such nice work, an' time would come when the great-grandchildren would give their eyeteeth to have the old meetin' house look just as it did then. But haul the inside to pieces they would and did."

"There come to be a real fight over it, didn't there?" agreed Mrs. Trimble soothingly. "Well, 'twa'n't good taste. I remember the old house well. I come here as a child to visit a cousin o' mother's, an' Mr. Trimble's folks was neighbors, an' we was drawed to each other then, young's we was. Mr. Trimble spoke of it many's the time,—the first time he ever see me, in a leghorn hat with a feather; 'twas one that mother had, an' pressed over."

"When I think of them old sermons that used to be preached in that old meetin' house of all, I'm glad it's altered over, so's not to remind folks," said Miss Rebecca Wright, after a suitable pause. "Them old brimstone discourses, you know, Mis' Trimble. Preachers is far more reasonable, nowadays. Why, I set an' thought, last Sabbath, as I listened, that if old Mr. Longbrother an' Deacon Bray could hear the difference they'd crack the ground over 'em like pole beans, an' come right up 'longside their headstones."

Mrs. Trimble laughed heartily, and shook the reins three or four times by way of emphasis. "There's no gitting round you," she said, much pleased. "I should think Deacon Bray would want to rise, anyway, if 'twas so he could, an' knew how his poor girls was farin'. A man ought to provide for his folks he's got to leave behind him, specially if they're women. To be sure, they had their little home; but we've seen how, with all their industrious ways, they hadn't means to keep it.

I s'pose he thought he'd got time enough to lay by, when he give so generous in collections; but he didn't lay by, an' there they be. He might have took lessons from the squirrels; even them little wild creatur's makes them their winter hoards, an' men folks ought to know enough if squirrels does. 'Be just before you are generous'; that's what was always set for the B's in the copybooks, when I was to school, and it often runs through my mind."

" 'As for man, his days are as grass,'—that was for A; the two go well together," added Miss Rebecca Wright soberly. "My good gracious, ain't this a starved-lookin' place? It makes me ache to think them nice Bray girls has to brook it here."

The sorrel horse, though somewhat puzzled by an unexpected deviation from his homeward way, willingly came to a stand by the gnawed corner of the dooryard fence, which evidently served as hitching place. Two or three ragged old hens were picking about the yard, and at last a face appeared at the kitchen window, tied up in a handkerchief, as if it were a case of toothache. By the time our friends reached the side door next this window, Mrs. Janes came disconsolately to open it for them, shutting it again as soon as possible, though the air felt more chilly inside the house.

"Take seats," said Mrs. Janes briefly. "You'll have to see me just as I be. I have been suffering these four days with the ague, and everything to do. Mr. Janes is to court, on the jury. 'Twas inconvenient to spare him. I should be pleased to have you lay off your things."

Comfortable Mrs. Trimble looked about the cheerless kitchen, and could not think of anything to say; so she smiled blandly and shook her head in answer to the invitation. "We'll just set a few minutes with you, to pass the time o' day, an' then we must go in an' have a word with the Miss Brays, bein' old acquaintance. It ain't been so we could git to call on 'em before. I don't know's you're acquainted with Miss R'becca Wright. She's been out of town a good deal."

"I heard she was stopping over to Plainfields with her brother's folks," replied Mrs. Janes, rocking herself with irregular motion, as she sat close to the stove. "Got back some time in the fall, I believe?"

"Yes'm," said Miss Rebecca, with an undue sense of guilt and conviction. "We've been to the installation over to the

East Parish, an' thought we'd stop in; we took this road home to see if 'twas any better. How is the Miss Brays gittin' on?"

"They're well's common," answered Mrs. Janes grudgingly. "I was put out with Mr. Janes for fetchin' of 'em here, with all I've got to do, an' I own I was kind o' surly to 'em 'long to the first of it. He gits the money from the town, an' it helps him out; but he bid 'em off for five dollars a month, an' we can't do much for 'em at no such price as that. I went an' dealt with the selec'men, an' made 'em promise to find their firewood an' some other things extra. They was glad to git rid o' the matter the fourth time I went, an' would ha' promised 'most anything. But Mr. Janes don't keep me half the time in ovenwood, he's off so much; an' we was cramped o' room, any way. I have to store things up garrit a good deal, an' that keeps me trampin' right through their room. I do the best for 'em I can, Mis' Trimble, but 'tain't so easy for me as 'tis for you, with all your means to do with."

The poor woman looked pinched and miserable herself, though it was evident that she had no gift at house or home keeping. Mrs. Trimble's heart was wrung with pain, as she thought of the unwelcome inmates of such a place; but she held her peace bravely, while Miss Rebecca again gave some brief information in regard to the installation.

"You go right up them back stairs," the hostess directed at last. "I'm glad some o' you church folks has seen fit to come an' visit 'em. There ain't been nobody here this long spell, an' they've aged a sight since they come. They always send down a taste out of your baskets, Mis' Trimble, an' I relish it. I tell you. I'll shut the door after you, if you don't object. I feel every draught o' cold air."

"I've always heard she was a great hand to make a poor mouth. Wa'n't she from somewheres up Parsley way?" whispered Miss Rebecca, as they stumbled in the half-light.

"Poor meechin' body, wherever she come from," replied Mrs. Trimble, as she knocked at the door.

There was silence for a moment after this unusual sound; then one of the Bray sisters opened the door. The eager guests stared into a small, low room, brown with age, and gray, too, as if former dust and cobwebs could not be made wholly to disappear. The two elderly women who stood there looked like captives. Their withered faces wore a look of apprehension, and the room itself was more bare and plain than was fitting to their evident refinement of character and self-respect. There was an uncovered small table in the middle of the floor, with some crackers on a plate; and, for some reason or other, this added a great deal to the general desolation.

But Miss Ann Bray, the elder sister, who carried her right arm in a sling, with piteously drooping fingers, gazed at the visitors with radiant joy. She had not seen them arrive. The one window gave only the view at the back of the house, across the fields, and their coming was indeed a surprise. The next minute she was laughing and crying together. "Oh, sister!" she said, "if here ain't our dear Mis' Trimble!—an' my heart o' goodness, 'tis 'Becca Wright, too! What dear good creatur's you be! I've felt all day as if somethin' good was goin' to happen, an' was just sayin' to myself 'twas most sundown now, but I wouldn't let on Mandany I'd give up hope quite yet. You see, the scissors stuck in the floor this very mornin', an' it's always a reliable sign. There, I've got to kiss ye both again!"

"I don't know where we can all set," lamented sister Mandana. "There ain't but the one chair an' the bed; t'other chair's too rickety; an' we've been promised another these ten days; but first they've forgot it, an' next Mis' Janes can't spare it,—one excuse an' another. I'm goin' to git a stump o' wood an' nail a board on to it, when I can git outdoor again," said Mandana, in a plaintive voice. "There, I ain't goin' to complain o' nothin', now you've come," she added; and the guests sat down, Mrs. Trimble, as was proper, in the one chair.

"We've sat on the bed many's the time with you, 'Becca, an' talked over our girl nonsense, ain't we? You know where 'twas,—in the little back bedroom we had when we was girls, an' used to peek out at our beaux through the strings o' mornin'-glories," laughed Ann Bray delightedly, her thin face shining more and more with joy. "I brought some o' them mornin'-glory seeds along when we come away, we'd raised 'em so many years; an' we got 'em started all right, but the hens found 'em out. I declare I chased them poor hens, foolish as 'twas; but the mornin'-glories I'd counted on a sight to remind me o' home. You see, our debts was so large, after my long sickness an' all, that we didn't feel 'twas right to keep back anything we could help from the auction."

It was impossible for anyone to speak for a moment or two; the sisters felt their own uprooted condition afresh, and their guests for the first time really comprehended the piteous contrast between that neat little village house, which now seemed a palace of comfort, and this cold, unpainted upper room in the remote Janes farmhouse. It was an unwelcome thought to Mrs. Trimble that the well-to-do town of Hampden could provide no better for its poor than this, and her round face flushed with resentment and the shame of personal responsibility. "The girls shall be well settled in the village before another winter, if I pay their board myself," she made an inward resolution, and took another almost tearful look at the broken stove, the miserable bed, and the sisters' one hair-covered trunk, on which Mandana was sitting. But the poor place was filled with a golden spirit of hospitality.

Rebecca was again discoursing eloquently of the installation; it was so much easier to speak of general subjects, and the sisters had evidently been longing to hear some news. Since the late summer they had not been to church, and presently Mrs. Trimble asked the reason.

"Now, don't you go to pouring out our woes, Mandy!" begged little old Ann, looking shy and almost girlish, and as if she insisted upon playing that life was still all before them and all pleasure. "Don't you go to spoilin' their visit with our complaints! They know well's we do that changes must come, an' we'd been so wonted to our home things that this come hard at first; but then they felt for us, I know just as well's can be. 'Twill soon be summer again, an' 'tis real pleasant right out in the fields here, when there ain't too hot a spell. I've got to know a sight o' new singin' birds since we come."

"Give me the folks I've always known," sighed the younger sister, who looked older than Miss Ann, and less even-tempered. "You may have your birds, if you want 'em. I do re'lly long to go to meetin' an' see folks go by up the aisle. Now, I will speak of it, Ann, whatever you say. We need, each of us, a pair o' good stout shoes an' rubbers,—ours are all wore out; an' we've asked an' asked, an' they never think to bring 'em, an' "—

Poor old Mandana, on the trunk, covered her face with her arms and sobbed aloud. The elder sister stood over her, and patted her on the thin shoulder like a child, and tried to comfort her. It crossed Mrs. Trimble's mind that it was not the first time one had wept and the other had comforted. The sad scene must have been repeated many times in that long, drear winter. She would see them forever after in her mind as fixed as a picture, and her own tears fell fast.

"You didn't see Mis' Janes's cunning little boy, the next one to the baby, did you?" asked Ann Bray, turning round quickly at last, and going cheerfully on with the conversation. "Now, hush, Mandy, dear; they'll think you're childish! He's a dear, friendly little creatur', an' likes to stay with us a good deal, though we feel's if 'twas too cold for him, now we are waitin' to get us more wood."

"When I think of the acres o' woodland in this town!" groaned Rebecca Wright. "I believe I'm goin' to preach next Sunday, 'stead o' the minister, an' I'll make the sparks fly. I've always heard the saying, 'What's everybody's business is nobody's business,' an' I've come to believe it."

"Now, don't you, 'Becca. You've happened on a kind of a poor time with us, but we've got more belongings than you see here, an' a good large cluset, where we can store those things there ain't room to have about. You an' Miss Trimble have happened on a kind of poor day, you know. Soon's I git me some stout shoes an' rubbers, as Mandy says, I can fetch home plenty o' little dry boughs o' pine; you remember I was always a great hand to roam in the woods? If we could only have a front room, so 't we could look out on the road an' see the passin', an' was shod for meetin', I don't know's we should complain. Now we're just goin' to give you what we've got, an' make out with a good welcome. We make more tea 'n we want in the mornin', an' then let the fire go down, since 't has been so mild. We've got a *good* cluset" (disappearing as she spoke), "an' I know this to be good tea, 'cause it's some o' yourn, Mis' Trimble. An' here are our sprigged chiny cups that R'becca knows by sight, if Mis' Trimble don't. We kep' out four of 'em, an' put the even half dozen with the rest of the auction stuff. I've often wondered who'd get 'em, but I never asked, for fear 'twould be somebody that would distress us. They was mother's, you know."

The four cups were poured, and the little table pushed to the bed, where Rebecca Wright still sat, and Mandana, wiping her eyes, came and joined her. Mrs. Trimble sat in her chair at the end, and Ann trotted about the room in pleased content for a while, and in and out of the closet, as if she still had much to do; then she came and stood opposite Mrs. Trimble. She was very short and small, and there was no painful sense of her being obliged to stand. The four cups were not quite full of cold tea, but there was a clean old tablecloth folded double, and a plate with three pairs of crackers neatly piled, and a small—it must be owned, a very small—piece of hard white cheese. Then, for a treat, in a glass dish, there was a little preserved peach, the last—Miss Rebecca knew it instinctively—of the household stores brought from their old home. It was very sugary, this bit of peach; and as she helped her guests and sister Mandy, Miss Ann Bray said, half unconsciously, as she often had said with less reason in the old days, "Our preserves ain't so good as usual this year; this is beginning to candy." Both the guests protested, while Rebecca added that the taste of it carried her back, and made her feel young again. The Brays had always managed to keep one or two peach trees alive in their corner of a garden. "I've been keeping this preserve for a treat," said her friend. "I'm glad to have you eat some, 'Becca. Last summer I often wished you was home an' could come an' see us, 'stead o' being away off to Plainfields."

The crackers did not taste too dry. Miss Ann took the last of the peach on her own cracker; there could not have been quite a small spoonful, after the others were helped, but she asked them first if they would not have some more. Then there was a silence, and in the silence a wave of tender feeling rose high in the hearts of the four elderly women. At this moment the setting sun flooded the poor plain room with light; the unpainted wood was all of a golden-brown, and Ann Bray, with her gray hair and aged face, stood at the head of the table in a kind of aureole. Mrs. Trimble's face was all a-quiver as she looked at her; she thought of the text about two or three being gathered together, and was half afraid.

"I believe we ought to 've asked Mis' Janes if she wouldn't come up," said Ann. "She's real good feelin', but she's had it very hard, an' gits discouraged. I can't find that she's ever had anything real pleasant to look back to, as we have. There, next time we'll make a good heartenin' time for her too."

The sorrel horse had taken a long nap by the gnawed fence rail, and the cool air after sundown made him impatient to be gone. The two friends jolted homeward in the gathering darkness, through the stiffening mud, and neither Mrs. Trimble nor Rebecca Wright said a word until they were out of sight as well as out of sound of the Janes house. Time must elapse before they could reach a more familiar part of the road and resume conversation on its natural level.

"I consider myself to blame," insisted Mrs. Trimble at last. "I haven't no words of accusation for nobody else, an' I ain't one to take comfort in calling names to the board o' selec'*men*. I make no reproaches, an' I take it all on my own shoulders; but I'm goin' to stir about me, I tell you! I shall begin early tomorrow. They're goin' back to their own house,—it's been standin' empty all winter,—an' the town's goin' to give 'em the rent an' what firewood they need; it won't come to more than the board's payin' out now. An' you an' me'll take this same horse an' wagon, an' ride an' go afoot by turns, an' git means enough together to buy back their furniture an' whatever was sold at that plaguy auction; an' then we'll put it all back, an' tell 'em they've got to move to a new place, an' just carry 'em right back again where they come from. An' don't you never tell, R'becca, but here I be a widow woman, layin' up what I make from my farm for nobody knows who, an' I'm goin' to do for them Bray girls all I'm a mind to. I should be sca't to wake up in heaven, an' hear anybody there ask how the Bray girls was. Don't talk to me about the town o' Hampden, an' don't ever let me hear the name o' town poor! I'm ashamed to go home an' see what's set out for supper. I wish I'd brought 'em right along."

"I was goin' to ask if we couldn't git the new doctor to go up an' do somethin' for poor Ann's arm," said Miss Rebecca. "They say he's very smart. If she could get so's to braid straw or hook rugs again, she'd soon be earnin' a little somethin'. An' maybe he could do somethin' for Mandy's eyes. They did use to live so neat an' ladylike. Somehow I couldn't speak to tell 'em there that 'twas I bought them six best cups an' saucers, time of the auction; they went very low, as everythin' else did, an' I thought I could save it some other way. They shall have 'em back an' welcome. You're real wholehearted, Mis' Trimble. I expect Ann'll be sayin' that her father's child'n wa'n't goin' to be left desolate, an' that all the bread he cast on the waters's comin' back through you."

"I don't care what she says, dear creatur'!" exclaimed Mrs. Trimble. "I'm full o' regrets I took time for that installation, an' set there seepin' in a lot o' talk this whole day long, except for its kind of bringin' us to the Bray girls. I wish to my heart 'twas tomorrow mornin' a'ready, an' I a-startin' for the selec'*men*."

MARY WILKINS FREEMAN was born in Randolph, Massachusetts, in 1852, but moved with her parents to Brattleboro, Vermont, when she was fifteen. She grew up and began writing against the backdrop of the New England Congregational Church and her parents' chronic financial reverses. A regular churchgoer to six-hour-long Sunday services, she knew the ethical stance of New England Protestantism in her bones. As the only surviving child of a father who suffered one business failure after another, she knew the pinch of poverty intimately. She wrote at first to help out her parents by earning money, but she did not achieve regular and wide publication of her stories until after their deaths in the 1880s. Both these influences of her childhood and adolescence—and her understanding of the dignity of the poor—are evident in the story that follows, "A Mistaken Charity." Also a palpable force in this story is the writer's love of the independent spirit of the two sisters who are up against impossible odds but remain unconverted to the conventional wisdom on the subject of poverty. Their circumstances neither frighten nor paralyze these women. In this story, the sisterly bond is a source of strength and survival.

Once her literary reputation was established, Mary Wilkins Freeman won prizes and awards as well as the admiration of her contemporaries Sarah Orne Jewett and Henry James. As a middle-aged woman, she left New England for Metuchen, New Jersey, to marry a medical doctor who was also an alcoholic. After twenty years of unhappy marriage and writing less distinguished than she had once published, Mary Wilkins Freeman separated from her husband. At the time of her death in 1930 she had had forty volumes of fiction published, both novels and collections of short stories, the most famous of which is probably *A New England Nun and Other Stories*.

A Mistaken Charity

by
Mary Wilkins Freeman

There were in a green field a little, low, weather-stained cottage, with a foot-path leading to it from the highway several rods distant, and two old women—one with a tin pan and old knife searching for dandelion greens among the short young grass, and the other sitting on the door-step watching her, or, rather, having the appearance of watching her.

"Air there enough for a mess, Harriét?" asked the old woman on the door-step. She accented oddly the last syllable of the Harriet, and there was a curious quality in her feeble, cracked old voice. Besides the question denoted by the arrangement of her words and the rising inflection, there was another, broader and subtler, the very essence of all questioning, in the tone of her voice itself; the cracked, quavering notes that she used reached out of themselves, and asked, and groped like fingers in the dark. One would have known by the voice that the old woman was blind.

The old woman on her knees in the grass searching for dandelions did not reply; she evidently had not heard the question. So the old woman on the door-step, after waiting a few minutes with her head turned expectantly, asked again, varying her question slightly, and speaking louder:

"Air there enough for a mess, do ye s'pose, Harriét?"

The old woman in the grass heard this time. She rose slowly and laboriously; the effort of straightening out the rheumatic old muscles was evidently a painful one; then she eyed the greens heaped up in the tin pan, and pressed them down with her hand.

"Wa'al, I don't know, Charlotte," she replied, hoarsely. "There's plenty on 'em here, but I 'ain't got near enough for a mess; they do bile down so when you get 'em in the pot; an' it's all I can do to bend my j'ints enough to dig 'em."

"I'd give consider'ble to help ye, Harriét," said the old woman on the door-step.

But the other did not hear her; she was down on her knees in the grass again, anxiously spying out the dandelions.

So the old woman on the door-step crossed her little shrivelled hands over her calico knees, and sat quite still, with the soft spring wind blowing over her.

The old wooden door-step was sunk low down among the grasses, and the whole house to which it belonged had an air of settling down and mouldering into the grass as into its own grave.

When Harriet Shattuck grew deaf and rheumatic, and had to give up her work as tailoress, and Charlotte Shattuck lost her eyesight, and was unable to do any more sewing for her livelihood, it was a small and trifling charity for the rich man who held a mortgage on the little house in which they had been born and lived all their lives to give them the use of it, rent and interest free. He might as well have taken credit to himself for not charging a squirrel for his tenement in some old decaying tree in his woods.

So ancient was the little habitation, so wavering and mouldering, the hands that had fashioned it had lain still so long in their graves, that it almost seemed to have fallen below its distinctive rank as a house. Rain and snow had filtered through its roof, mosses had grown over it, worms had eaten it, and birds built their nests under its eaves; nature had almost completely overrun and obliterated the work of man, and taken her own to herself again, till the house seemed as much a natural ruin as an old tree-stump.

The Shattucks had always been poor people and common people; no especial grace and refinement or fine ambition had ever characterized any of them; they had always been poor and coarse and common. The father and his father before him had simply lived in the poor little house, grubbed for their living, and then unquestioningly died. The mother had been of no rarer stamp, and the two daughters were cast in the same mould.

After their parents' death Harriet and Charlotte had lived along in the old place from youth to old age, with the one hope of ability to keep a roof over their heads, covering on their backs, and victuals in their mouths—an all-sufficient one with them.

Neither of them had ever had a lover; they had always seemed to repel rather than attract the opposite sex. It was not merely because they were poor, ordinary, and homely; there were plenty of men in the place who would have matched them well in that respect; the fault lay deeper—in their characters. Harriet, even in her girlhood, had a blunt, defiant manner that almost amounted to surliness, and was well calculated to alarm timid adorers, and Charlotte had always had the reputation of not being any too strong in her mind.

Harriet had gone about from house to house doing tailor-work after the primitive country fashion, and Charlotte had done plain sewing and mending for the neighbors. They had been, in the main, except when pressed by some temporary anxiety about their work or the payment thereof, happy and contented, with that negative kind of happiness and contentment which comes not from gratified ambition, but a lack of ambition itself. All that they cared for they had had in tolerable abundance, for Harriet at least had been swift and capable about her work. The patched, mossy old roof had been kept over their heads, the coarse, hearty food that they loved had been set on their table, and their cheap clothes had been warm and strong.

After Charlotte's eyes failed her, and Harriet had the rheumatic fever, and the little hoard of earnings went to the doctors, times were harder with them, though still it could not be said that they actually suffered.

When they could not pay the interest on the mortgage they were allowed to keep the place interest free; there was as much fitness in a mortgage on the little house, anyway, as there would have been on a rotten old apple-tree; and the people about, who were mostly farmers, and good friendly folk, helped them out with their living. One would donate a barrel of apples from his abundant harvest to the two poor old women, one a barrel of potatoes, another a load of wood for the winter fuel, and many a farmer's wife had bustled up the narrow foot-path with a pound of butter, or a dozen fresh eggs, or a nice bit of pork. Besides all this, there was a tiny garden patch behind the house, with a straggling row of currant bushes in it, and one of gooseberries, where Harriet contrived every year to raise a few pumpkins, which were the pride of her life. On the right of the garden were two old apple-trees, a Baldwin and a Porter, both yet in a tolerably good fruit-bearing state.

The delight which the two poor old souls took in their own pumpkins, their apples and currants, was indescribable. It was not merely that they contributed largely towards their living; they were their own, their private share of the great wealth of nature, the little taste set apart for them alone out of her bounty, and worth more to them on that account, though they were not conscious of it, than all the richer fruits which they received from their neighbors' gardens.

This morning the two apple-trees were brave with flowers, the currant bushes looked alive, and the pumpkin seeds were in the ground. Harriet cast complacent glances in their direction from time to time, as she painfully dug her dandelion greens. She was a short, stoutly built old woman, with a large face coarsely wrinkled, with a suspicion of a stubble of beard on the square chin.

When her tin pan was filled to her satisfaction with the sprawling, spidery greens, and she was hobbling stiffly towards her sister on the door-step, she saw another woman standing before her with a basket in her hand.

"Good-morning, Harriet," she said, in a loud, strident voice, as she drew near. "I've been frying some doughnuts, and I brought you over some warm."

"I've been tellin' her it was real good in her," piped Charlotte from the door-step, with an anxious turn of her sightless face towards the sound of her sister's footstep.

Harriet said nothing but a hoarse "Good-mornin', Mis' Simonds." Then she took the basket in her hand, lifted the towel off the top, selected a doughnut, and deliberately tasted it.

"Tough," said she. "I s'posed so. If there is anything I 'spise on this airth it's a tough doughnut."

"Oh, Harriét!" said Charlotte, with a frightened look.

"They air tough," said Harriet, with hoarse defiance, "and if there is anything I 'spise on this airth it's a tough doughnut."

The woman whose benevolence and cookery were being thus ungratefully received only laughed. She was quite fleshy, and had a round, rosy, determined face.

"Well, Harriet," said she, "I am sorry they are tough, but perhaps you had better take them out on a plate, and give me my basket. You may be able to eat two or three of them if they are tough."

"They air tough—turrible tough," said Harriet, stubbornly; but she took the basket into the house and emptied it of its contents nevertheless.

"I suppose your roof leaked as bad as ever in that heavy rain day before yesterday?" said the visitor to Harriet, with an inquiring squint towards the mossy shingles, as she was about to leave with her empty basket.

"It was turrible," replied Harriet, with crusty acquiescence—"turrible. We had to set pails an' pans everywheres, an' move the bed out."

"Mr. Upton ought to fix it."

"There ain't any fix to it; the old ruff ain't fit to nail new shingles on to; the hammerin' would bring the whole thing down on our heads," said Harriet, grimly.

"Well, I don't know as it can be fixed, it's so old. I suppose the wind comes in bad around the windows and doors too?"

"It's like livin' with a piece of paper, or mebbe a sieve, 'twixt you an' the wind an' the rain," quoth Harriet, with a jerk of her head.

"You ought to have a more comfortable home in your old age," said the visitor, thoughtfully.

"Oh, it's well enough," cried Harriet, in quick alarm, and with a complete change of tone; the woman's remark had brought an old dread over her. "The old house'll last as long as Charlotte an' me do. The rain ain't so bad, nuther is the wind; there's room enough for us in the dry places, an' out of the way of the doors an' windows. It's enough sight better than goin' on the town." Her square, defiant old face actually looked pale as she uttered the last words and stared apprehensively at the woman.

"Oh, I did not think of your doing that," she said, hastily and kindly. "We all know how you feel about that, Harriet, and not one of us neighbors will see you and Charlotte go to the poorhouse while we've got a crust of bread to share with you."

Harriet's face brightened. "Thank ye, Mis' Simonds," she said, with reluctant courtesy. "I'm much obleeged to you an' the neighbors. I think mebbe we'll be able to eat some of them doughnuts if they air tough," she added, mollifyingly, as her caller turned down the foot-path.

"My, Harriét," said Charlotte, lifting up a weakly, wondering, peaked old face, "what did you tell her them doughnuts was tough fur?"

"Charlotte, do you want everybody to look down on us, an' think we ain't no account at all, just like any beggars, 'cause they bring us in vittles?" said Harriet, with a grim glance at her sister's meek, unconscious face.

"No, Harriét," she whispered.

"Do you want *to go to the poor-house?*"

"No, Harriét." The poor little old woman on the door-step fairly cowered before her aggressive old sister.

"Then don't hender me agin when I tell folks their doughnuts is tough an' their pertaters is poor. If I don't kinder keep up an' show some sperrit, I sha'n't think nothing of myself, an' other folks won't nuther, and fust thing we know they'll kerry us to the poorhouse. You'd 'a been there before now if it hadn't been for me, Charlotte."

Charlotte looked meekly convinced, and her sister sat down on a chair in the doorway to scrape her dandelions.

"Did you git a good mess, Harriét?" asked Charlotte, in a humble tone.

"Toler'ble."

"They'll be proper relishin' with that piece of pork Mis' Mann brought in yesterday. O Lord, Harriét, it's a chink!"

Harriet sniffed.

Her sister caught with her sensitive ear the little contemptuous sound. "I guess," she said, querulously, and with more pertinacity than she had shown in the matter of the doughnuts, "that if you was in the dark, as I am, Harriét, you wouldn't make fun an' turn up your nose at chinks. If you had seen the light streamin' in all of a sudden through some little hole that you hadn't known of before when you set down on the door-step this mornin', and the wind with the smell of the apple blows in it came in your face, an' when Mis' Simonds brought them hot doughnuts, an' when I thought of the pork an' greens jest now—O Lord, how it did shine in! An' it does now. If you was me, Harriét, you would know there was chinks."

Tears began starting from the sightless eyes, and streaming pitifully down the pale old cheeks.

Harriet looked at her sister, and her grim face softened. "Why, Charlotte, hev it that thar *is* chinks if you want to. Who cares?"

"Thar *is* chinks, Harriét."

"Wa'al, thar *is* chinks, then. If I don't hurry, I sha'n't get these greens in in time for dinner."

When the two old women sat down complacently to their meal of pork and dandelion greens in their little kitchen they did not dream how destiny slowly and surely was introducing some new colors into their web of life, even when it was almost completed, and that this was one of the last meals they would eat in their old home for many a day. In about a week from that day they were established in the "Old Ladies' Home" in a neighboring city. It came about in this wise: Mrs. Simonds, the woman who had brought the gift of hot doughnuts, was a smart, energetic person, bent on doing good, and she did a great deal. To be sure, she always did it in her own way. If she chose to give hot doughnuts, she gave hot doughnuts; it made not the slightest difference to her if the recipients of her charity would infinitely have preferred ginger cookies. Still, a great many would like hot doughnuts, and she did unquestionably a great deal of good.

She had a worthy coadjutor in the person of a rich and childless elderly widow in the place. They had fairly entered into a partnership in good works, with about an equal capital on both sides, the widow furnishing the money, and Mrs. Simonds, who had much the better head of the two, furnishing the active schemes of benevolence.

The afternoon after the doughnut episode she had gone to the widow with a new project, and the result was that entrance fees had been paid, and old Harriet and Charlotte made sure of a comfortable home for the rest of their lives. The widow was hand in glove with officers of missionary boards and trustees of charitable institutions. There had been an unusual mortality among the inmates of the "Home" this spring, there were several vacancies, and the matter of the admission of Harriet and Charlotte was very quickly and easily arranged. But the matter which would have seemed the least difficult—inducing the two old women to accept the bounty which Providence, the widow, and Mrs. Simonds were ready to bestow on them—proved the most so. The struggle to persuade them to abandon their tottering old home for a better was a terrible one. The widow had pleaded with mild surprise, and Mrs. Simonds with benevolent determination; the counsel and reverend eloquence of the minister had been called in; and when they yielded at last it was with a sad grace for the recipients of a worthy charity.

It had been hard to convince them that the "Home" was not an almshouse under another name, and their yielding at length to anything short of actual force was only due probably to the plea, which was advanced most eloquently to Harriet, that Charlotte would be so much more comfortable.

The morning they came away, Charlotte cried pitifully, and trembled all over her little shrivelled body. Harriet did not cry. But when her sister had passed out the low, sagging door she turned the key in the lock, then took it out and thrust it slyly into her pocket, shaking her head to herself with an air of fierce determination.

Mrs. Simonds's husband, who was to take them to the depot, said to himself, with disloyal defiance of his wife's active charity, that it was a shame, as he helped the two distressed old souls into his light wagon, and put the poor little box, with their homely clothes in it, in behind.

Mrs. Simonds, the widow, the minister, and the gentleman from the "Home" who was to take charge of them, were all at the depot, their faces beaming with the delight of successful benevolence. But the two poor old women looked like two forlorn prisoners in their midst. It was an impressive illustration of the truth of the saying "that it is more blessed to give than to receive."

Well, Harriet and Charlotte Shattuck went to the "Old Ladies' Home" with reluctance and distress. They stayed two months, and then—they ran away.

The "Home" was comfortable, and in some respects even luxurious; but nothing suited those two unhappy, unreasonable old women.

The fare was of a finer, more delicately served variety than they had been accustomed to; those finely flavored nourishing soups for which the "Home" took great credit to itself failed to please palates used to common, coarser food.

"O Lord, Harriét, when I set down to the table here there ain't no chinks," Charlotte used to say. "If we could hev some cabbage, or some pork an' greens, how the light would stream in!"

Then they had to be more particular about their dress. They had always been tidy enough, but now it had to be something more; the widow, in the kindness of her heart, had made it possible, and the good folks in charge of the "Home," in the kindness of their hearts, tried to carry out the widow's designs.

But nothing could transform these two unpolished old women into two nice old ladies. They did not take kindly to white lace caps and delicate neckerchiefs. They liked their new black cashmere dresses well enough, but they felt as if they broke a commandment when they put them on every afternoon. They had always worn calico with long aprons at home, and they wanted to now; and they wanted to twist up their scanty gray locks into little knots at the back of their heads, and go without caps, just as they always had done.

Charlotte in a dainty white cap was pitiful, but Harriet was both pitiful and comical. They were totally at variance with their surroundings, and they felt it keenly, as people of their stamp always do. No amount of kindness and attention—and they had enough of both—sufficed to reconcile them to their new abode. Charlotte pleaded continually with her sister to go back to their home.

"O Lord, Harriét," she would exclaim (by the way, Charlotte's "O Lord," which, as she used it, was innocent enough, had been heard with much disfavor in the "Home," and she, not knowing at all why, had been remonstrated with concerning it), "let us go home. I can't stay here no ways in this world. I don't like their vittles, an' I don't like to wear a cap; I want to go home and do different. The currants will be ripe, Harriét. O Lord, thar was almost a chink, thinking about 'em. I want some of 'em; an' the Porter apples will be gittin' ripe, an' we could have some apple-pie. This here ain't good; I want merlasses fur sweeting. Can't we get back no ways, Harriét? It ain't far, an' we could walk, an' they don't lock us in, nor nothin'. I don't want to die here; it ain't so straight up to heaven from here. O Lord, I've felt as if I was slantendicular from heaven ever since I've been here, an' it's been so awful dark. I ain't had any chinks. I want to go home, Harriét."

"We'll go to-morrow mornin'," said Harriet, finally; "we'll

pack up our things an' go; we'll put on our old dresses, an' we'll do up the new ones in bundles, an' we'll just shy out the back way to-morrow mornin'; an' we'll go. I kin find the way, an' I reckon we kin git thar, if it is fourteen mile. Mebbe somebody will give us a lift."

And they went. With a grim humor Harriet hung the new white lace caps with which she and Charlotte had been so pestered, one on each post at the head of the bedstead, so they would meet the eyes of the first person who opened the door. Then they took their bundles, stole slyly out, and were soon on the high-road, hobbling along, holding each other's hands, as jubilant as two children, and chuckling to themselves over their escape, and the probable astonishment there would be in the "Home" over it.

"O Lord, Harriét, what do you s'pose they will say to them caps?" cried Charlotte, with a gleeful cackle.

"I guess they'll see as folks ain't goin' to be made to wear caps agin their will in a free kentry," returned Harriet, with an echoing cackle, as they sped feebly and bravely along.

The "Home" stood on the very outskirts of the city, luckily for them. They would have found it a difficult undertaking to traverse the crowded streets. As it was, a short walk brought them into the free country road—free comparatively, for even here at ten o'clock in the morning there was considerable travelling to and from the city on business or pleasure.

People whom they met on the road did not stare at them as curiously as might have been expected. Harriet held her bristling chin high in air, and hobbled along with an appearance of being well aware of what she was about, that led folks to doubt their own first opinion that there was something unusual about the two old women.

Still their evident feebleness now and then occasioned from one and another more particular scrutiny. When they had been on the road a half-hour or so, a man in a covered wagon drove up behind them. After he had passed them, he poked his head around the front of the vehicle and looked back. Finally he stopped, and waited for them to come up to him.

"Like a ride, ma'am?" said he, looking at once bewildered and compassionate.

"Thankee," said Harriet, "we'd be much obleeged."

After the man had lifted the old women into the wagon, and established them on the back seat, he turned around, as he drove slowly along, and gazed at them curiously.

"Seems to me you look pretty feeble to be walking far," said he. "Where were you going?"

Harriet told him with an air of defiance.

"Why," he exclaimed, "it is fourteen miles out. You could never walk it in the world. Well, I am going within three miles of there, and I can go on a little farther as well as not. But I don't see— Have you been in the city?"

"I have been visitin' my married darter in the city," said Harriet, calmly.

Charlotte started, and swallowed convulsively.

Harriet had never told a deliberate falsehood before in her life, but this seemed to her one of the tremendous exigencies of life which justify a lie. She felt desperate. If she could not contrive to deceive him in some way, the man might turn directly around and carry Charlotte and her back to the "Home" and the white caps.

"I should not have thought your daughter would have let you start for such a walk as that," said the man. "Is this lady your sister? She is blind, isn't she? She does not look fit to walk a mile."

"Yes, she's my sister," replied Harriet, stubbornly: "an' she's blind; an' my darter didn't want us to walk. She felt reel bad about it. But she couldn't help it. She's poor, and her husband's dead, an' she's got four leetle children."

Harriet recounted the hardships of her imaginary daughter with a glibness that was astonishing. Charlotte swallowed again.

"Well," said the man, "I am glad I overtook you, for I don't think you would ever have reached home alive."

About six miles from the city an open buggy passed them swiftly. In it were seated the matron and one of the gentlemen in charge of the "Home." They never thought of looking into the covered wagon—and indeed one can travel in one of those vehicles, so popular in some parts of New England, with as much privacy as he could in his tomb. The two in the buggy were seriously alarmed, and anxious for the safety of the old women, who were chuckling maliciously in the wagon they soon left far behind. Harriet had watched them breathlessly until they disappeared on a curve of the road; then she whispered to Charlotte.

A little after noon the two old women crept slowly up the foot-path across the field to their old home.

"The clover is up to our knees," said Harriet; "an' the sorrel and the white-weed; an' there's lots of yaller butterflies."

"O Lord, Harriét, thar's a chink, an' I do believe I saw one of them yaller butterflies go past it," cried Charlotte, trembling all over, and nodding her gray head violently.

Harriet stood on the old sunken door-step and fitted the key, which she drew triumphantly from her pocket, in the lock, while Charlotte stood waiting and shaking behind her.

Then they went in. Everything was there just as they had left it. Charlotte sank down on a chair and began to cry. Harriet hurried across to the window that looked out on the garden.

"The currants air ripe," said she, "*an'* them pumpkins hev run all over everything."

"O Lord,Harriét," sobbed Charlotte, "thar is so many chinks that they air all runnin' together!"

ELIZABETH BOWEN was born in Dublin in 1899 and spent her childhood at Bowen's Court in Kildorrery, County Cork. She attended school in England and married in 1923. She lived in London during World War II, working for the Ministry of Information by day and as an air-raid warden at night. She wrote prodigiously during the war years, "the only interruption," she said, "being the necessity to clean up my house from time to time when it had been blasted." With the publication of *The Heat of the Day* (1949), her novel about London during the blitz and the last volume of her major trilogy (it began with *The House in Paris* and *The Death of the Heart*), the critic David Daiches says she moved "out of the ranks of interesting minor writers to become a major modern novelist," joining the company of Virginia Woolf, Katherine Mansfield, and Henry James. In his introduction to *The Collected Stories of Elizabeth Bowen*, published in 1981, Angus Wilson expresses the special power of her fiction: "Anyone so elegant and civilized, so certain of values that to state them would seem to her inept and naive, so concerned for lack of show—even the bravery that man needs so desperately in a precarious world must never assert itself too crudely . . . so concerned that compassion should never show a sloppy side—any such person inevitably seems to fit very little with Rousseau's noble savage, yet the instinctive artist is there at the very heart of her work and gives a strength, a fierceness and a depth to her elaborations . . ." "A Queer Heart," the story that follows, is a luminous reflection of this motif of Bowen's best fiction, the strength and health of the loving heart, and the death-in-life that defines the heart consumed by jealousy. The two sisters, Hilda and Rosa, embody this stark contrast and come to their appropriate, Bowenesque ends.

In *Why Do I Write*, Bowen (along with V. S. Pritchett and Graham Greene) has written with characteristic grace and intelligence on the art of fiction. She has written that her art was always a matter of life and breath. "I wrote my first short stories when I was twenty. From the moment that my pen touched paper, I thought of nothing but writing and since then I have thought of practically nothing else. I have been idle for months, or even for a year, at a time; but when I have nothing to write, I feel only half alive."

At the time of her death in 1973, she had received honorary degrees and the highest recognition from the two places that nourished her Anglo-Irish sensibility throughout her life, Ireland's Trinity College, Dublin, and Oxford University.

A Queer Heart

by

Elizabeth Bowen

Mrs. Cadman got out of the bus backwards. No amount of practice ever made her more agile; the trouble she had with her big bulk amused everyone, and herself. Gripping the handles each side of the bus door so tightly that the seams of her gloves cracked, she lowered herself cautiously, like a climber, while her feet, overlapping her smart shoes, uneasily scrabbled at each step. One or two people asked why the bus made, for one passenger, such a long, dead stop. But on the whole she was famous on this line, for she was constantly in and out of town. The conductor waited behind her, smiling, holding her basket, arms wide to catch her if she should slip.

Having got safe to the ground, Mrs. Cadman shook herself like a satisfied bird. She took back her shopping-basket from the conductor and gave him a smile instead. The big, kind, scarlet bus once more ground into movement, off up the main road hill: it made a fading blur in the premature autumn dusk. Mrs. Cadman almost waved after it, for with it went the happy part of her day. She turned down the side road that led to her gate.

A wet wind of autumn, smelling of sodden gardens, blew in her face and tilted her hat. Leaves whirled along it, and one lime leaf, as though imploring shelter, lodged in her fur collar. Every gust did more to sadden the poor trees. This was one of those roads outside growing provincial cities that still keep their rural mystery. They seem to lead into something still not known. Traffic roars past one end, but the other end is in silence: you see a wood, a spire, a haughty manor gate, or your view ends with the turn of an old wall. Here some new, raw-looking villas stood with spaces between them; in the spaces were orchards and market-gardens. A glasshouse roof reflected the wet grey light; there was a shut chapel farther along. And, each standing back in half an acre of ground, there were two or three stucco houses with dark windows, sombre but at the same time ornate, built years ago in this then retired spot. Dead lime leaves showered over their grass plots and evergreens. Mrs. Cadman's house, Granville, was one of these: its name was engraved in scrolls over the porch. The solid house was not large, and Mrs. Cadman's daughter, Lucille, could look after it with a daily help.

The widow and her daughter lived here in the state of cheerless meekness Lucille considered suitable for them now. *Mr.* Cadman had liked to have everything done in style. But twelve years ago he had died, travelling on business, in an hotel up in the North. Always the gentleman, he had been glad to spare them this upset at home. He had been brought back to the Midlands for his impressive funeral, whose size showed him a popular man. How unlike Mr. Cadman was Rosa proving herself. One can be most unfriendly in one's way of dying. Ah, well, one chooses one's husband; one's sister is dealt out to one by fate.

Mrs. Cadman, thumb on the latch of her own gate, looked for a minute longer up and down the road—deeply, deeply unwilling to go in. She looked back at the corner where the bus had vanished, and an immense sigh heaved up her coat lapels and made a cotton carnation, pinned to the fur, brush a fold of her chin. Laced, hooked, buttoned so tightly into her clothes, she seemed to need to deflate herself by these sudden sighs, by yawns or by those explosions of laughter that often vexed Lucille. Through her face—embedded in fat but still very lively, as exposed, as ingenuous as a little girl's—you could see some emotional fermentation always at work in her. Her smiles were frequent, hopeful and quick. Her pitching walk was due to her tight shoes.

When she did go in she went in with a sort of rush. She let the door bang back on the hall wall, so that the chain rattled and an outraged clatter came from the letter-box. Immediately, she knew she had done wrong. Lucille, appalled, looked out of the dining-room. "*Shissssh!* How can you, mother?" she said

"Ever so sorry, dear," said Mrs. Cadman, cast down.

"She's just dropped off," said Lucille. "After her bad night and everything. It really does seem hard."

Mrs. Cadman quite saw that it did. She glanced nervously up the stairs, then edged into the dining-room. It was not cheerful in here: a monkey puzzle, too close to the window, drank the last of the light up; the room still smelt of dinner; the fire smouldered resentfully, starved for coal. The big mahogany furniture lowered, with no shine. Mrs. Cadman, putting her basket down on the table, sent an uncertain smile across at Lucille, whose glasses blankly gleamed high up on her long face. She often asked herself where Lucille could have come from. *Could* this be the baby daughter she had borne, and tied pink bows on, and christened a pretty name? In the sun in this very bow window she had gurgled into sweet-smelling creases of Lucille's neck—one summer lost in time.

"You *have* been an age," Lucille said.

"Well, the shops were quite busy. I never *saw*," she said with irrepressible pleasure, "I never *saw* so many people in town!"

Lucille, lips tighter than ever shut, was routing about, unpacking the shopping basket, handling the packages. Chemist's and grocer's parcels. Mrs. Cadman watched her with apprehension. Then Lucille pounced; she held up a small, soft parcel in frivolous wrappings. "Oho," she said. "So you've been in at Babbington's?"

"Well, I missed one bus, so I had to wait for the next. So I just popped in there a minute out of the cold. And, you see, I've been wanting a little scarf—"

"Little scarf!" said Lucille. "I don't know what to make of you, mother. I don't really. How *could* you, at such a time? How you ever could have the heart!" Lucille, standing the other side of the table, leaned across it, her thin weight on her knuckles. This brought her face near her mother's. "Can't you understand?" she said. "Can't you take *anything* in? The next little scarf *you'll* need to buy will be black!"

"What a thing to say!" exclaimed Mrs. Cadman, profoundly offended. "With that poor thing upstairs now, waiting to have her tea."

"Tea? She can't take her tea. Why, since this morning she can't keep a thing down."

Mrs. Cadman blenched and began unbuttoning her coat. Lucille seemed to feel that her own prestige and Aunt

Rosa's entirely hung on Aunt Rosa's approaching death. You could feel that she and her aunt had thought up this plan together. These last days had been the climax of their complicity. And there was Mrs. Cadman—as ever, as usual—put in the wrong, frowned upon, out of things. Whenever Rosa arrived to stay Mrs. Cadman had no fun in her home, and now Rosa was leaving for ever it seemed worse. A perverse kick of the heart, a flicker of naughtiness, made Mrs. Cadman say: "Oh, well, while there's life there's hope."

Lucille said: "If you won't face it, you won't. But I just say it does fall heavy on me . . . We had the vicar round here this afternoon. He was up with Aunt for a bit, then he looked in and said he did feel I needed a prayer too. He said he thought I was wonderful. He asked where you were, and he seemed to wonder you find the heart to stay out so long. I thought from his manner he wondered a good deal."

Mrs. Cadman, with an irrepressible titter, said: "Give him something to think about! Why if I'd ha' shown up that vicar'd have popped out as fast as he popped in. Thinks I'd make a mouthful of him. Why, I've made him bolt down the street. Well, well. He's not *my* idea of a vicar. When your father and I first came here we had a rural dean. Oh, he was as pleasant as anything."

Lucille, with the air of praying for Christian patience, folded her lips. Jabbing her fingers down the inside of her waistbelt, she more tightly tucked in her tight blouse. She liked looking like Mrs. Noah—no, *Miss* Noah. "The doctor's not been again. We're to let him know of any change."

"Well, let's do the best we can," said Mrs. Cadman. "But don't keep on *talking*. You don't make things any better, keeping on going on. My opinion is one should keep bright to the last. When my time comes, oh, I would like a cheery face."

"It's well for you . . ." began Lucille. She bit the remark off and, gathering up the parcels, stalked scornfully out of the dining-room. Without comment she left exposed on the table a small carton of goodies Mrs. Cadman had bought to cheer herself up with and had concealed in the toe of the shopping bag. Soon, from the kitchen came the carefully muffled noises of Lucille putting away provisions and tearing the wrappings off the chemist's things. Mrs. Cadman, reaching out for the carton, put a peppermint into each cheek. She, oh so badly, wanted a cup of tea but dared not follow Lucille into the kitchen in order to put the kettle on.

Though, after all, Granville *was* her house . . .

You would not think it was her house—not when Rosa was there. While Lucille and her mother were *tête à tête* Lucille's disapproval was at least fairly tacit. But as soon as Rosa arrived on one of these yearly autumn visits—always choosing the season when Mrs. Cadman felt in her least good form, the fall of the leaf—the aunt and niece got together and found everything wrong. Their two cold natures ran together. They found Mrs. Cadman lacking; they forbade the affection she would have offered them. They censured her the whole time. Mrs. Cadman could date her real alienation from Lucille from the year when Rosa's visits began. During Mr. Cadman's lifetime Rosa had never come for more than an afternoon. Mr. Cadman had been his wife's defence from her sister—a great red kind of rumbustious fortification. He had been a man who kept every chill wind out. Rosa, during those stilted afternoon visits, had adequately succeeded in conveying that she found marriage *low*. She might just have suffered a pious marriage; she openly deprecated this high living, this state of fleshly bliss. In order not to witness it too closely she lived on in lodgings in her native town . . . But once widowhood left her sister exposed, Rosa started flapping round Granville like a doomful bird. She instituted these yearly visits, which, she made plain at the same time, gave her not much pleasure. The journey was tedious, and by breaking her habits, leaving her lodgings, Rosa was, out of duty, putting herself about. Her joyless and intimidating visits had, therefore, only one object—to protect the interests of Lucille.

Mrs. Cadman had suspected for some time that Rosa had something the matter with her. No one looks as yellow as that for nothing. But she was not sufficiently intimate with her sister to get down to the cosy subject of insides. This time, Rosa arrived looking worse than ever, and three days afterwards had collapsed. Lucille said now she had known her aunt was poorly. Lucille said now she had always known. "But of course you wouldn't notice, mother," she said.

Mrs. Cadman sat down by the fire and, gratefully, kicked off her tight shoes. In the warmth her plump feet uncurled, relaxed, expanded like sea-anemones. She stretched her legs out, propped her heels on the fender and wiggled her toes voluptuously. They went on wiggling of their own accord: they seemed to have an independent existence. Here, in her home, where she felt so "put wrong" and chilly, they were like ten stout, confidential friends. She said, out loud: "Well, *I* don't know what I've done."

The fact was: Lucille and Rosa resented her. (She'd feel better when she had had her tea.) She should *not* have talked as she had about the vicar. But it seemed so silly, Lucille having just him. She did wish Lucille had a better time. No young man so much as paused at the gate. Lucille's aunt had wrapped her own dank virginity round her like someone sharing a mackintosh.

Mrs. Cadman had had a good time. A real good time always lasts: you have it with all your nature and all your nature stays living with it. She had been a pretty child with long, blonde hair that her sister Rosa, who was her elder sister, used to tweak when they were alone in their room. She had grown used, in that childish attic bedroom, to Rosa's malevolent silences. Then one had grown up, full of great uppish curves. Hilda Cadman could sing. She had sung at parties and sung at charity concerts, too. She had been invited from town to town, much fêted in business society. She had sung in a dress cut low at the bosom, with a rose or carnation tucked into her hair. She had drunk port wine in great red rooms blazing with chandeliers. Mr. Cadman had whisked her away from her other gentlemen friends, and not for a moment had she regretted it. Nothing had been too good for her: she had gone on singing. She had felt warm air on her bare shoulders; she still saw the kind, flushed faces crowding round. Mr. Cadman and she belonged to the jolly set. They all thought the world of her, and she thought the world of them.

Mrs. Cadman, picking up the poker, jabbed the fire into a spurt of light. It does not do any good to sit and think in the dark.

The town was not the same now. They had all died, or lost their money, or gone. But you kept on loving the town for its dear old sake. She sometimes thought: Why not move and live at the seaside, where there would be a promenade and a band? But she knew her nature clung to the old scenes; where you had lived, you lived—your nature clung like a cat. While there was *something* to look at she was not one to repine. It kept you going to keep out and about. Things went, but then new things came in their place. You can't cure yourself of the habit of loving life. So she drank up the new pleasures—the big cafés, the barging buses, the cinemas, the shops dripping with colour, almost all built of glass. She could be perfectly happy all alone in a café, digging into a cream bun with a fork, the band playing, smiling faces all round. The old faces had not gone: they had dissolved, diluted into the ruddy blur through which she saw everything.

Meanwhile, Lucille was hard put to it, living her mother down. Mother looked ridiculous, always round town like that.

Mrs. Cadman heard Lucille come out of the kitchen and go upstairs with something rattling on a tray. She waited a minute more, then sidled into the kitchen, where she cautiously started to make tea. The gas-ring, as though it were a spy of Lucille's, popped loudly when she applied the match.

"Mother, she's asking for you."

"Oh, dear—do you mean she's—?"

"She's much more herself this evening," Lucille said implacably.

Mrs. Cadman, at the kitchen table, had been stirring sugar into her third cup. She pushed her chair back, brushed crumbs from her bosom and followed Lucille like a big, unhappy lamb. The light was on in the hall, but the stairs led up into shadow: she had one more start of reluctance at their foot. Autumn draughts ran about in the top storey: up there the powers of darkness all seemed to mobilize. Mrs. Cadman put her hand on the banister knob. "Are you sure she *does* want to see me? Oughtn't she to stay quiet?"

"You should go when she's asking. You never know . . ."

Breathless, breathing unevenly on the top landing, Mrs. Cadman pushed open the spare-room—that was the sick-room—door. In there—in here—the air was dead, and at first it seemed very dark. On the ceiling an oil-stove printed its flower-pattern; a hooded lamp, low down, was turned away from the bed. On that dark side of the lamp she could just distinguish Rosa, propped up, with the sheet drawn to her chin.

"Rosa?"

"Oh, it's you?"

"Yes; it's me, dear. Feeling better this evening?"

"Seemed funny, you not coming near me."

"They said for you to keep quiet."

"My own sister . . . You never liked sickness, did you? Well, I'm going. I shan't trouble you long."

"Oh, don't talk like that!"

"I'm glad to be going. Keeping on lying here . . . We all come to it. Oh, give over crying, Hilda. Doesn't do any good."

Mrs. Cadman sat down, to steady herself. She fumbled in her lap with her handkerchief, perpetually, clumsily knocking her elbows against the arms of the wicker chair. "It's such a shame," she said. "It's such a pity. You and me, after all . . ."

"Well, it's late for all that now. Each took our own ways." Rosa's voice went up in a sort of ghostly sharpness. "There were things that couldn't be otherwise. I've tried to do right by Lucille. Lucille's a good girl, Hilda. You should ask yourself if you've done right by her."

"Oh, for shame, Rosa," said Mrs. Cadman, turning her face through the dark towards that disembodied voice. "For shame, Rosa, even if you *are* going. You know best what's come between her and me. It's been you and her, you and her. I don't know where to turn sometimes—"

Rosa said: "You've got such a shallow heart."

"How should you know? Why, you've kept at a distance from me ever since we were tots. Oh, I know I'm a great silly, always after my fun, but I never took what was yours; I never did harm to you. I don't see what call we have got to judge each other. You didn't want my life that I've had."

Rosa's chin moved: she was lying looking up at her sister's big rippling shadow, splodged up there by the light of the low lamp. It is frightening, having your shadow watched. Mrs. Cadman said: "But what did I do to you?"

"I *could* have had a wicked heart," said Rosa. "A vain, silly heart like yours. I could have fretted, seeing you take everything. One thing, then another. But I was shown. God taught me to pity you. God taught me my lesson . . . You wouldn't even remember that Christmas tree."

"What Christmas tree?"

"No, you wouldn't even remember. Oh, I thought it was lovely. I could have cried when they pulled the curtains open, and there it was, all blazing away with candles and silver and everything—"

"Well, isn't that funny? I—"

"No; you've had all that pleasure since. All of us older children couldn't take it in, hardly, for quite a minute or two. It didn't look real. Then I looked up, and there was a fairy doll fixed on the top, right on the top spike, fixed on to a star. I set my heart on her. She had wings and long, fair hair, and she was shining away. I couldn't take my eyes off her. They cut the presents down; but she wasn't for anyone. In my childish blindness I kept praying to God. If I am not to have her, I prayed, let her stay there."

"And what did God do?" Hilda said eagerly.

"Oh, He taught me and saved me. You were a little thing in a blue sash; you piped up and asked might you have the doll."

"Fancy me! Aren't children awful!" said Mrs. Cadman. "Asking like that."

"They said: 'Make her sing for it.' They were taken with you. So you piped up again, singing. You got her, all right. I went off where they kept the coats. I've thanked God ever since for what I had to go through! I turned my face from vanity from that very night. I had been shown."

"Oh, what a shame!" said Hilda. "Oh, I think it was cruel; you poor little mite."

"No; I used to see that doll all draggled about the house till no one could bear the sight of it. I said to myself: that's how those things end. Why, I'd learnt more in one evening than you've ever learnt in your life. Oh, yes, I've watched you, Hilda. Yes, and I've pitied you."

"Well, you showed me no pity."

"You asked for no pity—all vain and set up."

"No wonder you've been against me. Fancy me not knowing. I didn't *mean* any harm—why, I was quite a little thing. I don't even remember."

"Well, you'll remember one day. When you lie as I'm

lying you'll find that everything comes back. And you'll see what it adds up to."

"Well, if I do?" said Hilda. "I haven't been such a baby; I've seen things out in my own way; I've had my ups and downs. It hasn't been all jam." She got herself out of the armchair and came and stood uncertainly by the foot of the bed. She had a great wish to reach out and turn the hooded lamp round, so that its light could fall on her sister's face. She felt she should *see* her sister, perhaps for the first time. Inside the flat, still form did implacable disappointment, then, stay locked? She wished she could give Rosa some little present. Too late to give Rosa anything pretty now: she looked back—it had always, then, been too late? She thought: you poor queer heart; you queer heart, eating yourself out, thanking God for the pain. She thought: I did that to her; then what have I done to Lucille?

She said: "You're ever so like me, Rosa, really, aren't you? Setting our hearts on things. When you've got them you don't notice. No wonder you wanted Lucille . . . You did ought to have had that fairy doll."

JESSAMYN WEST, born in Indiana of Quaker parents in 1902, grew up and was educated in California. She graduated from Whittier College and continued her studies in England and at the University of California. In her twenties she suffered and survived a long bout with tuberculosis. In her autobiographical memoir *The Woman Said Yes: Encounters With Life and Death*, she confesses her own suicide plans during this illness; she attributes her spiritual recovery, her determination to live, to her mother's bravery and infectious determination that her daughter recover. After her illness, West did give up her academic studies to pursue the writing career she had always desired. Over the years she authored nineteen books, including novels, memoirs, short stories, and poetry. Among her best-known works are *The Friendly Persuasion*, *The Massacre at Fall Creek*, and *Cress Delahanty*, still a highly regarded novel about adolescence. West's fiction and nonfiction have appeared in many distinguished and popular periodicals, including *The New Yorker*, *Atlantic Monthly*, *Harper's*, and *McCall's*. Essayist, reviewer, screenwriter, lecturer, and teacher, she was awarded six honorary doctorates in humane letters and literature. Until her death in February 1984 she lived with her husband, Harry Maxwell McPherson, in Napa, California. The recent publication of *The Collected Short Stories of Jessamyn West* was received with spirited critical acclaim, a testament to West's enduring contribution to American letters.

Reverdy
by
Jessamyn West

I never see asters without remembering her, never the haze of their pink and lavender blossoming as summer dies, but her name is in my heart: Reverdy, Reverdy.

I never say her name—not to anyone. When people ask about her, as they do occasionally even now, I say "she" and "her." "She is still gone." "We do not hear from her." "Yes, she was very beautiful," I say. But not her name.

Not Reverdy. That is buried deep, deep in my heart. Where the blood is warmest and thickest . . . where it has a sound to me like bells, or water running, or the doves whose voices in the evening wind are like smoke among the madrones and eucalyptus.

I have longed all these years to tell her how it was the night she left. You may scarcely believe it, but it is worse to have a good thing that is not true believed about you, than a bad. To be thanked for an act you meant to be harmful—every year those words sharpen until at last they cut like knives.

You mustn't think she was like me. She wasn't in the least. Not inside or out. She had dark hair like a cloud. Yes, really. It wasn't curly, but it didn't hang straight. It billowed out. And her face—oh, you mustn't think it was anything like mine. She had hazel eyes and a pointed chin. And you've seen lots of people, haven't you, with very live, animated faces and dead eyes? It was just the other way with Reverdy. Her face was always quiet, but her eyes were so alive they glowed. Oh, she was the most beautiful, most alive, and most loved girl in the world, and she was my sister.

I cannot bear for people to say we were alike. She was really good, and I was just a show-off.

Mother—she was better later, and gentler, but then she

was bad, cruel and suspicious with Reverdy. Everybody loved Reverdy. Not just the boys. But Mother wouldn't see that. She always acted as if Reverdy were boy-crazy, as if Reverdy tried to entice the boys to her. But it wasn't true. Reverdy never lifted a finger to a boy, though they were around her all the time from the day she was ten. Bringing her May baskets, or valentines, or ponies to ride.

And the big, tough boys liked her, too. When she was twelve and thirteen, big eighteen-year-olds would come over and sit on the steps and smoke and talk to Reverdy. They never said anything out of the way. I know because most of the time I was with them. Reverdy didn't care. She never wanted to be alone with them. Reverdy would listen to them until she got tired, then she'd say, "Good-bye for now." She'd always say, "Good-bye for now," and then she'd go out and play—maybe "Run, sheep, run"—with the little kids my age. And the little kids would all shout when Reverdy came out to play with them. If the game had been about to die, it would come to life again. If some of the kids had gone home, they'd yell, "Hey, Johnnie" or "Hey, Mary," or whoever it was, "Reverdy's going to play," and then everyone would come back, and in a minute or two the game would be better than ever.

I used to be awfully proud of being her sister. I don't know what I would have done without her. I was a terribly plain little frump—I wore glasses and had freckles. If I hadn't been Reverdy's sister, I'd have had to sit and play jacks by myself, until Joe came along. But boys would try to get Reverdy's attention by doing things for me. They'd say to her, "Does your sister want to ride on my handlebars?" And Reverdy would say, all glowing, happier than if she'd been asked, "Do you, Sister?" Of course I did, and when the boy came back, she'd ride with him just to thank him.

I don't know why people, why the boys, liked her so. Of course, she was beautiful, but I think it was more that she was so much—well, whatever she was at the moment; she never pretended. She talked with people when she wanted to, and when she got tired of them, she didn't stay on pretending, but said, "Good-bye for now," and left.

But Mother would never believe she wasn't boy-crazy, and I would hear her talking to Reverdy about girls who got in trouble, and how she'd rather see a daughter of hers in her grave. I didn't know what she was talking about, but it would make my face burn and scalp tingle just to hear her. She wouldn't talk sorrowfully or lovingly to Reverdy, but with hate. It wasn't Reverdy she hated, but you couldn't tell that, looking at her. She would bend over Reverdy and shake her finger and there would be long ugly lines from her nose to her mouth, and her eyebrows would be drawn down until you could see the bony ridges they were supposed to cover, all bare and hard. It used to make me tremble to see her. Then Reverdy would get mad. I don't think she knew half the time what Mother was talking about, either—only that Mother was full of hate and suspicion. She'd wait until Mother had finished, then she'd go to the foothills for a walk, even if it was dark, and stay for a long time. And then Mother would think she was out with some boy again.

I remember one time my mother came to me and said, "Clare, I want you to tiptoe out to the arbor and see what's going on there. Reverdy's out there with Sam Foss, and I haven't heard a sound out of them for an hour or more."

The arbor was a kind of little bower covered with honeysuckle. There was only a tiny little door, and the honeysuckle strands hung so thick over it the arbor was a kind of dark, sweet-smelling cave. Reverdy and I used to play house there. I knew I ought to say I wouldn't go spying on Reverdy, but I wanted to please Mother, so I went creeping out toward the arbor, holding my breath, walking on my toes. I didn't know then—but I've found out since—you can't do a thing without becoming that thing. When I started out to look for Reverdy I was her little sister, loving her. But creeping that way, holding my breath, spying, I became a spy. My hands got heavy and hot and my mouth dry, and I wanted to see her doing . . . whatever it was Mother was fearful of.

And then when I got to the arbor and peeped in, I saw that Chummie, our ten-year-old brother, was there with them, and they were all practicing sign language. Deaf-and-dumb language was the rage with kids that summer, and there was that big Sam Foss sitting crosslegged, practicing sign language so hard he was sweating. They had oranges rolled until they were soft, and straws stuck in them to suck the juice out.

That's all they were doing. Practicing deaf-and-dumb language, and sucking oranges that way, playing they were bottles of pop. I guess they'd taken a vow not to talk, because nobody said a word. Even when Reverdy saw me peeping in, she didn't say anything, just spelled out, "Hello, Sister." But my hands felt so hot and swollen I couldn't spell a thing, and I just stood there and stared until I heard Mother call me to her, where she was standing strained and waiting on the back steps.

"They're playing sign language with Chummie," I told her.

"Is Chummie with them?" she asked, and her face relaxed and had a sort of shamed look on it, I thought.

I went in the house and put on the old dress I went swimming in, and floated around in the irrigation canal until supper was over, so I wouldn't have to sit and look across the table at Reverdy.

Things like that were always happening. I loved Reverdy more than anybody, and I hated Mother sometimes for spying and suspecting and lecturing. But I wanted people to love me. And especially you want your mother to love you—isn't that true? And no one loved me the way Reverdy was loved. I wasn't beautiful and spontaneous, I had to work hard and do good deeds to be loved. I couldn't be free the way Reverdy was. I was always thinking of the effect I was making. I couldn't say, "Good-bye for now," and let people go to hell if they didn't like me. I was afraid they'd never come back, and I'd be left . . . alone. But Reverdy didn't care. She liked being alone—and that's the reason people loved her, I guess.

One evening in October, when it was almost dark, I was coming home from the library, coasting across lots in the hot dry Santa Ana that had been blowing all day. Cool weather had already come, and then three days of this hot wind. Dust everywhere. Under your eyelids, between your fingers, in your mouth. When we went to school in the morning the first thing we'd do would be to write our names in the dust on our desks. I had on a skirt full of pleats that evening, and I pulled the pleats out wide so the skirt made a sort of sail and the wind almost pushed me along. I watched the tumbleweeds blowing, and listening to the wind in the clump of eucalyptus by the barn, and felt miserable and gritty. Then I saw Reverdy walking up and down the driveway by the house, and I felt suddenly glad. Reverdy loved the wind, even Santa Ana's, and she was always out walking or running when the wind blew, if she didn't have any work to do. She liked to carry a scarf in her hand and hold it up in the wind so she could feel it tug and snap. When I saw Reverdy, I forgot how dusty and hot the wind was and remembered only how alive it was and how Reverdy loved it. I ran toward her, but she didn't wave or say a word, and when she reached the end of the driveway she turned her back on me and started walking toward the barn.

Before I had a chance to say a word to her, Mother came to the door and called to me to come in and not to talk to Reverdy. As soon as I heard her voice, before I could see her face, I knew there was some trouble—some trouble with Reverdy—and I knew what kind of trouble, too. I went in the house and shut the door. The sound of Reverdy's footsteps on the pepper leaves in the driveway outside stopped, and Mother put her head out the window and said, "You're to keep walking, Reverdy, and not stop. Understand? I want to hear footsteps and I want them to be brisk." Then she closed the window, though it was hard to do against the wind.

I stood with my face to the window and looked out into the dusty, windy dark where I could just see Reverdy in her white dress walking up and down, never stopping, her head bent, not paying any attention to the wind she loved. It made me feel sick to see her walking up and down there in the dusty dark like a homeless dog, while we were snug inside.

But Mother came over to the window and took the curtain out of my hand and put it back over the glass. Then she put her arm around my shoulders and pressed me close to her and said, "Mother's own dear girl who has never given her a moment's trouble."

That wasn't true. Mother had plenty of fault to find with me usually—but it was sweet to have her speak lovingly to me, to be cherished and appreciated. Maybe you can't understand that, maybe your family was always loving, maybe you were always dear little daughter, or maybe a big golden wonder-boy. But not me and not my mother. So try to understand how it was with me then, and how happy it made me to have Mother put her arms around me. Yes, I thought, I'm mother's comfort. And I forgot I couldn't make a boy look at me if I wanted to, and blamed Reverdy for not being able to steer clear of them the way I did. She just hasn't any consideration for any of us, I decided. Oh, I battened on Reverdy's downfall all right.

Then Father and Chummie came in, and Mother took Father away to the kitchen and talked to him there in a fast, breathless voice. I couldn't hear what she was saying, but I knew what she was talking about, of course. Chummie and I sat there in the dark. He whirled first one way and then another on the piano stool.

"What's Reverdy doing walking up and down outside there?" he asked.

"She's done something bad again," I told him.

Mother's voice got higher and higher, and Chummie said he'd have to go feed his rabbits, and I was left alone in the dark listening to her, and to Reverdy's footsteps on the pepper leaves. I decided to light the lights, but when I did—we had acetylene lights—the blue-white glare was so terrible I couldn't stand it. Not to sit alone in all that light and look at the dusty room and listen to the dry sound of the wind in the palms outside, and see Reverdy's books on the library table where she'd put them when she got home from school, with a big bunch of wilted asters laid across them. Reverdy always kept her room filled with flowers, and if she couldn't get flowers, she'd have leaves or grasses.

No, I couldn't stand that, so I turned out the lights and sat in the dark and listened to Reverdy's steps, not fast or light now, but heavy and slow—and I sat there and thought I was Mother's comforter, not causing her trouble like Reverdy.

Pretty soon I heard Mother and Father go outside, and then their voices beneath the window. Father was good, and he was for reason, but with Mother he lost his reason. He was just like me, I guess. He wanted Mother to love him, and because he did he would go out and say to Reverdy the things Mother wanted him to say.

Chummie came back from feeding his rabbits and sat with me in the dark room. Then I got the idea of a way to show Mother how much I was her comfort and mainstay, her darling younger daughter, dutiful and harmonious as hell.

Mother wanted me and Chummie to be musical—she'd given up with Reverdy—but Chummie and I had taken lessons for years. Usually we kicked and howled at having to play; so I thought, If we play now, it will show Mother how thoughtful and reliable we are. It will cheer her up while she's out there in the wind talking to that bad Reverdy. Yes, she will think, I have one fine, dependable daughter anyway.

So I said to Chummie, "Let's play something for Mother." So he got out his violin, and we played that piece I've ever afterward hated. Over and over again, just as sweet as we could make it. Oh, I felt smug as hell as I played. I sat there on the piano stool with feet just so, and my hands just so, and played carefully, every note saying, "Mother's comfort. Mother's comfort. Played by her good, fine, reliable daughter."

We could hear Mother's high voice outside the window and Reverdy's low murmur now and then. Chummie finally got tired of playing—the music wasn't saying anything to him—and went out to the kitchen to get something to eat. I went too, but the minute I took a bite I knew I wasn't hungry, and Chummie and I both went to bed. I lay in bed a long time waiting to hear Mother and Reverdy come in, but there wasn't any sound but the wind.

I was asleep when Reverdy did come in. She sat down on the side of my bed, and it was just her sitting there that finally woke me. Then, when I was awake, she picked up my hand and began to press my fingertips one by one, and spoke in the sweetest, kindest voice. You'd never have thought to hear her that she had just spent four or five hours the way she did.

She said, "I'll never forget your playing for me, Sister. Never. Never. It was kind and beautiful of you. Just when I thought I was all alone, I heard you telling me not to be sad." Then she leaned over and kissed me and said, "Good night, now. I've put some asters in water for you. They're a little wilted but I think they'll be all right by morning. Go to sleep, now. I'll never forget, Clare."

If I could only have told her, if I could only have told her then. If I could have said to her, "I was playing for Mother, Reverdy. I guess I was jealous of your always having the limelight. I wanted to be first for once." If I could only have said, "I love you more than anything, Reverdy, but I have a mean soul," she would have put her cheek to mine and said, "Oh, Clare, what a thing to say."

But I couldn't do it, and next morning she was gone. And there on the table by my bed were the asters she had left for me, grown fresh overnight.

JEAN STAFFORD was born in 1915 in Covina, California, and educated in Colorado. Although she spent most of her adult professional life in the Northeast, she once said that her "roots remain in the semi-fictitious town of Adams, Colorado." As the first wife of poet Robert Lowell she was part of a circle that included R. P. Blackmur, Delmore Schwartz, and Randall Jarrell. She was the author of three outstanding novels, *Boston Adventure* (1944), *The Mountain Lion* (1947), and *The Catherine Wheel* (1952), and two volumes of short stories, many of which appeared originally in *The New Yorker*. *The Collected Stories of Jean Stafford* (1969) won the Pulitzer Prize for Literature in 1970. Critics have compared the intellectuality of Stafford's fiction with that of Mary McCarthy; the style and sensitivity of her work is said to be reminiscent of Katherine Anne Porter. "In the Zoo," the story that follows here, received the O. Henry Memorial Award for the best short story of 1955. Joyce Carol Oates wrote in her review of *The Collected Stories* that in Stafford's stories, which are exquisitely wrought and sensitively imagined like glass flowers, according to the Jamesian-Chekhovian-Joycean model in which most "literary" writers wrote during those years, the heroines despair of striking free. But in the finest of the stories—"In the Zoo"—the protagonist is never morbid or self-pitying. Indeed, Oates writes, though the narrator of this story confesses that "my pain becomes intolerable," the story concludes "with an outburst of paranoia that manages to be comic." Such a twist is not unusual in Stafford's fiction: her best work is memorable especially for its bracing social irreverence. She died in 1979 in East Hampton, Long Island, where she had lived for many years.

In the Zoo

by
Jean Stafford

Keening harshly in his senility, the blind polar bear slowly and ceaselessly shakes his head in the stark heat of the July and mountain noon. His open eyes are blue. No one stops to look at him; an old farmer, in passing, sums up the old bear's situation by observing, with a ruthless chuckle, that he is a "back number." Patient and despairing, he sits on his yellowed haunches on the central rock of his pool, his huge toy paws wearing short boots of mud.

The grizzlies to the right of him, a conventional family of father and mother and two spring cubs, alternately play the clown and sleep. There is a blustery, scoundrelly, half-likable bravado in the manner of the black bear on the polar's left; his name, according to the legend on his cage, is Clancy, and he is a rough-and-tumble, brawling blowhard, thundering continually as he paces back and forth, or pauses to face his audience of children and mothers and release from his great, gray-tongued mouth a perfectly Vesuvian roar. If he were to be reincarnated in human form, he would be a man of action, possibly a football coach, probably a politician. One expects to see his black hat hanging from a branch of one of his trees; at any moment he will light a cigar.

The polar bear's next-door neighbors are not the only ones who offer so sharp and sad a contrast to him. Across a reach of scrappy grass and litter is the convocation of conceited monkeys, burrowing into each other's necks and chests for fleas, picking their noses with their long, black, finicky fingers, swinging by their gifted tails on the flying trapeze, screaming bloody murder. Even when they mourn—one would think the male orangutan was on the very brink of suicide—they are comedians; they only fake depression, for they are firmly secure in their rambunctious tribalism and in their appalling insight and contempt. Their flibbertigibbet gambolling is a sham, and, stealthily and shiftily, they are really watching the pitiful polar bear ("Back number," they quote the farmer. "That's *his* number all right," they snigger), and the windy black bear ("Life of the party. Gasbag. Low I.Q.," they note scornfully on his dossier), and the stupid, bourgeois grizzlies ("It's feed the face and hit the sack for them," the monkeys say). And they are watching my sister and me, two middle-aged women, as we sit on a bench between the exhibits, eating popcorn, growing thirsty. We are thoughtful.

A chance remark of Daisy's a few minutes before has turned us to memory and meditation. "I don't know why," she said, "but that poor blind bear reminds me of Mr. Murphy." The name "Mr. Murphy" at once returned us both to childhood, and we were floated far and fast, our later lives diminished. So now we eat our popcorn in silence with the ritualistic appetite of childhood, which has little to do with hunger; it is not so much food as a sacrament, and in tribute to our sisterliness and our friendliness I break the silence to say that this is the best popcorn I have ever eaten in my life. The extravagance of my statement instantly makes me feel self-indulgent, and for some time I uneasily avoid looking at the blind bear. My sister does not agree or disagree; she simply says that popcorn is the only food she has ever really liked. For a long time, then, we eat without a word, but I know, because I know her well and know her similarity to me, that Daisy is thinking what I am thinking; both of us are mournfully remembering Mr. Murphy, who, at one time in our lives, was our only friend.

This zoo is in Denver, a city that means nothing to my sister and me except as a place to take or meet trains. Daisy lives two hundred miles farther west, and it is her custom, when my every-other-year visit with her is over, to come across the mountains to see me off on my eastbound train. We know almost no one here, and because our stays are short, we have never bothered to learn the town in more than the most desultory way. We know the Burlington uptown office and the respectable hotels, a restaurant or two, the Union Station, and, beginning today, the zoo in the city park.

But since the moment that Daisy named Mr. Murphy by name our situation in Denver has been only corporeal; our minds and our hearts are in Adams, fifty miles north, and we are seeing, under the white sun at its pitiless meridian, the streets of that ugly town, its parks and trees and bridges, the bandstand in its dreary park, the roads that lead away from it, west to the mountains and east to the plains, its mongrel and multitudinous churches, its high school shaped like a loaf of bread, the campus of its college, an oasis of which we had no experience except to walk through it now and then, eying the woodbine on the impressive buildings. These things are engraved forever on our minds with a legibility so insistent that you have only to say the name of the town aloud to us to rip the rinds from our nerves and leave us exposed in terror and humiliation.

We have supposed in later years that Adams was not so bad as all that, and we know that we magnified its ugliness because we looked upon it as the extension of the possessive, unloving, scornful, complacent foster mother, Mrs. Placer, to whom, at the death of our parents within a month of each other, we were sent like Dickensian grotesqueries—cowardly, weak-stomached, given to tears, backward in school. Daisy was ten and I was eight when, unaccompanied, we made the long trip from Marblehead to our benefactress, whom we had never seen and, indeed, never heard of until the pastor of our church came to tell us of the arrangement our father had made on his deathbed, seconded by our mother on hers. This man, whose name and face I have forgotten and whose parting speeches to us I have not forgiven, tried to dry our tears with talk of Indians and of buffaloes; he spoke, however, at much greater length, and in preaching cadences, of the Christian goodness of Mrs. Placer. She was, he said, childless and fond of children, and for many years she had been a widow, after the lingering demise of her tubercular husband, for whose sake she had moved to the Rocky Mountains. For his support and costly medical care, she had run a boarding house, and after his death, since he had left her nothing, she was obliged to continue running it. She had been a girlhood friend of our paternal grandmother, and our father, in the absence of responsible relatives, had made her the beneficiary of his life insurance on the condition that she lodge and rear us.

The pastor, with a frankness remarkable considering that he was talking to children, explained to us that our father had left little more than a drop in the bucket for our care, and he enjoined us to give Mrs. Placer, in return for her hospitality and sacrifice, courteous help and eternal thanks. "Sacrifice" was a word we were never allowed to forget.

And thus it was, in grief for our parents, that we came cringing to the dry Western town and to the house where Mrs. Placer lived, a house in which the square, uncushioned furniture was cruel and the pictures on the walls were either dour or dire and the lodgers, who lived in the upper floors among shadowy wardrobes and chiffoniers, had come through the years to resemble their landlady in appearance as well as in deportment.

After their ugly-colored evening meal, Gran—as she bade us call her—and her paying guests would sit, rangy and aquiline, rocking on the front porch on spring and summer and autumn nights, tasting their delicious grievances: those slights delivered by ungrateful sons and daughters, those impudences committed by trolley-car conductors and uppity salegirls in the ready-to-wear, all those slurs and calculated elbow-jostlings that were their daily crucifixion and their staff of life. We little girls, washing the dishes in the cavernous kitchen, listened to their even, martyred voices, fixed like leeches to their solitary subject and their solitary creed—that life was essentially a matter of being done in, let down, and swindled.

At regular intervals, Mrs. Placer, chairwoman of the victims, would say, "Of course, I don't care; I just have to laugh," and then would tell a shocking tale of an intricate piece of skulduggery perpetrated against her by someone she did not even know. Sometimes, with her avid, partial jury sitting there on the porch behind the bitter hopvines in the heady mountain air, the cases she tried involved Daisy and me, and, listening, we travailed, hugging each other, whispering, "I wish she wouldn't! Oh, how did she find out?" How *did* she? Certainly we never told her when we were snubbed or chosen last on teams, never admitted to a teacher's scolding or to the hoots of laughter that greeted us when we bit on silly, unfair jokes. But she knew. She knew about the slumber parties we were not invited to, the beefsteak fries at which we were pointedly left out; she knew that the singing teacher had said in so many words that I could not carry a tune in a basket and that the sewing superintendent had said that Daisy's fingers were all thumbs. With our teeth chattering in the cold of our isolation, we would hear her protestant, litigious voice defending our right to be orphans, paupers, wholly dependent on her—except for the really ridiculous pittance from our father's life insurance—when it was all she could do to make ends meet. She did not care, but she had to laugh that people in general were so small-minded that they looked down on fatherless, motherless waifs like us and, by association, looked down on her. It seemed funny to her that people gave her no credit for taking on these sickly youngsters who were not even kin but only the grandchildren of a friend.

If a child with braces on her teeth came to play with us, she was, according to Gran, slyly lording it over us because our teeth were crooked, but there was no money to have them straightened. And what could be the meaning of our being asked to come for supper at the doctor's house? Were the doctor and his la-di-da New York wife and those pert girls with their solid-gold barrettes and their Shetland pony going to shame her poor darlings? Or shame their poor Gran by making them sorry to come home to the plain but honest life that was all she could provide for them?

There was no stratum of society not reeking with the effluvium of fraud and pettifoggery. And the school system was almost the worst of all: if we could not understand fractions, was that not our teacher's fault? And therefore what right had she to give us F? It was as plain as a pikestaff to Gran that the teacher was only covering up her own inability to teach. It was unlikely, too—highly unlikely—that it was by accident that time and time again the free medical clinic was closed for the day just as our names were about to be called out, so that nothing was done about our bad tonsils, which meant that we were repeatedly sick in the winter, with Gran fetching and carrying for us, climbing those stairs a jillion times a day with her game leg and her heart that was none too strong.

Steeped in these mists of accusation and hidden plots and double meanings, Daisy and I grew up like worms. I think no one could have withstood the atmosphere in that house where everyone trod on eggs that a little bird had told them were bad. They spied on one another, whispered behind doors, conjectured, drew parallels beginning "With all due respect . . ." or "It is a matter of indifference to *me* but . . ." The vigilantes patrolled our town by day, and by night returned to lay their goodies at their priestess's feet and wait for her oracular interpretation of the innards of the butcher, the baker, the candlestick maker, the soda jerk's girl, and the barber's unnatural deaf white cat.

Consequently, Daisy and I also became suspicious. But it was suspicion of ourselves that made us mope and weep and grimace with self-judgment. Why were we not happy when Gran had sacrificed herself to the bone for us? Why did we not cut dead the paper boy who had called her a filthy name? Why did we persist in our willful friendliness with the grocer who had tried, unsuccessfully, to overcharge her on a case of pork and beans?

Our friendships were nervous and surreptitious; we sneaked and lied, and as our hungers sharpened, our debasement deepened; we were pitied; we were shifty-eyed, always on the lookout for Mrs. Placer or one of her tattletale lodgers; we were hypocrites.

Nevertheless, one thin filament of instinct survived, and Daisy and I in time found asylum in a small menagerie down by the railroad tracks. It belonged to a gentle alcoholic ne'er-do-well, who did nothing all day long but drink bathtub gin in rickeys and play solitaire and smile to himself and talk to his animals. He had a little, stunted red vixen and a deodorized skunk, a parrot from Tahiti that spoke Parisian French, a woebegone coyote, and two capuchin monkeys, so serious and humanized, so small and sad and sweet, and so religious-looking with their tonsured heads that it was impossible not to think their gibberish was really an ordered language with a grammar that someday some philologist would understand.

Gran knew about our visits to Mr. Murphy and she did not object, for it gave her keen pleasure to excoriate him when we came home. His vice was not a matter of guesswork; it was an established fact that he was half-seas over from dawn till midnight. "With the black Irish," said Gran, "the taste for drink is taken in with the mother's milk and is never mastered. Oh, I know all about those promises to join the temperance movement and not to touch another drop. The way to Hell is paved with good intentions."

We were still little girls when we discovered Mr. Murphy, before the shattering disease of adolescence was to make our bones and brains ache even more painfully than before, and we loved him and we hoped to marry him when we grew up. We loved him, and we loved his monkeys to exactly the same degree and in exactly the same way; they were husbands and fathers and brothers, these three little, ugly, dark, secret men who minded their own business and let us mind ours. If we stuck our fingers through the bars of the cage, the monkeys would sometimes take them in their tight, tiny hands and look into our faces with a tentative, somehow absent-minded sorrow, as if they terribly regretted that they could not place us but were glad to see us all the same. Mr. Murphy, playing a solitaire game of cards called "once in a blue moon" on a kitchen table in his back yard beside the pens, would occasionally look up and blink his beautiful blue eyes and say, "You're peaches to make over my wee friends. I love you for it." There was nothing demanding in his voice, and nothing sticky; on his lips the word "love" was jocose and forthright, it had no strings attached. We would sit on either side of him and watch him regiment his ranks of cards and stop to drink as deeply as if he were dying of thirst and wave to his animals and say to them, "Yes, lads, you're dandies."

Because Mr. Murphy was as reserved with us as the capuchins were, as courteously noncommittal, we were surprised one spring day when he told us that he had a present for us, which he hoped Mrs. Placer would let us keep; it was a puppy, for whom the owner had asked him to find a home—half collie and half Labrador retriever, blue-blooded on both sides.

"You might tell Mrs. Placer—" he said, smiling at the name, for Gran was famous in the town. "You might tell Mrs. Placer," said Mr. Murphy, "that this lad will make a fine watchdog. She'll never have to fear for her spoons again. Or her honor." The last he said to himself, not laughing but tucking his chin into his collar; lines sprang to the corners of his eyes. He would not let us see the dog, whom we could hear yipping and squealing inside his shanty, for he said that our disappointment would weigh on his conscience if we lost our hearts to the fellow and then could not have him for our own.

That evening at supper, we told Gran about Mr. Murphy's present. A dog? In the first place, why a dog? Was it possible that the news had reached Mr. Murphy's ears that Gran had just this very day finished planting her spring garden, the very thing that a rampageous dog would have in his mind to destroy? What sex was it? A male! Females, she had heard, were more trustworthy; males roved and came home smelling of skunk; such a consideration as this, of course, would not have crossed Mr. Murphy's fuddled mind. Was this young male dog housebroken? We had not asked? That was the limit!

Gran appealed to her followers, too raptly fascinated by Mr. Murphy's machinations to eat their Harvard beets. "Am I being farfetched or does it strike you as decidedly queer that Mr. Murphy is trying to fob off on my little girls a young cur that has not been trained?" she asked them. "If it were housebroken, he would have said so, so I feel it is safe to assume that it is not. Perhaps cannot *be* housebroken. I've heard of such cases."

The fantasy spun on, richly and rapidly, with all the skilled helping hands at work at once. The dog was tangibly in the room with us, shedding his hair, biting his fleas, shaking rain off himself to splatter the walls, dragging some dreadful carcass across the floor, chewing up slippers, knocking over chairs with his tail, gobbling the chops from the platter, barking, biting, fathering, fighting, smelling to high heaven of carrion, staining the rug with his muddy feet, scratching the floor with his claws. He developed rabies; he bit a child, two children! Three! Everyone in town! And Gran and her poor darlings went to jail for harboring this murderous, odoriferous, drunk, Roman Catholic dog.

And yet, astoundingly enough, she came around to agreeing to let us have the dog. It was, as Mr. Murphy had predicted, the word "watchdog" that deflected the course of the trial. The moment Daisy uttered it, Gran halted, marshalling her reverse march; while she rallied and tacked and reconnoitred, she sent us to the kitchen for the dessert. And by the time this course was under way, the uses of a dog, the enormous potentialities for investigation and law enforcement in a dog trained by Mrs. Placer, were being minutely and passionately scrutinized by the eight upright bloodhounds sitting at the table wolfing their brown Betty as if it were fresh-killed rabbit. The dog now sat at attention beside his mistress, fiercely alert, ears cocked, nose aquiver, the protector of widows, of orphans, of lonely people who had no homes. He made short shrift of burglars, homicidal maniacs, Peeping Toms, gypsies, bogus missionaries, Fuller Brush men with a risqué spiel. He went to the store and brought back groceries, retrieved the evening paper from the awkward place the boy had meanly thrown it, rescued cripples from burning houses, saved children from drowning, heeled at command, begged, lay down, stood up, sat, jumped through a hoop, ratted.

Both times—when he was a ruffian of the blackest delinquency and then a pillar of society—he was full-grown in his prefiguration, and when Laddy appeared on the following day, small, unsteady, and whimpering lonesomely, Gran and her lodgers were taken aback; his infant, clumsy paws embarrassed them, his melting eyes were unapropos. But it could never be said of Mrs. Placer, as Mrs. Placer her own self said, that she was a woman who went back on her word, and her darlings were going to have their dog, softheaded and feckless as he might be. All the first night, in his carton in the kitchen, he wailed for his mother, and in the morning, it was true, he had made a shambles of the room—fouled the floor, and pulled off the tablecloth together with a ketchup bottle, so that thick gore lay everywhere. At breakfast, the lodgers confessed they had had a most amusing night, for it had actually been funny the way the dog had been determined not to let anyone get a wink of sleep. After that first night, Laddy slept in our room, receiving from us, all through our delighted, sleepless nights, pats and embraces and kisses and whispers. He was our baby, our best friend, the smartest, prettiest, nicest dog in the entire wide world. Our soft and rapid blandishments excited him to yelp at us in pleased bewilderment, and then we would playfully grasp his muzzle, so that he would snarl, deep in his throat like an adult dog, and shake his head violently, and, when we freed him, nip us smartly with great good will.

He was an intelligent and genial dog and we trained him quickly. He steered clear of Gran's radishes and lettuce after she had several times given him a brisk comeuppance with a strap across the rump, and he soon left off chewing shoes and the laundry on the line, and he outgrew his babyish whining. He grew like a weed; he lost his spherical softness, and his coat, which had been sooty fluff, came in stiff and rusty black; his nose grew aristocratically long, and his clever, pointed ears stood at attention. He was all bronzy, lustrous black except for an Elizabethan ruff of white and a tip of white at the end of his perky tail. No one could deny that he was exceptionally handsome and that he had as well, great personal charm and style. He escorted Daisy and me to school in the morning, laughing interiorly out of the enormous pleasure of his life as he gracefully cantered ahead of us, distracted occasionally by his private interest in smells or unfamiliar beings in the grass but, on the whole, engrossed in his role of chaperon. He made friends easily with other dogs, and sometimes he went for a long hunting weekend into the mountains with a huge and bossy old red hound named Mess, who had been on the county most of his life and had made a good thing of it, particularly at the fire station.

It was after one of these three-day excursions into the high country that Gran took Laddy in hand. He had come back spent and filthy, his coat a mass of cockleburs and ticks, his eyes bloodshot, loud *râles* in his chest; for half a day he lay motionless before the front door like someone in a hangover, his groaning eyes explicitly saying "Oh, for God's sake, leave me be" when we offered him food or bowls of water. Gran was disapproving, then affronted, and finally furious. Not, of course, with Laddy, since all inmates of her house enjoyed immunity, but with Mess, whose caddish character, together with that of his nominal masters, the firemen, she examined closely under a strong light, with an air of detachment, with her not caring but her having, all the same, to laugh. A lodger who occupied the back west room had something to say about the fire chief and his nocturnal visits to a certain house occupied by a certain group of young women, too near the same age to be sisters and too old to be the daughters of the woman who claimed to be their mother. What a story! The exophthalmic librarian—she lived in one of the front rooms—had some interesting insinuations to make about the deputy marshal, who had borrowed, significantly, she thought, a book on hypnotism. She also knew—she was, of course, in a most useful position in the town, and from her authoritative pen in the middle of the library her mammiform and azure eyes and her eager ears missed nothing—that the fire chief's wife was not as scrupulous as she might be when she was keeping score on bridge night at the Sorosis.

There was little at the moment that Mrs. Placer and her disciples could do to save the souls of the Fire Department and their families, and therefore save the town from holocaust (a very timid boarder—a Mr. Beaver, a newcomer who was not to linger long—had sniffed throughout this recitative as if he were smelling burning flesh), but at least the unwholesome bond between Mess and Laddy could and would be severed once and for all. Gran looked across the porch at Laddy, who lay stretched at full length in the darkest corner, shuddering and baying abortively in his throat as he chased jack rabbits in his dreams, and she said, "A dog can have morals like a human." With this declaration Laddy's randy, manly holidays were finished. It may have been telepathy that woke him; he lifted his heavy head from his paws, laboriously got up, hesitated for a moment, and then padded languidly across the porch to Gran. He stood docilely beside her chair, head down, tail drooping as if to say, "O.K., Mrs. Placer, show me how and I'll walk the straight and narrow."

The very next day, Gran changed Laddy's name to Caesar, as being more dignified, and a joke was made at the supper table that he had come, seen, and conquered Mrs. Placer's heart—for within her circle, where the magnanimity she lavished upon her orphans was daily demonstrated, Mrs. Placer's heart was highly thought of. On that day also, although we did not know it yet, Laddy ceased to be our dog. Before many weeks passed, indeed, he ceased to be anyone we had ever known. A week or so after he became Caesar, he took up residence in her room, sleeping alongside her bed. She broke him of the habit of taking us to school (temptation to low living was rife along those streets; there was a chow—well, never mind) by the simple expedient of chaining him to a tree as soon as she got up in the morning. This discipline, together with the stamina-building cuffs she gave his sensitive ears from time to time, gradually but certainly remade his character. From a sanguine, affectionate, easygoing Gael (with the fits of melancholy that alternated with the larkiness), he turned into an overbearing, military, efficient, loud-voiced Teuton. His bark, once wide of range, narrowed to one dark, glottal tone.

Soon the paper boy flatly refused to serve our house after Caesar efficiently removed the bicycle clip from his pants leg; the skin was not broken, or even bruised, but it was a matter of principle with the boy. The milkman approached the back door in a seizure of shakes like St. Vitus's dance. The metermen, the coal men, and the garbage collector crossed themselves if they were Catholics and, if they were not, tried whistling in the dark. "Good boy, good Caesar," they carolled, and, unctuously lying, they said they knew his bark was worse than his bite, knowing full well that it was not, considering the very nasty nip, requiring stitches, he had given a representative of the Olson Rug Company, who had had the folly to pat him on the head. Caesar did not molest the lodgers, but he disdained them and he did not brook being personally addressed by anyone except Gran. One night, he wandered into the dining room, appearing to be in search of something he had mislaid, and, for some reason that no one was ever able to divine, suddenly stood stock-still and gave the easily upset Mr. Beaver a long and penetrating look. Mr. Beaver, trembling from head to toe, stammered, "Why—er, hello there, Caesar, old boy, old boy," and Caesar charged. For a moment, it was touch and go, but Gran saved Mr. Beaver, only to lose him an hour later when he departed, bag and baggage, for the Y.M.C.A. This rout and the consequent loss of revenue would more than likely have meant Caesar's downfall and his deportation to the pound if it had not been that a newly widowed druggist, very irascible and very much Gran's style, had applied for a room in her house a week or so before, and now he moved in delightedly, as if he were coming home.

Finally, the police demanded that Caesar be muzzled and they warned that if he committed any major crime again—they cited the case of the Olson man—he would be shot on sight. Mrs. Placer, although she had no respect for the law, knowing as much as she did about its agents, obeyed. She obeyed, that is, in part; she put the muzzle on Caesar for a few hours a day, usually early in the morning when the traffic was light and before the deliveries had started, but the rest of the time his powerful jaws and dazzling white sabre teeth were free and snapping. There was between these two such preternatural rapport, such an impressive conjugation of suspicion, that he, sensing the approach of a policeman, could convey instantly to her the immediate necessity of clapping his nose cage on. And the policeman, sent out on the complaint of a terrorized neighbor, would be greeted by this law-abiding pair at the door.

Daisy and I wished we were dead. We were divided between hating Caesar and loving Laddy, and we could not give up the hope that something, someday, would change him back into the loving animal he had been before he was appointed vice-president of the Placerites. Now at the meetings after supper on the porch he took an active part, standing rigidly at Gran's side except when she sent him on an errand. He carried out these assignments not with the air of a servant but with that of an accomplice. "Get me the paper, Caesar," she would say to him, and he, dismayingly intelligent and a shade smart-alecky, would open the screen door by himself and in a minute come back with the *Bulletin*, from which Mrs. Placer would then read an item, like the Gospel of the day, and then read between the lines of it, scandalized.

In the deepening of our woe and our bereavement and humiliation, we mutely appealed to Mr. Murphy. We did not speak outright to him, for Mr. Murphy lived in a state of indirection, and often when he used the pronoun "I," he seemed to be speaking of someone standing a little to the left of him, but we went to see him and his animals each day during the sad summer, taking what comfort we could from the cozy, quiet indolence of his back yard, where small black eyes encountered ours politely and everyone was half asleep. When Mr. Murphy inquired about Laddy in his bland, inattentive way, looking for a stratagem whereby to shift the queen of hearts into position by the king, we would say, "Oh, he's fine," or "Laddy is a nifty dog." And Mr. Murphy, reverently slaking the thirst that was his talent and his concubine, would murmur, "I'm glad."

We wanted to tell him, we wanted his help, or at least his sympathy, but how could we cloud his sunny world? It was awful to see Mr. Murphy ruffled. Up in the calm clouds as he generally was, he could occasionally be brought to earth with a thud, as we had seen and heard one day. Not far from his house, there lived a bad troublemaking boy of twelve, who was forever hanging over the fence trying to teach the parrot obscene words. He got nowhere, for she spoke no English and she would flabbergast him with her cold eye and sneer, "*Tant pis.*" One day, this boorish fellow went too far; he suddenly shot his head over the fence like a jack-in-the-box and aimed a water pistol at the skunk's face. Mr. Murphy leaped to his feet in a scarlet rage; he picked up a stone and threw it accurately, hitting the boy square in the back, so hard that he fell right down in a mud puddle and lay there kicking and squalling and, as it turned out, quite badly hurt. "If you ever come back here again, I'll kill you!" roared Mr. Murphy. I think he meant it, for I have seldom seen an anger so resolute, so brilliant, and so voluble. "How dared he!" he cried, scrambling into Mallow's cage to hug and pet and soothe her. "He must be absolutely mad! He must be the Devil!" He did not go back to his game after that but paced the yard, swearing a blue streak and only pausing to croon to his animals, now as frightened by him as they had been by the intruder, and to drink straight from the bottle, not bothering with fixings. We were fascinated by this unfamiliar side of Mr. Murphy, but we did not want to see it ever again, for his face had grown so dangerously purple and the veins of his forehead seemed ready to burst and his eyes looked scorched. He was the closest thing to a maniac we had ever seen. So we did not tell him about Laddy; what he did not know would not hurt him, although it was hurting us, throbbing in us like a great, bleating wound.

But eventually Mr. Murphy heard about our dog's conversion, one night at the pool hall, which he visited from time to time when he was seized with a rare but compelling garrulity, and the next afternoon when he asked us how Laddy was and we replied that he was fine, he tranquilly told us, as he deliberated whether to move the jack of clubs now or to bide his time, that we were sweet girls but we were lying in our teeth. He did not seem at all angry but only interested, and all the while he questioned us, he went on about his business with the gin and the hearts and spades and diamonds and clubs. It rarely happened that he won the particular game he was playing, but that day he did, and when he saw all the cards laid out in their ideal pattern, he leaned back, looking disappointed, and he said, "I'm damned." He then scooped up the cards, in a gesture unusually quick and tidy for him, stacked them together, and bound them with a rubber band. Then he began to tell us what he thought of Gran. He grew as loud and apoplectic as he had been that other time, and though he kept repeating that he knew *we* were innocent and he put not a shred of the blame on us, we were afraid he might suddenly change his mind, and, speechless, we cowered against the monkeys' cage. In dread, the monkeys clutched the fingers we offered to them and made soft, protesting noises, as if to say, "Oh, stop it, Murphy! Our nerves!"

As quickly as it had started, the tantrum ended. Mr. Murphy paled to his normal complexion and said calmly that the only practical thing was to go and have it out with Mrs. Placer. "At once," he added, although he said he bitterly feared that it was too late and there would be no exorcising the fiend from Laddy's misused spirit. And because he had given the dog to us and not to her, he required that we go along with him, stick up for our rights, stand on our mettle, get up our Irish, and give the old bitch something to put in her pipe and smoke.

Oh, it was hot that day! We walked in a kind of delirium through the simmer, where only the grasshoppers had the energy to move, and I remember wondering if ether smelled like the gin on Mr. Murphy's breath. Daisy and I, in one way or another, were going to have our gizzards cut out along with our hearts and our souls and our pride, and I wished I were as drunk as Mr. Murphy, who swam effortlessly through the heat, his lips parted comfortably, his eyes half closed. When we turned in to the path at Gran's house, my blood began to scald my veins. It was so futile and so dangerous and so absurd. Here we were on a high moral mission, two draggletailed, gumptionless little girls and a toper whom no one could take seriously, partly because he was little more than a gurgling bottle of booze and partly because of the clothes he wore. He was a sight, as he always was when he was out of his own yard. There, somehow, in the carefree disorder, his clothes did not look especially strange, but on the streets of the town, in the barbershop or the post office or on Gran's path, they were fantastic. He wore a pair of hound's tooth pants, old but maintaining a vehement pattern, and with them he wore a collarless blue flannelette shirt. His hat was the silliest of all, because it was a derby three sizes too big. And as if Shannon, too, was a part of his funny-paper costume, the elder capuchin rode on his shoulder, tightly embracing his thin red neck.

Gran and Caesar were standing side by side behind the screen door, looking as if they had been expecting us all along. For a moment, Gran and Mr. Murphy faced each other across the length of weedy brick between the gate and the front porch, and no one spoke. Gran took no notice at all of Daisy and me. She adjusted her eyeglasses, using both hands, and then looked down at Caesar and matter-of-factly asked, "Do you want out?"

Caesar flung himself full-length upon the screen and it sprang open like a jaw. I ran to meet and head him off, and Daisy threw a library book at his head, but he was on Mr. Murphy in one split second and had his monkey on his shoulder and had broken Shannon's neck in two shakes. He would have gone on nuzzling and mauling and growling over the corpse for hours if Gran had not marched out of the house and down the path and slapped him lightly on the flank and said, in a voice that could not have deceived an idiot, "Why, Caesar, you scamp! You've hurt Mr. Murphy's monkey! Aren't you ashamed!"

Hurt the monkey! In one final, apologetic shudder, the life was extinguished from the little fellow. Bloody and covered with slather, Shannon lay with his arms suppliantly stretched over his head, his leather fingers curled into loose, helpless fists. His hind legs and his tail lay limp and helter-skelter on the path. And Mr. Murphy, all of a sudden reeling drunk, burst into the kind of tears that Daisy and I knew well—the kind that time alone could stop. We stood aghast in the dark-red sunset, killed by our horror and our grief for Shannon and our unforgivable disgrace. We stood upright in a dead faint, and an eon passed before Mr. Murphy picked up Shannon's body and wove away, sobbing, "I don't believe it! I don't *believe it!*"

The very next day, again at morbid, heavy sunset, Caesar died in violent convulsions, knocking down two tall hollyhocks in his throes. Long after his heart had stopped, his right hind leg continued to jerk in aimless reflex. Madly methodical, Mr. Murphy had poisoned some meat for him, had thoroughly envenomed a whole pound of hamburger, and early in the morning, before sunup, when he must have been near collapse with his hangover, he had stolen up to Mrs. Placer's house and put it by the kitchen door. He was so stealthy that Caesar never stirred in his fool's paradise there on the floor by Gran. We knew these to be the facts, for Mr. Murphy made no bones about them. Afterward, he had gone home and said a solemn Requiem for Shannon in so loud a voice that someone sent for the police, and they took him away in the Black Maria to sober him up on strong green tea. By the time he was in the lockup and had confessed what he had done, it was far too late, for Caesar had already gulped down the meat. He suffered an undreamed-of agony in Gran's flower garden, and Daisy and I, unable to bear the sight of it, hiked up to the red rocks and shook there, wretchedly ripping to shreds the sand lilies that grew in the cracks. Flight was the only thing we could think of, but where could we go? We stared west at the mountains and quailed at the look of the stern white glacier; we wildly scanned the prairies for escape. "If only we were something besides kids! Besides girls!" mourned Daisy. I could not speak at all; I huddled in a niche of the rocks and cried.

No one in town, except, of course, her lodgers, had the slightest sympathy for Gran. The townsfolk allowed that Mr. Murphy was a drunk and was fighting Irish, but he had a heart and this was something that could never be said of Mrs. Placer. The neighbor who had called the police when he was chanting the *Dies Irae* before breakfast in that deafening monotone had said, "The poor guy is having some kind of a spell, so don't be rough on him, hear?" Mr. Murphy became, in fact, a kind of hero; some people, stretching a point, said he was a saint for the way that every day and twice on Sunday he sang a memorial Mass over Shannon's grave, now marked with a chipped, cheap plaster figure of Saint Francis. He withdrew from the world more and more, seldom venturing into the streets at all, except when he went to the bootlegger to get a new bottle to snuggle into. All summer, all fall, we saw him as we passed by his yard, sitting at his dilapidated table, enfeebled with gin, graying, withering, turning his head ever and ever more slowly as he maneuvered the protocol of the kings and the queens and the knaves. Daisy and I could never stop to visit him again.

It went on like this, year after year. Daisy and I lived in a mesh of lies and evasions, baffled and mean, like rats in a maze. When we were old enough for beaux, we connived like sluts to see them, but we would never admit to their existence until Gran caught us out by some trick. Like this one, for example: Once, at the end of a long interrogation, she said to me, "I'm more relieved than I can tell you that you *don't* have anything to do with Jimmy Gilmore, because I happen to know that he is after only one thing in a girl," and then, off guard in the loving memory of sitting in the movies the night before with Jimmy, not even holding hands, I defended him and defeated myself, and Gran, smiling with success, said, "I *thought* you knew him. It's a pretty safe rule of thumb that where there's smoke there's fire." That finished Jimmy and me, for afterward I was nervous with him and I confounded and alarmed and finally bored him by trying to convince him, although the subject had not come up, that I did not doubt his good intentions.

Daisy and I would come home from school, or, later, from our jobs, with a small triumph or an interesting piece of news, and if we forgot ourselves and, in our exuberance, told Gran, we were hustled into court at once for cross-examination. Once, I remember, while I was still in high school, I told her about getting a part in a play. How very nice for me, she said, if that kind of make-believe seemed to me worth while. But what was my role? An old woman! A widow woman believed to be a witch? She did not care a red cent, but she did have to laugh in view of the fact that Miss Eccles, in charge of dramatics, had almost run her down in her car. And I would forgive her, would I not, if she did not come to see the play, and would not think her eccentric for not wanting to see herself ridiculed in public?

My pleasure strangled, I crawled, joy-killed, to our third-floor room. The room was small and its monstrous furniture was too big and the rag rugs were repulsive, but it was bright. We would not hang a blind at the window, and on this day I stood there staring into the mountains that burned with the sun. I feared the mountains, but at times like this their massiveness consoled me; they, at least, could not be gossiped about.

Why did we stay until we were grown? Daisy and I ask ourselves this question as we sit here on the bench in the municipal zoo, reminded of Mr. Murphy by the polar bear, reminded by the monkeys not of Shannon but of Mrs. Placer's insatiable gossips at their post-prandial feast.

"But how could we have left?" says Daisy, wringing her buttery hands. "It was the depression. We had no money. We had nowhere to go."

"All the same, we could have gone," I say, resentful still of the waste of all those years. "We could have come here and got jobs as waitresses. Or prostitutes, for that matter."

"I wouldn't have wanted to be a prostitute," says Daisy.

We agree that under the circumstances it would have been impossible for us to run away. The physical act would have been simple, for the city was not far and we could have stolen the bus fare or hitched a ride. Later, when we began to work as salesgirls in Kress's, it would have been no trick at all to vanish one Saturday afternoon with our week's pay, without so much as going home to say goodbye. But it had been infinitely harder than that, for Gran, as we now see, held us trapped by our sense of guilt. We were vitiated, and we had no choice but to wait, flaccidly, for her to die.

You may be sure we did not unlearn those years as soon as we put her out of sight in the cemetery and sold her house for a song to the first boob who would buy it. Nor did we forget when we left the town for another one, where we had jobs at a dude camp—the town where Daisy now lives with a happy husband and two happy sons. The succubus did not relent for years, and I can still remember, in the beginning of our days at the Lazy S 3, overhearing an edgy millionaire say to his wife, naming my name, "That girl gives me the cold shivers. One would think she had just seen a murder." Well, I had. For years, whenever I woke in the night in fear or pain or loneliness, I would increase my suffering by the memory of Shannon, and my tears were as bitter as poor Mr. Murphy's.

We have never been back to Adams. But we see that house plainly, with the hopvines straggling over the porch.

The windows are hung with the cheapest grade of marquisette, dipped into coffee to impart to it an unwilling color, neither white nor tan but individual and spitefully unattractive. We see the wicker rockers and the swing, and through the screen door we dimly make out the slightly veering corridor, along one wall of which stands a glass-doored bookcase; when we were children, it had contained not books but stale old cardboard boxes filled with such things as W.C.T.U. tracts and anti-cigarette literature and newspaper clippings relating to sexual sin in the Christianized islands of the Pacific.

Even if we were able to close our minds' eyes to the past, Mr. Murphy would still be before us in the apotheosis of the polar bear. My pain becomes intolerable, and I am relieved when Daisy rescues us. "We've got to go," she says in a sudden panic. "I've got asthma coming on." We rush to the nearest exit of the city park and hail a cab, and, once inside it, Daisy gives herself an injection of adrenalin and then leans back. We are heartbroken and infuriated, and we cannot speak.

Two hours later, beside my train, we clutch each other as if we were drowning. We ought to go out to the nearest policeman and say, "We are not responsible women. You will have to take care of us because we cannot take care of ourselves." But gradually the storm begins to lull.

"You're sure you've got your ticket?" says Daisy. "You'll surely be able to get a roomette once you're on."

"I don't know about that," I say. "If there are any V.I.P.s on board, I won't have a chance. 'Spinsters and Orphans Last' is the motto of this line."

Daisy smiles. "I didn't care," she says, "but I had to laugh when I saw that woman nab the redcap you had signalled to. I had a good notion to give her a piece of my mind."

"It will be a miracle if I ever see my bags again," I say, mounting the steps of the train. "Do you suppose that blackguardly porter knows about the twenty-dollar gold piece in my little suitcase?"

"Anything's possible!" cries Daisy, and begins to laugh. She is so pretty, standing there in her bright-red linen suit and her black velvet hat. A solitary ray of sunshine comes through a broken pane in the domed vault of the train shed and lies on her shoulder like a silver arrow.

"So long, Daisy!" I call as the train begins to move.

She walks quickly along beside the train. "Watch out for pickpockets!" she calls.

"You, too!" My voice is thin and lost in the increasing noise of the speeding train wheels. "Goodbye, old dear!"

I go at once to the club car and I appropriate the writing table, to the vexation of a harried priest, who snatches up the telegraph pad and gives me a sharp look. I write Daisy approximately the same letter I always write her under this particular set of circumstances, the burden of which is that nothing for either of us can ever be as bad as the past before Gran mercifully died. In a postscript I add: "There is a Roman Catholic priest (that is to say, he is *dressed* like one) sitting behind me although all the chairs on the opposite side of the car are empty. I can only conclude that he is looking over my shoulder, and while I do not want to cause you any alarm, I think you would be advised to be on the lookout for any appearance of miraculous medals, scapulars, papist booklets, etc., in the shops of your town. It really makes me laugh to see the way he is pretending that all he wants is for me to finish this letter so that he can have the table."

I sign my name and address the envelope, and I give up my place to the priest, who smiles nicely at me, and then I move across the car to watch the fields as they slip by. They are alfalfa fields, but you can bet your bottom dollar that they are chockablock with marijuana.

I begin to laugh. The fit is silent but it is devastating; it surges and rattles in my rib cage, and I turn my face to the window to avoid the narrow gaze of the Filipino bar boy. I must think of something sad to stop this unholy giggle, and I think of the polar bear. But even his bleak tragedy does not sober me. Wildly I fling open the newspaper I have brought and I pretend to be reading something screamingly funny. The words I see are in a Hollywood gossip column: "How a well-known starlet can get a divorce in Nevada without her crooner husband's consent, nobody knows. It won't be worth a plugged nickel here."

MAEVE BRENNAN was born in Ireland in 1917 and moved to America with her family when she was seventeen. As a girl in convent school she secretly kept a journal and wrote poems until the nuns found them. Her first writing job was at *Harper's Bazaar. The New Yorker* editor William Shawn hired her to write the Long-Winded Lady column in the magazine's "Talk of the Town" section. For twenty years she wrote about the city, getting up at dawn to people-watch and eavesdrop, with an open book for camouflage. "Nobody ever noticed," she said, "that I never turn the page." She loves New York "because the chances for being invisible are so much greater." Throughout her years at *The New Yorker* she wrote short stories, which were set in Dublin as well as in New York, and originally appeared in the magazine. Her first collection of fiction, *In and Out of Never-Never Land,* (1969) was highly acclaimed; it was followed five years later by another collection, *Christmas Eve*, from which the story that follows is taken. It is difficult to exaggerate her mastery of the art of fiction. Her sense of the spirit underlying the tangible world comes through so powerfully that reading her stories is always an experience of seeing life as if for the first time and feeling deeply. One must go carefully through her work in order not to miss the wit and the quick soundings of the hidden reserves of tenderness. "The Springs of Affection," a story about a marriage and the relationship between a single sister and her married brother and new sister-in-law, is told with simplicity and grace; it suggests an imagination rooted in rich and ancient soil. Like her Irish literary ancestors, Yeats and Joyce and John Millington Synge, she is able to bring to life the extraordinariness of the ordinary with a sureness that makes her art seem sacramental.

The Springs of Affection

by

Maeve Brennan

Delia Bagot died suddenly and quietly, alone in her bed, with the door shut, and six years later, after eight months of being bedridden, Martin, her husband, died, attended by a nursing nun and his eighty-seven-year-old twin sister, Min. And at last Min was released from the duty she had imposed on herself, to remain with him as long as he needed her. She could go home now, back to her flat in Wexford, and settle into the peace and quiet she had enjoyed before Delia's death summoned her to the suburbs of Dublin. To the suburbs of Dublin and the freedom of that house where she had wandered so often in her fancy. For fifty years she had wandered in their private lives, ever since Delia appeared out of the blue and fascinated Martin, the born bachelor, into marrying her. Min wasn't likely to forget that wedding day, the misery of it, the anguish of it, the abomination of deprivation as she and her mother stood together and looked at him, the happy bridegroom, standing there grinning his head off as though he had ascended into Heaven. She and her mother and her two sisters, all three of them gone now, and Martin, too, gone. Min thought of the neat graves, one by one—a sister's grave, a sister's grave, a mother's grave, a brother's grave—all gone, all present, like medals on the earth. And she thought it was fitting that she should be the one to remain alive, because out of them all she was the one who was always faithful to the family. She was the only one of the lot of them who hadn't gone off and got married. She had never wanted to assert herself like that, never needed to. She had wondered at their lack of shame as they exhibited themselves, Clare and Polly with their husbands and Martin with poor Delia, the poor thing. They didn't seem to care what anybody thought of them when they got caught up in that excitement, like animals. It was disgusting, and they seemed to know it, the way they pretended their only concern was with the new clothes they'd have and the flowers they'd grow in their very own gardens. And now it was over for them, and they might just as well have controlled themselves, for all the good they had of it. And she, standing alone as always, had lived to sum them all up. It was a great satisfaction to see finality rising up like the sun. Min thought not many people knew that satisfaction. To watch the end of all was not much different from watching the beginning of things, and if you weren't ever going to take part anyway, then to watch the end was far and away better. You could be jealous of people who were starting out, but you could hardly be jealous of the dead.

Not that I was ever jealous, Min thought. God forbid that I should encourage small thoughts in myself, but I couldn't help but despise Delia that day, the way she stood looking up at Martin as though she was ready to fall down on her knees before him. She made a show of herself that day. We were late getting out for the wedding. We were late getting started, and then, we were all late getting there and they were all waiting for us. And after it was over and they were married and we were all in the garden, she came running up to my mother and she said, "Oh, I was afraid you weren't coming. I began to imagine Martin had changed his mind about me. I thought I would burst with impatience and longing. I had such a longing to see his face, and then, when I saw you driving up, I still had a great fear something might come between us. I'll never forget how impatient I was—I see it would be easy to go mad with love." She said that to my mother. "Mad with love," she said. My mother just looked at her, and when she flew off, all full of herself as she was that day, my mother turned and looked at me, and said to me, "Min, I am an old woman, but never in my life have I spoken like that. Never in my life have I said the like of that. All the years I've lived, and I've never, never allowed myself to feel like that about anybody, let alone be that open about it. That girl has something the matter with her. My heart goes out to Martin, I can tell you. There's something lacking in her."

Min remembered that Martin's wedding day was a very long day, with many different views and scenes, country roads, country lanes, gardens and orchards and fields and streams, and a house with rooms that multiplied in recollection, because she only visited them that one time, and they attracted her very much—dim, old rooms that maintained an air of simple, implacable formality. She envied the way the rooms were able to remain unknown even when you were standing in them. It was the same with the people out there in the country—even when they were most friendly and open they kept a lot of themselves hidden. Min thought they were like a strange tribe that only shows up in force on festival days.

The days before the wedding were a great strain, and Min always said she never understood how they got themselves out of the house the morning of the wedding. If it had not been that Markey was standing outside with the horse and car they had hired, they might all have stayed in the house and let Martin find his way out to Oylegate as best he could. He might have changed his mind then, and remained at home where he belonged. Driving out of the town of Wexford, they crossed the bridge at Ferrycarrig and there was the Slaney pouring away under them, flowing straight for the harbor as unconcernedly as though it was any old day. And then the long drive out to Oylegate. And when they got to Oylegate the chapel yard was waiting for them, looking more like an arena than a religious place. And the chapel itself, all solemn and hedged in with flowers so full in bloom that they seemed to be overflowing their petals, color flowing freely through the air. Min drew deep breaths, filling her lungs with fright. The fright built up inside her chest—she could feel it beginning to smother her. There was no air in the place. She said to her mother later, "I nearly got a headache in the chapel. I thought I might have to walk outside. It was too close in there. I began to feel weak. I thought we'd never get away out of the place." Polly was listening. Polly always seemed to be listening in time to turn your own words against you.

Polly said, "You always tell everybody you never had a headache in your life. You always say you never had time to have a headache. You leave the headaches to the rest of us. Clare and Polly have time for all that kind of nonsense, imagining themselves to be delicate—that's what you always say. And then in the next breath, every time anything goes against you, you tell us you *almost* got a headache. If you almost got a headache it would show on your face. You're overcome by your own bad humor—that's all that's the matter with you."

"In the name of God," their mother said, "this is not the time for the two of you to start fighting. Do you want to make a show of us all, have them all laughing at us more than they're laughing already?"

They were walking through the chapel yard after the wedding and Min went ahead, looking hurried, as though she had left something outside in the road and wanted to look for it. In Polly's voice she heard the enmity that had been oppressing her all day, enmity that came at her out of the streets of the town as they started to drive out here, distant, incomprehensible enmity that rose up at her from the bridge at Ferrycarrig, and from the road itself, and from the fields and trees and cottages they passed, and even from the sky itself, blue and white and summery though it was. Even the faraway sky looked satisfied to see her in the condition she was in. Min didn't know what condition she was in. She knew that she couldn't say a word without being misunderstood. She knew that something had happened that deprived her of an approbation so natural that she had always taken it for granted. She only noticed it now that she missed it—it was as though the whole world had turned against her. Polly must have rehearsed that speech—Polly was very spiteful. But where had Polly found that tone of voice, so hard and condescending? She's very sure of herself all of a sudden, Min thought. I must have given myself away, somehow. But what was there to give away—Min knew she had done nothing to earn that tone of contempt from a younger sister. She had an awful feeling of being in disgrace with somebody she had never seen and who had never liked her very much, never, not even when she was a little mite trying to help her mother with the younger children. No, wherever it came from, this impersonal dislike had been lying in wait for her all her life. And it was clear from the way people were looking at her that everybody knew about it. She couldn't even say a word to her mother about a headache without being attacked as though she was a scoundrel. All the good marks she had won at school were forgotten. Nothing was known about her now except that she had presumed to a place far above her station in life.

She had believed she could fly sky-high, with her brains for wings. Nobody notices me as I am, Min thought; all they can see is the failure. I was done out of my right, but they'd rather say, She got too big for her boots, and Pride must have a fall. She had to face up to it. There was nothing she could say in her own defense, and she condemned herself if she remained silent. It is impossible to prove you are not a disappointed old maid.

Min remembered Martin's wedding day as the day when everything changed in their lives at home. My mother was never the same after Martin married, she thought, and it was then, too, that Clare and Polly became restless and hard to get along with, and stopped joining in the conversation we always had about the family fortunes and talked instead about what they were going to do with their own lives. *Their* lives—and what about sticking together as a family, as we had been brought up to do? They got very selfish all of a sudden, and the house seemed very empty, as though he had died. After the wedding he never came back again except as a visitor. They lived only around the corner but it wasn't the same, knowing he was not sleeping in his own bed.

There was eight years between Delia and Martin, and then, since he lived six years after her, there was fourteen years between them, and now that they were both gone none of it mattered at all. They might have been born hundreds of years apart, Min thought with satisfaction. But it was not likely that Martin would ever have belonged to any family except his own, or that he would ever have had sisters who were not Min and Clare and Polly, or that he would ever have had another woman for his mother than their own mother, who had sacrificed everything for them and asked in return only that they stick together as a family, and build themselves up, and make a wall around themselves that nobody could see through, let alone climb. What she had in mind was a fort, a fortress, where they could build themselves up in private and strengthen their hold on the earth, because in the long run that is what matters—a firm foothold and a roof over your head. But all that hope ended and all their hard work was mocked when Delia Kelly walked into their lives. She smashed us up, Min thought, and got us all out into the open where blood didn't count anymore, and where blood wasn't thicker than water, and where the only mystery was, what did he see in her. It was like the end of the world, knowing he was at the mercy of somebody outside the family. A farmer's daughter is all she was, even if she had attended the Loreto convent and owned certificates to show what a good education she had.

Min sat beside her own gas fire in her own flat in Wexford and considered life and crime and punishment according to the laws of arithmetic. She counted up and down the years, and added and subtracted the questions and answers, and found that she came out with a very tidy balance in her favor. She glanced over to the old brown chest that now held those certificates, still in the big brown paper envelope that Delia had kept them in. Min intended to do away with the certificates, but not yet. She liked looking at them—especially at the one given for violin playing. It was strange that in spite of her good memory she had quite forgotten that Delia had a little reputation as a musician when she first met Martin. A *very* little reputation, and she had come by it easily, because she had been given every chance. All the chances in Min's own family had gone to Martin, because he was the boy, and he took all their chances with him when he left. And spoiled his own chances for good, because he did nothing for the rest of his life, tied down as he was, slaving to support a wife and children, turning himself into a nobody. After all that promise and all that talk and all those plans he made nothing of himself. A few pounds in the bank, a few sticks of furniture, a few books, and a garden that still bloomed although it had gone untended for six years—that was the sum of his life, all he had to show for himself. He would have done better to think of his mother, and stay at home, and benefit from the encouragement of his own family, all of them pushing for him in everything he did. With his ability and his brains and the nice way he had about him, he could have done anything. He could have risen to any height, a natural leader like him, able to be at ease anywhere with anybody. As it was, he died friendless. How could he have friends when he was ashamed to invite anybody to the house? He was ashamed of Delia and ashamed of the house, and more than anything else, he was unwilling to let people know of his unhappiness. He was like all of us in that, Min thought, proud and sensitive and fond of our privacy. Delia came from another class of people altogether. They were a different breed, more coarse-grained than we are, country people, accustomed to being out in all weathers, plowing, and gathering in the hay, and dealing with animals. They had no thoughts in their heads beyond saving the corn. They tried to be friendly; Min gave them that much. She wanted to be fair. But she didn't trust them, and in any case they were rejoicing over herself and her mother, because Martin made himself such an easy catch. Min didn't like to see mother being made a fool of, and Martin too being made a fool of, because he didn't know what he was doing when he turned around and got married. He went out of his head about that girl, mad with longing, all decency gone. He was like somebody in a delirium. Min couldn't help feeling a bit contemptuous of him, to see him so helpless. And then the same thing overcame Clare and Polly, Clare marrying a dirty shabby fellow nearly old enough to be her father, and Polly marrying a commercial traveller and having one child after another until she nearly had her mother and Min out in the street with the expense she put on them. But Martin started it all, vanishing out of their lives as casually as though he had never been more than a lodger in the house.

It was a shame, what happened, all their plans gone for nothing. By that time they were all out working—Polly in the knitting factory, Clare in the news agent's, Martin in the County Surveyor's office, and Min in the dressmaking business. She was a dressmaker from the beginning, through no choice of her own, and she made a good job of it. Everybody said she was very reliable and that she had good style. As soon as she could manage it she moved the sewing machine out of her mother's front parlor and into the rooms on the Main Street, where she now lived. One way and another, she had had a title to these rooms for almost sixty years. The house changed owners, but Min remained on. She had no intention of giving up her flat, especially since her rent included the three little atticky rooms on the third floor, the top floor of the house. She showed great foresight when she had those top-floor rooms included in her original arrangement, all those many years ago. Now she had made the top floor into a little flat, makeshift but very nice. She found young couples liked it for the first years or so of their married lives. And she still had the lease of the little house at the corner of Georges Street and Oliver Plunkett Street, where her mother had taken them all to live when they were still babies. That little house Min had turned, in her informal way, into two flats, and she had the rent from them. And she had her old-age pension, and something in the bank—nobody knew how much, although there were many guesses. Some said she was too clever, too sharp altogether. The butcher downstairs under her flat hated her. She didn't care. She had the last laugh. He could stand in the doorway of his shop and watch her coming up the street, and give her all the black looks he liked—she didn't care. She couldn't help laughing when she thought of how sure he was when he bought the house that he would be able to get rid of her simply by telling her she wasn't wanted, and that he needed the whole house for his growing family. She wasn't going to die to suit him and she didn't care whether he wanted her or not. It was presumptuous of him to imagine she would care whether he wanted her there or didn't want her there. He even had the impertinence to tell her that he and his wife had the greatest respect for her. Min didn't know the wife but she knew the people the wife came from. No need to see people of that class to know what they were, and what their "respect" was worth. She told the butcher to his face that he might as well leave her alone. She wasn't going to budge. Of course, it would be very nice and convenient for him only to have to walk upstairs to his tea at night after he shut up the shop, but he was going to have to wait for his convenience. A narrow gate alongside his shop entrance led into a covered passage, and there was her downstairs front door at the side of the house, as private as you please. She was very well off there. The place was nicely fixed up. She liked being there in the flat alone, with the downstairs door locked and the door of her flat locked and the fire going and the electric reading lamp at her shoulder and an interesting book to read and the day's paper to hand, in case she felt like going over it again. And she had Delia's little footstool to keep her feet off the floor. She thought it was like a miracle the way things had evened out in the end. She had gone around and around and up and down for all those years, doing her duty and observing the rules of life as far as she knew them, and her feet had stopped walking on the exact spot where her road ended—here in this room, with everything gathered around her, and everything in its right place. Her mother had always said that Min was the one who would keep the flag flying no matter what. Min had never in her life been content to sit down and do nothing, but now she was quite content to sit idle. What she saw about her in the room was a job well done. She had not known until now that a job well done creates an eminence that you can rest on.

The room where she sat beside the fire, and where she spent nearly all of her time, had been her workroom in the old days. It was the front room, running the whole width of the narrow old house, and it had a high ceiling and three tall windows. The windows were curtained in thin blue stuff that showed gaps of darkness outside when she pulled them together at night. Min didn't care. Often she didn't bother to pull them but just left them open. The house opposite was all given over to offices, dead at night, and in any case, she told herself, she had nothing to hide. . . . It was only a manner of speaking with her, that she had nothing to hide: she meant that she wasn't afraid to be alone at night with the windows wide open to the night.

There were three doors in the wall that faced the three windows. Two of the doors led into the two smaller rooms of the flat, and the middle door led out into the hall. One of the smaller rooms used to be her fitting room, and the tall gilt mirror was still attached to the wall there. It was Min's bedroom now, although more and more she slept on the narrow studio couch against the wall in her big room. The gas fire was on so much, the big room was always warm. She craved the warmth. She believed the climate in Wexford to be warmer than in Dublin, and she blamed the six years she had spent living with her brother for the colds that plagued her life now. She wore two cardigans and sometimes a shawl as well, over her woollen pullover. She buttoned only the top button of the outer cardigan. The inner cardigan she buttoned from top to bottom. Her pullover had long sleeves, and so she appeared with thick stuffed arms that ended at the wrist in three worn edges—green of the pullover, beige of the inner cardigan, and mottled brown of the outer cardigan, which was of very heavy wool, an Aran knit, Min called it. Her hands were mottled too, brown on pink, and she had very small yellow nails that were always cut short. She was very small and thin, and only a little stooped, and in the street she walked quickly, with no hesitation. She went out every day to buy a newspaper, and she bought food. Bread, milk, sometimes a slice of cooked ham or a tomato. She liked hard-boiled eggs. She nodded to very few people as she went along, and very few people spoke to her. She was a tiny old woman, dressed in black, wearing a scrap of a hat that she had made herself and decorated with an eye veil.

She read a good deal, leaning attentively back toward the weak light given by the lamp she had taken from Delia's bedside table. Before getting the lamp she had relied on a naked bulb screwed into a socket in the middle of the ceiling. She was very saving in her ways—she had never lost the habit of rigid economy, and in fact she enjoyed pinching her pennies. She hadn't amassed a great fortune, but it was the amassing she enjoyed as she watched her wealth grow. She looked at people with calculation not for what she might get from them but for what they might take from her if she gave them their chance. She wasn't inclined to gossip. She admitted to disliking or hating people only to the degree in which they reminded her of a certain type or class. "Oh I *hates* that class of person," she would say, or "Oh that's not a nice class of person at all." Grimaces, winks, nods, and gestures indicating mock alarm, mock shyness, mock anger, and mock piety were her repertoire, together with a collection of sarcastic or humorous phrases she had found useful in her youth. But she saw few people.

In the days when this was her workroom, the furniture had been sewing machines, ironing boards, storage shelves, and, down the center of the room, the huge cutting table that was always having to be cleared of its litter of fashion books and paper patterns, and cups of tea, and scissors, and scraps and ribbons of cloth. Underfoot there was always a field of thread and straight pins. Mountains of color and acres of texture were submerged in that room under the flat, tideless peace of Min's old age. The gas fire glowed red and orange—it was her only extravagance. On the floor was a flowered carpet that had once been the pride of Delia's front sitting room in Dublin, and the room was furnished with Min's souvenirs—Delia's books, Martin's books, Delia's low chair, Martin's armchair. She had Delia's sewing basket, and Martin's framed map of Dublin. On the fourth finger of her left hand she wore Martin's wedding ring. She had slipped it from his dead hand. She told herself she wanted to save it from grave robbers.

If she lifted her eyes from her book she could see, down a length of narrow side street, the sky over the harbor, and if she stood up and walked to the window she could see the water. Below her windows there was the Main Street. The streets in Wexford are very narrow, and crooked rather than winding. At some points the Main Street is only wide enough to allow one car to pass, and the side path for pedestrians shrinks to the width of a plank. There are always children bobbing along with one foot in the street and one on the path, and children dodging and running, making intricacies among the slowly moving bicycles and cars. It is a small, worn, angular town with plain unmatched houses that are dried into color by the sun and washed into color by the rain. There is nothing dark about Wexford. The sun comes up very close to the town, and sometimes seems to be rising from among the houses. The wind scatters seeds against the walls and along the edges of the roofs, so that you can look up and see marigolds blooming between you and the sky.

Min's father had been a good deal older than her mother, Bridget, and he could neither read nor write. He was silent with his vivacious, quick-tempered wife, who read Dickens and Scott and Maria Edgeworth with her children, and he worked at odd jobs, when he could get them. It was the dream of his life to make money exporting pigs to the English market, and to everyone's surprise he succeeded on one occasion in getting hold of enough money to buy a few pigs and rent a pen to keep them in. He discovered at once that possession of the pigs brought him automatically into the company of a little crowd of amateurs like himself, who gathered together in serious discussion of their animals, their ambitions, their hopes, and their chances. The pigs were young and trim and pink and healthy, and they were very greedy. He found he very much enjoyed giving them their food and that he didn't mind cleaning up after them. He began talking about how clean they were, and how well mannered, and how friendly. He marvelled at the way they opened and shut their mouths, and he thought their big round nostrils were very natural-looking, not pig-like at all. He liked to see them lift their heads and look up at him with their tiny, blind-looking eyes. He said a lot of lies had been told about pigs. He interpreted their grunts and squeals as words of affection for him, and after a day or two Bridget told the children their father had gone off to live with the pigs. "He likes the pigs better than he likes his own children," she said. He did like the pigs. He liked having a place of his own to go to, outside the house. He liked being a man of affairs. He began smiling around at his children, as though he was keeping a little secret from them. Martin kept his accounts for him, writing down the number of pigs, the price he had paid for them, and the price he expected to get for them. Once Martin visited the pen and saw the pigs. He was forbidden to go a second time. Bridget said that one lunatic in the family was enough. Martin cried and said he wanted a dog of his own. He knew better than that. There was never a dog or a cat in that house. Bridget said she had enough to do, keeping their own mouths fed.

The great day dawned when the pigs were to be sold. Their father was gone before any of them were awake, and he didn't come home until long after the hour when they were supposed to be in bed. They weren't in bed. They all waited up for him. When he came in they were all sitting around the stove in the kitchen waiting for him. They heard him coming along the passage from the door at the Georges Street side of the house and, as their mother had instructed them to do, they remained very quiet, so that he thought there was nobody up. At the doorway he saw them all and he looked surprised and not very pleased. Then he put his hand in his top pocket and took out the money, which he had wrapped in brown paper, and he walked over to the kitchen table and put it down.

"There's the money," he said to Bridget. "Blood money."

He looked very cold, but instead of getting near the stove to warm himself he sat down at the table and put his elbows on the table and his head in his hands.

"What sort of acting is this?" Bridget asked. "What ails you now, talking about blood money in front of the children. Will you answer me?"

"I'm no better than a murderer," he said. "I'll never forget the look in their eyes till the day I die. I shouldn't have sold them. I lay awake all last night thinking of ways to keep them, and all day today after I sold them I kept thinking of ways I could have kept them in hiding someplace where nobody would know about them—I got that fond of them. They knew me when they saw me."

Bridget stood up and walked to the table and picked up the money and put it into her apron pocket. She was a very small, stout, vigorous woman with round blue eyes and straight black hair, and she was proud of the reputation she had for speaking her mind. She was proud, cunning, suspicious, and resourceful, and where her slow, stumbling husband was concerned she was pitiless. She didn't want the children to grow up to be like him. She didn't want them to be seen with him. She told them she didn't want them dragging around after him. She had long ago grown tired of trying to understand what it was that was holding him back, and so, impeding them all. But tonight, for once, it was clear to her that he was going to make an excuse of the pigs for doing nothing at all about anything for weeks or even months to come. It would be laughable if it wasn't for the bad effect his laziness might have on the children. But he was useful to her around the house, as a bad example. The children were half afraid of him, because they were afraid of being drawn into his bad luck. They were ashamed of him. Min thought anybody could tell by the way her father spoke that he couldn't read or write. Maybe that was the great attraction between him and the pigs. He always seemed to be begging for time until his speech could catch up with his memory, and he never seemed to have come to any kind of an understanding with himself. He always seemed to be looking around as though somebody might arrange that understanding for him, and tell him about it.

On the night he came back so late after having sold the pigs, he was so distressed that he forgot to take off his hat. It was a hat he had worn so long as any of the children could remember, and Bridget told them he had been wearing it the first time she ever set eyes on him. She said she was so impressed by the hat that she hardly noticed him at first. It was a big, wide-brimmed black hat, a very distinguished-looking hat, although it was conspicuous now for its shabbiness. It was green with age, and the greenness showed up very much in the lamplight that night as he sat by the table with his face in his hands, grieving for his pigs. He never went out without first putting his hat on. He was never without it. He depended on it, and the children depended on being able to spot it in time to avoid meeting him outside on the street someplace. When the money was safe in Bridget's deep pocket she reached out and snatched the hat off her husband's head. "Haven't I told you never to wear that hat in the house?" she said.

He looked up at her in bewilderment and then he stood up and reached out his hand for the hat. "Give me back my hat," he said, looking at her as though he was ready to smile.

Min hated her father's weak, foolish smile. Sometimes Martin smiled like that, when he was trying to prove he understood something he couldn't understand. She thought Martin and her father were both like cowards alongside her mother. She wished her mother would throw the hat in her father's face and make him go away. She wished everything could be different—no pigs, no old hat, no struggling and scheming. She wished her mother hadn't snatched the hat off her father's head. She didn't like it when her mother started fighting, and sometimes it seemed she was always fighting. She even went out of the house sometimes and went into the house of somebody who had annoyed her and started fighting there. Then she would come home and tell the children what she'd said and what had been said to her.

One time Bridget's sister Mary came storming into the house. Bridget and Mary hated one another. They began fighting, and then they began hitting one another. Bridget hit the hardest and Mary ran out of the house with her children screaming at her heels. Martin and Min saw it all and they told their mother she was very brave, but they were frightened. Afterward, when Bridget told the story of the battle, she always ended by saying, "And there was my sister Mary with her precious blood running down her face." Min despised her father, but she hoped her mother wouldn't hit him. She didn't want to see his precious blood running down his face. She began to cry, and when Clare and Polly saw their formidable older sister crying they began crying along with her. Martin stood up and begged, "Give him the hat, Mam, give him his hat!" And then he began crying and lifting his feet up and down as though he was getting ready to run a race.

"You'll frighten the wits out of the children," their father said, and for once in his life he sounded as though he knew what he was saying. "Give me that hat this minute. I'm going out. I'm getting out of here." And he made a grab for the hat, which Bridget was holding behind her back.

She struck out at him. "Don't defy me, I'm warning you!" she screamed. But he dodged her hand and reached behind her to snatch the hat away, and then he hurried out of the kitchen, and they heard the Georges Street door bang after him.

He didn't come home again that night, but he was there in the morning, sitting at the kitchen table, and Bridget gave him his tea as usual. The children looked around for the hat. It was in its usual place, where he always left it, on top of a cupboard that stood to one side of the door that led out into the yard. He used to lift the hat from his head and toss it up on top of the cupboard in one gesture. Always, when he walked in from outside, he threw the hat up, as though he was saluting the wall of the house. And when he was going out, in one gesture he lifted his arm to reach the hat and put it on his head, often without even looking at it. One afternoon, when they were all in the kitchen after school, Bridget decided to play a little trick on their father, a joke. She said he needed a new hat anyway, and that a cap would suit him better. A cap would be better for keeping out the rain—a nice dark-blue or dark-grey cap. He looked a sketch in the old hat, and it was time he got rid of it. Once he was rid of it, he would be glad, and he would thank them all, but there was no use trying to persuade him to get rid of it himself—he would only say no. He could feel loyalty for anything, even an old hat. Look at the way he had gone on about those pigs. He wasn't able to deal with his own feelings, that was his weakness. There are only certain things a person can be true to, but he didn't know that. Once the hat was gone he'd soon forget about it, and it was a shame to see him going around with that monstrosity on his head. She had an idea. They would take the hat down and cut the crown away from the brim and then put the whole hat back on the top of the cupboard and see what happened when he lifted it down the next time he was going out. They got the hat down and Bridget cut the brim away, but she left a thin strip of the velours—hardly more than a thread—to hold the two parts of the hat together when their father lifted it down onto his head. It all happened just as they expected—the brim tumbled down around their father's face and hung around his neck. He put his hands up and felt around his face and neck to see what had happened, and then he took the hat off and looked at it.

"Which of you did this?" he said.

"We all did it," Bridget said.

He held the hat up and looked at it. "It's done for," he said, but he didn't seem angry—just puzzled. Then he went out, carrying the hat in his hand, and they heard no more about it.

Not long after that, Bridget went to see a man she knew who worked in Vernon's on the Main Street, and he arranged for her to buy a sewing machine on the installment plan, and she set about teaching herself to make dresses. Min was the one who helped her mother, so Min was sentenced to a lifetime of sewing, when she had her heart set on going to a college and becoming a teacher. Min wanted to teach. She wanted to have a dignified position in the town, to be appointed secretary to different committees, to meet important people who came to Wexford, and to have numbers of mothers and fathers deferring to her because she had their children under her thumb. But she learned to cut a pattern and run a sewing machine, and the only committee she ever sat on was the Committee of One she established in her own place on the Main Street. She always thought if her father had gone ahead with the pigs, and learned to control his feelings, and if he had cared anything about her, she would have had a better chance. But all the chances in the family had to go to Martin, because he was the boy, and because he had the best brains, and because he was the only hope they had of struggling up out of the poverty they lived in. He was doing very well and turning out to have a good business head when he threw it all away to get married. The best part of their lives ended the day Martin met Delia. Min remembered the nights they all used to sit around talking, sometimes till past midnight.

They were happy in those years, when they were all out working, and at night they had so much to talk about that they didn't know where to start or when to stop. Clare used to bring all the new books and papers and weeklies home from the news agent's on the sly for them to read. Polly and Martin had joined the Amateur Dramatics and they were always off at rehearsals and recitations, and they began to talk knowledgeably about scenery and costumes and dialogue and backgrounds. They talked about nothing but plays and acting, and they knew everything that was going to happen—they had all the information about concerts and performances and competitions that were coming off, not merely in Wexford but in Dublin. Min thought the future was much more interesting when you knew at least a few of the things that were going to happen. There was something going on every minute, and it was really very nice being in the swim. People went out of their way to say hello to the Bagots in the street. They had a piano now, second-hand but very good. It was the same shape as their tiny parlor and it took up half the space there. They took turns picking out tunes, but Clare had the advantage over all, because she had had a few lessons from the daughter of a German family that lived in the street for a short time. The Germans knew their music—you had to admit that. Clare felt that with a few more lessons she might have made a good accompanist. They all liked to sing—they got that from Bridget. Martin went off by himself to Dublin once in a while, just for the night, and he always brought back something new—a song sheet, or a book. He always went to a concert, or a play, or to hear a lecture.

Martin and Polly liked to act out scenes, and Min used to get behind them and imitate their gestures until her mother said that she'd rather watch Min than the real thing any day. Min was glad she had found a way to join in the fun. She hadn't as much voice as the others and serious acting was beyond her.

In one way it was a pity their father wasn't there to witness their prosperity, but in another way it was just as well, because he would have done something to spoil things—not meaning any harm but because he couldn't help himself. Min remembered how irritating it used to be to have him hanging around, like a skeleton at the feast. And he got on their mother's nerves, because they all knew he didn't understand a word of what they talked about. And he had a peaceful death. He must have been glad to go. He was never more than a burden to himself and to everybody else.

Min always remembered how stalwart and kind Martin was, comforting her mother after their father's death, and she never could understand how he could be so thoughtful, and make the promises he made, and pretend the way he did, and then run off and leave them all the first chance he got. She always said, "I can get along without the menfolk. They are more trouble and annoyance than they're worth." But she had liked very much having Martin in her life. She liked it very much when he crept upstairs to her workroom in the Main Street and stood outside the door and called out, "There's a man in the house. Will you let me in, Min?" And he would stand outside making jokes while all the women scurried about pretending to be alarmed and making themselves decent. The women used to tease her about having such a handsome brother, and ask her if she wasn't afraid some girl would steal him away. And Min always replied that Martin thought far too much of his mother ever to leave home.

"He's devoted to my mother," she always said, lowering her eyes to her work in a way that showed Martin's devotion to be of such magnitude that it was almost sacred, so that the mere mention of it made her want silence in the room. Silence or an end to that kind of careless, meddlesome talk.

"Martin has no time to spend gadding around," she said to a customer who teased her too pointedly.

"Oh, Min, you're a real old maid," the customer said. "Martin's going to surprise you all one of these days. Some girl will come along and sweep him off his feet. Wait and see."

Min told her mother about that remark. "Pay no attention to her, Min," Bridget said. "Martin's no fool. He knows when he's well off. He's too comfortable ever to want to leave home. He's as set in his ways as a man of forty. Martin's a born bachelor."

And of course, the next thing they knew, Martin was married and gone. And then Polly ran off with the commercial traveller, a Protestant, and it turned out he was tired of travelling and wanted to settle down. Being settled didn't suit him either; he was never able to make a go of anything. And Clare married another Protestant, an old fellow who made a sort of living catching rabbits, and he used to walk into the house as if he owned it, with the rabbits hanging from his hand, dripping blood all over Bridget's clean floor.

Min never understood how things could come to an end so fast and so quietly. It was as though a bad trick had been played on them all. There was an end to order and thrift and books and singing, and the house seemed to fill up with detestable confusion and noise. Everywhere you turned, there was Clare's husband or Polly's children, he with his dead rabbits and his smelly pipe and the children always wanting a bag of sweets or wanting to go to the lavatory or falling down and having to be picked up screaming. She couldn't stick any of them, couldn't stand the sight of them. And then Martin moved off to Dublin in anger, telling them that his mother wouldn't let Delia have a minute's peace, that Delia had no life at all in this place, and that there was no future in Wexford anyway. Bridget always said that Delia had ruined Martin's life, and Min agreed with her, except that Min said Delia ruined all their lives. They were a good team before Delia arrived on the scene. The saying was that when a couple got married they went off by themselves and closed the door on the world, but Min thought that in her family what they did was to get married and let the whole world into the house so that there wasn't a quiet minute or a sensible thought left in this life for anybody. Such a din those marriages made, such racket and confusion and expense and quarrelling. She thought it was awful that brothers and sisters could shape your whole life with doings that had nothing at all to do with you. She felt they were all tugging at her, and that her mother was on their side.

When Min got back to Wexford after Martin's death, and got her flat all cleared out and arranged with her new acquisitions—Delia's things, Martin's things, their set of wedding furniture and their books and pictures and lamps—she suddenly realized that she was at home for good. There was nobody left who mattered to her, nobody to disturb her. The family circle was closed. She was the only one left of them. She could only think of them as the crowd in the kitchen at home long ago, and she felt it was they who had finally died, not the men and women they had turned into, who had been such an aggravation to her. She dismissed Delia. Delia was just a long interlude that had separated Martin from his twin, but the twins were joined at the end as they had been at the beginning. Min was Martin's family now.

It was hard to believe that only nine years had elapsed between her father's death and Martin's marriage. Those were the best years. She remembered the day her father died, giving them all a great fright. None of them really missed him. It was a relief not to have to worry about him—an old man not able to write his name, going around looking for work, or pretending to look for work. He couldn't stay in the house. He was gone before any of them got up in the morning, but he was always there to spoil their dinnertime, and to spoil their teatime. And often in the evening he was there listening to them, although they all knew he couldn't understand a word they said. What was most annoying to Min was that he took it for granted he had a right to come in and join them and sit down in the corner and settle himself as though he had something to offer. He had nothing to offer except his restlessness. He always seemed to be on the point of leaving. He even interrupted their conversations to describe long journeys he might take, but he never went anywhere in particular. He just wandered. The restlessness that brought him to Wexford afflicted him till the day he died.

Maybe if he'd learned to read he would have been more content. He could have learned if he'd wanted to. Bridget would have taught him to read when they were first married, but he said no, he'd wait till the children were big enough and then learn when they were learning. But the children weren't pleased to have him sit down with them when they were doing their homework, and he said himself that he felt in the way. Bridget felt that he was indeed in the way, and that he was depriving the children of a part of something they needed a good deal more than he needed it. Bridget was surprised at how strongly she felt that he should not look into their books. She was afraid he might hold the children back. She despised him, the way he went on talking about his dream of being a sailor, when everybody knew he was afraid of water. Oh, he was a great trial to them all, and toward the end of his life people got to be a bit fearful of him, and even the children seemed to know there was something not quite right about him.

It was probably the same restlessness that made their father queer that drove Martin to go off and get married on impulse, the way he did. He made up his mind in two seconds, and there was no arguing with him. Min would never forget that wedding day, the struggle they had to get Bridget dressed. She was dressed in black from head to toe, as though she was going to a funeral. She generally wore black, very suitable for a middle-aged woman who was a widow, but that day the black seemed blacker than usual. Min made her a new bonnet for the wedding, of black satin with jet beads, and a shoulder cape of black satin, with jet beads around the neck. It made a very fetching outfit, but Bridget spoiled the effect by carrying her old prayer book stuffed with holy pictures and leaflets and memory cards, and she wound her black rosary beads around the prayer book so that the big metal crucifix dangled free. She looked very smart, quite the Parisienne, until she got the prayer book in her hand. Her iron-grey hair was pulled up into a tight knot on top of her head, the same as every day, and the bonnet, skewered with long hatpins, crowned the knot and gave her a few more inches extra height. Min and her sisters wore stiff-brimmed white hats and white blouses with their grey costumes, and Min felt they gave the country wedding a cosmopolitan touch. But of course Clare had to spoil it all by saying to anybody who would listen to her, "We're Martin's sisters. We have the name of being short on beauty but long on brains." Clare always said the wrong thing at the wrong time. It was her way of trying to get on the right side of people. It didn't matter whether she liked a person or not, Clare had to curry favor. She couldn't help herself. You could trust her to make a fool not only of herself but of you. And Polly got fed up and said, "Oh, it's well known that Martin's the beauty of the family." And naturally there was no one at the wedding but friends and relatives of Delia and her family; Bridget invited nobody, because it wasn't at all certain, she said, that Martin would go through with it.

It was true that Martin, with his glossy black curls and his bright-blue eyes, was the beauty of the family. On him the features that were angular in Clare and lumpy in Polly and pinched in Min became regular and harmonious. Before he got married, when they all used to go around together, the three girls took lustre from Martin's face, and that was fair enough, because their faces reflected his so faithfully that one could say, "He shows what they really look like." But after he left them the likeness between them became one they did not want attention for. Instead of being reflections of Martin they became copies of one another, or three not very fortunate copies of a face that was gone. It was as though Martin was the family silver. They all went down in value when he went out of their lives.

Martin's wedding day always opened up in Min's memory as though it had started as an explosion. It was because they had been so full of dread driving out in the car they'd hired, and then, when they arrived in Oylegate, there was everybody ready and waiting, the priests and all the strangers, and candles and flowers, and the terrible sense of being caught up in the ceremony and of having to go on and on and on, knowing all the time that you had no voice in the matter and that it didn't matter what you did now. That was a terrible drive out to Oylegate that day. When they finally succeeded in getting their mother out of the house and into the car, she closed her eyes and kept them closed until she got out at the chapel gates. Up to the last minute she had been hoping Martin would change his mind.

"Martin, I'm asking you for your own good," she said. "Couldn't you put it off till tomorrow? I'll never get used to losing my little son, but I might feel stronger tomorrow." She even offered Martin the fare to go to Dublin and start up on his own, away from all of them, at least until any fuss there was blew over.

"Ah, what's the use of this, Mother?" Min said. "Come on, now, and we'll all go out together with big smiles on our faces, not to let everybody in the town know how cut up you are."

Min was angling for a grateful look from Martin, and she got it. She thought how easily swayed he was, for all his brains. Oh, she could have kept him and given me his chances, she thought. But Min could not really have been accused of holding a grudge against Martin. She could be angry with him, but she couldn't hate him or even dislike him. He was her twin. There should have been only one of us, she thought, in despair, and saw Delia Kelly making free with a part of Min Bagot, who had known more about hard work when she was ten years old than Delia Kelly could ever know. She wondered what Delia really saw when she looked at Martin. She wondered what Delia saw and how much she noticed with those queer, cloud green eyes. All the Bagots had bright-blue eyes, very keen eyes, and they all had coal-black hair, but only Martin's was curly. The Kellys were much fairer in coloring; they didn't look Irish at all, Bridget said. And except for Delia they were all bigger than the Bagots, big and strong-looking, country people. Min felt defeated by them, and she didn't know why. She felt that what mattered to her could never matter a bit to them, and she didn't know what mattered to them. They were friendly enough, and why wouldn't they be, with Martin taking one of the girls off their hands. They're not our sort at all, she thought. East is East and West is West. In a way, it was worse than if Martin had married a girl from a foreign country.

On the way out to the wedding Bridget made Markey go slow. They jogged along, and they were late already; they were late leaving the house. The horse kept flicking his tail as though he was impatient with them. Markey was irritated, because he'd had such a long wait outside the house, but he tried to put a good face on it with philosophical chat about weddings and marriages and young men, and on and on. Bridget lost patience with him and asked him whether he charged extra for the conversational accompaniment. Markey was so insulted he started to stand up, which shook the car and made the horse try to turn his head to look back at them, and Polly squealed with fear and asked her mother if she was out to have them all killed with a runaway horse. Bridget replied, "I wouldn't mind."

It was an inside car, and they sat three on each seat, Markey and Clare on one side with Min in between, and, facing them, Bridget and Polly with Martin in the middle. Markey looked at Polly when she spoke, and then he winked at her and sat down without saying a word, and they continued on at the same slow rate until they got to the chapel gate.

Entering Oylegate, they passed the top of the lane that

led with ups and downs and various curves to the house where Delia lived. The lane was on their left and on their right there was a prosperous-looking grocery with a public house attached to it. There was a gap between the grocery and a row of whitewashed cottages with thatched roofs. Outside one of these an old white-haired woman sat crouched on a short wooden bench. The narrow door of her cottage stood open behind her, showing how much darkness can gather in a small room on a bright day in June. She had a piece of sacking tied around her waist for an apron, and on her head she wore a man's cloth cap. She smoked a clay pipe and regarded the carful of Bagots with an amusement that was as empty of malice as it was of innocence. Markey touched his hat to her and said, "Fine day, Ma'am." The others didn't notice her—their eyes were ahead to the little knot of people at the chapel gates. Min knew Delia must be waiting, and she thought, One good thing, we've given her a few anxious minutes. Martin looked as if he had felt a twinge of doubt about what he was doing. He said, "I feel like a great stranger all of a sudden."

"There's time yet, Martin," Min said. "We can hurry the horse and go on past them all and go to Enniscorthy and take the train back to Wexford and never see any of them again."

Bridget turned her head and opened her eyes and looked at Martin. "Come on home with us, darling," she said, "and you'll never hear another word about it."

Markey pulled the horse up and said to Martin, "Here you are, now."

Martin stood up, making the little car suddenly flimsy, and he pushed his way between their skirts and jumped out onto the road. It was at that moment, when she heard his feet land on the ground, that the day began whirling in Min's memory. She had known perfectly well that the day would be hateful, but she had not known that it would all be so unnatural, or that she herself would feel worn and dry and unable to manage, because the only thing she wanted was to escape from it all, and she couldn't leave her mother's side. Min had never felt trapped before that day. She felt like a prisoner. She longed to be back in her workroom, where she was monarch of all she surveyed. She didn't like the voices of the people out here in the country. They were hard to understand. She knew they were discussing her behind her back and she tried to let them know she was on to them by the knowing way she looked at them. Martin behaved as though he had forgotten she was alive. She thought it was strange that the world lit up in moments of joy but that everything remained exactly the same when disaster struck. Martin turned into a different person when he jumped out of the car at the chapel gate. From now on there would be nothing more between her and him than running into each other in the street once in a while.

After the wedding ceremony was over, they all drove out a very long way along the road to Enniscorthy, and then off that road onto a rough country road that took them to the Slaney River. Delia's mother's family, her old brother and her three old sisters, lived by the Slaney in a very big farmhouse, whitewashed, with a towering thatched roof. The size of the house and the prosperous appearance of the place impressed Min. Delia's aunts and her uncle were all unmarried, and they had all been born here. Min heard the house was very old, and that the family had been in this lovely spot beside the Slaney for centuries. She and her mother were amazed by the furniture they saw in the parlor and in the rooms beyond the parlor. It was grandeur to have furniture like this.

"This house must have a great upstairs," Bridget whispered to Min, and Min felt very sorry for her mother. The best her mother had been able to do was to struggle out of a district where the people were down and out and into a street where the poor lived—self-respecting people, but poor. And here they were, at Martin's wedding, surrounded by women who were mistresses of farms, some of them owning more than one house, all of them in possession of so many acres, and even the least of them with a firm hold on the house she lived in, even if it was only a cottage, or even a half acre.

Min glanced about. These people out here in the country all belonged to one another and they were related to one another from the distant past. These families went a long way back in time, and they remembered marriages that had taken place a hundred years before. They didn't talk, as Min understood talk. Here in the country they wove webs with names and dates and places. The dead were mentioned in the same voice with the living, so that fathers and sisters and cousins who had been gone for decades could have trooped through the house and through the orchards and gardens and found themselves at home, the same as always, and they could even have counted on finding their own names and their own faces registered faithfully somewhere among the generations that had succeeded them. Min thought of all the dead who had been familiar here, and she wished her name could have been woven into talk somehow. She noticed there were no children in sight—they must have been sent off to play by themselves. There was plenty of room for children here—the farm was big, a hundred acres.

She thought many acres seemed to have been given to the orchard—there was no end to it, and from where she stood the view was more like a forest than like a field of fruit trees, which is what she understood an orchard to be. The ground was uneven, for one thing, slanting this way and that. In her reading, she had always imagined an orchard to be a geometrical place, square or oblong, with the trees spaced evenly. This orchard was wild and looked unknown, as though it had been laid out and cultivated long ago and then forgotten until this wedding day. Min thought of the town of Wexford, of the trees and houses and shops, and she thought of the harbor. Even in the dead of night when people were asleep, the town remained alive and occupied, waiting to be reclaimed in the morning, and the harbor was always restless. The town was always the same, very old and always on the go, with people around every corner, and no matter who they were you knew you had as much right there as they had. Min knew every inch of Wexford and every lift of the water in the harbor, and she thought that even if everybody belonging to her was dead and gone she would never feel lost or out of place as long as she could walk about in the streets she had known all her life. Out here in the country, things were different. You had to own your place—not merely the house but some of the land. And the houses were miles apart from one another, and the families lived according to laws of succession that were known only to them, and people had to depend for recognition on a loose web of relationships, a complicated genealogy that they kept in their heads and reinforced by repetition on days like today when they were all gathered together.

Min thought it would be pleasant to walk around the orchard once in a while when the weather was fine, but for a nice interesting walk she would take the streets of Wexford any time.

Min stood on a narrow path that led from the orchard's entrance to nowhere—it seemed to pause and fade under grass somewhere among the trees. There were rounded grassy banks on either side of the path, but they disappeared into high ground beyond the point where the path gave out. Near the edge of the bank, which was not very high, Min's mother sat talking with two of Delia's aunts—Aunt Mag and Aunt Annie. Some of the lads had carried out three kitchen chairs so that the ladies could rest themselves while they looked at the orchard. The ladies talked comfortably, all of them glad to have something to divert them from the marriage that had brought them together. Bridget lost something of her edginess and made complimentary remarks about the house, and said it was a treat to get out into the country on a day like this. The day grew in beauty, coming in like the tide, minute by minute. There were a lot of butterflies. Min saw a bronze-and-gold one she would have liked for a dress, except that she was not likely to have occasion to wear such colors, and it would be hard to find a design like that anyway, even in the best silk.

"Oh, Min has good sense. She is a born old maid. I can always depend on Min," she heard her mother say, but she kept her eyes on the ground as though she was deep in thought. She didn't care what they said and she wasn't going to be drawn into their talk. She thought of wandering off toward the garden. Most of the younger people were there, and she supposed Martin was there too, with Delia at his side. She wondered when Martin and Delia would be leaving for the station. They were taking the train to Dublin. They were going to a hotel there. Well, she wasn't going to the station to see them off. She would get out of that little demonstration, even if it meant she had to walk back to Wexford. She would go on toward the garden now, not to have to listen to her mother talking nonsense to these strangers. There were times when her mother was as bad as Clare.

There was a stone wall around the garden and inside the wall a rich green box hedge that grew very tall and was clipped into a round arch over the narrow gate at the garden entrance. A similar green box arch showed the way into the orchard, but the orchard had no gate. When Min and her mother walked into the orchard earlier, Min had the impression, just for a second, that she was coming out of a dark tunnel, the green box was so thick at her sides and over her head—so dense, you might say—and that they were walking into an unfamiliar, brilliantly illuminated place full of shadows and green caves and a floor of broken sunlight that seemed to undulate before their dazzled eyes. The boys who carried the chairs out from the kitchen were going to put them in an open space where the ground dipped—a very suitable-looking grassy sward, Min thought it. But Delia's Aunt Mag wanted to sit close to a particular tree she said was her favorite, and that is where her chair was placed, with the two other chairs nearby. The boys couldn't get the chair close enough to the tree to suit Delia's Aunt Mag, and when she sat down she moved her body sideways in a very adroit quick way, and then she put her arm around the tree and her face up against the trunk as though she was cuddling it. "I love my old tree," she said. She looked up into the tree, stretching her head back, and she began laughing. "The best parts of the sky show through this tree. Now you know my secret." Min thought she was a bit queer.

She told them the tree bore cooking apples that were as big as your head and too sour to eat. Delia's Aunt Mag and her three sisters, including Delia's mother, all wore long-sleeved, high-necked black dresses cut to show the rigidity of their busts and waists, and the straightness of their backs. They were big women, and the sweeping motion of their long heavy skirts gave them the appearance of nuns. Yes, they looked like women belonging to a religious order. Min thought them very forbidding, all four of them, and she was surprised at the change in Aunt Mag once she got her arm around the tree. Her face got much younger and she looked a bit mischievous. She was a strange, wayward old woman, and Min wondered if Delia took after her. There was something dreamy about Delia that Min didn't really trust.

Thirty years later, when Min was obliged to have Clare locked up in the Enniscorthy lunatic asylum, she remembered Delia's Aunt Mag, and she wondered how many people were abroad in the world who should by rights be locked up out of harm's way. By then, of course, Bridget was dead. Bridget had always said that their father would have ended up in the poorhouse if he had been left to himself. Min thought he might have been very well off in the poorhouse. Maybe that was where his place was. There were people who couldn't manage in the world. But Bridget would never have let Clare go into the lunatic asylum. She always said, "Poor Clare, she takes after her father." Min couldn't see that at all. Their father had been very silent. But Clare never shut up, and all she did was pray for them all. It got on Min's nerves to hear the rosary going day and night. Clare's rabbit-chasing husband was no help at all. He just laughed, probably pleased in his heart to hear the prayers mocked. Min finally lost patience when she found out that Clare had given away every piece but one of the blue-and-white German china their mother had treasured. Only the soup tureen remained, with its heavy lid. Min never got over the loss of that china. She would have gone and demanded it back, but Clare wouldn't tell her who had it. It was gone for good, no hope of ever seeing it again. Clare claimed the china was hers, and that where it went was none of Min's business. Min knew otherwise. Clare didn't live many years after being shut up, and Min brought her body back to Wexford and buried her there where they would all be buried. All but Martin. Martin and Delia were buried together in St. Jerome's in Dublin.

During the years she lived with him after Delia died, Min found Martin very changed. Fifty years with Delia had left their mark on him. He wasn't the brother she remembered. She had seen other men like that—so buried in habit that their lives were worth nothing to them when the wife was gone. Martin would begin to read, and then his hand would sink down, with the book in it, and he would stare over to the side of his chair, as though he was trying to remember something. More likely he was trying to understand something, Min thought. He had had a habit like that when he was young, of staring away at the wall, or at nothing, when things were going against him. He didn't want her in the house with him—that was obvious—but he had to put up with her. She didn't care. She was being loyal to their mother, that was the main thing. He continued to take his walk every day till his legs gave out. He never went out in the garden, never, but every once in a while he would go to the big window that looked out on the garden and he would stand there staring and always turn away saying, "The garden misses her."

Min got tired of that, and one day she burst out, "Oh, she was a good gardener. That is what she had a talent for. She was good at gardening." He turned from the window and he said to her, "What did you say? What was that you said?" She repeated what she had said. She wasn't afraid of him. "I said, she was a good gardener. That is what she was good at, I said." Min was shocked at what he said to her then. "And what were you ever good at, may we ask?" he said. Martin of all people ought to know she had always been good at anything she chose to put her hand to. All the times she came here to visit them, he used to hold her up as an example to Delia. He used to tell Delia that Min could have done wonders if she hadn't been tied to the sewing machine. Martin ought to be ashamed of himself, but she said nothing to defend herself now. He was an old man, wandering in his mind like their father.

Martin was restless too, and the more feeble he became, the less he wanted to stay in the house. He said he wanted to see the water again. He wanted to go to the sea. He wanted to walk on the strand. He even talked about paying a last visit to the west of Ireland. He wanted to walk by the Atlantic Ocean once again. He said the air there would put new life into him. Once he began talking about Connemara and Kerry there was no stopping him. He liked to recall the adventures he'd had on the holidays he used to take by himself in Connemara and Kerry long ago. He used to go on long walking tours by himself. He'd stay away for a week at a time. He liked to recall those days when he was on his own. He seemed proud of having gone off on his own, away from this house and from Delia and the children, away from all he knew. He sounded like a conjurer describing some magical rope trick when he talked about how he left the house at such and such an hour, and what So-and-So had said to him on the train, and how he carried nothing with him but his knapsack and his blackthorn stick. Min didn't like hearing about it. She knew his adventures, and she had no sympathy with him. If he was all that anxious to have a change from Delia—and nobody could blame him for that—

why hadn't he come to Wexford to see his mother, and to see his sisters, and to go about the town and have a word with all the old crowd? Most of them were still there at that time.

He could have taken a walk about the town with me, Min thought. It would have set me up, in those days, to be seen with him, show off a bit. Many a time he could have come down to see us, but no, he was off to Connemara, or to Kerry, to enjoy another holiday by himself with the Atlantic Ocean. The Irish Sea wasn't good enough for him anymore, and Wexford Harbour was nothing compared with the beauties of Galway Bay. He talked about the wild Mayo coast as though wildness was a sort of virtue, and one you didn't find in the scenery in Wexford. She reminded him that he had once been in love with their own strand at Rosslare, and she described to him how he used to spend half his life out there, riding out on his bicycle every chance he got. Every free minute he could get he spent at Rosslare. He listened to her, but as though he was being patient with her. "I'd be very glad to see Rosslare again," he said when she had finished talking.

Then he gave up talking about Connemara and Kerry, and he began to wish for a day out at Dun Laoghaire. And he said he'd like to have a day at Greystones. And he wanted to go out to Killiney for a day. Which would Min like best? Maybe they could manage it. Min didn't see how they were going to manage it. A whole day out of the house, and no guarantee of what the weather might be like. They might not be able to find shelter so easy in case of a sudden shower. If he got his feet wet there'd be the devil to pay. They had no car, even if they could drive, and it was an awful drag out to Killiney and back on the bus, or on the train, if they took the train. It would be foolish to go to the expense of hiring a car. She didn't see how they were going to do it.

He seemed to let go of the idea, and then one day he said, "Min, do you remember the lovely view of the Slaney from the garden that day? Do you remember how the Slaney looked that day, flowing past us into Wexford? And we all stood looking at it? I thought of the passage of time. I stood there, and I thought for a minute that the garden was moving along with the river. And then later on when Delia and I were at Edermine station waiting for the train to Dublin, there were all the flowers in the station, and the stationmaster laughing at us and talking to us, and the white stones spelling out the name of the station. Delia said an expert gardener must have planted the bed of flowers beside the station house, and the stationmaster said he'd done it all himself, getting the place ready for her. But the garden they had there by the Slaney—that was magnificent. Wasn't it, Min?"

Min remembered standing in the garden, surrounded by roses with big heavy heads, and hearing her mother say that she would like very much to have a bunch of flowers to take back to Wexford with her. They all got bunches of flowers to take home. And there was a bunch of flowers for Markey to take to his wife. The car was filled with flowers, and still the garden looked as though it hadn't been touched.

"That was a grand place they had there," Min said, and she was glad to know that the garden was in ruins now, and that the house stood empty with the roof falling in and that the door there stood open to display the vacant rooms and the cold hearth in the kitchen. "It's all gone now," she said.

"It was a marvellous day," Martin said. "I never forgot what Delia's Aunt Mag said to me. Do you remember—she said the air was like mother o' pearl. Wasn't that a funny thing for an old country woman to say? I wonder what put a thought like that in her head. 'The air is like mother o' pearl today,' she said, looking at me as though we were the same age and had known one another all our lives."

"She didn't look at me that way," Min said. "But I remember her saying that. She was a bit affected, I think—inclined to talk above herself. I didn't care for her. Something about her made me very uneasy."

"Ah, no," Martin said. "Delia was very fond of her."

"Oh, Delia," Min said impatiently. "Delia said the first thing that came into her head. You told her so often enough, to her face, with me sitting here in this room listening to you barging at her. She couldn't open her mouth to suit you. There was no harm in Delia, but she never knew what she said. Half the time she made no sense. There was nothing to Delia."

The minute she finished speaking, she was sorry. She didn't want to start a row. But Martin was silent, and then he said, "Nothing to Delia. That's true. I never thought that. But as Shakespeare says, It's true. It's true, it's a pity, and pity 'tis it's true. Nothing to Delia. Shakespeare was right that time."

"Shakespeare didn't say it. I said it," Min cried furiously.

"You or Shakespeare, what matter now. It's true, there was nothing to Delia. Wasn't she a lovely girl, though."

"Are you going to make a song out of it?" Min said. "What's got into you, Martin?"

She looked at him sitting across the hearth from her. His snowwhite curls floated on his head. His narrow face was the same shape as her own face. His blue eyes watched her through his rimless spectacles, and he smiled easily, as though they were discussing something pleasant from the past. She thought of Clare singing "You stick to the boats, lads . . ." that morning when she was being driven off in the car that took her to the asylum. They told Min later that Clare stopped singing quick enough when she saw where she was going. Min wondered if the queer strain that was in Clare had touched Martin and she was glad that she herself was free of it. Martin seemed to follow her thoughts.

"You put poor Clare into the asylum," he said gently.

"She was off her head, driving us all to distraction, trying to give the house away!" Min said indignantly. "What help were you, up here in Dublin, away from all the unpleasantness?"

"Clare was mad," Martin said. "There was nothing to Delia. That's a weight off my mind. I know where I am now. I always knew where I was with her, even though I didn't know what she was, and now I still don't know what she was, and God knows I don't know where I am without her. But there was nothing to her."

"My mother said Delia didn't amount to much," Min said spitefully. "Right from the beginning, she said that."

"Nothing to her. You said it yourself," Martin said. "I'll show you a picture of her, taken when she was sixteen years old."

He pulled himself slowly to his feet, and made his way across the room to the cupboard, which had glass doors on top and solid wooden doors underneath. Behind the glass doors Delia's Waterford glass bowls and her Waterford glass jug shimmered dimly. They had a shelf to themselves. Another shelf held her good Arklow china. Martin bent painfully to open the lower doors, and when they were open wide he reached in and took out a large brown envelope. He pushed the doors shut and made his way back to where Min sat in Delia's chair on Delia's side of the fire. He unfastened the envelope and slid the photograph out carefully, holding it as though it was thin glass. His hands are trembling more these days, Min thought. When the photograph was free, he held it up for Min to see.

"There she is," he said. "That's what she looked like. Look at the hair she had. Who ever had hair like that, that color? Nobody else in that family had hair like that. They said she took after her father. He died young. Look at that, Min."

"That photograph glorifies her," Min said.

"She was very good," Martin said. "I remember that day we got married, I was standing off to myself, looking at the Slaney. I was lost in admiration. I was looking through a gap in the hedge—one of the children had pulled open a place there, to look through. The river seemed very close up to the garden, under my feet. It was very close. Even then the water was eating in under the garden, and the little strand they told me they had there at one time was gone, or nearly gone. I remember I was there by myself—the water was dazzling. I didn't know where I was. I was inside a dream, and everything was safe, I know. The Slaney was very broad that day, and powerful, sure and strong—you know the way it used to be. An Irish river of great importance, the inspector said the day he visited the school. But I felt grand, looking at the Slaney that day. To know it was my own native river and was so, long before I was born. I was standing there like that, when Delia's Aunt Mag came up alongside me. 'I was looking for you,' she said. My God, how well I remember her voice, as if it was five minutes ago. We might still be there. 'I was looking for you,' she said. She saw the break in the hedge. 'Ah, you found a spy hole,' she said. And do you know what she did? She put her arm around my shoulders. She was taller than me—they were big women in that family—and she stuck her face out past me so that she could see what I was looking at. I started to move to the side, to give her room, but she held on to me. 'Stay where you are,' she said. I said, 'I'm in your way.' 'You're not in my way, child,' she said. 'Haven't you more right to stand here than anybody? I only want to have a little look before Willie comes along and finds this hole and starts to patch it up. "The lads have been up to mischief again"—that's what Willie will say. He says they're tearing down the hedge, helping the garden into the river. The river is eating up the garden, you know—if it wasn't for Willie always on guard, we'd be swallowed up.' I said, 'It's great to see the Slaney like this.' 'I have a great fondness for the water,' she said. 'I couldn't be content any place but here where I was born and brought up. I've never spent a night away from this house in my life, do you know that? It's a blessing the day turned out so grand. And nobody was sick or anything. Everybody was able to come see Delia married. The Slaney is in full flood, and the springs of affection are rising around us.' She spoke the truth. The Slaney was in full flood that day."

"That's sheer nonsense," Min said. "How could the Slaney be in full flood on a fine day in June? The Slaney was the same as any other day."

Martin went to his own chair and sat down. "My legs aren't getting any better," he said. "I can't stand on my own feet these days."

"You've tired yourself out making speeches," Min said.

Martin still held the photograph of Delia. He lifted it, to see it better. He's trembling too much, Min thought. She wondered if she could get him to go to his room and lie down. "You're wearing yourself out," she said.

Martin gazed at the shaking photograph. "It's very like her," he said. Then he fitted it back into its envelope, pressing his lips together and frowning, like a foolish old man making an effort to do something that was beyond him.

"I'll do that for you," she said, getting ready to stand up and go over to him.

"You stay where you are," he said, and when he had the photograph safe he placed the envelope on the low shelf under his table. "I shouldn't have stood up so long," he said, and then he took his book from the table and began reading, but after a minute he got up and went out of the room, carrying the book with him. "I'm going to my room," he said without looking at her. "I might lie down for a bit."

Min was glad to see him go. There would be peace now,

for a while. She didn't like to see him getting into these states where he talked so much. All that raking up of the past was a bad sign. She would have asked the priest to come in and talk to him, but she knew Martin would fight the priest's coming until he could fight no more. Martin didn't want the priest in the house. His mind was made up to that, and there was no use arguing with him. Min only hoped she would be able to get the priest in time, when the time came. She didn't want her brother dying without the Last Sacraments. She didn't understand Martin's bitter attitude toward the Church. Polly went very much the same way, of course. Min would never forget Polly's blasphemous language when the third-eldest child died, the little one they called Mary. Min was trying to comfort Polly by telling her the baby would be well taken care of in Heaven, when Polly burst out laughing and crying and saying she could take care of her own child better than God and His Blessed Mother and all the saints and angels put together. "They might have left poor little Mary with her own Mammy!" Polly said. "They must have seen the way she was holding on to my hand, wanting to stay with me. They have very hard hearts up there, if you ask me." Martin had never gone that far in his talk against the Church. At least, as far as Min knew he'd never gone that far, but she knew she was going to have to do a bit of scheming to get the priest into the house. "The springs of affection are rising." She didn't like to hear him talking like that. What Min remembered of that day in the garden by the Slaney was that she felt worn out and dried up, and trapped, crushed in by people who were determined to see only the bright surface of the occasion. They could call it a wedding or anything they liked, but she knew it was a holocaust and that she was the victim, although nobody would ever admit that.

She thought they were all very clumsy. It wasn't that she wanted to be noticed. But she knew that any notice she got was pity, or derision. Nothing she could say was right. She was out of it, and nothing could convince those people that she wanted to be out of it. She would ten times rather have been back in Wexford working as usual, but she had to go to the wedding or cause a scandal. Now here they were. Bridget was giving every evidence of enjoying herself, and so were Polly and Clare, and in Min's opinion they were letting the side down. She had been dragged out here like a victim of war at the back of a chariot, and all to bolster Martin up, and he didn't need bolstering up.

She stood outside the garden gate. The children had all vanished and she imagined they had gone to play somewhere by themselves, but suddenly the place was full of children running around, and she thought they must have been having their dinner. Children always had to be fed, no matter what. These children were a healthy-looking lot, fair-haired or red-headed, most of them. Min remembered how black she and Martin had been as children, Martin with his black curls and she with her straight black plait. They were a skinny pair, very different from these children. A little boy ran up to her so suddenly that she thought he was going to crash into her, but he stopped just in time and stared up at her. He was about five years old, a very solid-looking little fellow. His eyes were so blue that it was like two flowers looking at you, and he had a very short nose, and there was sweat on his forehead. His hair was nearly white. He wore a little suit of clothes, a little coat and trousers and a white shirt, and black stockings pulled up on his legs under the trousers. He opened his mouth, but he said nothing, just stared at her. Min gave him no encouragement. She didn't dislike children, but she had no great fondness for them, and she didn't want a whole crowd of them trooping along after him and asking her questions and making her conspicuous. He turned red, and he threw his arm up over his eyes, and peered up at her from under his sleeve, and began to smile. She smiled at him. He was a nice little fellow. She ought to say something to him.

"Are you a good boy?" she asked him. He turned and ran off, flapping his arms at his sides like a farmyard bird, and when he was a little distance away he turned and looked back to see if she was watching him. Then he ran off out of the garden. She didn't see him again.

The next thing she remembered was a moment of terrible unhappiness—it gave her a shock. What happened was that Martin and one of Delia's brothers and a woman she didn't even know came up to her and began talking about the train. They kept saying that it wouldn't do for Delia and Martin to miss the train. Min never knew the woman's name, but she remembered that she made a great fuss, as though she imagined that the day depended on her. There were always people like that everywhere, trying to boss things. She wanted to tell that woman to mind her own business. All these strangers were taking Martin over. They thought they owned him now.

"The springs of affection are rising." It would be those people who would say a thing like that, including everybody in their inspirations, everybody, even people who didn't want to be included. Min thought of that garden. She thought of the green box hedge and the monkey-puzzle tree and the pink and white roses and all the big dark and white star-shaped flowers, and she thought of Delia's Aunt Mag on the kitchen chair under the cooking-apple tree, and she remembered Delia's brothers and sisters and Delia's mother, and the white-haired child. She had forgotten nothing of that glittering day, and she saw it all enclosed in a radiant fountain that rushed up through a rain of sunlight to meet with and rejoice with whatever was up there—Heaven, God the Father, the Good Shepherd, everything everybody ever wanted, wonderful prizes, happiness.

Min knew it was only the transfiguration of memory. She was no fool and she was not likely to mistake herself for a visionary. The lovely fountain was like a mirage, except that in a mirage people saw what they wanted and were starving for, and in the fountain Min saw what she did not want and never had wanted. Why was it nobody ever believed her when she told them she wanted nothing to do with all that hullabaloo? The fortunes of war condemned her to a silence that misrepresented her as thoroughly as the words she was too proud to speak would have done, and she knew all that. Martin's lightmindedness had changed the course of her life, and there wasn't one single thing she could do about it. He turned all their lives around. He cared no more about his mother and sisters and what happened to them than if he had been a stranger passing through the house on his way to a far better place, where the people were more interesting.

He made his mother cry. For a wedding present, Bridget wanted to give Martin the good dining-room set that she had paid for penny by penny at a time when she couldn't afford it. A big round mahogany table and four matching chairs that must have had pride of place in some great house at one time. She kept that furniture up to the nines, polished and waxed till you could see to do your hair in it. But Martin turned up his nose at it. No second-hand stuff for him and Delia, and the mahogany was too big and heavy anyway. He didn't want it. He and Delia went and ordered furniture made just for them; new furniture, all walnut—a bed, a chest of drawers, a wardrobe, a washstand, and two sitting-room chairs so that Delia could hold court in style when they had visitors. Those were Martin's very words. "Now Delia can hold court in style," he said, and never noticed the look on his mother's face. Min noticed the bed had vanished out of the house in Dublin and she was never able to find out what happened to it. But the other things were still there. Above all, the two sitting-room chairs were still there—Martin sat in his own, and she sat in Delia's. She would take the whole lot back to Wexford when the time came. She would bring the furniture back where it belonged. It was never too late to make things right.

In Wexford, in her own flat, she sat in Delia's chair, and sometimes for a change sat propped up with pillows in Martin's big chair, his armchair. It was nice to have the two chairs. The wardrobe and the chest of drawers went into her bedroom, and the washstand into the room she used for a kitchen. Delia's old sitting-room carpet was threadbare, but the colors held up well, and it looked nice on the floor, almost like an antique carpet. And the hearthrug from the house in Dublin looked very suitable in front of Min's old fireplace, where so many girls and ladies had warmed themselves when they came in to be measured for a dress, or to have a fitting.

Against the end wall, facing down the room to the fireplace, Delia's bookshelves were ranged along, filled with Delia's books, and with some of Martin's books. Some of Martin's books Min wouldn't have in the house, and she had sold them. She was glad now that she had never spent money on books; these had been waiting for her. The room looked very distinguished, very literary. It was what she should always have had. She wished they could all see it. There was room for them, and a welcome. There was even a deep, dim corner there between the end wall and the far window where her father could steal in and sit down and listen to them with his silence, as he used to do. There was a place here for all of them—a place for Polly, a place for poor Clare. A place in the middle for Bridget. A place for Martin in his own chair. They could come in any time and feel right at home, although the room was warmer and the furniture a bit better than anything they had been used to in the old days.

CARSON MCCULLERS was born Lula Carson Smith in Columbus, Georgia, in 1917. As a child, she practiced the piano five hours a day, planning to be a concert pianist. At the age of fifteen, however, an attack of rheumatic fever forced her to give up the demands of a musical career. At seventeen, she arrived in New York to study writing at New York University and at Columbia, supporting herself as a waitress and typist. Upon the publication of her first novel, *The Heart Is a Lonely Hunter*, when she was twenty-three, she became famous, winning the friendship and admiration of such established writers as Richard Wright, W. H. Auden, and Jane Bowles. In the opinion of Tennessee Williams, she was the only great talent to appear in America since the generation of major writers that emerged in the twenties (Crane, Porter, cummings, Faulkner, Hemingway, Fitzgerald, and Eliot).

McCullers suffered from poor health all her life. During the decades when she was writing and publishing such highly acclaimed works as *Reflections in a Golden Eye* (1941), *The Ballad of the Sad Café* (1944), *The Member of the Wedding* (1946), *The Square Root of Wonderful* (1958), and *Clock Without Hands* (1961), she also suffered a series of strokes, a heart attack, pneumonia, and breast cancer. She also knew the strain and torment of two difficult marriages to the same man as well as the constant need for money to pay her medical bills. As her recent biographer Virginia Spencer Carr has noted, the dark, almost sinister moodiness of McCuller's work reflects the grief and trouble of her own life. In much of her best-known work, troubled adolescents in particular, such as the narrator in "Like That," the posthumously published story that follows here, are the dominant voice, yearning for the simple time and world before the sexual confusions of puberty destroyed the mythic wonders and kinships of childhood.

McCullers' reputation is as solid in Europe as in America. Dame Edith Sitwell wrote that she "has a great poet's eye and mind and senses, together with a great prose writer's sense of construction and character. She is a transcendental writer." McCullers once wrote that love was "the main generator of all good writing," including her own. "Love, passion, compassion, are all welded together." After a final series of strokes, she died at the age of fifty.

Like That

by
Carson McCullers

Even if Sis is five years older than me and eighteen we used always to be closer and have more fun together than most sisters. It was about the same with us and our brother Dan, too. In the summer we'd all go swimming together. At nights in the wintertime maybe we'd sit around the fire in the living room and play three-handed bridge or Michigan, with everybody putting up a nickel or a dime to the winner. The three of us could have more fun by ourselves than any family I know. That's the way it always was before this.

Not that Sis was playing down to me, either. She's smart as she can be and has read more books than anybody I ever knew—even school teachers. But in High School she never did like to priss up flirty and ride around in cars with girls and pick up the boys and park at the drugstore and all that sort of thing. When she wasn't reading she'd just like to play around with me and Dan. She wasn't too grown up to fuss over a chocolate bar in the refrigerator or to stay awake most of Christmas Eve night either, say, with excitement. In some ways it was like I was heaps older than her. Even when Tuck started coming around last summer I'd sometimes have to tell her she shouldn't wear ankle socks because they might go down town or she ought to pluck out her eyebrows above her nose like the other girls do.

In one more year, next June, Tuck'll be graduated from college. He's a lanky boy with an eager look to his face. At college he's so smart he has a free scholarship. He started coming to see Sis the last summer before this one, riding in his family's car when he could get it, wearing crispy white linen suits. He came a lot last year but this summer he came even more often—before he left he was coming around for Sis every night. Tuck's O.K.

It began getting different between Sis and me a while

back, I guess, although I didn't notice it at the time. It was only after a certain night this summer that I had the idea that things maybe were bound to end like they are now.

It was late when I woke up that night. When I opened my eyes I thought for a minute it must be about dawn and I was scared when I saw Sis wasn't on her side of the bed. But it was only the moonlight that shone cool looking and white outside the window and made the oak leaves hanging down over the front yard pitch black and separate seeming. It was around the first of September, but I didn't feel hot looking at the moonlight. I pulled the sheet over me and let my eyes roam around the black shapes of the furniture in our room.

I'd waked up lots of times in the night this summer. You see Sis and I have always had this room together and when she would come in and turn on the light to find her nightgown or something it woke me. I liked it. In the summer when school was out I didn't have to get up early in the morning. We would lie and talk sometimes for a good while. I'd like to hear about the places she and Tuck had been or to laugh over different things. Lots of times before that night she had talked to me privately about Tuck just like I was her age—asking me if I thought she should have said this or that when he called and giving me a hug, maybe, after. Sis was really crazy about Tuck. Once she said to me: "He's so lovely—I never in the world thought I'd know anyone like him—"

We would talk about our brother too. Dan's seventeen years old and was planning to take the co-op course at Tech in the fall. Dan had gotten older by this summer. One night he came in at four o'clock and he'd been drinking. Dad sure had it in for him the next week. So he hiked out to the country and camped with some boys for a few days. He used to talk to me and Sis about diesel motors and going away to South America and all that, but by this summer he was quiet and not saying much to anybody in the family. Dan's real tall and thin as a rail. He has bumps on his face now and is clumsy and not very good looking. At nights sometimes I know he wanders all around by himself, maybe going out beyond the city limits sign into the pine woods.

Thinking about such things I lay in bed wondering what time it was and when Sis would be in. That night after Sis and Dan had left I had gone down to the corner with some of the kids in the neighborhood to chunk rocks at the street light and try to kill a bat up there. At first I had the shivers and imagined it was a smallish bat like the kind in Dracula. When I saw it looked just like a moth I didn't care if they killed it or not. I was just sitting there on the curb drawing with a stick on the dusty street when Sis and Tuck rode by slowly in his car. She was sitting over very close to him. They weren't talking or smiling—just riding slowly down the street, sitting close, looking ahead. When they passed and I saw who it was I hollered to them. "Hey, Sis!" I yelled.

The car just went on slowly and nobody hollered back. I just stood there in the middle of the street feeling sort of silly with all the other kids standing around.

That hateful little old Bubber from down on the other block came up to me. "That your sister?" he asked.

I said yes.

"She sure was sitting up close to her beau," he said.

I was mad all over like I get sometimes. I hauled off and chunked all the rocks in my hand right at him. He's three years younger than me and it wasn't nice, but I couldn't stand him in the first place and he thought he was being so cute about Sis. He started holding his neck and bellering and I walked off and left them and went home and got ready to go to bed.

When I woke up I finally began to think of that too and old Bubber Davis was still in my mind when I heard the sound of a car coming up the block. Our room faces the street with only a short front yard between. You can see and hear everything from the sidewalk and the street. The car was creeping down in front of our walk and the light went slow and white along the walls of the room. It stopped on Sis's writing desk, showed up the books there plainly and half a pack of chewing gum. Then the room was dark and there was only the moonlight outside.

The door of the car didn't open but I could hear them talking. Him, that is. His voice was low and I couldn't catch any words but it was like he was explaining something over and over again. I never heard Sis say a word.

I was still awake when I heard the car door open. I heard her say, "Don't come out." And then the door slammed and there was the sound of her heels clopping up the walk, fast and light like she was running.

Mama met Sis in the hall outside our room. She had heard the front door close. She always listens out for Sis and Dan and never goes to sleep when they're still out. I sometimes wonder how she can just lie there in the dark for hours without going to sleep.

"It's one-thirty, Marian," she said. "You ought to get in before this."

Sis didn't say anything.

"Did you have a nice time?"

That's the way Mama is. I could imagine her standing there with her nightgown blowing out fat around her and her dead white legs and the blue veins showing, looking all messed up. Mama's nicer when she's dressed to go out.

"Yes, we had a grand time," Sis said. Her voice was funny—sort of like a piano in the gym at school, high and sharp on your ear. Funny.

Mama was asking more questions. Where did they go? Did they see anybody they knew? All that sort of stuff. That's the way she is.

"Goodnight," said Sis in that out of tune voice.

She opened the door of our room real quick and closed it. I started to let her know I was awake but changed my mind. Her breathing was quick and loud in the dark and she did not move at all. After a few minutes she felt in the closet for her nightgown and got in the bed. I could hear her crying.

"Did you and Tuck have a fuss?" I asked.

"No," she answered. Then she seemed to change her mind. "Yeah, it was a fuss."

There's one thing that gives me the creeps sure enough—and that's to hear somebody cry. "I wouldn't let it bother me. You'll be making up tomorrow."

The moon was coming in the window and I could see her moving her jaw from one side to the other and staring up at the ceiling. I watched her for a long time. The moonlight was cool looking and there was a wettish wind coming cool from the window. I moved over like I sometimes do to snug up with her, thinking maybe that would stop her from moving her jaw like that and crying.

She was trembling all over. When I got close to her she jumped like I'd pinched her and pushed me over quick and kicked my legs over. "Don't," she said. "Don't."

Maybe Sis had suddenly gone batty, I was thinking. She

was crying in a slower and sharper way. I was a little scared and I got up to go to the bathroom a minute. While I was in there I looked out the window, down toward the corner where the street light is. I saw something then that I knew Sis would want to know about.

"You know what?" I asked when I was back in the bed.

She was lying over close to the edge as she could get, stiff. She didn't answer.

"Tuck's car is parked down by the street light. Just drawn up to the curb. I could tell because of the box and the two tires on the back. I could see it from the bathroom window."

She didn't even move.

"He must be just sitting out there. What ails you and him?"

She didn't say anything at all.

"I couldn't see him but he's probably just sitting there in the car under the street light. Just sitting there."

It was like she didn't care or had known it all along. She was as far over the edge of the bed as she could get, her legs stretched out stiff and her hands holding tight to the edge and her face on one arm.

She used always to sleep all sprawled over on my side so I'd have to push at her when it was hot and sometimes turn on the light and draw the line down the middle and show her how she really was on my side. I wouldn't have to draw any line that night, I was thinking. I felt bad. I looked out at the moonlight a long time before I could get to sleep again.

The next day was Sunday and Mama and Dad went in the morning to church because it was the anniversary of the day my aunt died. Sis said she didn't feel well and stayed in bed. Dan was out and I was there by myself so naturally I went into our room where Sis was. Her face was white as the pillow and there were circles under her eyes. There was a muscle jumping on one side of her jaw like she was chewing. She hadn't combed her hair and it flopped over the pillow, glinty red and messy and pretty. She was reading with a book held up close to her face. Her eyes didn't move when I came in. I don't think they even moved across the page.

It was roasting hot that morning. The sun made everything blazing outside so that it hurt your eyes to look. Our room was so hot that you could almost touch the air with your finger. But Sis had the sheet pulled up clear to her shoulders.

"Is Tuck coming today?" I asked. I was trying to say something that would make her look more cheerful.

"Gosh! Can't a person have *any* peace in this house?"

She never did used to say mean things like that out of a clear sky. Mean things, maybe, but not grouchy ones.

"Sure," I said. "Nobody's going to notice you."

I sat down and pretended to read. When footsteps passed on the street Sis would hold onto the book tighter and I knew she was listening hard as she could. I can tell between footsteps easy. I can even tell without looking if the person who passes is colored or not. Colored people mostly make a slurry sound between the steps. When the steps would pass Sis would loosen the hold on the book and bite at her mouth. It was the same way with passing cars.

I felt sorry for Sis. I decided then and there that I never would let any fuss with any boy make me feel or look like that. But I wanted Sis and me to get back like we'd always been. Sunday mornings are bad enough without having any other trouble.

"We fuss lots less than most sisters do," I said. "And when we do it's all over quick, isn't it?"

She mumbled and kept staring at the same spot on the book.

"That's one good thing," I said.

She was moving her head slightly from side to side—over and over again, with her face not changing. "We never do have any real long fusses like Bubber Davis's two sisters have—"

"No." She answered like she wasn't thinking about what I'd said.

"Not one real one like that since I can remember."

In a minute she looked up the first time. "I remember one," she said suddenly.

"When?"

Her eyes looked green in the blackness under them and like they were nailing themselves into what they saw. "You had to stay in every afternoon for a week. It was a long time ago."

All of a sudden I remembered. I'd forgotten it for a long

time. I hadn't wanted to remember. When she said that it came back to me all complete.

It was really a long time ago—when Sis was about thirteen. If I remember right I was mean and even more hardboiled than I am now. My aunt who I'd liked better than all my other aunts put together had had a dead baby and she had died. After the funeral Mama had told Sis and me about it. Always the things I've learned new and didn't like have made me mad—mad clean through and scared.

That wasn't what Sis was talking about, though. It was a few mornings after that when Sis started with what every big girl has each month, and of course I found out and was scared to death. Mama then explained to me about it and what she had to wear. I felt then like I'd felt about my aunt, only ten times worse. I felt different toward Sis, too, and was so mad I wanted to pitch into people and hit.

I never will forget it. Sis was standing in our room before the dresser mirror. When I remembered her face it was white like Sis's there on the pillow and with the circles under her eyes and the glinty hair to her shoulders—it was only younger.

I was sitting on the bed, biting hard at my knee. "It shows," I said. "It does too!"

She had on a sweater and a blue pleated skirt and she was so skinny all over that it did show a little.

"Anybody can tell. Right off the bat. Just to look at you anybody can tell."

Her face was white in the mirror and did not move.

"It looks terrible. I wouldn't ever ever be like that. It shows and everything."

She started crying then and told Mother and said she wasn't going back to school and such. She cried a long time. That's how ugly and hardboiled I used to be and am still sometimes. That's why I had to stay in the house every afternoon for a week a long time ago . . .

Tuck came by in his car that Sunday morning before dinner time. Sis got up and dressed in a hurry and didn't even put on any lipstick. She said they were going out to dinner. Nearly every Sunday all of us in the family stay together all day, so that was a little funny. They didn't get home until almost dark. The rest of us were sitting on the front porch drinking ice tea because of the heat when the car drove up again. After they got out of the car Dad, who had been in a very good mood all day, insisted Tuck stay for a glass of tea.

Tuck sat on the swing with Sis and he didn't lean back and his heels didn't rest on the floor—as though he was all ready to get up again. He kept changing the glass from one hand to the other and starting new conversations. He and Sis didn't look at each other except on the sly, and then it wasn't at all like they were crazy about each other. It was a funny look. Almost like they were afraid of something. Tuck left soon.

"Come sit by your Dad a minute, Puss," Dad said. Puss is a nickname he calls Sis when he feels in a specially good mood. He still likes to pet us.

She went and sat on the arm of his chair. She sat stiff like Tuck had, holding herself off a little so Dad's arm hardly went around her waist. Dad smoked his cigar and looked out on the front yard and the trees that were beginning to melt into the early dark.

"How's my big girl getting along these days?" Dad still likes to hug us up when he feels good and treat us, even Sis, like kids.

"O.K.," she said. She twisted a little bit like she wanted to get up and didn't know how to without hurting his feelings.

"You and Tuck have had a nice time together this summer, haven't you, Puss?"

"Yeah," she said. She had begun to see-saw her lower jaw again. I wanted to say something but couldn't think of anything.

Dad said: "He ought to be getting back to Tech about now, oughtn't he? When's he leaving?"

"Less than a week," she said. She got up so quick that she knocked Dad's cigar out of his fingers. She didn't even pick it up but flounced on through the front door. I could hear her half running to our room and the sound the door made when she shut it. I knew she was going to cry.

It was hotter than ever. The lawn was beginning to grow dark and the locusts were droning out so shrill and steady that you wouldn't notice them unless you thought to. The sky was bluish grey and the trees in the vacant lot across the street were dark. I kept on sitting on the front porch with Mama and Papa and hearing their low talk without listening to the words. I wanted to go in our room with Sis but I was afraid to. I wanted to ask her what was really the matter. Was hers and Tuck's fuss so bad as that or was it that she was so crazy about him that she was sad because he was leaving? For a minute I didn't think it was either one of those things. I wanted to know but I was scared to ask. I just sat there with the grown people. I never have been so lonesome as I was that night. If ever I think about being sad I just remember how it was then—sitting there looking at the long bluish shadows across the lawn and feeling like I was the only child left in the family and that Sis and Dan were dead or gone for good.

It's October now and the sun shines bright and a little cool and the sky is the color of my turquoise ring. Dan's gone to Tech. So has Tuck gone. It's not at all like it was last fall, though. I come in from High School (I go there now) and Sis maybe is just sitting by the window reading or writing to Tuck or just looking out. Sis is thinner and sometimes to me she looks in the face like a grown person. Or like, in a way, something has suddenly hurt her hard. We don't do any of the things we used to. It's good weather for fudge or for doing so many things. But no she just sits around or goes for long walks in the chilly late afternoon by herself. Sometimes she'll smile in a way that really gripes—like I was such a kid and all. Sometimes I want to cry or to hit her.

But I'm hardboiled as the next person. I can get along by myself if Sis or anybody else wants to. I'm glad I'm thirteen and still wear socks and can do what I please. I don't want to be any older if I'd get like Sis has. But I wouldn't. I wouldn't like any boy in the world as much as she does Tuck. I'd never let any boy or any thing make me act like she does. I'm not going to waste my time and try to make Sis be like she used to be. I get lonesome—sure—but I don't care. I know there's no way I can make myself stay thirteen all my life, but I know I'd never let anything really change me at all—no matter what it is.

I skate and ride my bike and go to the school football games every Friday. But when one afternoon the kids all got quiet in the gym basement and then started telling certain things—about being married and all—I got up quick so I wouldn't hear and went up and played basketball.

And when some of the kids said they were going to start wearing lipstick and stockings I said I wouldn't for a hundred dollars.

You see I'd never be like Sis is now. I wouldn't. Anybody could know that if they knew me. I just wouldn't, that's all. I don't want to grow up—if it's like that.

NADINE GORDIMER, the daughter of an English mother and a Jewish father who emigrated to Africa from a Baltic town, was born in 1923 at Springs, near Johannesburg in South Africa. At convent school she was a good student with a "bossy vitality" that made her popular, restless, and a frequent truant.

With the publication of her critically acclaimed novels *A Guest of Honour* (1970), *Burger's Daughter* (1979), and *July's People* (1981) and eight volumes of short stories, she has achieved an international reputation of the highest order. Diane Johnson has described her as a mature and brilliant artist whose "writing has the tough precision of poetry and the closely observed naturalness of everyday life." In Gordimer's native South Africa her books have been banned on and off over the years because of their author's condemnation as an artist and activist of the system of *apartheid*. Her short stories, especially, reflect her sensitivity and opposition to the corrosive effects of imperialist attitudes on both political structures and personal relationships.

Gordimer has said that a writer's purpose is to make sense of life. "Even the most esoteric of linguistic innovations, the wildest experiments with form, are an expression of this purpose. The only dictum I always remember is André Gide's—'Salvation, for the writer, lies in being sincere even against one's better judgement.' "

Married and the mother of two children, Gordimer has often visited the United States, where she has been an instructor of writing at Columbia University and a guest lecturer at the Poetry Center of the 92nd Street Y in New York City.

La Vie Bohème

by
Nadine Gordimer

She got off the tram where she had been told, at Minos' New Tearoom, and looked around her at the streets she didn't know. Turn to the left past the tearoom and carry straight on. She crossed the road slowly and recognized in precognition the windows set with a mosaic of oranges, licorice sticks, and chewing gum in packets. This was it, then.

As she walked up the street, her eyes ready for the name of the building, she kept saying over and over to herself snatches of the conversation she had had with her sister yesterday. She saw her sister in her white blouse and red peasant skirt coming in to the exhibition, she felt again the curious suffocating excitement of looking up hard at her and meeting her black eyes—she heard again the surprised cry "Baby!": her sister's voice, not heard for eighteen months, so familiar, yet striking her ear afresh, showing her she had forgotten. And her sister looked just the same. Just the same. And yet in between she had left home, quarreled with her parents, married her student *without any money at all.*

Well, how are you getting on? she had said, because she really couldn't think what would be tactful to say. And her sister laughed: Body and soul together, you know. We've got a little flat—oh very small—minute, not really a flat.—In "Glenorin." There's a balcony.

Live in one room. *Without any money.*—Mother said that, she remembered; kept saying it over and over, until she had felt the awfulness of what her sister was doing. *One room.*—But there, you see, it wasn't one room; it was a small flat, and it had a balcony.

I couldn't believe for a moment that it could be you, Baby.—I was still thinking of you as being at school. . . .

Of course—she had been still at school, when it happened. And her sister never had thought about her much; she was so much younger, and there were a brother and another sister in between. Besides, her sister hadn't ever been a "family" person. She felt the natural ties of affinity rather than the conventional blind ties of the blood.

Come and see me! Why don't you? Come and see my child.—You're not afraid of the family wrath?

That was a compliment. Meeting her at an architectural exhibition, finding that she had grown up, her sister felt perhaps they were of a kind, after all. . . .

With a balcony. Not that building over there? No—wrong side of the street. Besides there were potted plants on the ledge—how her sister always disliked the sword ferns in the bay window at home! It would be something like a studio, inside, she supposed. Warmly untidy. Lived in. God, this room! her sister used to say at home; what a thicket of lace curtains and firescreens and knick-knackery through which to peer out half-seeing at the world. . . .

People drop in. You might meet someone who would interest you. Anyway . . . Her sister always looked so interesting, with her black smooth hair and her contrasting expanses of clear, bright colors; that had always been her way of dressing: as if she had been painted by Gauguin, or even Raoul Dufy.—But why did she persist in this notion, this fancy of seeing her sister against a painted backdrop of an abstract "artist's life." Her sister was not an artist; she was a schoolteacher. And the young student she had married was not an artist; he was studying medicine. Yet her sister brought to mind the black, bright center of a flower, set off within a corolla of the many-colored and curiously distinct petals each resting and overlapping in a curve one upon the other—the pictures she had of an artist's way of life. The simplicity of it—no lounge chairs uncovered for visitors, no halls, no pantries; one room, and in the room, everything. The books that start the ideas; the ideas that start the wonderful talk; the friends who talk. She saw her sister moving amongst all this. . . . Medical student or no medical student. Hadn't her sister's friends—whom she had refused to bring home at all after a while, because her father asked them such banal and stupid questions at table—always been people who wrote, acted or painted?

The building was on the left side of the street and the

name was spelled out over the entrance in red cut-out letters, like children's alphabetical blocks. She went in with her heart beating suddenly hotly, looking at the names on the board and reading Mr. and Mrs., Mr. and Mrs., over and over very quickly until she stopped at the name. Second floor. There was a lift, the paint worn off its metal sides so that being inside was like standing in a biscuit tin, and when she pressed the button, it moved off with a belch that drifted into a sigh and died to a stop at the second floor.

Her sister in the red skirt and white blouse . . . She suddenly felt worried and ashamed of home, of that awful stuffy "nice" home that she was sure clung about her, left its mark imprinted on her face and clothes. And her sister would recognize it at once, and smile to herself, curl her lip. She felt very anxious to impress upon her sister that she *knew* home was awful, a kind of tomb overgrown with impenetrable mediocrity, walking along the cold high passage that leaned over the deep well of a courtyard, looking for Number 11, she calculated urgently how she might let her sister know that *she* was not taken in by home.

Number 11 was a green door, like all the others, but there was a knocker on this one, a little black mask with its tongue out. Of course!

Her smile was ready on her face as she clacked the knocker down.

The door opened to the smell of burned milk and bright warm sleepy yellow light from the wide windows; full in her face it came, making a dark outline of dazzle round her sister, standing there with a soapy hand stiff away from her face, holding back a strand of loose hair awkwardly with the knob of her bent wrist. She was wearing the same red skirt and an old pair of creaking leather sandals threaded in and out her toes. She waved her visitor in, talking, shrugging, holding out her dripping hands. On the right wall above the big divan there was a wonderful picture; her eye leaped to it, in excitement! Ah—! An enormous picture: an Indian child, sitting fawn-colored, cross-legged, with her arms round a great sheaf of arum lilies with their white throats lifted. There were bookshelves, sagging; a great pile of papers, gramophone records. A radio with an elongated, slit-eyed terra-cotta head on it. A kind of tall boy with a human skull wearing an old military cap lopsided.

You mustn't mind all this, said her sister, urging her to the divan. I'm in a mess, the washgirl hasn't turned up for the baby's things. Of course you had to catch me like this. She looked at herself as if she wanted to draw attention to her own boldness of not caring.

Feeling rude as a fascinated child, she dragged her eyes away from the picture, vaguely. Oh there, in the corner: a door was open. The tides of light that washed continuously, in deeps of orange and shallows of pale yellow all about the room, stopped there as at the foot of a glowering little cave. Inside she could see only a confused, cellar-like gloom, whitish things hanging quite dead from the lowness of the ceiling, splashes of white, feeble flashes of nickel. If there's anything I hate doing, said her sister, clicking on a light. —There in the flare of a small globe it was a bathroom, hung with napkins sodden on crisscrossed lines of string, a bath and lavatory and washbasin fitted in one against the other, and just room enough for her sister to stand. A chipped enamel pail on the floor held unwashed napkins, and wet ones lay beneath the scum of pricking soap bubbles in the basin.

Oh, go ahead, she said. Don't worry about me.

Her sister's long hands disappeared beneath the scum; she washed and talked, vivacious as ever.

And she sat on the divan looking intensely round the room, looking, looking, whilst she pretended to talk. From point to point her eyes raced; the cushions with brick-colored and white stalking figures like bushman paintings; the woolly white rugs shaded with stains; the lovely green head of Pan that was a wall vase and that her sister had had at home, and that there had been an argument about because her mother didn't like the wall spoiled with the nail that held it up. There were three dead anemones hanging out of its mouth. Something was pressing into her back, and she found that she was leaning against a big book. She picked it up; whooshed the hundreds of cool pages falling back smooth and close to solidity: FORENSIC MEDICINE it said on the cover, and beneath it, his name. She looked curiously at the curves of his handwriting: realizing that some of the unknown elements of the room were also this signature.

When she just doesn't turn up like this, her sister was

saying, I could wring her neck. In theory, why should another woman wash my child's napkins for me; but in practice . . . She gave a little snort of knowing better now.

Can you imagine what mother would say, she said from the divan, suddenly easily, laughing. They paused: I told you so, they called out together, laughing. Her sister held up her soapy hands; she leaned back on her elbow against a cushion, shaking her head. And their laughter faded companionably down.

Her sister had turned back to the basin, letting the water out with a gurgle. How peculiarly her sister stood, with her feet splayed out in those sandals, clinging to the floor flatly, the Achilles tendon at the back of each ankle pulled taut, strong and thin. . . . The washgirl at home stood just like that, endlessly before the tub on Monday mornings. . . ? The recognition came like a melting inside her. She looked quickly away: sticking out beneath the cushion at her elbow she saw a baby's knitted coat. With a smile she pulled it out, tugged at the little ribbon bedraggled and chewed at the neck.

The baby's? she said, holding it up.

Oh Lord—give here, said her sister—While I'm at it—

A few minutes later, whilst her sister was drying her hands, the cushion fell off the divan, and she saw a small vest and bib, that had been hiding innocently beneath it. She picked them up; the bib smelled sour where the baby had brought up some milk on it. She put them back under the cushion.

I'll hang them out in the courtyard later, said her sister, closing the bathroom door on the napkins. She stood in the room, pleased, a little uncertainly, pushing back her cuticles.

You know, now that I look at you, I think you've got thinner, or taller or something . . . , she said.

Have I? said her sister, smiling. Yes, perhaps—she smoothed her hips. Now I'll make some tea, and then we can talk.

Can't I go and see the baby? she asked. Her sister had said he was asleep on the balcony.

Oh for God's sake don't wake him *now*, said her sister. Let's have some peace. She went over to a curtained recess next to the bathroom door. Is that curtain hand-woven? she asked her sister, admiring the clay, green and black horses on it. Mmm, said her sister, made by a girl called Ada Leghorn who ate with us—for nothing, needless to say—for five months before she went off to South America to paint.—Anyway—And she pulled it on a little two-plate stove with tin legs and a shelf piled and crammed with pots, boxes of cereal, tins, a piece of polony end-down on a saucer, two or three tomatoes, unwashed glasses misted with milk.

Can I help? she asked.

I think you could wash two cups for us, said her sister.

She got up and went to the little square sink, that stood close against the stove. Out of the breakfast dishes thinly coated with the hard dry lacquer of egg, she found two cups and ran the tap over them. On the ledge at the side of the sink she found a swab, and picked it up to wipe the cups; but it was sodden, and unidentifiable bits of soggy food clung to it. She put it down again quickly, not wanting to be noticed. But her eye wandered back to the slimy rag and her sister's followed it. Her sister made an impatient noise with her tongue: Oh—look at that—she said, and quickly snatched up something the other hadn't noticed until then: a square of newspaper sandwiched over a filling of shaving soap lather, grayish with the powderings of a day's beard. *Never* remembers to throw *anything* away!

He's working so terribly hard, poor child, she said after a moment.

Yes, I suppose so, she said, shyly, drying the cups.

You must come when he's here, her sister said gaily. It's ridiculous—not even knowing my own sister!

Yes! she said enthusiastically, and was suddenly afraid she would not like him.

Do you cook here? she asked—And then the moment she said it she heard with the sharp cringe of regret that it had come out in her mother's voice; she had said it just the way her mother spoke. I mean—all your meals . . . ? she stumbled.

Yes! Yes-s! said her sister loudly, against the splutter of the tap splurting water into a small pot. She planked the pot down on the little stove, taking a lid from another saucepan, much larger, with which to cover it, saying with a short snort of a laugh, Not one of those dinners of mother's at home, that are prayed over and anointed like a sacrifice being prepared for the gods—we eat. Food isn't all that important.

Of course not, she agreed, in contempt of the mother.

Her sister turned round, paused, looking at her, searching: And then we just go out for a really decent meal when we feel like it. —Naturally . . .

I always think of you when we have steak-and-kidney pie, she smiled.

My yes! exclaimed her sister. It was marvelous! The crust! . . . Some day when I've got an oven I'm going to learn how to make it. I'll eat a whole one myself.

They had tea on a tray between them on the divan. Her sister tore open a packet of biscuits. Now! she said.

It's funny to think of you domesticated, she smiled at her sister.

The mechanics of life . . . , said her sister, watching the tea flow into a cup.

Of course, yes, you have to get *through them* to other things, she said, urging her understanding.

Getting through them's the thing, said her sister.

". . . By the time I've got the house cleaned the way I want it, and put three meals on the table . . ." She heard her mother. A familiar phrase of music played on a different instrument.

When he qualifies, said her sister, sitting back with her tea, we're going away . . . to travel. Perhaps to Kenya for a bit. And of course, I'm still determined to go to Italy. We even started to learn Italian. She laughed.—It petered out, though. We want to go to Italy, and Switzerland. . . . But what we'll do with the baby, God knows. . . . At the thought she frowned, accusing the invisible; put the whole thing away in some part of her mind where she kept it.

Did you see the exhibition of modern Italian art last week? she asked eagerly, ready for the talk. What did you think of it?

Didn't even know there was one, said her sister. I don't know, I don't seem to get beyond the headlines of the paper, most of the time.

Oh, she said. There was an oil that reminded me of that picture of yours—she twisted her head to the Indian child and the lilies.

That's a gouache, said her sister, her eyes on the balcony.

She tilted her head. Was that a grumble from the pram . . . ? She looked questioningly.

I didn't hear anything, she said, subsiding back.

I *hope* not, said her sister.

I rather hope he *will* cry, she laughed, I want to see him.

Her sister looked at her very attentively, her eyes held very wide, the impressive, demanding way she had looked at her when they were children, and her sister was the big sister directing the game: Look here, she said, I'm afraid you'll have to see him next time, if you don't mind. I have to go out to give a child a lesson just now, and Alan has to rush back from a ward round to be here with the baby. It's bad enough he has to interrupt his work as it is; if he's got to be here, he's got to get some swotting done at least—and he can't do that if the baby's awake. I try to get him off to sleep and then I pray he'll stay asleep till I get back. So if you don't mind—her hands were trembling a little on the teacup.

Of course not! she protested. I'll see him next time. I didn't know . . . It doesn't matter at all.

No, said her sister, smiling now, friendly, careless, you'll come often.

Did that mean she must go now?

Are you going out soon? she said.

Yes, said her sister, I must get myself tidied up. . . . You can wander round behind me. Then as soon as he comes, I can rush off.

All at once she wanted to go; she must get away before He came. It was quite ridiculous how agitated she felt lest He should come whilst she was still there. She whimpered inwardly to go, like a child in a strange place. She followed her sister distractedly around, unable to think of anything else but her impulse to go. She thought she heard a step; she thought she heard the door, every minute.

Her sister changed her sandals for shoes, went into the bathroom to smooth her hair. The bathroom was steamy with wet napkins; standing there with her sister, she felt hot and hardly able to breathe. I must hang them out before I go . . . , said her sister, her mouth full of hairpins; her eyes were curiously distracted, as if all the time her attention was divided, pulled this way and that. And I should get the vegetables ready for tonight. . . . Her hands fumbled with haste, remembering.

Was that the clang of the lift gate? Her heart beat up inside her. . . . No. You know, I really think I should go now, she said, smiling, to her sister.

Well, all right, then, Baby, said her sister, turning with her old smile, her old slow, superior smile. Next time come in the evening, it'll be more interesting for you. Alan'll be here—that is, we'd better make it a week-end evening, when he hasn't got to work. . . . But if you wait just another few minutes he'll be here—she encouraged.

No, she said, I've got to go now; I've got to get something for mother, in town. So I'd better . . .

They stood smiling at one another for a moment.

Mother . . . , said her sister . . . God, always something to get for mother. . . . She shook her hair freely, with a little gesture of release; then with long, sure movements, pinned it up.

—Well, I'll leave you then, she said, dodging beneath napkins to the door. With the napkins and the vegetables and the lesson to go to, she didn't say.

And as she turned at the door she noticed something on the bathroom shelf that suddenly lifted her strong sense of depression for her sister; something that signaled out to her that all was not lost. It was quite an ordinary thing; a box of talcum powder. The special kind of talcum powder with a special light sweet perfume of honeysuckle that her sister had always used; that had always been snowed about the bathroom for mother to mop up and grumble over. You still use it! she cried with pleasure—The same old kind in the flowered box! I haven't smelled it since you left!

What? said her sister, not listening.

Your bath powder in those big messy boxes! she laughed.

Her sister's eyes wandered tolerantly to the shelf. Oh *that*! she said. She looked at it: It's just the empty box—Alan keeps his shaving things in it. Fourteen-and-six on bath powder! I didn't know what to spend money on next, in those days. . . . Good-by! she called out from the door.

Good-by, shouted out her sister from the bathroom. Don't forget—

No, I won't, she called back, Good-by!

The lift wasn't on that floor so she didn't wait for it but

ran down the stairs and went straight out of the building and down the street and past Minos' tearoom to the tram stop. In the tram she sat, slowly unclenching herself and thinking fool, fool, what is the matter with you? She was terribly, terribly pleased because she hadn't met Him. She was really quite foolishly pleased. When she thought how ridiculously pleased she was, she felt a strong sense of guilt toward her sister. The more pleased, the more strong the pang for her sister. As if her not wanting to meet Him made him not good enough for her sister. Oh her poor, poor sister . . .

Quite suddenly she rang, got off the tram and went into a chemist shop. Strained and trembling so that the assistant looked at her curiously, she bought a large box of the special bath powder. She caught the next tram back to Minos' tearoom and rushed along the street and swept into the building and into the lift. In the presence of the lift she stood stiffly, clutching the parcel. The lift seemed discreetly to ignore her nervous breathing. Out of the lift and along the passage to Number 11, and as she brought down the knocker, it came to her with a cold start—He might be there. Too late it came to her. . . . As it came, the door opened.

Look, said a dark young man—Come in, won't you—just a minute—and leaving her standing, disappeared on to the balcony. She could hear a baby crying; holding its breath and then releasing all the force of its lungs in a long diminishing bellow. In a moment the young man came back. It's all right, he said, with a wave of his hand. He was holding a pair of glasses; his brown eyes were faintly red-rimmed. He looked at her enquiringly.

Good afternoon, she said foolishly.

Good afternoon! he said kindly. Did you want to see me? Or is it for my wife . . . ?

I—I just wanted to leave something—she said—something . . .

He saw the parcel. You want to leave something for my wife, he said helpfully.

Yes—she said—thank you, if you will—and gave him the parcel.

She knows about it, does she? he said. I mean she knows who it's from?

She nodded her head violently. Thanks—then, she said, stepping back.

Righto, said the young man. He was in a hurry. He gave her a brief explanatory smile and closed the door.

She hadn't said it. She hadn't told Him. I'm her sister, I'm her sister. She kept saying it over and over silently inside herself, the way she should have said it to Him . . . And in between she told herself, Fool, fool . . .

ELIZABETH JOLLEY was born in 1923 in the industrial Midlands of England and brought up in a household "half English and three quarters Viennese" and later in a Quaker boarding school. She describes her childhood and early education in the very poignant memoir "A Child Went Forth," the final selection in her latest collection of stories. In 1959 she moved to Western Australia with her husband and their three children. Since then she has worked as a nurse, a door-to-door salesperson (failed), a realtor (failed), and a flying domestic. She is currently cultivating a small orchard and is a tutor at the Fremantle Arts Centre and at the Western Australian Institute of Technology. One of Australia's leading contemporary writers of fiction, she has published three collections of short fiction, *Five Acre Virgin, The Travelling Entertainer,* and *Woman in a Lampshade,* and six novels, *Palomino, Mr. Scobie's Riddle, The Newspaper of Claremont Street, Miss Peabody's Inheritance, Foxybaby,* and *The Sugar Mother*. She has been highly praised in her own country and in the United States and England for her humor, pathos, and radiant originality. In the words of the reviewer in the *Washington Post Book World,* "the hallmark of her writing is irony, even fantasy, so beautifully controlled that the reader is ricocheted between the pitiable, the hilarious, and the profound in a quite dizzying way. Elizabeth Jolley joins the handful of Australian writers of whom it may be said that their books are able to alter the direction of one's inner life." The writer Robert Coover has observed that she "seems to have a lot of fun when she writes. She lets herself go, laughs a lot, cries a lot, dances every chance she gets . . . gets playfully inventive, then spooks herself with the uncanny, celebrates outrageous behavior and eccentric voices, mocks Paradise, eats an apricot, throws a goofy wedding party, commits a murder or two, hovers about hospitals and old folks' homes because she loves the people there, loves people everywhere, to tell the truth, though there's no hope for them, sadly enough, crippled as they are with guilt and poverty and stupidity and mortality, no hope and not all that much dignity either, but they *are* a treat to listen to." Angela Carter remarks neatly: "Her fiction shines and shines and shines, like a good deed in a naughty world."

Dingle the Fool

by

Elizabeth Jolley

"No one can tell what is taken up from the earth by a lemon tree." Deirdre's mother said it didn't matter where the roots of the tree were, the lemons would take what they needed.

"What if they are in the drain?" Deirdre asked.

"What if they are," her mother replied. "Can you see drains on any of them lemons? Can you?"

Deirdre stood under the tree. It was fragrant with flower and fruit at the same time, she liked to be sent to fetch a lemon.

When Deirdre took off the cushion covers to wash them before Christmas, roses and peacocks from her childhood spilled out, frayed, from the worn covers underneath reminding her of the tranquillity in that expectation of happiness as she and her sister Joanna, years ago, sat on the back verandah twisting tinsel and making red and green paper chains.

Now Deirdre remembered her mother most around Christmas. At that time of the year the sisters stole mulberries from the tree in the garden next to theirs and their mother, approving, made pies.

"Take Dingle to the river while I'm baking," Mother called them, so they took their brother out with them. They called him Dingle, it was his own name for himself. "Dingle!" Mother called him softly, smiling at his gentle face. "Always look after Dingle," she told the girls. "Remember people will say he is a fool and will try to take away anything he's got. And he will give them everything."

He loved the river. He shouted on the shore and waded into the brackish water waving his thin arms and following the other children, he wanted to play with them. The other children swam and Dingle followed them, unable to swim. He waded deeper and the gentle waves slapped his knees and then caressed his waist and he held up his arms as he went deeper and then the water was round his neck and over his face and his round mouth gasped as the water closed and parted rippling over his shorn head.

"Dingle!" Deirdre shouted and ran into the river and grabbed him. She had to carry him home, her dress, sopping wet, embarrassed because she was big and her breasts showed up round and heavy under the wet clinging material.

After the death of their mother the three of them lived on in the old weatherboard and iron house. And, for the time being, after they were married the sisters continued to share the house. Dingle had the two attics in the gable of the house, a cramped spaciousness all his own. They could hear him moving about up there for he was a heavy man and they often could hear his thick voice mumbling to and fro as he talked to the secret people in his secret world in the roof.

The sisters spent their time looking after their babies which had been born within a few weeks of each other. Every day when they had bathed the babies and were washed themselves and dressed in freshly ironed clothes—they were always washing and ironing—they went out from the dark ring of trees around the house into the sunshine and, crossing the road, they walked, brushing against hibiscus and lantana with their hips and thighs up the hill to the shops. Joanna had a little pram but Deirdre carried her son, his dark fuzzy head nestled against the creamy skin of her plump neck. The sisters gazed at the things in the shops and they met people they had known all their lives and they showed off their lovely babies.

Everything was peaceful in the household except when the conversation turned as it often did, to land prices and whether they should sell the house and the land. All round them the old houses had been sold and blocks of flats and two-storey townhouses with car parks instead of gardens were being built. Joanna longed for a modern house on one of the estates, she had magazines full of glossy pictures and often sat looking at them.

"Look at this all electric kitchen Deirdre," she would say. "Just look at all these cupboards fitting in to the walls!" But Deirdre wanted to stay in the house; as well as being fond of the place where she had always lived, she had a deep wish to go on with a continuation of something started years ago.

Sometimes she pictured to herself the people who first built the house and she thought of them planting trees and making paths and as she trod the paths she rested on these thoughts. And of course the house with the big tangled garden was the only world Dingle could have. And the house did belong to all three of them.

"The value of the land's gone up again!" Joanna said at breakfast. "Why don't we sell now and build? Oh do let's!" Deirdre moved the milk jug and pushed aside the bread. "I want to stay here," she said.

How would Dingle be on a new housing estate where no one knew or understood him? She imagined him pressing the old tennis ball, which he thought contained happiness, on complete strangers. It was all right at the bowling club where he went sometimes to trim the lawns, they knew him there and would take the dirty old ball and thank him and then give it back. Sometimes Dingle lost his ball and Deirdre and Joanna, scolding, had to leave their house work and help him search for it in the fallen leaves beneath the overgrown pomegranates, and, in the fragrance of the long white bells of the datura, they parted stems and flowers searching for happiness for Dingle.

"What about Dingle?" Deirdre asked, her voice trembled. She was afraid Freddy, Joanna's neat quick husband, would insist they have a place of their own. Freddy and Joanna had more money, and in any case, Joanna was entitled to her share of the house and land.

"There would be enough from the sale," Spiro, Deirdre's husband said, he spoke slowly with a good-natured heaviness. They had to wait while he slowly chewed another mouthful. "With his share, your fool of a brother could be very comfortable in some nice home." Spiro did not mean to be unkind, Deirdre knew this, but she could not bear what he said. She felt they were all against her. More than anything she wanted to stay in the house and she wanted for Dingle to be able to stay but she and Spiro had no money with which to pay Joanna and Freddy their share. So Deirdre said nothing, she got up from the table and started to go about her work and the talk was dropped for the time being.

Their lives went on as usual and the two sisters were kept busy with their babies.

One day Spiro came home in the middle of the afternoon.

He walked straight through the kitchen and into the room which was their bedroom and he shut the door. The two sisters looked at each other and Deirdre put her baby down in his basket and went after her husband.

"He's not feeling well," she said, coming back after a few minutes.

"Why? What's wrong?"

"Nothing much, but I think he's had words with the Boss. He's going to have a sleep."

Joanna shrugged.

"There's nothing like a good sleep," she said. "We'd better keep quiet."

"Yes a good sleep," Deirdre agreed. Mostly the two sisters agreed. Their mother too had been an agreeable woman hard working and thrifty, she had wisdom too.

"Sisters give things to each other," she said when Joanna wanted to sell her sequined party bag to Deirdre.

"Give the bag," Mother said. "Sisters don't buy and sell with each other. They share things. Sisters share."

And she had left them the house to share, Dingle included of course. But when Deirdre thought about it, how could she expect Joanna to give her her share of the house.

Deirdre's husband continued to stay at home. He seemed to step on plastic toys and lemons and he was bored with all the washing and ironing and the disorder brought about by the two babies. For though the sisters kept the shabby house clean, there was a certain untidiness which was comfortable but Deirdre, as Spiro stumbled crossly, began to see squalor everywhere. The verandahs needed sweeping every day, paint peeled and fell in flakes and there were rusty marks. For some reason wheat was growing wild in the rough laundry tubs and they had to wash clothes in the bathroom. Joanna worked hard too but she complained and kept on wishing for a modern house. She reproached Deirdre.

Deirdre felt annoyed with Spiro for being at home all the time when she wanted to clean the house. As well as being annoyed she was worried that he might not have any work, and then how would they manage. She avoided her husband.

And then the two sisters began to quarrel over small things.

"If you don't want to make your bed," Deirdre shouted

at Joanna, "at least close your door so the whole world needn't see what a pig sty your room is!"

"Who cares! Bossy Boots!" Joanna tossed her head, and their voices rose as they flung sharp words at each other. They moved saucepans noisily and scraped chairs and there was no harmony in their movements when they prepared the dinner.

Joanna began to do things for Deirdre's husband. She made tea for him in the middle of the long hot afternoon, she sat talking to him, her pretty head turned to one side as she gazed attentively while he replied in his slow speech. Deirdre saw that she sat there with her blouse still unfastened after feeding her baby. And it seemed to Deirdre that Spiro was watching Joanna and looking with admiration at her small white breasts which were delicately veined and firm with the fullness of milk.

Deirdre went out shopping alone.

"I'm leaving Robbie," she called out to her husband. "Watch him when he wakes will you."

She had several things to buy from the supermarket. It would have been wiser to ask Spiro to go with her. She took upon herself the burden of the shopping and in her present unhappiness she thought she wouldn't buy a Christmas tree.

The two sisters had taken some time to find husbands. Deirdre, nine years older than Joanna and with her straight cut dull hair and sullen expression, had taken somewhat longer. Spiro had come just in time into Deirdre's life for the two sisters to be married on the same day.

Deirdre wished she could be alone with Spiro and persuade him to go back to his work before Christmas even if only for half a day to make everything all right for after the holiday. But she knew he was a quiet man and proud, and besides, he was enjoying a kind of new discovery in her sister. Nothing like this had ever happened in the household before. Joanna's husband was deeply in love with his wife. He was always kind to Dingle and roguishly polite to Deirdre, admired her baby and her cooking, but really he only cared about Joanna and their own baby daughter. Joanna took all his love, basking, cherished, she seemed to glow more every day with the love she had from Freddy and now here she was trying to attract her own sister's husband, as if she wanted both men to pay every attention to her.

Unhappiness and jealousy rose in Deirdre and she trembled as she put packages in her bag and she thought again she wouldn't bother to have a tree this year. But on the way home she passed a watered heap of Christmas trees sheltered from the sun by a canvas screen.

"How much are the trees?" she asked the boy.

"Dollar fifty," he looked at her hopefully.

"I'll take one," she said, sparing the money from her purse, wondering whether she should.

"Which'll you want?" he reached into the heap and shook out one tree after another till she chose one with a long enough stem. Slowly she dragged it home.

They put the tree in the hall, it seemed the best place for it though they had to squeeze by. It seemed to Deirdre when the tree was decorated with the little glittering treasures saved from their childhood that there was an atmosphere of peace in the tranquil depths of the branches, and, as she brushed against it, a fragrance which seemed to come from previous years soothed her. The corners of the rooms and the woodwork seemed as if smoothed and rounded, the brown linoleum and the furniture, polished for so many years, were mellow and pleasant to look upon because of this fragrance from the tree. She felt better and wondered why she had been so unhappy.

"I think I can smell rain," she said smiling as she stepped on to the back verandah. "It must be raining somewhere."

"Yes, there's weather coming up," Freddy agreed and they paused to breathe in the sharp fragrance of rain-laden air. Later they played table tennis; the old boards creaked and the house seemed to shake but the contented babies and Dingle the Fool slept in spite of the noise.

For some reason Joanna had put on a stupid frock. It had no shoulder straps or sleeves and she kept missing the ball and spoiling the game because she kept tugging up her frock saying it was slipping down. And every time she missed the ball she dissolved into laughter and the two men laughed too and Deirdre noticed how her husband only looked at Joanna. Usually he was impatient if any one played badly but tonight he was laughing with Joanna.

"Oh I'm too tired to play any more," Deirdre put her bat down suddenly.

"I'll take on the two men then," Joanna cried. Deirdre

wanted to shake Joanna, but she tried to control her anger, her voice trembled.

"No Joanna," she said as quietly as she could. "I want to talk about the house."

"Oh Deirdre!" Joanna said. "The agent was here again this morning while you were out, they're going to start building on the block next door quite soon. He promised us a really good price if only we'll sell!"

"Be quiet Joanna!" Deirdre said. "I want to say how a house has such history, such meaning. Places, especially houses are important, they matter," somehow she couldn't go on, she kept thinking about Dingle.

They had to wait, Spiro was speaking, his broken English more noticeable.

"It's what a person really wants that has meaning," Spiro said slowly. "For you Deirdre, this house. For Joanna it is a new house," he shrugged his shoulders lazily. "It is the wanting that matters," he said. Deirdre's sallow face flushed a dull red.

"I know you and Freddy want a modern home of your own," she said. "We'll sell this place," she forced out the words; she had been preparing them all evening.

"Oh Deirdre!" Joanna hugged her sister. "Shall we really!" she was shrill with excitement. "Mr. Rusk, you know, the agent, said our two acres could be a gold mine if only we'd sell now!"

"Oh be quiet Joanna!" Deirdre said, she couldn't stop thinking of Dingle. "There's no more to be said," she snapped. "Sisters share," her mother had said. Deirdre couldn't share Spiro with Joanna.

"We'll sell," she made herself say it again.

"Oh Deirdre!" Joanna hitched up her frock. "Oh we'll go on Sunday and look at the show houses on the Greenlawns Estate. Do let's!"

"Perhaps," Deirdre said shortly. Joanna got out her magazines. "Look at these kitchens." She was showing her treasures to the two men long after Deirdre had gone, sleepless, to bed.

The two sisters sat together in the humid heat.

"I hope it'll be cooler on Christmas Day," Joanna said. They fed their babies and drank cold water greedily taking turns to drink from a big white jug while their babies sucked.

Spiro was out. Deirdre felt comforted. He was driving a load of baled lucerne hay, it was only work for one day, but it was something. She leaned over to smile at Joanna's baby.

The air was heavy with the over ripe mulberries fermenting and dropping, replenishing the earth. Soon the tree next door would be gone, the house had already been pulled down.

Dingle the Fool came in, his hands and face stained red.

"Oh let us get some mulberries too!" Joanna laid her baby in her basket and Deirdre put her little son down quickly.

Soon the three of them were lost and laughing in the great tree, it was as big as a house itself.

They pushed in between the gnarled branches and twigs climbing higher and deeper into the tree, pausing one after the other on the big forked branch where Dingle often slept on hot nights. All round them were green leaves, green light and green shade. For every ripe berry Deirdre picked three more fell through her fingers splashing her face and shoulders, they dropped, lost to the earth. She felt restored in the tree, as if she could go on through the thick leaves and emerge suddenly in some magic place beyond. And, as she picked and ate the berries one after the other, she wondered why she had let things worry her so much.

"Here's a beauty!" Joanna cried. "If only I could get it," she leaned, cracking twigs. "Oh I missed it! Here's another. Oh Beauty!" The tree was full of their voices.

"Here's another!" Deirdre heard Joanna just above her and then Dingle slithered laughing beside her smearing her white bare legs with the red juice. From above Joanna showered them both with berries and soon they were having a mulberry fight as they did when they were children together. Dingle could lose what little wits he had for joy.

Breathless and laughing they stood at last on the ground stained all over with the stolen fruit.

"Anyone for a swim?" Spiro was back, he had the truck till the next day. His face widened with his good natured smile as he saw them.

"Oh I can't," Deirdre said. And he remembered the mysterious things about the women after their childbirths and he was about to go off on his own.

"Wait for me! I'll come!" Joanna cried. "Watch Angela for me, Deirdre, we'll not be long. Wait Spiro! I'm coming!"

In the kitchen Deirdre stuck cloves into an onion and an orange. Slowly and heavily she began preparations for the Christmas cooking tomorrow. Reluctantly she greased a pudding basin. Sadness began again to envelop her. Joanna had scrambled up so quickly beside Spiro in the cabin of the truck. Deirdre tried to think of the mulberry fight instead.

Dingle came in, he had washed himself and flattened his colourless hair with water. He picked things up from the table and put them down, he examined the orange and the onion, he pulled out a clove and chewed it noisily.

"Oh Dingle don't!" Impatiently Deirdre snatched them from him.

So then he began striking matches, one match after another. He watched the brief little flame with pleasure.

"Oh Dingle don't keep on wasting matches. Stop it!" Deirdre spoke sharply and then she tried to explain to him about the house being sold but he didn't seem to understand.

"You'll sleep in the Doctor's nice bed," she told him and tears came into her eyes as she spoke. Dingle came over to the table.

"Here," he said to Deirdre. "You have this," he held out the old tennis ball to his sister.

"No no Dingle," Deirdre was impatient. "Try and listen, we are selling the house—No! I don't want your old ball!"

"Go on!" Dingle interrupted. "You have it, there's happiness inside." He bounced the ball and gave it to her. She took it, her hand covered in flour.

"Thank you," and she tried to give it back to him.

"No, you have it, keep it," he insisted, his voice was thick and indistinct but Deirdre always knew what he said. She refused to keep the ball. Flour fell on the floor.

Dingle drew a chair up to the table close to where she was working, he took her vegetable knife and began to cut the ball in half.

"No Dingle you Fool. Don't!" Deirdre cried out and she tried to take the knife, but Dingle had strength and he held on to the knife and began working it right into the ball.

"Dingle, you don't understand!"

"I understand," he muttered, "I understand, half each, you have half."

He cut the ball and stared at the two empty halves of it. He looked at Deirdre and he looked at the two halves and, perplexed, he shook his head. He sat shaking his head and, as he realized the emptiness of the ball, his face crumpled and he cried, sobbing like a child except that he had white hair and a man's voice.

Deirdre had not seen him cry for years, she saw his mouth all square as he cried and it reminded her of Joanna's mouth when she cried and she could hardly bear to be reminded like this.

"Don't cry Dingle. Please don't cry," she spoke softly trying to comfort him. But it seemed there was nothing she could do.

In the night Joanna was thirsty and she got up to go for water. The hall was full of smoke.

"There's a fire!" she called, terrified in the smoke-filled darkness. "The Christmas tree's burning! Deirdre! Quick! The house is on fire. Freddy! Spiro!"

The whole house seemed full of smoke and they couldn't tell which part was burning the most. They saved their babies and most of their clothes.

"Where is Dingle?" Deirdre hardly had breath to call out. Her eyes were blind with pain from the smoke.

Spiro tried to rush up to the attic but the heat and the burning timber falling forced him back out into the garden.

There was nothing any one could do to save Dingle and nothing to do to save the house. They stood in the ring of trees. The Norfolk pines, the cape lilacs, the jacarandas and the kurrajong and the great mulberry tree in the next garden were all lit up in the hot light of the flames. The noise of the fire seemed to make a storm in the trees. They stood, helpless little people, beside the big fire, their bare feet seeking out the coolness of fallen hibiscus flowers which had curled up slowly in their damp sad ragged dying on the grass.

There was nothing they could do to save Dingle. "He will have suffocated from the smoke before the fire could reach him," Spiro spoke slowly, he tried to comfort them. Deirdre saw his hands bursting with the burns he had received and she saw how he was hardly able to bear the pain of them and she persuaded him to go with a neighbour to have them bandaged. They all allowed themselves to be looked after, quietly, as if they couldn't understand what had happened.

And later, Deirdre, wandering in the half light of dawn while the others slept on the vinyl cushions in the lounge of the bowling club, went back to the smouldering soaked remains of the house. She half hoped her brother would be dead but how could she hope for him to be burned to death. In her unhappiness she felt the burden of his life. His life was too much for her but the pain of wishing him burned in the fire was even worse. She felt she must search in the remains of the house and was afraid of what she might find. It would be easier if he had slept on and on in the smoke as Spiro said he had.

She thought she saw him in the forked branch of the mulberry tree. She paused, shivering and hoped it was only his old washed-out shirt that was there, left behind after the mulberry fight. Dingle sometimes forgot his clothes and Deirdre often went about last thing at night gathering up his shoes and things.

She stood now and tried to see what was in the fork of the tree. She began, with hope and with fear to climb into the quiet branches, the cool damp leaves brushed her face and her arms and legs.

It was not just his shirt up there. Gently she woke him, empty match boxes fell as she shook him.

"Dingle, wake up!" He was asleep in the tree after all. Dingle the Fool stretched himself along the friendly branch. His face was as if stained with red tears. Deirdre hugged her brother clumsily, crying and kissing him. How could she have wished him dead?

"Another mulberry fight?" Dingle asked in his strange thick voice and he made a noise and Deirdre was unable to tell whether he was laughing or crying.

They thought they might as well choose a motel right on the sea front. They had only a short time to wait for their new houses to be ready. So every day they lay on the sand, even the babies sunbathed in their baskets.

"The quick brown fox," Deirdre thought to herself as she

watched Freddy put up the beach umbrella to make the best shade for Spiro who was still unwell after his burns.

Lazily they spent the days talking about nothing in particular and swimming and eating. They bought fried chicken and hamburgers to eat while watching television in the motel. There wasn't any point in wondering about the fire so they didn't talk about it.

Deirdre couldn't help thinking about Dingle. When she took him to the hospital he sat so awkwardly on the edge of the white bed. She wondered whatever could he do there. She went to the window.

"You can watch the road from here," she said. Dingle got up and came to the window and obediently looked out at the corner of the road. There were no grass plots, Deirdre wished there was some grass and she could have asked if he could trim the edges. It was something he always enjoyed. She thought about him watching the empty street. What would he be doing now, Deirdre wondered. She watched Joanna and Freddy laughing in the sea. Joanna looked so happy, the green water curled handsomely round her lovely body. Deirdre envied Joanna, she envied her sister's innocence.

"The land's more valuable than ever with the house and sheds gone and on top there's all the insurance!" Deirdre seemed to hear Joanna's excited voice ringing, she envied her happiness but more enviable was her innocence. Joanna had never wished her brother burned to death.

"Where's that Fool of a brother of yours?" Spiro often asked this question when he came in, sometimes he had something for Dingle, a cake or some apples, sometimes he wanted Dingle to help him move a heavy box or shift the load in his truck with him.

Everyone called Dingle a fool, their mother said he would give everything he had and people would take it.

Deirdre had taken everything from him, she had made him give everything. Freddy and Joanna seemed hilarious in the water and Spiro, sitting with both hands bandaged, was laughing and laughing and all the time he watched Joanna.

"It's the wanting that really matters," Spiro had said it himself.

Deirdre longed to talk about Dingle. She wanted to ask

Spiro if he thought Dingle would be all right. She wanted comfort and reassurance but did not ask.

Near them on the beach was a bread carter woman eating her lunch. She looked so carefree and sunburned and strong, Deirdre almost spoke to her.

"I have a brother—" but she didn't. In a little while the bread carter would eat her last mouthful and be gone, taking with her her strength and vitality.

Deirdre lay back, she heard the sea come up the sand with a little sigh. Tears welled up under her closed eyelids. Joanna and Freddy came running from the water and Deirdre turned her face away so that they shouldn't see the tears spill over her cheeks.

ALICE MUNRO was born in Wingham, Ontario, in 1931. She was educated in Canada and London. She began publishing short stories in the early fifties. After the publication of her first collection, *Dance of the Happy Shades* (1968), she received the first of the three Governor General's Awards for Literature she was to be awarded over the next twenty years. *The Progress of Love* (1986)—the title story follows here—is her fifth collection of short stories in twenty years. Though her novel *Lives of Girls and Women* was highly praised, Alice Munro now writes short stories exclusively, many of which appear originally in *The New Yorker*. "I no longer feel attracted to the well-made novel," she has written. "I want to write the story that will zero in and give you intense but not connected moments of experience. I guess that's the way I see life. People remake themselves bit by bit and do things they don't understand. The novel has to have a coherence which I don't see anymore in the lives around me." In "The Progress of Love," Munro reveals her belief in the utter subjectivity of truth by having the two sisters remember the incident of their mother's attempted suicide from completely opposite points of view. Munro demonstrates her view that memory distorts reality; what the sisters know about their mother is basically what each has imagined on her own. All of Munro's stories are set in the southwestern Ontario region where she has spent most of her life. Readers now call the farmlands and little towns east of Lake Huron "Alice Munro Country." Joyce Carol Oates has said that on the emotional landscape of Munro's fiction "life is heartbreak, but it is also uncharted moments of kindness and reconciliation."

The Progress of Love

by
Alice Munro

I got a call at work, and it was my father. This was not long after I was divorced and started in the real-estate office. Both of my boys were in school. It was a hot enough day in September.

My father was so polite, even in the family. He took time to ask me how I was. Country manners. Even if somebody phones up to tell you your house is burning down, they ask first how you are.

"I'm fine," I said. "How are you?"

"Not so good, I guess," said my father, in his old way—apologetic but self-respecting. "I think your mother's gone."

I knew that "gone" meant "dead." I knew that. But for a second or so I saw my mother in her black straw hat setting off down the lane. The word "gone" seemed full of nothing but a deep relief and even an excitement—the excitement you feel when a door closes and your house sinks back to normal and you let yourself loose into all the free space around you. That was in my father's voice, too—behind the apology, a queer sound like a gulped breath. But my mother hadn't been a burden—she hadn't been sick a day—and far from feeling relieved at her death, my father took it hard. He never got used to living alone, he said. He went into the Netterfield County Home quite willingly.

He told me how he found my mother on the couch in the kitchen when he came in at noon. She had picked a few tomatoes, and was setting them on the windowsill to ripen; then she must have felt weak, and lain down. Now, telling this, his voice went wobbly—meandering, as you would expect—in his amazement. I saw in my mind the couch, the old quilt that protected it, right under the phone.

"So I thought I better call you," my father said, and he waited for me to say what he should do now.

* * *

My mother prayed on her knees at midday, at night, and first thing in the morning. Every day opened up to her to have God's will done in it. Every night she totted up what she'd done and said and thought, to see how it squared with Him. That kind of life is dreary, people think, but they're missing the point. For one thing, such a life can never be boring. And nothing can happen to you that you can't make use of. Even if you're racked by troubles, and sick and poor and ugly, you've got your soul to carry through life like a treasure on a platter. Going upstairs to pray after the noon meal, my mother would be full of energy and expectation, seriously smiling.

She was saved at a camp meeting when she was fourteen. That was the same summer that her own mother—my grandmother—died. For a few years, my mother went to meetings with a lot of other people who'd been saved, some who'd been saved over and over again, enthusiastic old sinners. She could tell stories about what went on at those meetings, the singing and hollering and wildness. She told about one old man getting up and shouting, "Come down, O Lord, come down among us now! Come down through the roof and I'll pay for the shingles!"

She was back to being just an Anglican, a serious one, by the time she got married. She was twenty-five then, and my father was thirty-eight. A tall good-looking couple, good dancers, good card-players, sociable. But serious people—that's how I would try to describe them. Serious the way hardly anybody is anymore. My father was not religious in the way my mother was. He was an Anglican, an Orangeman, a Conservative, because that's what he had been brought up to be. He was the son who got left on the farm with his parents and took care of them till they died. He met my mother, he waited for her, they married; he thought himself lucky then to have a family to work for. (I have two brothers, and I had a baby sister who died.) I have a feeling that my father never slept with any woman before my mother, and never with her until he married her. And he had to wait, because my mother wouldn't get married until she had paid back to her own father every cent he had spent on her since her mother died. She had kept track of everything—board, books, clothes—so that she could pay it back. When she married, she had no nest egg, as teachers usually did, no hope chest, sheets, or dishes. My father used to say, with a somber, joking face, that he had hoped to get a woman with money in the bank. "But you take the money in the bank, you have to take the face that goes with it," he said, "and sometimes that's no bargain."

The house we lived in had big, high rooms, with dark-green blinds on the windows. When the blinds were pulled down against the sun, I used to like to move my head and catch the light flashing through the holes and cracks. Another thing I liked looking at was chimney stains, old or fresh, which I could turn into animals, people's faces, even distant cities. I told my own two boys about that, and their father, Dan Casey, said, "See, your mom's folks were so poor, they couldn't afford TV, so they got these stains on the ceiling—your mom had to watch the stains on the ceiling!" He always liked to kid me about thinking poor was anything great.

When my father was very old, I figured out that he didn't mind people doing new sorts of things—for instance, my getting divorced—as much as he minded them having new sorts of reasons for doing them.

Thank God he never had to know about the commune.

"The Lord never intended," he used to say. Sitting around with the other old men in the Home, in the long, dim porch behind the spirea bushes, he talked about how the Lord never intended for people to tear around the country on motorbikes and snowmobiles. And how the Lord never intended for nurses' uniforms to be pants. The nurses didn't mind at all. They called him "Handsome," and told me he was a real old sweetheart, a real old religious gentleman. They marvelled at his thick black hair, which he kept until he died. They washed and combed it beautifully, wet-waved it with their fingers.

Sometimes, with all their care, he was a little unhappy. He wanted to go home. He worried about the cows, the fences, about who was getting up to light the fire. A few flashes of meanness—very few. Once, he gave me a sneaky, unfriendly look when I went in; he said, "I'm surprised you haven't worn all the skin off your knees by now."

I laughed. I said, "What doing? Scrubbing floors?"
"Praying!" he said, in a voice like spitting.
He didn't know who he was talking to.

I don't remember my mother's hair being anything but white. My mother went white in her twenties, and never saved any of her young hair, which had been brown. I used to try to get her to tell what color brown.

"Dark."

"Like Brent, or like Dolly?" Those were two workhorses we had, a team.

"I don't know. It wasn't horsehair."

"Was it like chocolate?"

"Something like."

"Weren't you sad when it went white?"

"No. I was glad."

"Why?"

"I was glad that I wouldn't have hair anymore that was the same color as my father's."

Hatred is always a sin, my mother told me. Remember that. One drop of hatred in your soul will spread and discolor everything like a drop of black ink in white milk. I was struck by that and meant to try it, but knew I shouldn't waste the milk.

All these things I remember. All the things I know, or have been told, about people I never even saw. I was named Euphemia, after my mother's mother. A terrible name, such as nobody has nowadays. At home they called me Phemie, but when I started to work, I called myself Fame. My husband, Dan Casey, called me Fame. Then in the bar of the Shamrock Hotel, years later, after my divorce, when I was going out, a man said to me, "Fame, I've been meaning to ask you, just what is it you are famous for?"

"I don't know," I told him. "I don't know, unless it's for wasting my time talking to jerks like you."

After that I thought of changing it altogether, to something like Joan, but unless I moved away from here, how could I do that?

In the summer of 1947, when I was twelve, I helped my mother paper the downstairs bedroom, the spare room. My mother's sister, Beryl, was coming to visit us. These two sisters hadn't seen each other for years. Very soon after their mother died, their father married again. He went to live in Minneapolis, then in Seattle, with his new wife and his younger daughter, Beryl. My mother wouldn't go with them. She stayed on in the town of Ramsay, where they had been living. She was boarded with a childless couple who had been neighbors. She and Beryl had met only once or twice since they were grown up. Beryl lived in California.

The paper had a design of cornflowers on a white ground. My mother had got it at a reduced price, because it was the end of a lot. This meant we had trouble matching the pattern, and behind the door we had to do some tricky fitting with scraps and strips. This was before the days of pre-pasted wallpaper. We had a trestle table set up in the front room, and we mixed the paste and swept it onto the back of the paper with wide brushes, watching for lumps. We worked with the windows up, screens fitted under them, the front door open, the screen door closed. The country we could see through the mesh of screens and the wavery old window glass was all hot and flowering—milkweed and wild carrot in the pastures, mustard rampaging in the clover, some fields creamy with the buckwheat people grew then. My mother sang. She sang a song she said her own mother used to sing when she and Beryl were little girls.

> *"I once had a sweetheart, but now I have none.*
> *He's gone and he's left me to weep and to moan.*
> *He's gone and he's left me, but contented I'll be,*
> *For I'll get another one, better than he!"*

I was excited because Beryl was coming, a visitor, all the way from California. Also, because I had gone to town in late June to write the Entrance Examinations, and was hoping to hear soon that I had passed with honors. Everybody who had finished Grade 8 in the country schools had to go into town to write those examinations. I loved that—the rustling sheets of foolscap, the important silence, the big stone high-school building, all the old initials carved in the desks, darkened with varnish. The first burst of summer outside, the green and yellow light, the townlike chestnut trees, and honeysuckle. And all it was was this same town, where I have lived now more than half my life. I wondered at it. And at myself, drawing maps with ease and solving problems, knowing quantities of answers. I thought I was so clever. But I wasn't clever enough to understand the simplest thing. I didn't even understand that examinations made no difference in my case. I wouldn't be going to high school. How could I? That was before there were school buses; you had to board in town. My parents didn't have the money. They operated on very little cash, as many farmers did then. The payments from the cheese factory were about all that came in regularly. And they didn't think of my life going in that direction, the high-school direction. They thought that I would stay at home and help my mother, maybe hire out to help women in the neighborhood who were sick or having a baby. Until such time as I got married. That was what they were waiting to tell me when I got the results of the examinations.

You would think my mother might have a different idea, since she had been a schoolteacher herself. But she said God didn't care. God isn't interested in what kind of job or what kind of education anybody has, she told me. He doesn't care two hoots about that, and it's what He cares about that matters.

This was the first time I understood how God could become a real opponent, not just some kind of nuisance or large decoration.

My mother's name as a child was Marietta. That continued to be her name, of course, but until Beryl came I never heard her called by it. My father always said Mother. I had a childish notion—I knew it was childish—that Mother suited my mother better than it did other mothers. Mother, not Mama. When I was away from her, I could not think what my mother's face was like, and this frightened me. Sitting in school, just over a hill from home, I would try to picture my mother's face. Sometimes I thought that if I couldn't do it, that might mean my mother was dead. But I had a sense of her all the time, and would be reminded of her by the most unlikely things—an upright piano, or a tall white loaf of bread. That's ridiculous, but true.

Marietta, in my mind, was separate, not swallowed up in my mother's grownup body. Marietta was still running around loose up in her town of Ramsay, on the Ottawa River. In that town, the streets were full of horses and puddles, and darkened by men who came in from the bush on weekends. Loggers. There were eleven hotels on the main street, where the loggers stayed, and drank.

The house Marietta lived in was halfway up a steep street climbing from the river. It was a double house, with two bay windows in front, and a wooden trellis that separated the two front porches. In the other half of the house lived the Sutcliffes, the people Marietta was to board with after her mother died and her father left town. Mr. Sutcliffe was an Englishman, a telegraph operator. His wife was German. She always made coffee instead of tea. She made strudel. The dough for the strudel hung down over the edges of the table like a fine cloth. It sometimes looked to Marietta like a skin.

Mrs. Sutcliffe was the one who talked Marietta's mother out of hanging herself.

Marietta was home from school that day, because it was Saturday. She woke up late and heard the silence in the house. She was always scared of that—a silent house—and as soon as she opened the door after school she would call, "Mama! Mama!" Often her mother wouldn't answer. But she would be there. Marietta would hear with relief the rattle of the stove grate or the steady slap of the iron.

That morning, she didn't hear anything. She came downstairs, and got herself a slice of bread and butter and molasses, folded over. She opened the cellar door and called. She went into the front room and peered out the window, through the bridal fern. She saw her little sister, Beryl, and some other neighborhood children rolling down the bit of grassy terrace to the sidewalk, picking themselves up and scrambling to the top and rolling down again.

"Mama?" called Marietta. She walked through the house to the back yard. It was late spring, the day was cloudy and mild. In the sprouting vegetable gardens, the earth was damp, and the leaves on the trees seemed suddenly full-sized, letting down drops of water left over from the rain of the night before.

"Mama?" calls Marietta under the trees, under the clothesline.

At the end of the yard is a small barn, where they keep

firewood, and some tools and old furniture. A chair, a straight-backed wooden chair, can be seen through the open doorway. On the chair, Marietta sees her mother's feet, her mother's black laced shoes. Then the long, printed cotton summer work dress, the apron, the rolled-up sleeves. Her mother's shiny-looking white arms, and neck, and face.

Her mother stood on the chair and didn't answer. She didn't look at Marietta, but smiled and tapped her foot, as if to say, "Here I am, then. What are you going to do about it?" Something looked wrong about her, beyond the fact that she was standing on a chair and smiling in this queer, tight way. Standing on an old chair with back rungs missing, which she had pulled out to the middle of the barn floor, where it teetered on the bumpy earth. There was a shadow on her neck.

The shadow was a rope, a noose on the end of a rope that hung down from a beam overhead.

"Mama?" says Marietta, in a fainter voice. "Mama. Come down, please." Her voice is faint because she fears that any yell or cry might jolt her mother into movement, cause her to step off the chair and throw her weight on the rope. But even if Marietta wanted to yell she couldn't. Nothing but this pitiful thread of a voice is left to her—just as in a dream when a beast or a machine is bearing down on you.

"Go and get your father."

That was what her mother told her to do, and Marietta obeyed. With terror in her legs, she ran. In her nightgown, in the middle of a Saturday morning, she ran. She ran past Beryl and the other children, still tumbling down the slope. She ran along the sidewalk, which was at that time a board-walk, then on the unpaved street, full of last night's puddles. The street crossed the railway tracks. At the foot of the hill, it intersected the main street of the town. Between the main street and the river were some warehouses and the buildings of small manufacturers. That was where Marietta's father had his carriage works. Wagons, buggies, sleds were made there. In fact, Marietta's father had invented a new sort of sled to carry logs in the bush. It had been patented. He was just getting started in Ramsay. (Later on, in the States, he made money. A man fond of hotel bars, barber-shops, harness races, women, but not afraid of work—give him credit.)

Marietta did not find him at work that day. The office was empty. She ran out into the yard where the men were working. She stumbled in the fresh sawdust. The men laughed and shook their heads at her. No. Not here. Not a-here right now. No. Why don't you try upstreet? Wait. Wait a minute. Hadn't you better get some clothes on first?

They didn't mean any harm. They didn't have the sense to see that something must be wrong. But Marietta never could stand men laughing. There were always places she hated to go past, let alone into, and that was the reason. Men laughing. Because of that, she hated barbershops, hated their smell. (When she started going to dances later on with my father, she asked him not to put any dressing on his hair, because the smell reminded her.) A bunch of men standing out on the street, outside a hotel, seemed to Marietta like a clot of poison. You tried not to hear what they were saying, but you could be sure it was vile. If they didn't say anything, they laughed and vileness spread out from them—poison—just the same. It was only after Marietta was saved that she could walk right past them. Armed by God, she walked through their midst and nothing stuck to her, nothing scorched her; she was safe as Daniel.

Now she turned and ran, straight back the way she had come. Up the hill, running to get home. She thought she had made a mistake leaving her mother. Why did her mother tell her to go? Why did she want her father? Quite possibly so that she could greet him with the sight of her own warm body swinging on the end of a rope. Marietta should have stayed—she should have stayed and talked her mother out of it. She should have run to Mrs. Sutcliffe, or any neighbor, not wasted time this way. She hadn't thought who could help, who could even believe what she was talking about. She had the idea that all families except her own lived in peace, that threats and miseries didn't exist in other people's houses, and couldn't be explained there.

A train was coming into town. Marietta had to wait. Passengers looked out at her from its windows. She broke out wailing in the faces of those strangers. When the train passed, she continued up the hill—a spectacle, with her hair uncombed, her feet bare and muddy, in her nightgown, with a wild, wet face. By the time she ran into her own yard, in sight of the barn, she was howling. "Mama!" she was howling. "Mama!"

Nobody was there. The chair was standing just where it had been before. The rope was dangling over the back of it. Marietta was sure that her mother had gone ahead and done it. Her mother was already dead—she had been cut down and taken away.

But warm, fat hands settled down on her shoulders, and Mrs. Sutcliffe said, "Marietta. Stop the noise. Marietta. Child. Stop the crying. Come inside. She is well, Marietta. Come inside and you will see."

Mrs. Sutcliffe's foreign voice said, "Mari-et-cha," giving the name a rich, important sound. She was as kind as could be. When Marietta lived with the Sutcliffes later, she was treated as the daughter of the household, and it was a household just as peaceful and comfortable as she had imagined other households to be. But she never felt like a daughter there.

In Mrs. Sutcliffe's kitchen, Beryl sat on the floor eating a raisin cookie and playing with the black-and-white cat, whose name was Dickie. Marietta's mother sat at the table, with a cup of coffee in front of her.

"She was silly," Mrs. Sutcliffe said. Did she mean Marietta's mother or Marietta herself? She didn't have many English words to describe things.

Marietta's mother laughed, and Marietta blacked out. She fainted, after running all that way uphill, howling, in the warm, damp morning. Next thing she knew, she was taking black, sweet coffee from a spoon held by Mrs. Sutcliffe. Beryl picked Dickie up by the front legs and offered him as a cheering present. Marietta's mother was still sitting at the table.

Her heart was broken. That was what I always heard my mother say. That was the end of it. Those words lifted up the story and sealed it shut. I never asked, Who broke it? I never asked, What was the men's poison talk? What was the meaning of the word "vile"?

Marietta's mother laughed after not hanging herself. She sat at Mrs. Sutcliffe's kitchen table long ago and laughed. Her heart was broken.

I always had a feeling, with my mother's talk and stories,

of something swelling out behind. Like a cloud you couldn't see through, or get to the end of. There was a cloud, a poison, that had touched my mother's life. And when I grieved my mother, I became part of it. Then I would beat my head against my mother's stomach and breasts, against her tall, firm front, demanding to be forgiven. My mother would tell me to ask God. But it wasn't God, it was my mother I had to get straight with. It seemed as if she knew something about me that was worse, far worse, than ordinary lies and tricks and meanness; it was a really sickening shame. I beat against my mother's front to make her forget that.

My brothers weren't bothered by any of this. I don't think so. They seemed to me like cheerful savages, running around free, not having to learn much. And when I just had the two boys myself, no daughters, I felt as if something could stop now—the stories, and griefs, the old puzzles you can't resist or solve.

Aunt Beryl said not to call her Aunt. "I'm not used to being anybody's aunt, honey. I'm not even anybody's momma. I'm just me. Call me Beryl."

Beryl had started out as a stenographer, and now she had her own typing and bookkeeping business, which employed many girls. She had arrived with a man friend, whose name was Mr. Florence. Her letter had said that she would be getting a ride with a friend, but she hadn't said whether the friend would be staying or going on. She hadn't even said if it was a man or a woman.

Mr. Florence was staying. He was a tall, thin man with a long, tanned face, very light-colored eyes, and a way of twitching the corner of his mouth that might have been a smile.

He was the one who got to sleep in the room that my mother and I had papered, because he was the stranger, and a man. Beryl had to sleep with me. At first we thought that Mr. Florence was quite rude, because he wasn't used to our way of talking and we weren't used to his. The first morning, my father said to Mr. Florence, "Well, I hope you got some kind of a sleep on that old bed in there?" (The spare-room bed was heavenly, with a feather tick.) This was Mr. Florence's cue to say that he had never slept better.

Mr. Florence twitched. He said, "I slept on worse."

His favorite place to be was in his car. His car was a royal-blue Chrysler, from the first batch turned out after the war. Inside it, the upholstery and floor covering and roof and door padding were all pearl gray. Mr. Florence kept the names of those colors in mind and corrected you if you said just "blue" or "gray."

"Mouse skin is what it looks like to me," said Beryl rambunctiously. "I tell him it's just mouse skin!"

The car was parked at the side of the house, under the locust trees. Mr. Florence sat inside with the windows rolled up, smoking, in the rich new-car smell.

"I'm afraid we're not doing much to entertain your friend," my mother said.

"I wouldn't worry about him," said Beryl. She always spoke about Mr. Florence as if there was a joke about him that only she appreciated. I wondered long afterward if he had a bottle in the glove compartment and took a nip from time to time to keep his spirits up. He kept his hat on.

Beryl herself was being entertained enough for two. Instead of staying in the house and talking to my mother, as a lady visitor usually did, she demanded to be shown everything there was to see on a farm. She said that I was to take her around and explain things, and see that she didn't fall into any manure piles.

I didn't know what to show. I took Beryl to the icehouse, where chunks of ice the size of dresser drawers, or bigger, lay buried in sawdust. Every few days, my father would chop off a piece of ice and carry it to the kitchen, where it melted in a tin-lined box and cooled the milk and butter.

Beryl said she had never had any idea ice came in pieces that big. She seemed intent on finding things strange, or horrible, or funny.

"Where in the world do you get ice that big?"

I couldn't tell if that was a joke.

"Off of the lake," I said.

"Off of the lake! Do you have lakes up here that have ice on them all summer?"

I told her how my father cut the ice on the lake every winter and hauled it home, and buried it in sawdust, and that kept it from melting.

Beryl said, "That's amazing!"

"Well, it melts a little," I said. I was deeply disappointed in Beryl.

"That's really amazing."

Beryl went along when I went to get the cows. A scarecrow in white slacks (this was what my father called her afterward), with a white sun hat tied under her chin by a flaunting red ribbon. Her fingernails and toenails—she wore sandals—were painted to match the ribbon. She wore the small, dark sunglasses people wore at that time. (Not the people I knew—they didn't own sunglasses.) She had a big red mouth, a loud laugh, hair of an unnatural color and a high gloss, like cherry wood. She was so noisy and shiny, so glamorously got up, that it was hard to tell whether she was good-looking, or happy, or anything.

We didn't have any conversation along the cowpath, because Beryl kept her distance from the cows and was busy watching where she stepped. Once I had them all tied in their stalls, she came closer. She lit a cigarette. Nobody smoked in the barn. My father and other farmers chewed tobacco there instead. I didn't see how I could ask Beryl to chew tobacco.

"Can you get the milk out of them or does your father have to?" Beryl said. "Is it hard to do?"

I pulled some milk down through the cow's teat. One of the barn cats came over and waited. I shot a thin stream into its mouth. The cat and I were both showing off.

"Doesn't that hurt?" said Beryl. "Think if it was you."

I had never thought of a cow's teat as corresponding to any part of myself, and was shaken by this indecency. In fact, I could never grasp a warm, warty teat in such a firm and casual way again.

Beryl slept in a peach-colored rayon nightgown trimmed with écru lace. She had a robe to match. She was just as careful about the word "écru" as Mr. Florence was about his royal blue and pearl gray.

I managed to get undressed and put on my nightgown without any part of me being exposed at any time. An awkward business. I left my underpants on, and hoped that Beryl had done the same. The idea of sharing my bed with a grownup was a torment to me. But I did get to see the contents of what Beryl called her beauty kit. Hand-painted glass jars contained puffs of cotton wool, talcum powder, milky lotion, ice-blue astringent. Little pots of red and mauve rouge—rather greasy-looking. Blue and black pencils. Emery boards, a pumice stone, nail polish with an overpowering smell of bananas, face powder in a celluloid box shaped like a shell, with the name of a dessert—Apricot Delight.

I had heated some water on the coal-oil stove we used in summertime. Beryl scrubbed her face clean, and there was such a change that I almost expected to see makeup lying in strips in the washbowl, like the old wallpaper we had soaked and peeled. Beryl's skin was pale now, covered with fine cracks, rather like the shiny mud at the bottom of puddles drying up in early summer.

"Look what happened to my skin," she said. "Dieting. I weighed a hundred and sixty-nine pounds once, and I took it off too fast and my face fell in on me. Now I've got this cream, though. It's made from a secret formula and you can't even buy it commercially. Smell it. See, it doesn't smell all perfumy. It smells serious."

She was patting the cream on her face with puffs of cotton wool, patting away until there was nothing to be seen on the surface.

"It smells like lard," I said.

"Christ Almighty, I hope I haven't been paying that kind of money to rub lard on my face. Don't tell your mother I swear."

She poured clean water into the drinking glass and wet her comb, then combed her hair wet and twisted each strand round her finger, clamping the twisted strand to her head with two crossed pins. I would be doing the same myself, a couple of years later.

"Always do your hair wet, else it's no good doing it up at all," Beryl said. "And always roll it under even if you want it to flip up. See?"

When I was doing my hair up—as I did for years—I sometimes thought of this, and thought that of all the pieces of advice people had given me, this was the one I had followed most carefully.

We put the lamp out and got into bed, and Beryl said, "I never knew it could get so dark. I've never known a dark that was as dark as this." She was whispering. I was slow to understand that she was comparing country nights to city nights, and I wondered if the darkness in Netterfield County could really be greater than that in California.

"Honey?" whispered Beryl. "Are there any animals outside?"

"Cows," I said.

"Yes, but wild animals? Are there bears?"

"Yes," I said. My father had once found bear tracks and droppings in the bush, and the apples had all been torn off a wild apple tree. That was years ago, when he was a young man.

Beryl moaned and giggled. "Think if Mr. Florence had to go out in the night and he ran into a bear!"

Next day was Sunday. Beryl and Mr. Florence drove my brothers and me to Sunday school in the Chrysler. That was at ten o'clock in the morning. They came back at eleven to bring my parents to church.

"Hop in," Beryl said to me. "You, too," she said to the boys. "We're going for a drive."

Beryl was dressed up in a satiny ivory dress with red dots, and a red-lined frill over the hips, and red high-heeled shoes. Mr. Florence wore a pale-blue summer suit.

"Aren't you going to church?" I said. That was what people dressed up for, in my experience.

Beryl laughed. "Honey, this isn't Mr. Florence's kind of religion."

I was used to going straight from Sunday school into church, and sitting for another hour and a half. In summer, the open windows let in the cedary smell of the graveyard and the occasional, almost sacrilegious sound of a car swooshing by on the road. Today we spent this time driving through country I had never seen before. I had never seen it, though it was less than twenty miles from home. Our truck went to the cheese factory, to church, and to town on Saturday nights. The nearest thing to a drive was when it went to the dump. I had seen the near end of Bell's Lake, because that was where my father cut the ice in winter. You couldn't get close to it in summer; the shoreline was all choked up with bulrushes. I had thought that the other end of the lake would look pretty much the same, but when we drove there today, I saw cottages, docks and boats, dark water reflecting the trees. All this and I hadn't known about it. This, too, was Bell's Lake. I was glad to have seen it at last, but in some way not altogether glad of the surprise.

Finally, a white frame building appeared, with verandas and potted flowers, and some twinkling poplar trees in front. The Wildwood Inn. Today the same building is covered with stucco and done up with Tudor beams and called the Hideaway. The poplar trees have been cut down for a parking lot.

On the way back to the church to pick up my parents, Mr. Florence turned in to the farm next to ours, which belonged to the McAllisters. The McAllisters were Catholics. Our two families were neighborly but not close.

"Come on, boys, out you get," said Beryl to my brothers. "Not you," she said to me. "You stay put." She herded the little boys up to the porch, where some McAllisters were watching. They were in their raggedy home clothes, because their church, or Mass, or whatever it was, got out early. Mrs. McAllister came out and stood listening, rather dumbfounded, to Beryl's laughing talk.

Beryl came back to the car by herself. "There," she said. "They're going to play with the neighbor children."

Play with McAllisters? Besides being Catholics, all but the baby were girls.

"They've still got their good clothes on," I said.

"So what? Can't they have a good time with their good clothes on? I do!"

My parents were taken by surprise as well. Beryl got out and told my father he was to ride in the front seat, for the legroom. She got into the back, with my mother and me. Mr. Florence turned again onto the Bell's Lake road, and Beryl announced that we were all going to the Wildwood Inn for dinner.

"You're all dressed up, why not take advantage?" she said. "We dropped the boys off with your neighbors. I thought they might be too young to appreciate it. The neighbors were happy to have them." She said with a further emphasis that it was to be their treat. Hers and Mr. Florence's.

"Well, now," said my father. He probably didn't have five dollars in his pocket. "Well, now. I wonder do they let the farmers in?"

He made various jokes along this line. In the hotel dining

room, which was all in white—white tablecloths, white painted chairs—with sweating glass water pitchers and high, whirring fans, he picked up a table napkin the size of a diaper and spoke to me in a loud whisper, "Can you tell me what to do with this thing? Can I put it on my head to keep the draft off?"

Of course he had eaten in hotel dining rooms before. He knew about table napkins and pie forks. And my mother knew—she wasn't even a country woman, to begin with. Nevertheless this was a huge event. Not exactly a pleasure—as Beryl must have meant it to be—but a huge, unsettling event. Eating a meal in public, only a few miles from home, eating in a big room full of people you didn't know, the food served by a stranger, a snippy-looking girl who was probably a college student working at a summer job.

"I'd like the rooster," my father said. "How long has he been in the pot?" It was only good manners, as he knew it, to joke with people who waited on him.

"Beg your pardon?" the girl said.

"Roast chicken," said Beryl. "Is that okay for everybody?"

Mr. Florence was looking gloomy. Perhaps he didn't care for jokes when it was his money that was being spent. Perhaps he had counted on something better than ice water to fill up the glasses.

The waitress put down a dish of celery and olives, and my mother said, "Just a minute while I give thanks." She bowed her head and said quietly but audibly, "Lord, bless this food to our use, and us to Thy service, for Christ's sake. Amen." Refreshed, she sat up straight and passed the dish to me, saying, "Mind the olives. There's stones in them."

Beryl was smiling around at the room.

The waitress came back with a basket of rolls.

"Parker House!" Beryl leaned over and breathed in their smell. "Eat them while they're hot enough to melt the butter!"

Mr. Florence twitched, and peered into the butter dish. "Is that what this is—butter? I thought it was Shirley Temple's curls."

His face was hardly less gloomy than before, but it was a joke, and his making it seemed to convey to us something of the very thing that had just been publicly asked for—a blessing.

"When he says something funny," said Beryl—who often referred to Mr. Florence as "he" even when he was right there—"you notice how he always keeps a straight face? That reminds me of Mama. I mean of our mama, Marietta's and mine. Daddy, when he made a joke you could see it coming a mile away—he couldn't keep it off his face—but Mama was another story. She could look so sour. But she could joke on her deathbed. In fact, she did that very thing. Marietta, remember when she was in bed in the front room the spring before she died?"

"I remember she was in bed in that room," my mother said. "Yes."

"Well, Daddy came in and she was lying there in her clean nightgown, with the covers off, because the German lady from next door had just been helping her take a wash, and she was still there tidying up the bed. So Daddy wanted to be cheerful, and he said, 'Spring must be coming. I saw a crow today.' This must have been in March. And Mama said quick as a shot, 'Well, you better cover me up then, before it looks in that window and gets any ideas!' The German lady—Daddy said she just about dropped the basin. Because it was true, Mama was skin and bones; she was dying. But she could joke."

Mr. Florence said, "Might as well when there's no use to cry."

"But she could carry a joke too far, Mama could. One time, one time, she wanted to give Daddy a scare. He was supposed to be interested in some girl that kept coming around to the works. Well, he was a big good-looking man. So Mama said, 'Well, I'll just do away with myself, and you can get on with her and see how you like it when I come back and haunt you.' He told her not to be so stupid, and he went off downtown. And Mama went out to the barn and climbed on a chair and put a rope around her neck. Didn't she, Marietta? Marietta went looking for her and she found her like that!"

My mother bent her head and put her hands in her lap, almost as if she was getting ready to say another grace.

"Daddy told me all about it, but I can remember anyway. I remember Marietta tearing off down the hill in her nightie, and I guess the German lady saw her go, and she came out and was looking for Mama, and somehow we all ended up in the barn—me, too, and some kids I was playing with—and there was Mama up on a chair preparing to give Daddy the fright of his life. She'd sent Marietta after him. And the German lady starts wailing, 'Oh, Missus, come down Missus, think of your little *kindren'—'kindren'* is the German for 'children'—'think of your *kindren*,' and so on. Until it was me standing there—I was just a little squirt, but I was the one noticed that rope. My eyes followed that rope up and up and I saw it was just hanging over the beam, just flung there—it wasn't tied at all! Marietta hadn't noticed that, the German lady hadn't noticed it. But I just spoke up and said, 'Mama, how are you going to manage to hang yourself without that rope tied around the beam?' "

Mr. Florence said, "That'd be a tough one."

"I spoiled her game. The German lady made coffee and we went over there and had a few treats, and, Marietta, you couldn't find Daddy after all, could you? You could hear Marietta howling, coming up the hill, a block away."

"Natural for her to be upset," my father said.

"Sure it was. Mama went too far."

"She meant it," my mother said. "She meant it more than you give her credit for."

"She meant to get a rise out of Daddy. That was their whole life together. He always said she was a hard woman to live with, but she had a lot of character. I believe he missed that, with Gladys."

"I wouldn't know," my mother said, in that particularly steady voice with which she always spoke of her father. "What he did say or didn't say."

"People are dead now," said my father. "It isn't up to us to judge."

"I know," said Beryl. "I know Marietta's always had a different view."

My mother looked at Mr. Florence and smiled quite easily and radiantly. "I'm sure you don't know what to make of all these family matters."

The one time that I visited Beryl, when Beryl was an old woman, all knobby and twisted up with arthritis, Beryl said, "Marietta got all Daddy's looks. And she never did a thing with herself. Remember her wearing that old navy-blue crêpe dress when we went to the hotel that time? Of course, I know it was probably all she had, but did it have to be all she had? You know, I was scared of her somehow. I couldn't stay in a room alone with her. But she had outstanding looks." Trying to remember an occasion when I had noticed my mother's looks, I thought of the time in the hotel, my mother's pale-olive skin against the heavy white, coiled hair, her open, handsome face smiling at Mr. Florence—as if he was the one to be forgiven.

I didn't have a problem right away with Beryl's story. For one thing, I was hungry and greedy, and a lot of my attention went to the roast chicken and gravy and mashed potatoes laid on the plate with an ice-cream scoop and the bright diced vegetables out of a can, which I thought much superior to those fresh from the garden. For dessert, I had a butterscotch sundae, an agonizing choice over chocolate. The others had plain vanilla ice cream.

Why shouldn't Beryl's version of the same event be different from my mother's? Beryl was strange in every way—everything about her was slanted, seen from a new angle. It was my mother's version that held, for a time. It absorbed Beryl's story, closed over it. But Beryl's story didn't vanish; it stayed sealed off for years, but it wasn't gone. It was like the knowledge of that hotel and dining room. I knew about it now, though I didn't think of it as a place to go back to. And indeed, without Beryl's or Mr. Florence's money, I couldn't. But I knew it was there.

The next time I was in the Wildwood Inn, in fact, was after I was married. The Lions Club had a banquet and dance there. The man I had married, Dan Casey, was a Lion. You could get a drink there by that time. Dan Casey wouldn't have gone anywhere you couldn't. Then the place was remodelled into the Hideaway, and now they have strippers every night but Sunday. On Thursday nights, they have a male stripper. I go there with people from the real-estate office to celebrate birthdays or other big events.

The farm was sold for five thousand dollars in 1965. A man from Toronto bought it, for a hobby farm or just an investment. After a couple of years, he rented it to a commune. They stayed there, different people drifting on and off, for a dozen years or so. They raised goats and sold the milk to the health-food store that had opened up in town. They painted a rainbow across the side of the barn that faced the road. They hung tie-dyed sheets over the windows, and let the long grass and flowering weeds reclaim the yard. My parents had finally got electricity in, but these people didn't use it. They preferred oil lamps and the wood stove, and taking their dirty clothes to town. People said they wouldn't know how to handle lamps or wood fires, and they would burn the place down. But they didn't. In fact, they didn't manage badly. They kept the house and barn in some sort of repair and they worked a big garden. They even dusted their potatoes against blight—though I heard that there was some sort of row about this and some of the stricter members left. The place actually looked a lot better than many of the farms round about that were still in the hands of the original families. The McAllister son had started a wrecking business on their place. My own brothers were long gone.

I knew I was not being reasonable, but I had the feeling that I'd rather see the farm suffer outright neglect—I'd sooner see it in the hands of hoodlums and scroungers—than see that rainbow on the barn, and some letters that looked Egyptian painted on the wall of the house. That seemed a mockery. I even disliked the sight of those people when they came to town—the men with their hair in ponytails, and with holes in their overalls that I believed were cut on purpose, and the women with long hair and no makeup and their meek, superior expressions. What do you know about life, I felt like asking them. What makes you think you can come here and mock my father and mother and their life and their poverty? But when I thought of the rainbow and those letters, I knew they weren't trying to mock or imitate my parents' life. They had displaced that life, hardly knowing it existed. They had set up in its place these beliefs and customs of their own, which I hoped would fail them.

That happened, more or less. The commune disintegrated. The goats disappeared. Some of the women moved to town, cut their hair, put on makeup, and got jobs as waitresses or cashiers to support their children. The Toronto man put the place up for sale, and after about a year it was sold for more than ten times what he had paid for it. A young couple from Ottawa bought it. They have painted the outside a pale gray with oyster trim, and have put in skylights and a handsome front door with carriage lamps on either side. Inside, they've changed it around so much that I've been told I'd never recognize it.

I did get in once, before this happened, during the year that the house was empty and for sale. The company I work for was handling it, and I had a key, though the house was being shown by another agent. I let myself in on a Sunday afternoon. I had a man with me, not a client but a friend—Bob Marks, whom I was seeing a lot at the time.

"This is that hippie place," Bob Marks said when I stopped the car. "I've been by here before."

He was a lawyer, a Catholic, separated from his wife. He thought he wanted to settle down and start up a practice here in town. But there already was one Catholic lawyer. Business was slow. A couple of times a week, Bob Marks would be fairly drunk before supper.

"It's more than that," I said. "It's where I was born. Where I grew up." We walked through the weeds, and I unlocked the door.

He said that he had thought, from the way I talked, that it would be farther out.

"It seemed farther then."

All the rooms were bare, and the floors swept clean. The woodwork was freshly painted—I was surprised to see no smudges on the glass. Some new panes, some old wavy ones. Some of the walls had been stripped of their paper and painted. A wall in the kitchen was painted a deep blue, with an enormous dove on it. On a wall in the front room, giant sunflowers appeared, and a butterfly of almost the same size.

Bob Marks whistled. "Somebody was an artist."

"If that's what you want to call it," I said, and turned back to the kitchen. The same wood stove was there. "My mother once burned up three thousand dollars," I said. "She burned three thousand dollars in that stove."

He whistled again, differently. "What do you mean? She threw in a check?"

"No, no. It was in bills. She did it deliberately. She went into town to the bank and she had them give it all to her, in a shoebox. She brought it home and put it in the stove. She put it in just a few bills at a time, so it wouldn't make too big a blaze. My father stood and watched her."

"What are you talking about?" said Bob Marks. "I thought you were so poor."

"We were. We were very poor."

"So how come she had three thousand dollars? That would be like thirty thousand today. Easily. More than thirty thousand today."

"It was her legacy," I said. "It was what she got from her father. Her father died in Seattle and left her three thousand dollars, and she burned it up because she hated him. She didn't want his money. She hated him."

"That's a lot of hate," Bob Marks said.

"That isn't the point. Her hating him, or whether he was bad enough for her to have a right to hate him. Not likely he was. That isn't the point."

"Money," he said. "Money's always the point."

"No. My father letting her do it is the point. To me it is. My father stood and watched and he never protested. If anybody had tried to stop her, he would have protected her. I consider that love."

"Some people would consider it lunacy."

I remember that that had been Beryl's opinion, exactly.

I went into the front room and stared at the butterfly, with its pink-and-orange wings. Then I went into the front bedroom and found two human figures painted on the wall. A man and a woman holding hands and facing straight ahead. They were naked, and larger than life size.

"It reminds me of that John Lennon and Yoko Ono picture," I said to Bob Marks, who had come in behind me. "That record cover, wasn't it?" I didn't want him to think that anything he had said in the kitchen had upset me.

Bob Marks said, "Different color hair."

That was true. Both figures had yellow hair painted in a solid mass, the way they do it in the comic strips. Horsetails of yellow hair curling over their shoulders and little pigs' tails of yellow hair decorating their not so private parts. Their skin was a flat beige pink and their eyes a staring blue, the same blue that was on the kitchen wall.

I noticed that they hadn't quite finished peeling the wallpaper away before making this painting. In the corner, there was some paper left that matched the paper on the other walls—a modernistic design of intersecting pink and gray and mauve bubbles. The man from Toronto must have put that on. The paper underneath hadn't been stripped off when this new paper went on. I could see an edge of it, the cornflowers on a white ground.

"I guess this was where they carried on their sexual shenanigans," Bob Marks said, in a tone familiar to me. That thickened, sad, uneasy, but determined tone. The not particularly friendly lust of middle-aged respectable men.

I didn't say anything. I worked away some of the bubble paper to see more of the cornflowers. Suddenly I hit a loose spot, and ripped away a big swatch of it. But the cornflower paper came, too, and a little shower of dried plaster.

"Why is it?" I said. "Just tell me, why is it that no man can mention a place like this without getting around to the subject of sex in about two seconds flat? Just say the words 'hippie' or 'commune' and all you guys can think about is screwing! As if there wasn't anything at all behind it but orgies and fancy combinations and non-stop screwing! I get so sick of that—it's all so stupid it just makes me sick!"

In the car, on the way home from the hotel, we sat as before—the men in the front seat, the women in the back. I was in the middle, Beryl and my mother on either side of me. Their heated bodies pressed against me, through cloth; their smells crowded out the smells of the cedar bush we passed through, and the pockets of bog, where Beryl exclaimed at the water lilies. Beryl smelled of all those things in pots and bottles. My mother smelled of flour and hard soap and the warm crêpe of her good dress and the kerosene she had used to take the spots off.

"A lovely meal," my mother said. "Thank you, Beryl. Thank you, Mr. Florence."

"I don't know who is going to be fit to do the milking," my father said. "Now that we've all ate in such style."

"Speaking of money," said Beryl—though nobody actually had been—"do you mind my asking what you did with yours? I put mine in real estate. Real estate in California—you can't lose. I was thinking you could get an electric stove, so you wouldn't have to bother with a fire in summer or fool with that coal-oil thing, either one."

All the other people in the car laughed, even Mr. Florence.

"That's a good idea, Beryl," said my father. "We could use it to set things on till we get the electricity."

"Oh, Lord," said Beryl. "How stupid can I get?"

"And we don't actually have the money, either," my mother said cheerfully, as if she was continuing the joke.

But Beryl spoke sharply. "You wrote me you got it. You got the same as me."

My father half turned in his seat. "What money are you talking about?" he said. "What's this money?"

"From Daddy's will," Beryl said. "That you got last year. Look, maybe I shouldn't have asked. If you had to pay something off, that's still a good use, isn't it? It doesn't matter. We're all family here. Practically."

"We didn't have to use it to pay anything off," my mother said. "I burned it."

Then she told how she went into town in the truck, one day almost a year ago, and got them to give her the money in a box she had brought along for the purpose. She took it home, and put it in the stove and burned it.

My father turned around and faced the road ahead.

I could feel Beryl twisting beside me while my mother talked. She was twisting, and moaning a little, as if she had a pain she couldn't suppress. At the end of the story, she let out a sound of astonishment and suffering, an angry groan.

"So you burned up money!" she said. "You burned up money in the stove."

My mother was still cheerful. "You sound as if I'd burned up one of my children."

"You burned their chances. You burned up everything the money could have got for them."

"The last thing my children need is money. None of us need his money."

"That's criminal," Beryl said harshly. She pitched her voice into the front seat: "Why did you let her?"

"He wasn't there," my mother said. "Nobody was there."

My father said, "It was her money, Beryl."

"Never mind," Beryl said. "That's criminal."

"Criminal is for when you call in the police," Mr. Florence said. Like other things he had said that day, this created a little island of surprise and a peculiar gratitude.

Gratitude not felt by all.

"Don't you pretend this isn't the craziest thing you ever heard of," Beryl shouted into the front seat. "Don't you pretend you don't think so! Because it is, and you do. You think just the same as me!"

My father did not stand in the kitchen watching my mother feed the money into the flames. It wouldn't appear so. He did not know about it—it seems fairly clear, if I remember everything, that he did not know about it until that Sunday afternoon in Mr. Florence's Chrysler, when my mother told them all together. Why, then, can I see the scene so clearly, just as I described it to Bob Marks (and to others—he was not the first)? I see my father standing by the table in the middle of the room—the table with the drawer in it for knives and forks, and the scrubbed oilcloth on top—and there is the box of money on the table. My mother is carefully dropping the bills into the fire. She holds the stove lid by the blackened lifter in one hand. And my father, standing by, seems not just to be permitting her to do this but to be protecting her. A solemn scene, but not crazy. People doing something that seems to them natural and necessary. At least, one of them is doing what seems natural and necessary, and the other believes that the important thing is for that person to be free, to go ahead. They understand that other people might not think so. They do not care.

How hard it is for me to believe that I made that up. It seems so much the truth it is the truth; it's what I believe about them. I haven't stopped believing it. But I have stopped telling that story. I never told it to anyone again after telling it to Bob Marks. I don't think so. I didn't stop just because it wasn't, strictly speaking, true. I stopped because I saw that I had to give up expecting people to see it the way I did. I had to give up expecting them to approve of any part of what was done. How could I even say that I approved of it myself? If I had been the sort of person who approved of that, who could do it, I wouldn't have done all I have done—run away from home to work in a restaurant in town when I was fifteen, gone to night school to learn typing and bookkeeping, got into the real-estate office, and finally become a licensed agent. I wouldn't be divorced. My father wouldn't have died in the county home. My hair would be white, as it has been naturally for years, instead of a color called Copper Sunrise. And not one of these things would I change, not really, if I could.

Bob Marks was a decent man—good-hearted, sometimes with imagination. After I had lashed out at him like that, he said, "You don't need to be so tough on us." In a moment, he said, "Was this your room when you were a little girl?" He thought that was why the mention of the sexual shenanigans had upset me.

And I thought it would be just as well to let him think that. I said yes, yes, it was my room when I was a little girl. It was just as well to make up right away. Moments of kindness and reconciliation are worth having, even if the parting has to come sooner or later. I wonder if those moments aren't more valued, and deliberately gone after, in the setups some people like myself have now, than they were in those old marriages, where love and grudges could be growing underground, so confused and stubborn, it must have seemed they had forever.

JOYCE CAROL OATES was born in Lockport, New York, in 1938, to Irish-Catholic working-class parents. Since graduating Phi Beta Kappa from Syracuse University and receiving an M.A. in English from the University of Wisconsin, she has had an academic career that includes teaching at the University of Detroit and at Princeton and a prolific publishing record: she is the author of more than fifty works which include the novels *Them* (1969), *Do with Me What You Will* (1973), *Unholy Loves* (1979), *Bellefleur* (1980), and *A Bloodsmoor Romance* (1982), as well as short-story collections such as *Upon the Sweeping Flood* (1966), *Marriages and Infidelities* (1972), and *Raven's Wing* (1986), from which the following story is taken. Some of her many short stories have been referred to as fictionalized documentaries of the grotesque violence of contemporary family life as well as of the nihilism of adolescent culture. Teenaged nihilism suffuses her widely anthologized story "Where Are You Going, Where Have You Been?" and the connection between such lovelessness and the physical waste of the contemporary landscape is, in her view, what literature is all about. "Great art," she has written, "is always cathartic; it is always moral. . . . The greatest works of literature deal with the human soul caught in the stampede of time, unable to gauge the profundity of what passes over it, like the characters of Yeats who live through terrifying events but who cannot understand them; in this way history passes over most of us. Society is caught in a convulsion, whether of growth or of death, and ordinary people are destroyed. They do not, however, understand that they are destroyed."

Double Solitaire

by

Joyce Carol Oates

They were sisters but they had never been friends, so when the telephone call came late one weekday evening Anita didn't recognize Miriam's voice at first. Miriam was calling to say she was scheduled to check into Detroit General the next day, she'd be operated on the following morning, yes it was serious but she didn't expect to die, nobody expected her to die, she just thought that Anita, being her sister, should be informed.

Anita wasn't certain she had heard correctly, Miriam's voice was so hoarse and muffled. She turned down the radio volume, her hand trembling, and asked Miriam what was wrong, what kind of operation was it?—and Miriam repeated that it was serious but not all that serious, an operation many women have, she just thought that Anita should be informed. Anita said at once, "I'd better drive over, I can get off work if it's an emergency," and Miriam said quickly, "It isn't an emergency, nobody expects me to die or anything. I don't want Wayne and the kids upset," and Anita heard herself say for some reason, "No don't *die*," and from that point on the conversation was out of control: she and Miriam interrupted each other, spoke at the same time, misheard, misunderstood, came close to seriously quarreling. Anita was almost in tears, saying, "Look, please, I want to come—I'm coming." Miriam's words were beginning to slur, she might have been drunk, she might have been drugged, saying it wasn't an emergency, she knew Anita had a life of her own.

But by the time they hung up ten minutes later it was all settled: Anita would drive to Detroit, Anita would stay with them for as long as Miriam and the children needed her. "Please, I *want* to come," she insisted.

Afterward, Anita noticed that she had broken out in

perspiration, her hands were shaking badly. She resented that she should be so frightened when she'd spent half the days of her childhood wishing her sister would die.

There were two vivid memories from childhood that had to do with Miriam, Anita and Miriam together. Alone together.

Anita, five or six years old, being pushed in a playground swing by Miriam, who must have been about ten at the time: Anita, for fun, leaping from the swing in mid-air, not guessing how the swing seat would fly back and strike Miriam on the side of the head. (Had she cried? Anita wondered. She must have cried, it must have hurt her badly. But Anita hadn't any memory of Miriam crying—only of herself crying, in Miriam's presence.)

Anita, older, in seventh grade maybe, sitting in the kitchen with Miriam, playing double solitaire. Slapping the cards down. Noisy, silly, on the verge of bursting into wild laughter, because it was so late at night and no one knew or cared what they did, their father was dead and their mother was in bed drunk, their mother spent much of her time in bed, drunk, and she hadn't more than a few years more to live, and both Anita and Miriam seemed to know this fact. All one winter they'd played double solitaire at the kitchen table, drinking diet cola and eating doughnuts covered in confectioner's sugar, not minding that both decks of cards were sticky, frayed. Miriam won most of the games and though Anita guessed she was cheating—Anita herself cheated occasionally—she never said anything.

Anita left home at six-thirty in the morning and arrived at Miriam's house on the west side of Detroit in the early afternoon, in time to help her get ready for the hospital. When they embraced Anita smelled cigarette smoke and sweet red wine on her sister's breath.

She shook hands self-consciously with Miriam's husband, whom she'd met only once before, at the wedding. He was Miriam's second husband and no one in the family knew him very well. His name was Wayne; he was tall, stiff, silent, frightened; he had long narrow suspicious eyes and Indian-sharp facial bones. He thanked Anita for coming without moving his mouth and without exactly looking at her, and Anita heard herself say again, in a faltering voice, that she wanted to come. She wanted to help out with the children. It was the least, she said, not knowing what she said, she could do.

Both Anita's parents were dead now, her only brother had moved to Oregon eight years before, Anita supposed she went for weeks without thinking of Miriam though sometimes, in a weak, melancholy mood, she found herself thinking about Miriam's children—*her* little niece Julie, *her* little nephew Bobby—and wondering if they remembered her. Both the children were from Miriam's first marriage, which had ended when Miriam was twenty-six and Anita was finishing her last semester of college. The marriage had been a mistake from the start so Anita was relieved when it ended but she'd felt sorry for Julie and Bobby—Miriam hadn't told her any details about the divorce except that, at one point, she'd had to get a court injunction against her husband, to keep him from breaking into the house. "Once a man lives in a house," Miriam would say, as if giving Anita warning, "he won't just walk out the door. Nothing's that easy."

The children didn't remember her, or pretended they didn't, which hurt Anita at first. She was their *aunt*, wasn't she? Their only *aunt*.

But she was careful with them, cheery, playful, soft-spoken, not pushing herself on them, knowing her time would come.

The operation, Miriam's doctor said cautiously, had turned out well. Barring post-op complications.

Such words as *tumor, uterus, hysterectomy* sounded faintly comical, obscene, uttered so frankly in fluorescent-lit rooms and corridors. *Fibroid. Nonmalignant. Complete removal of.* Anita noted how Wayne shrank from speaking them, how he hunched his heavy shoulders when he heard them, how his face went hard and neutral . . . as if he happened to be part of these exchanges only by accident. As if, in his sheepskin jacket, his hands in his pockets, he'd only wandered in to hear the tail end of a conversation between strangers.

Anita and Wayne had spent most of the long morning together in the hospital coffee shop, waiting for Miriam to come down from surgery.

Anita wasn't frightened, Anita knew that Miriam couldn't die, but still she heard her voice vague and faltering and falsely bright, talking about the children, talking about Miriam "back home," while Wayne glanced through newspapers left behind by other customers. Where was Wayne from, was he from Detroit? . . . how had he and Miriam met? . . . was she still married at the time? . . . what sort of business did he own? . . . could she have a cigarette? . . . and she saw how automatically he pushed the pack toward her, how natural it was that, just for an instant, she touched his wrist, closed her fingers lightly about his wrist.

Afterward, after the consultation with the doctor, they went out for a drink at a place Wayne knew, just off the expressway, and both Anita and Wayne got pleasantly high. Just beer. One or two tequilas.

"Okay," said Wayne, "this is a celebration."

His spiky black hair was disheveled, there were deep depressions at the corners of his mouth, Anita liked the way he leaned forward against the bar and then turned, on his elbow, lazily, to face her. They'd been doing this for years, maybe. Anita and Wayne. Coming to this place off the expressway where the late-morning light didn't quite penetrate the grimy front windows and where everyone seemed to know Wayne but didn't waste his time by coming over.

Wayne's smile was slow and mocking. "You don't know how to drink tequila?" he said.

"Sure I do," said Anita.

For three days Miriam was so heavily sedated she didn't feel pain but then, on the fourth morning, it hit. She screamed at Wayne and Anita to get out, to take the children away, she didn't want anybody to see her like this.

They'd scooped out her insides, she said, and now there was nothing left.

"Hey don't *say* that," Anita said, embarrassed.

The incision was ten inches long and she was filled with staples—Christ, with *staples*, would you believe it!—and she had to sleep sitting up because it hurt too much to stretch out flat. Right now she didn't care whether she lived or died so don't anybody hand her bullshit about being lucky. "You think I'm *lucky*," she said, staring at Anita, tears in the corners of her eyes, "you get in this fucking bed and take my place."

Wayne had to be away, most days, from ten in the morning until late at night. He had business problems, he said.

People he couldn't always trust. So he wasn't able to make it down to the hospital more than twice, or was it three times, in the eight days Miriam was there. During that time Anita did all the visiting. Driving back and forth on the expressway, learning all the exits, which lanes to avoid and why, sometimes with Julie and Bobby, sometimes alone. When she was alone she turned the car radio up as loud as she could stand it. Weird spaced-out Detroit sounds, a heavy black beat, country-and-western, an announcer with an Ozark drawl whose voice sometimes dropped to a whisper. Anita knew them all.

When she was alone in the car her face felt elastic, she might have been a little girl again, her mouth just naturally turning up in a secret smile.

Closets. What was there about other women's closets.

Anita seemed always to be looking in them, didn't she, barefoot and half dressed and her hair in her eyes, fingering the sleeve of a black velveteen dress, pushing hangers aside to stare, critically, at a silk blouse with a ruffled front, jersey dresses, wool skirts, sweaters on hangers that are ruining the shoulders, pairs of shoes on the floor, neat, or jumbled together, depending. She never put on another woman's clothes, never even held anything (this maroon blazer, for instance, more Anita's style than Miriam's) up against her, looking in a mirror, not because none of the clothes appealed but because they all did.

In this case the closet belonged to her sister, not a stranger, but it made no difference because all the clothes were new to her.

Strange, Anita thought, brushing her sticky hair out of her eyes, how you only remember certain things at certain times. There'd been a married lover in Cleveland when she was just out of college, and another married lover in Pittsburgh, and, for the past three years, intermittently, the man who supervised her office. (She worked at a social welfare agency in Buffalo but she'd had to go on part-time salary because the state legislature had cut their budget, yes she was fortunate she had a job at all, yes she knew enough to be grateful.) One December day when it was dark at five in the afternoon this man brought her to his house on Delaware Avenue because his wife and children were away and they could be alone together. One of the things he said was, It's good you're here in this bed because God knows it's a place where I think about you all the time. In a while Anita was crying, though she wasn't unhappy, and then she was coming out of the shower, out of the adjoining bathroom, a towel wrapped around her, barefoot, her skin glowing, her eyes wild and darting . . . because her lover loved her so much . . . because she was alone for the moment in a room in which strangers slept . . . there was a mahogany bureau whose contents she didn't know, there were photographs on the wall of people she didn't know, there was a closet that ran the entire length of the room with white louvered doors, filled with clothes she didn't know. . . .

She went to the closet and looked through it hurriedly, a woman's clothes, so many clothes, a faint scent of wool, mothballs, stale perfume, expensive-looking shoes arranged in neat pairs on the floor, she had to move quickly, quickly, for fear her lover would discover her, for fear (was this possible?) he'd forget and call her by another woman's name.

Of course that never happened. He never called her anything but Anita.

Tomorrow Miriam was being discharged from the hospital and tonight why not go out for a few drinks, Wayne had completed a deal he felt good about, why not celebrate, why not make a night of it, as long as the kids were asleep (though Anita wondered if Julie, nervous little Julie, ever slept at all now); and Anita said, But is it safe to leave them all alone?—they're so little; and Wayne, car keys rattling in his hand, said, You coming or not?

An hour earlier, in his and Miriam's bed, he'd gripped Anita's buttocks hard, squeezing hard, his fingers had come away bright with blood, Anita was in the second day of her period. The hottest time, Wayne kept saying, c'mon, c'mon, it's the hottest time isn't it? short of breath, excited as she hadn't seen him before, not caring (as other men did) if he was hurting her, wasn't Anita a pool into which he plunged, exhilarated and wild and vengeful, no you couldn't say he was vengeful, he was just . . . what he was doing right now; and Anita was what was being done to her. She strained and strained until her heart hammered but the dim little kernel of sensation he'd aroused deep inside her never got any stronger and when they were finished she started crying, really sobbing, though she knew Wayne would hate it, Wayne was the kind of man who got bored with tears—hadn't Miriam said, Don't cry in front of him?—but she couldn't help crying because this was something he and Miriam knew to do and maybe one day (was *this* possible?) he'd tell Miriam about it, to hurt her feelings or to make her laugh.

The *Detroit News* had been running a series on fires in the city, suspected arson, a high percentage of the fires suspected arson, maybe for insurance purposes, maybe to get welfare tenants out of buildings, though of course—many of the houses being old, in disrepair—there were blameless fires as well, "blameless" in the sense of being no one's specific criminal intention.

Anita heard sirens in the night, Anita's head was buzzing, her heartbeat pleasantly quickened. Wayne knew more ways of getting high than Anita had read about or had been told at the social welfare agency but he was sparing, it might be said he had a certain professional discretion. She nudged her forehead against his and said, What if the house burns down while we're out, and Wayne laughed and said, Sweetheart that isn't going to happen, and Anita said, But what *if*, and Wayne said, Y'know you worry more than Miriam, and Anita said, That's because I'm not Miriam, and Wayne said, irritated, Okay sweetheart but you aren't their mother, are you, and Anita, stung, but remembering to keep it all light, said, *You* aren't their father, are you.

She lost track of the drinks, the bars, the parking lots, the men who greeted Wayne, there were two or three who actually called her Miriam, she lost track of the sirens she couldn't always hear fully, to know if they were fire trucks or just police or ambulances. It was a weekday night in Detroit but it wouldn't shut down for a long, long time. What if, Anita said under her breath, what *if*, but Wayne wasn't in the mood to humor her, anyway she knew she was being silly, a house doesn't catch fire so quickly, most of the time it has to be someone's fault. Miriam was the kind of mother who'd slap her kids if she caught them playing with matches, no nonsense about *her*, she'd said the other day in the hospital when Anita came, alone, to visit and was holding her hand for a while, just holding her hand, she'd said, trying not to cry, If it wasn't for Julie and Bobby, shit, I don't *know*. . . .

Anita told her it was natural to feel bad, to feel depressed, following surgery. It wasn't just the pain, it was the anesthetic too.

Wayne was crazy about her, he said, and wanted her to move to Detroit, couldn't she get a job here, couldn't she get an apartment here, maybe even move in with them, she and Miriam got along all right, didn't they? Anita had been thinking she wouldn't be able to leave Detroit just yet but she didn't want to take any of this too seriously because, well, she didn't want to take any of this too seriously, there she was crying and gagging in Wayne's arms in a cinder parking lot, just past closing time, four in the morning; then, making a joke of it, he gripped her under the arms like a big rag doll and tried to walk her to the car.

That was the night they pulled up in front of the darkened house Anita couldn't recognize, and Wayne said, nudging her, "See?—no fire," said Anita, blinking and squinting, couldn't remember what the subject was.

In Wayne's car on the way home from the hospital Miriam had her first cigarette, and her first glass of red wine she had in the kitchen, and her hands were shaking when she hugged the kids, hugged and kissed them. Julie said, Don't you never *never* go away, Mommy, and Bobby was sniveling over some worry, Bobby wasn't getting enough attention, in a few minutes he'd turn back to Aunt Anita, whom he'd gotten to like a lot, Aunt Anita who loved him more than Mommy did, but right now things were confused, right now it was strange, it was frightening, that Mommy should be crying but trying to laugh at the same time.

Wayne kept saying, Jesus it's good to have you back, Wayne was almost shy around her, fearful of touching her and hurting her. She had a three-week recovery period to get through, she said, and that was just the beginning. But, God, she *was* glad to get home, she felt a thousand times better just being home. . . .

Anita helped her walk, Anita helped her in the bathroom, dressing and undressing, getting ready for bed. Anita made dinner and Anita cleaned up afterward and Anita gave the kids their baths and Anita put them to bed and a half hour later Anita put Julie to bed again—Julie you little sneak, *I* see you!—and Anita slept on the sofa except she couldn't sleep, she put on the television, the volume low, and watched old movies, the tail end of the Carson show, her feet curled up beneath her. Very early in the morning when she finally fell asleep she heard someone, it must have been Wayne, in the bathroom, she heard the toilet flush, she wasn't asleep and she wasn't awake but she was telling him, laughing, "Look please honey *no*, Miriam will hear us."

Anita helped Miriam lower herself into the bathtub and Anita shampooed Miriam's hair and Anita set up a board—a breadboard, actually—so that Miriam could play solitaire in bed, propped up in bed, and Anita quieted the kids when they ran wild and Anita let Bobby sleep curved in her arms on the sofa and Anita went shopping at Kroger's on Livernois and Anita did the laundry and Anita tried to vacuum the place but the vacuum cleaner bag was clogged, stuffed full with dirt, and she'd never changed one quite like this before, and Miriam said, "Let me do it for Christ's sake," but of course she didn't dare bend over; she had a long way to go before she'd be able to bend over like that.

Anita said, "I guess I'd better make plans to leave."

Anita said, shakily, not looking at Wayne, "I don't think I should stay much longer," not looking at Wayne to read his expression, to see why he didn't answer.

And, hearing her, Miriam said with a sharp little laugh, "Hey, what do you *mean*?—you just came."

Anita became wise, even fussy, in the ways of the household; she learned how to scold the kids, even to "discipline" them (Bobby required a slap, Julie a light pinch), but she couldn't gauge how much her sister knew about her, not just her and Wayne but Anita's own life back in Buffalo. She had a job there, an apartment, even a lover. She had a life, there. It was real, it was waiting for her to come back to resume it.

Still, when she thought suddenly of her apartment—a certain angle of vision when she dressed hurriedly in the morning, looking slantwise into the mirror on the back of a closet door which reflected a window with a patched venetian blind—she felt a stab in her belly hard and frightening as sex. It *was* real, her life back there, her life alone, waiting for her.

One evening she and Miriam, putting the kids to bed, couldn't help overhearing Wayne on the telephone in the next room.

Was he angry?—no, maybe pretending.

Laughing, too.

But angry, yes.

His voice rose in a curious way—rage, elation, resignation—but Anita couldn't make out anything except: *"I'll be right over, you!"*

After he went out Anita asked Miriam, whom she didn't want to annoy (Miriam had been feeling rotten since morning), "What is Wayne's business exactly?" and Miriam looked at her and said, "Hasn't he told you?" and Anita felt the corners of her eyes tighten but she went on; she said, "No, he doesn't tell me much, I mean we don't talk much," and then, because Jesus God that sounded bad, she said, "I just mean Wayne and I don't see that much of each other."

Miriam was staring at her but she *was* smiling, so it must have been all right. She said, "Ask him, sometime. Maybe he'll tell you."

Two and a half weeks, and then three weeks, and Miriam had good days and bad days, and Anita learned to know (or was it to sense?) when her sister was feeling pain though they might be in separate rooms.

And one morning when the sisters were sitting in the kitchen, drinking coffee, eating stale cherry-jelly doughnuts, and playing at their old game of double solitaire, Miriam said suddenly, as if it had something to do with a card she'd just turned up, "Hey. I hope you don't think it means a damn thing."

"What means a damn thing . . . ?" Anita asked.

"You and Wayne," Miriam said.

Anita felt that stab of fear in her bowels but she continued with the cards, a jack of clubs, an ace of spades, she didn't miss a single beat though Miriam was watching. But her voice was faint, her voice gave everything away, when she said, "*What?* Me and *Wayne* . . . ?"

The apartment was always drafty these days so they'd put

the oven on, had the oven door down, the kitchen was warming up nicely, the coziest room of all despite the loose-fitting windows. The place was quiet—no radio right now, no television, not even any noise from the street—Julie and Bobby were at school—Wayne was away on business, wouldn't be back until the end of the week, in Toledo Anita remembered him saying but Miriam said it was Chicago: his most important contacts were in Chicago.

Anita had never asked Wayne what his business was, maybe she'd been afraid he would tell her.

"This is the coziest room I know," Anita said, about to giggle, "and it's only a *kitchen.*"

Then she cleared her throat. She said in a low careful voice, "I don't know what the hell you're talking about, Miriam, but it isn't funny."

"It *is* funny, in its way," Miriam said.

"I mean, I just don't know what you're talking about."

"Just so you don't think it means anything," Miriam said. She was no longer watching Anita, she was watching her cards, a single sharp crease between her eyes. "I've been through this before with that bastard and he always comes back whining, he always says he loves *me.*"

Anita wanted to say, But that was before you were operated on, wasn't it!—but of course she kept quiet. After a while she said, "I really don't know what you're talking about, but I don't think it's funny."

"You're the one who said it was funny."

"I'm *not.*"

For a few minutes they continued with their games, their double game, slapping down the cards. Anita thought as she'd thought many times in childhood that a special card—the queen of diamonds, for instance, the handsome jack of clubs—had to come a long way to get to her. She heard herself say suddenly, about to cry, "Look—I don't think I can leave here yet."

"I've been through it before," Miriam said. "He always comes back."

"Yes," said Anita. "But I don't think I can leave yet. For Buffalo."

"The kids aren't his but he loves them and they love him, he's very close to them," Miriam said, not looking up, "he just isn't the kind of man to show it. What do *you* know—you don't know a damn thing."

Miriam was breathing hard, her cheeks flushed. Anita held a six of clubs she didn't know what to do with, it seemed to be a card she'd drawn out of nowhere. She had forgotten how to play the game.

If Miriam reached out suddenly to touch her hand, to grab hold of her wrist, she knew she'd embarrass them both by crying but she wanted very badly for Miriam to reach out and touch her and tell her she couldn't go back home yet, it wasn't time.

"What do you know about it," Miriam whispered. Her breath had become audible.

"I don't know anything," Anita protested. She was staring at the card in her hand, not recognizing it, waiting.

MERRILL JOAN GERBER was born in Brooklyn in 1938 and now lives in California where she teaches fiction writing at Pasadena City College. The mother of three daughters, she has been the Stanford University Creative Writing fellow, and the story that follows here, "I Don't Believe This," was included in the *1986 O. Henry Prize Stories.* Gerber has published three novels, several novels for young adults, and more than fifty stories in magazines such as *The New Yorker, The Atlantic,* and *Redbook* that have also been collected in two volumes: *Stop Here, My Friend* (1965) and *Honeymoon* (1985). The writer Cynthia Ozick wrote of that collection, from which the following story is taken, that the "stories cast you into rapt absorption and an almost scary loss of self. To read these stories is to belong to them absolutely; their great art is to make you oblivious of their art, and passionate about their people." She re-creates with an absolute sureness the empathic connection between two sisters, especially as in "I Don't Believe This," when one sister is in trouble and the other is taking care; the mutual pain of the protecting sister and the battered sister comes across in this story with an insistent pulse that is as strong as a real heartbeat.

"I Don't Believe This"

by

Merrill Joan Gerber

After it was all over, one final detail emerged, so bizarre that my sister laughed crazily, holding both hands over her ears as she read the long article in the newspaper. I had brought it across the street to show it to her; now that she was my neighbor, I came to see her and the boys several times a day. The article said that the crematorium to which her husband's body had been entrusted for cremation, had been burning six bodies at a time, and dumping most of the bone and ash into plastic garbage bags which went directly into their dumpsters. A disgruntled employee had tattled.

"Can you imagine?" Carol said, laughing. "Even that! Oh, his poor mother! His poor *father*!" She began to cry. "I don't believe this," she said. That was what she had said on the day of the cremation when she sat in my backyard in a beach chair at the far end of the garden, holding on to a washcloth. I think she was prepared to cry so hard that an ordinary handkerchief would not do. But she remained dry-eyed. When I came outside after a while, she said, "I think of his beautiful face burning, of his eyes burning." She looked up at the blank blue sky and said, "I just don't believe this. I try to think of what he was feeling when he gulped in that stinking gas. What could he have been thinking? I know he was blaming me."

She rattled the newspaper. "A dumpster! Oh, Bard would have loved that. Even at the end, he couldn't get it right. Nothing ever went right for him, did it? And all along I've been thinking that I won't ever be able to swim in the ocean again, because his ashes are floating in it! Can you believe it? How that woman at the mortuary promised they would play Pachelbel's *Canon* on the little boat, and the remains would be scattered with 'dignity and taste'? His *mother* even came all the way down with that jar of his father's ashes that she had saved for thirty years, so father and son could be mixed together for all eternity. Plastic garbage baggies! You know," she said, looking at me, "life is just a joke, a bad joke, isn't it?"

Bard had not believed me when I'd told him that my sister was in a shelter for battered women. Afraid of *him*? Running away from *him*? The world was full of dangers from which only *he* could protect her! He had accused me of hiding her in my house. "Would I be so foolish?" I had said. "She knows it's the first place you'd look."

"You better put me in touch with her," he had said menacingly. "You both know I can't handle this for long."

It had gone on for weeks. On the last day he called me three times, demanding to be put in touch with her. "Do you understand me?" he threatened me. "If she doesn't call here in ten minutes, I'm checking out. Do you believe me?"

"I believe you," I said. "But you know she can't call you. She can't be reached in the shelter. They don't want the women there to be manipulated by their men. They want them to have space and time to think."

"Manipulated?" He was incredulous. "I'm checking *out*, this is *IT*. Goodbye forever!"

He hung up. It wasn't true that Carol couldn't be reached. I had the number. I had not only been calling her, but I had also been playing tapes for her of his conversations over the phone during the past weeks. This one I hadn't taped. The tape recorder was in a different room.

"Should I call her and tell her?" I asked my husband.

"Why bother?" he said. He and the children were eating dinner; he was becoming annoyed by this continual disruption in our lives. "He calls every day and says he's killing himself and he never does. Why should this call be any different?"

Then the phone rang. It was my sister. She had a fever and bronchitis. I could barely recognize her voice.

"Could you bring me some cough syrup with codeine tomorrow?" she asked.

"Is your cough very bad?"

"No, it's not too bad, but maybe the codeine will help me get to sleep. I can't sleep here at all. I just can't sleep."

"He just called."

"Really," she said. "What a surprise!" But the sarcasm didn't hide her fear. "What this time?"

"He's going to kill himself in ten minutes unless you call him."

"So what else is new?" She made a funny sound. I was frightened of her these days. I couldn't read her thoughts. I didn't know if the sound was a cough or a sob.

"Do you want to call him?" I suggested. I was afraid to be responsible. "I know you're not supposed to."

"I don't know," she said. "I'm breaking all the rules anyway."

The rules were very strict. No contact with the batterer, no news of him, no worrying about him. Forget him. Only female relatives could call, and they were not to relay any news of him—not how sorry he was, not how desperate he was, not how he had promised to reform and never do it again, not how he was going to kill himself if she didn't come home. Once I had called the shelter for advice, saying that I thought he was serious this time, that he was going to do it. The counselor there—a deep-voiced woman named Katherine—said to me, very calmly, "It might just be the best thing; it might be a blessing in disguise."

My sister blew her nose. "I'll call him," she said. "I'll tell him I'm sick and to leave you alone and to leave me alone."

I hung up and sat down to try to eat my dinner. My children's faces were full of fear. I could not possibly reassure them about any of this. Then the phone rang again. It was my sister.

"Oh, God," she said. "I called him. I told him to stop bothering you, and he said, *'I have to ask you one thing, just one thing, I have to know this. Do you love me?'* " My sister gasped for breath. "I shouted *No*—what else could I say? That's how I *felt*, I'm so sick, this is such a nightmare, and then he just hung up. A minute later I tried to call him back to tell him that I didn't mean it, that I did love him, that I *do*, but he was gone." She began to cry. "He was gone."

"There's nothing you can do," I said. My teeth were chattering as I spoke. "He's done this before. He'll call me tomorrow morning full of remorse for worrying you."

"I can hardly breathe," she said. "I have a high fever and the boys are going mad cooped up here." She paused to blow her nose. "I don't believe any of this. I really don't."

* * *

Afterward she moved right across the street from me. At first she rented the little house, but then it was put up for sale and my mother and aunt found enough money to make a down payment so she could be near me and I could take care of her till she got her strength back. I could see her bedroom window from my bedroom window—we were that close. I often thought of her trying to sleep in that house, alone there with her sons and the new, big watchdog. She told me that the dog barked at every tiny sound and frightened her when there was nothing to be frightened of. She was sorry she had gotten him. I could hear his barking from my house, at strange hours, often in the middle of the night.

I remembered when she and I had shared a bedroom as children. We giggled every night in our beds and made our father furious. He would come in and threaten to smack us. How could he sleep, how could he go to work in the morning, if we were going to giggle all night? That made us laugh even harder. Each time he went back to his room, we would throw the quilts over our heads and laugh till we nearly suffocated. One night our father came to quiet us four times. I remember the angry hunch of his back as he walked, barefooted, back to his bedroom. When he returned the last time, stomping like a giant, he smacked us, each once, very hard, on our upper thighs. That made us quiet. We were stunned. When he was gone, Carol turned on the light and pulled down her pajama bottoms to show me the marks of his violence. I showed her mine. Each of us had our father's handprint, five red fingers, on the white skin of her thigh. She had crept into my bed, where we clung to each other till the burning, stinging shock subsided and we could sleep.

Carol's sons, living on our quiet adult street, complained to her that they missed the shelter. They rarely asked about their father and occasionally said they wished they could see their old friends and their old school. For a few weeks they had gone to a school near the shelter; all the children had to go to school. But one day Bard had called me and told me he was trying to find the children. He said he wanted to take them out to lunch. He knew they had to be at some school. He was going to go to every school in the district and look in every classroom, ask everyone he saw if any of the children there looked like his children. He would find them. "You can't keep them from me," he said, his voice breaking. "They belong to me. They love me."

Carol had taken them out of school at once. An art therapist at the shelter held a workshop with the children every day. He was a gentle, soft-spoken man named Ned, who had the children draw domestic scenes and was never once surprised at the knives, bloody wounds, or broken windows that they drew. He gave each of them a special present, a necklace with a silver running-shoe charm, which only children at the shelter were entitled to wear. It made them special, he said. It made them part of a club to which no one else could belong.

While the children played with crayons, their mothers were indoctrinated by women who had survived, who taught the arts of survival. The essential rule was: *Forget him, he's on his own, the only person you have to worry about is yourself.* A woman who was in the shelter at the same time Carol was had had her throat slashed. Her husband had cut her vocal cords. She could only speak in a grating whisper. Her husband had done it in the bathroom with her son watching. Yet each night she sneaked out and called her husband from a nearby shopping center. She was discovered and disciplined by the administration; they threatened to put her out of the shelter if she called him again. Each woman was allowed space at the shelter for a month while she got legal help and made new living arrangements. Hard cases were allowed to stay a little longer. She said she was sorry, but he was the sweetest man, and when he loved her up, it was the only time she knew heaven.

Carol felt humiliated. Once each week the women lined up and were given their food: three very small whole frozen chickens, a package of pork hot dogs, some plain-wrap cans of baked beans, eggs, milk, margarine, white bread. The children were happy with the food. Carol's sons played in the courtyard with the other children. Carol had difficulty relating to the other mothers. One had ten children. Two had black eyes. Several were pregnant. She began to have doubts that what Bard had done had been violent enough to cause her to run away. Did mental violence or violence done to furniture really count as battering? She wondered if she had been too hard on her husband. She wondered if she hadn't been wrong to come here. All he had done—he said so himself, on the taped conversations, dozens of times—was to break a lousy hundred-dollar table. He had broken it before; he had fixed it before. Why was this time different from any of the others? She had pushed all his buttons, that's all, and he had gotten mad, and he had pulled the table away from the wall and smashed off its legs and thrown the whole thing outside into the yard. Then he had put his head through the wall, using the top of his head as a battering ram. He had knocked open a hole to the other side. Then he had bitten his youngest son on the scalp. What was so terrible about that? It was just a momentary thing. He didn't mean anything by it. When his son had begun to cry in fear and pain, hadn't he picked the child up and told him it was nothing? If she would just come home he would never get angry again. They'd have their sweet life. They'd go to a picnic, a movie, the beach. They'd have it better than ever before. He had just started going to a new church that was helping him to become a kinder and more sensitive man. He was a better person than he had ever been; he now knew the true meaning of love. Wouldn't she come back?

One day Bard called me and said, "Hey, the cops are here. You didn't send them, did you?"

"*Me?*" I said. I turned on the tape recorder. "What did you do?"

"Nothing. I busted up some public property. Can you come down and bail me out?"

"How can I?" I said. "My children. . . ."

"How can you *not*?"

I hung up and called Carol at the shelter. I told her, "I think he's being arrested."

"Pick me up," she said, "and take me to the house. I have to get some things. I'm sure they'll let me out of the shelter if they know he's in jail. I'll check to make sure he's really there. I have to get us some clean clothes, and some toys for the boys. I want to get my picture albums. He threatened to burn them."

"You want to go to the house?"

"Why not? At least we know he's not going to be there.

At least we know we won't find him hanging from a beam in the living room."

We stopped at a drugstore a few blocks away and called the house. No one was there. We called the jail. They said their records showed that he had been booked but they didn't know for sure whether he'd been bailed out. "Is there any way he can bail out this fast?" Carol asked.

"Only if he uses his own credit card," the man answered.

"I *have* his credit card," Carol said to me after she hung up. "We're so much in debt that I had to take it away from him. Let's just hurry. I hate this! I hate sneaking into my own house this way."

I drove to the house and we held hands going up the walk. "I feel his presence is here, that he's right here seeing me do this," she said, in the dusty, eerie silence of the living room. "Why do I give him so much power? It's as if he knows whatever I'm thinking, whatever I'm doing. When he was trying to find the children, I thought he had eyes like God, and he would go directly to the school where they were and kidnap them. I had to warn them, 'If you see your father anywhere, run and hide. Don't let him get near you!' Can you imagine telling your children that about their father? Oh, God, let's hurry."

She ran from room to room, pulling open drawers, stuffing clothes into paper bags. I stood in the doorway of their bedroom, my heart pounding as I looked at their bed with its tossed covers, at the phone he used to call me. Books were everywhere on the bed—books about how to love better, how to live better, books on the occult, on meditation, books on self-hypnosis for peace of mind. Carol picked up an open book and looked at some words underlined in red. *"You can always create your own experience of life in a beautiful and enjoyable way if you keep your love turned on within you—regardless of what other people say or do,"* she read aloud. She tossed it down in disgust. "He's paying good money for these," she said. She kept blowing her nose.

"Are you crying?"

"No!" she said. "I'm allergic to all this dust."

I walked to the front door, checked the street for his car, and went into the kitchen.

"Look at this," I called to her. On the counter was a row

of packages, gift-wrapped. A card was slipped under one of them. Carol opened it and read it aloud: "I have been a brute and I don't deserve you. But I can't live without you and the boys. Don't take that away from me. Try to forgive me." She picked up one of the boxes and then set it down. "I don't believe this," she said. "God, where are the children's picture albums! I can't *find* them." She went running down the hall. In the bathroom, I saw the boys' fish bowl, with their two goldfish swimming in it. The water was clear. Beside the bowl was a piece of notebook paper. Written on it in his hand were the words, *Don't give up, hang on, you have the spirit within you to prevail.*

Two days later he came to my house, bailed out of jail with money his mother had wired. He banged on my front door. He had discovered that Carol had been to the house. "Did *you* take her there?" he demanded. "*You* wouldn't do that to me, would you?" He stood on the doorstep, gaunt, hands shaking.

"Was she at the house?" I asked. "I haven't been in touch with her lately."

"Please," he said, his words slurred, his hands out for help. "Look at this." He showed me his arms; the veins in his forearms were black-and-blue. "When I saw that Carol had been home, I took the money my mother sent me for food and bought three packets of heroin. I wanted to OD. But it was lousy stuff, it didn't kill me. It's not so easy to die, even if you want to. I'm a tough bird. But please, can't you treat me like regular old me; can't you ask me to come in and have dinner with you? I'm not a monster. Can't anyone, *anyone,* be nice to me?"

My children were hiding at the far end of the hall, listening. "Wait here," I said. I went and got him a whole ham I had. I handed it to him where he stood on the doorstep and stepped back with distaste. Ask him in? Let my children see *this*? Who knew what a crazy man would do? He must have suspected that I knew Carol's exact whereabouts. Whenever I went to visit her at the shelter I took a circuitous route, always watching in my rearview mirror for his blue car. Now I had my tear gas in my pocket; I carried it with me all the time, kept it beside my bed when I slept. I thought of the things in my kitchen: knives, electric cords, mixers, graters, elements which could become white-hot and sear off a person's flesh.

He stood there like a supplicant, palms up, eyebrows raised in hope, waiting for a sign of humanity from me. I gave him what I could—a ham and a weak, pathetic little smile. I said, dishonestly, "Go home, maybe I can reach her today, maybe she will call you once you get home." He ran to his car, jumped in it, sped off, and I thought, coldly, *Good, I'm rid of him. For now we're safe.* I locked the door with three locks.

Later, Carol found among his many notes to her one which said, "At least your sister smiled at me, the only human thing that happened in this terrible time. I always knew she loved me and was my friend."

He became more persistent. He staked out my house, not believing I wasn't hiding her. "How could I possibly hide her?" I said to him on the phone. "You know I wouldn't lie to you."

"I know you wouldn't," he said. "I trust you." But on certain days I saw his blue car parked behind a hedge a block away, saw him hunched down like a private eye, watching my front door. One day my husband drove away with one of our daughters beside him, and an instant later the blue car tore by. I got a look at him then, curved over the wheel, a madman, everything at stake, nothing to lose, and I felt he would kill, kidnap, hold my husband and child as hostages till he got my sister back. I cried out. As long as he lived he would search for her, and if she hid, he would plague me. He had once said to her (she told me this), "You love your family? You want them alive? Then you'd better do as I say."

On the day he broke the table, after his son's face crumpled in terror, Carol told him to leave. He ran from the house. Ten minutes later he called my sister and said, in the voice of a wild creature, "I'm watching some men building a house, Carol. I'm never going to build a house for you now. Do you know that?" He was panting like an animal. "And I'm coming back for you. You're going to be with me one way or the other. You know I can't go on without you."

She hung up and called me. "I think he's coming back to hurt us."

"Then get out of there," I cried, miles away and helpless. "Run!"

By the time she called me again I had the number of the shelter for her. She was at a gas station with her children. Outside were two phone booths—she hid her children in one; she called the shelter from the other. I called the boys at the number in their booth and I read to them from a book called *Silly Riddles* while she made arrangements to be taken in. She talked for almost an hour to a counselor at the shelter. All the time I was sweating and reading riddles. When it was settled, she came into the children's phone booth and we made a date to meet in forty-five minutes at Sears so she could buy herself some underwear and her children some blue jeans. They were still in their pajamas.

Under the bright fluorescent lights in the department store, we looked at price tags, considered quality and style, while her teeth chattered. Our eyes met over the racks, and she asked me, "What do you think he's planning now?"

My husband got a restraining order to keep him from our doorstep, to keep him from dialing our number. Yet he dialed it, and I answered the phone, almost passionately, each time I heard it ringing, having run to the room where I had the tape recorder hooked up. "Why is she so afraid of me? Let her come to see me without bodyguards! What can happen? The worst I could do is kill her, and how bad could that be, compared with what we're going through now?"

I played her that tape. "You must never go back," I said. She agreed; she had to. I brought clean nightgowns to her at the shelter; I brought her fresh vegetables, and bread that had substance.

Bard had hired a psychic that last week, and had gone to Las Vegas to confer with him, bringing along a $500 money order. When he got home, he sent a parcel to Las Vegas, containing clothing of Carol's and a small gold ring which she often wore. A circular that Carol found later under the bed promised immediate results: *Gold has the strongest psychic power—you can work a love spell by burning a red candle and reciting, "In this ring I place my spell of love to make you return to me." This will also prevent your loved one from being unfaithful.*

* * *

Carol moved across the street from my house just before Halloween. We devised a signal so she could call me for help in case some maniac cut her phone lines. She would use the antique gas alarm which our father had given to me. It was a loud wooden clacker which had been used in the war. She would open her window and spin it. I could hear it easily. I promised her that I would look out of my window often and watch for suspicious shadows near the bushes under her windows. Somehow, neither of us believed he was really gone. Even though she had picked up his wallet at the morgue, the wallet he'd had with him while he breathed his car's exhaust through a vacuum cleaner hose, thought his thoughts, told himself she didn't love him and so he had to do this and do it now, even though his ashes were in the dumpster, we felt that he was still out there, still looking for her.

Her sons built a six-foot-high spider web out of heavy white yarn for a decoration, and nailed it to the tree in her front yard. They built a graveyard around the tree, with wooden crosses. At their front door they rigged a noose, and hung a dummy from it. The dummy, in their father's old blue sweatshirt with a hood, swung from the rope. It was still there long after Halloween, still swaying in the wind.

Carol said to me, "I don't like it, but I don't want to say anything to them. I don't think they're thinking about him. I think they just made it for Halloween, and they still like to look at it."

LEE SMITH was born in 1944 in Grundy, Virginia. Rural Virginia has been the setting for many of her award-winning novels and short stories that have prompted comparison with the writings of Carson McCullers, Eudora Welty, Harper Lee, and Ellen Glasgow. Her novels, which include *The Last Day the Dogbushes Bloomed* (1968), *Something in the Wind* (1971), *Fancy Strut* (1973), *Black Mountain Breakdown* (1980), and *Oral History* (1983), have been praised for their skill at evoking small-town Southern life and at portraying characters struggling to find their identities. Her most recent novel, especially, has been praised for its preservation of the language and stories of the people of Appalachia. The poet and critic Katha Pollitt has observed that Lee Smith is to Southern writing what the New South is to the South. "Hers is a South divested of mystery and broodings." Her heroines—like the scatterbrained Florrie of "Cakewalk," the story that follows here, whose disorderly household and homemade cakes express a full heart—these women sustain themselves by their own pluck and warmth.

Cakewalk

by
Lee Smith

They call Florrie the "cake lady" now and don't think Stella doesn't know it, even though of course no one has dared to say it to her face. Stella's face is smooth, strong, and handsome still—you'd have to say she's a handsome woman, instead of a pretty one—but her face is proud and standoffish, too, sealed up tight with Estée Lauder makeup, ear to ear. Stella has run the cosmetics department at Belk's for twenty years and looks like it. Florrie, on the other hand, doesn't care what she looks like or what anybody thinks about it, either, and never has. Florrie wears running shoes, at her age, and wooly white athletic socks that fall in crinkles down around her ankles, and whatever else her eye lights on when she wakes up. At least that's what she looks like. Sometimes she'll have on one of those old flowered dresses that button all the way up the front, or sometimes she'll have on turquoise toreador pants or a felt skirt with a poodle on it—stuff she must have kept around for years and years, since she never throws anything at all away, stuff Stella wouldn't be caught dead in, as Stella frequently remarks to her husband, Claude, but whatever Florrie puts on, you can be sure she'll have white smudges all over it, at the skirt or on the sleeve, like she's been out in her own private snowfall. That's flour. She's always making those cakes. And then you can see her going through town carrying them so careful, her tired plump little face all crackled up and smiling, those Adidas just skimming the ground. She never wears a coat.

Oh Stella knows what they say! Just like Florrie is some poor soul on the order of Red Marcus' son who used to ride his blue bike around and around the Baptist Church until he either had a fit or somebody stopped him, or Martin Quesenberry's wife, Eloise, who is hooked on arthritis dope and has not come out of her nice Colonial frame house for eleven years, Stella knows the type and you do, too: a town character. It breaks Stella's heart. Because they were not raised to be town characters, the Ludington girls, they were brought up in considerable refinement thanks entirely to their sweet mother, Miss Bett, and not a day went by that she did not impress upon them in some subtle or some not-so-subtle way their obligations in this town as the crème de la crème, which is what she called them, which is what they were. Miss Bett learned this expression, and others, when she resided for one solid year on a tree-lined street in Europe in her youth. "Resided"—that's what she said.

Florrie and Stella resided in the big gray house on the corner of Lambert and Pine, the house with the gazebo, the hand-carved banisters and heart pine floors, the same house that Florrie has made a shambles of and lives in, to this day, in the most perverse manner Stella can think of. But in those days it was the loveliest house in town and the Ludington family had always lived there, "aloft," as Stella told Claude, "on the top rung of the social crust."

So Stella was born with a natural gift for elegance, and this is why she loves Belk's. She goes in to work twenty minutes early every day with her own key on a special key ring by itself, a shiny brass key ring that spells out STELLA. After she lets herself in, she goes straight to the cosmetics department where everything is elegant, gleaming glass counters cleaned the night before by the hired help, all the shiny little bottles and tubes and perfume displays arranged just so, and she pours the tea from her thermos into a china cup and puts the thermos out of sight under the counter and settles herself on her high pink tufted stool and slowly sips her tea; she uses a saucer, too. The cosmetics department rises like an island on a rose pink carpet in the center of the store, close to the accessories but not too close, a long way from the bedspreads. After Stella has been there for about ten minutes or so, everybody else comes trickling in, too, and she speaks to them pleasantly one by one and pities their makeup and the way they look so thrown together, some of them, with their slips showing and sleep at the edges of their eyes. Then, five minutes before Mr. Thomas slides open the huge glass door to the rest of the mall, just when she has reached the hand-painted violet at the bottom of the china cup, then comes the moment she has been waiting for, the reason she gets up one whole hour before she has to and does her makeup by artificial light, which is not the way to do it, anybody can tell you that, and leaves the house in the pitch black frosty morning with Claude still sleeping humped up in the bed: this is it, the moment when Mr. Thomas flicks that master switch and her chandelier comes on. Of course, the cosmetics department is the only section in the store that has a chandelier, and it's a real beauty, hundreds and hundreds and maybe thousands of glass teardrops glowing like a million little stars, and all those shiny tubes and bottles winking back the light. The chandelier is as big as a Volkswagen, hanging right down over Stella, dead center at the soul of Belk's. It's just beautiful; Stella sighs when it comes on.

She checks her merchandise, then, and maybe she'll add something new or drape a bright silk scarf around a mirror. Stella carries Erno Laszlo, Estée Lauder, Revlon, Clinique—all the most exclusive lines, and she sells to the very best people in town. Nobody else can afford these cosmetics, and Stella keeps it that way. The ladies she helps are the crème de la crème, so she never rushes them, and they will linger for hours sometimes in the sweet-smelling pink air of the cosmetics department, trying teal eyeliner or fuchsia blush, in the soft glow of the chandelier. Stella is calm, aloof, and refined, and it's a pleasure, in this day and age, to deal with someone like that. She doesn't seem to care if anybody buys anything or not, so the ladies buy and buy, just to *show* her. Stella makes a mint, her salary plus commissions, and whatever you read about in *Vogue*, she's already got it, she ordered it last month. If Pearls-in-Your-Bath are in, for instance, Stella has some pearls thrown out on black velvet in a tasteful little way to catch your eye, and the product set up in a pyramid at the side. Stella says she keeps one foot on the pulse of the future, and it's true. Stella has always stayed up with the times.

Florrie doesn't, though. If she made any real money from all those cakes, that would be different. But the way Stella figures it, Florrie just barely covers expenses. She won't use a mix, for one thing. And the way she gets herself up looking so awful, and the people she deals with—why, Florrie will make a cake for anybody, any class of person, and that's the plain truth, awful as it is. Stella shudders, thinking of it on this mid-October day, this cool nippy day with a jerky wind that whistles and whistles around the corner of Belk's although not one teardrop of the chandelier above Stella's cosmetics counter ever moves. Stella shudders, because today is the day she has circled in her mind to go over there (since she gets off early on Thursdays anyway) and try to talk some sense into Florrie for the umpteenth time.

She's got it all worked out in her head: if Florrie will quit making those embarrassing cakes and running around town like a mental person, Stella is prepared to be generous and let bygones be bygones, to let Florrie move in with her and Claude where she can do the cooking, since she likes to cook so much, and then they can sell Mama's house for a pretty penny. And all of this might be good for Claude, too, who has acted so funny since he retired from the electric company two years ago. Claude just bats around the house these days with his pajama top on over his slacks, leaving coffee cups any old place, which makes rings on all the furniture, smoking his pipe and smelling up the house, or taking that boat of his up to Kerr Lake and driving it around in the water all day by himself. It would be one thing if he were fishing, but he's not. He's just driving around in the water and looking back at the wake. Stella has colitis—that's why she's switched to tea instead of coffee—and the very thought of Claude out in that boat goes straight to her bowels. Well. At least she can go over and talk some sense into Florrie, something she's been trying to do ever since she can remember.

She can't remember a time when Florrie didn't need it, either, but she *can* remember, or thinks she can, when Florrie started making those cakes. In fact Stella can recall precisely, because she's got such a good head for business, several cakes in particular, and she narrows her frosty green eyelids and totally ignores the tacky woman on the other side of the counter asking if they carry Cover Girl, which of course they do *not*, and recalls these cakes one by one.

To understand the circumstances of Florrie's first cake, which she made practically over her mama's dead body when she was in the eighth grade—it was the dessert for a Methodist Youth Fellowship Progressive Dinner—you have to understand the way they used to live then, in that fine old house on the corner of Lambert and Pine. The house was number one on the House Tour every year, and you couldn't find a speck of dust in it, either, or one thing out of place. That Miss Bett kept her house this way was a triumph of mind over matter, because she was not a well woman, ever, and it wore her out to keep things so straight. But she did it anyway, and held her head up high in the face of her husband's failings, and even the towels were ironed. So you can see why the idea of fifteen teenagers tromping in for dessert would have run her right up the wall.

"But Mama," Florrie said, "they're *coming*. It's all settled. We're going to have the first course at Rhonda's house, and the main course at Sue and Joey's, and then I invited them here for dessert. After that we'll go back to the church for the meeting."

"I never heard of such a thing," Miss Bett said. Miss Bett was a tall frail woman with jet black hair in a bun on the top of her head, and big dark eyes that could flash fire, as they did right then at Florrie. Miss Bett held famous dinner parties every year or so, which involved several weeks of preparations, all the silver polished and the china out, dinner parties that were so lovely that she had to go to bed for a day or two afterward to recover. "A Progressive Dinner!" she snorted. "The very idea!"

"Well, they're coming," Florrie said sweetly. That was her way—she never argued with her mother, or cried, just acted so sweet and did whatever she wanted to do. Stella wasn't fooled by this and neither was Miss Bett, but Florrie had everybody else in town eating out of the palm of her hand, including, of course, her daddy.

"Come on, Bett," Oliver Ludington said, standing in the kitchen doorway. "Don't embarrass her."

"I would talk about embarrassment if I were you," Miss Bett said. She stared at him until he said something under his breath and started to turn away, and then she looked back at her two daughters just in time to see Florrie give him a wink. That wink was the last straw.

"All right." She bit off the words. "Since Florrie has invited fifteen perfect strangers into our home, we will entertain them properly. Stella," she directed, "go out and cut some glads and some of those snapdragons next to the lily pond."

Florrie giggled. "We don't have to have *flowers*," she said.

"Stella!" said Miss Bett, and Stella went out, furious because she was three years older and had never joined the MYF in the first place, even though she was more religious than Florrie, and now she had to cut the flowers.

Miss Bett began removing vases from the sideboard, considering them one by one.

"I'll just make a cake," Florrie suggested. She knew it would take her mother hours to arrange the flowers.

"You've never made a cake in your life," said Miss Bett. "You don't know the first thing about it."

"I won't make a mess," Florrie said.

"Florrie—" their mother began.

But Oliver Ludington, from the parlor, said, "That's all right, honey, Bessie can clean it up."

"Bessie doesn't come until *Monday*," Miss Bett reminded everybody, and of course it was only Sunday afternoon.

"I think I'll make a yellow cake with white icing," Florrie said. She had taken all the cookbooks out of their drawer and piled them on the table in a heap, and now she was flipping through them in her disorganized way. "Where's that big flat cake pan?"

A sound that could have been a laugh, or maybe a cough, came from the parlor as Miss Bett found the pan and slammed it out on the table for Florrie.

"Stella, don't put the flowers right down on the counter like that, honey, put them on *newspaper*, they could have anything on them, and then please take sixteen salad forks out of the silver chest and polish them."

"Mama," Stella said, but after one look at Miss Bett, she did it.

By the time the members of the MYF arrived three hours later, the dining room looked just like a picture, silver forks and pink linen on the table and flowers in a cut-glass vase from Europe in the center. Stella was fit to be tied and refused to have dessert with the group, even though Florrie begged her, and Miss Bett had taken to her bed with a sick headache after one look at Florrie's cake. The cake would have been fine if Florrie had not gotten into the food coloring, which was never used in that house except at Christmas when Miss Bett made cookies for the help. But Florrie had found it, and she had tinted some of the white icing yellow and had made a great big wobbly cross in the center of the cake. Then she tinted the rest of the icing dark blue and wrote MYF on the cross, and put a little blue border all around its sides.

"Oh!" Miss Bett shrieked, and her hand fluttered up to her high pale forehead, and she turned without a word and climbed the steps, clutching the handsome banister all the way.

Florrie had cleaned up the kitchen the best she could, not really knowing how to do it, but she couldn't get the blue food coloring off her fingers so they stayed that way for the Progressive Dinner, even though she looked very nice otherwise, with her curly blond hair pinned back out of her eyes by silver barrettes, and wearing her pleated skirt. Oliver Ludington went upstairs and took a bath, singing "Bicycle Built for Two" as loud as he could, and then he appeared at the door in a sparkling white shirt, a red bow tie, and his best seersucker suit, just in time to welcome the whole Progressive Dinner to his house. "Come right in!" He bowed. "Glad to have you," he said, and Florrie smiled her full happy smile at him, showing her dimples, and giggled "Oh Daddy!" as she came through the hall trailed by the whole MYF in which all the boys had a crush on her, even then, and even then she knew how to flirt back, and laugh, and shake her blond curls, but that's *all* she did in those days—it was later, in high school, that boys became a problem.

Oliver Ludington died when Florrie was sixteen and Stella was off at college. He died of cirrhosis of the liver, as everyone knew he would, and it was a funny thing how many people showed up for his funeral, filling up the whole Methodist Church and then spilling out to fill up all that space between the church and the street. It was awful how Florrie took on. Miss Bett and Stella cried too, into their handkerchiefs, but to tell the truth everybody expected Miss Bett to be *relieved*, after it was all over, since Oliver Ludington drank so and since she had never been happy with the way he had refused to practice law and taught at the high school instead. But Miss Bett was not relieved, or at least she didn't seem to be. After Oliver died, all that fine dark fire went right out of her, and she crept around like a pastel ghost of herself for the rest of her life. It was like she had used herself completely up in her long constant struggle with Oliver, and lacking anybody to fight with or try to raise up by their bootstraps, she paled and died back like one of the flowers in her own garden, going to seed. She let the house go, too, even though Bessie still came in. The house seemed to sag at all its corners, the gazebo started to peel, worn places in the upholstery were left unrepaired, and a loose shutter flapped in the wind. She didn't even try to control Florrie, who went out with any boy who asked her, and when Stella tried to talk some sense into her, she didn't seem to hear.

"Mama," said Stella, just home from business school where she had a straight A average, "you have got to do something about Florrie. She's getting a *reputation.*" Stella paused significantly, but her mother's dark eyes were looking beyond her face. "I might as well come right out and say it, Mother, I think she's fast. And Daddy used to think she was so smart, but look at her grades now! They're terrible, and she'll never make it to college at the rate she's going. Besides, I don't like the crowd she hangs around with, for instance that Barbara Whitley. Those people are common."

Miss Bett's fingers trembled on her lap, like she was brushing some insect, or some speck, off the flowered voile. "You haven't asked me how my stomach is," she said to Stella.

Stella sat straight up in her chair. "Well, how *is* it?" she said.

"I have my good days and I have my bad days," Miss Bett told her. "I just eat like a bird. Sometimes I have a little rice or a breast of chicken"—but just then Florrie came in from the kitchen with her lipstick on crooked, bringing her mama some tea, and Miss Bett sighed like she was dying and then drank it up in one gulp.

"Come on and go to the sidewalk carnival," Florrie said to Stella. "It's for the Fire Department, and they've got a band."

"I think somebody should stay here with Mama," Stella said.

"I think I could stand another cup of tea with a little more lemon in it," Miss Bett said, and then Stella decided to go after all, and she changed her dress while Florrie fixed Miss Bett's tea.

Florrie had made a cake for the carnival, a white sheet cake with yellow icing and a fire engine outlined on it in red, the engine's wheels made out of chocolate nonpareils. The sisters walked downtown along the new sidewalk and Stella thought how the town was growing since the aluminum company had come, and how many new faces she saw. Everybody spoke to Florrie, though, and stopped to admire her cake, and Florrie introduced them all, complete strangers, to Stella. "She's away at school," Florrie would say.

"I wish you wouldn't do that," Stella told her finally, because she could tell after twenty minutes or so that there was no one she wanted to meet.

The square had been roped off for the carnival, and Florrie took her cake carefully up to the table in the center of it, a long table draped with red, white, and blue, and put it right down in the middle. Everybody went "ooh, ah," and Stella turned away and went to sit on the steps of the North Carolina National Bank where to her surprise she fell into a conversation with Claude Lambeth, a boy she hadn't seen since high school, a tall serious-looking boy who was studying electrical engineering at State. Now Stella was a beauty at that time. She had Miss Bett's looks and her own way of walking so straight and inclining her head. Stella and Claude Lambeth sat on the high steps of the bank, back from the action, and watched the crowd mill around and watched the kids dancing in front of the fountain to the band. They had a lot in common, Stella learned, as they talked and talked and watched the dancing. Florrie was like a little whirlwind out there. First she went with one and then another, and even Stella had to admit she was pretty, or would have been if her hair didn't fly out so much on the turns and she didn't look quite so messy in general.

"That's your sister, isn't it?" Claude Lambeth said to Stella, and Stella said yes it was. Claude Lambeth just shook his head, and then later at the cakewalk, he shook it again when the music stopped and five or six boys jumped on the painted red dot for Florrie's cake and the right to walk her home. The boy who ended up on the bottom was Harliss Reeves, who was generally up to no good, and when the whole cakewalk was over, Claude Lambeth told Harliss Reeves thanks anyway, he had promised their mother that he would drive Florrie and Stella home in his car. And he did, leaving Harliss on the sidewalk with his cake in both hands and his mouth wide open, Florrie mouthing apologies at him through the closed glass window of Claude Lambeth's car. "What'd you do *that* for?" she screamed at Claude, jerking her arm away from Stella, but Stella was taken with Claude and approved his action with all her heart.

Which was broken when Claude Lambeth failed to write to her and dated her little sister instead, all that spring and summer while Stella graduated and then worked so hard in her first job as a teller trainee in Charlotte. Stella was so mad she wouldn't come home at all, not even to try to talk some sense into Florrie when her mama wrote that Florrie refused to go to college and was selling toys in the five-and-dime, but then her mama wrote that Florrie and that nice Claude Lambeth were unfortunately no longer seeing each other, and Stella knew he had seen the light. She came home for a visit and married him on the spot, and Florrie made them a three-tiered Lady Baltimore wedding cake.

"You ought to charge," Stella told her, eyeing the cake at her wedding reception. "You'll never get anywhere at the five-and-dime," she said, and Florrie stopped playing with all their squealing little girl cousins long enough to say maybe she would.

Florrie never had a wedding cake of her own, poor thing, or a wedding reception either—she ran off in a snowstorm two years later with Earl Mingo, a drifter from northern Florida, and married him in a J.P.'s office in the middle of the night in Spartanburg, South Carolina, under a bare hanging light bulb. Now Earl Mingo was good looking, you would have to say that—but who knows what else she saw in him? Because Florrie could have had her pick in this town, and she didn't, she ran off with Earl Mingo instead, a man with Indian blood in him who had never made a decent living for himself or anybody else. He painted houses, or so he said, but if it was too cold, or too hot, or he didn't like the color of paint you had picked out, forget it. Earl Mingo kept guns and he went hunting a lot, out in the river woods or up on the mountain, and sometimes when you were trying to hire him he'd stare right past you, to where the road went off in the trees. Everybody knew who he was. He had men friends, hunting buddies, but they never asked him over for dinner, and neither did anyone else.

Stella didn't speak to Florrie for months after she did it, and Miss Bett had to be hospitalized it was such a shock. After her mother got out of the hospital, Stella used to drive over there to pick up Miss Bett and take her to church—of course Florrie and Earl didn't attend—and then she would drop her off again, but finally when Miss Bett told Stella that Florrie was pregnant, she decided to walk back in that house, meet Earl Mingo face to face, and make peace. Because Stella had had a baby herself by then, little Dawn Elizabeth, and this had softened her heart.

So finally, on this particular Sunday after church, Stella parked the car and walked her mother right up to the door in the pale March sunlight, her hand under Miss Bett's arm, and she couldn't help but notice now nobody had ever fixed that shutter, and how dirty the carpet was in the front hall. While her mother went upstairs to lie down, Stella stood at the last step, holding on to the banister, and hollered for Florrie.

Nobody answered.

But Stella smelled coffee and so she pressed her black patent leather purse up tight against her bosom and put her lips in one thin line and headed back toward the kitchen without another word. Forgive and forget, she thought. The swinging kitchen door was closed. When Stella pushed it open, the first thing she noticed was the *color*, of course, which her mother had never said the first word about and which was a big surprise as you can imagine, her mama's nice white kitchen painted bright blue like the sky. Now if it had been a kitchen color that would be one thing, such as pale blue or beige or yellow, but whoever heard of a sky blue kitchen? Even the cabinets were blue. Stella was too surprised to say a word, so she kept her mouth shut and blinked, and then she saw what she would have seen right away if that color hadn't been such a shock: Earl Mingo seated big as life at the kitchen table with Florrie on his lap, both their faces hidden by Florrie's tumbling yellow hair. Florrie was laughing and Earl Mingo was saying something too low for Stella to hear. Earl Mingo didn't even have a shirt on, and the kitchen table was cluttered with dishes that no one had bothered to wash.

When Stella said "Good morning!" though, Florrie jumped up giggling and pulled the tie of her pink chenille robe around her and tied it as fast as she could, but not before Stella could see she was naked as a jaybird underneath. This was in the *afternoon*, close to one o'clock.

"Stella, this is Earl," Florrie said exactly as if people ran around in nothing but pink chenille robes all day long.

"I'm pleased to meet you." Earl stood up in his bare chest and stuck out his hand to Stella, who seized it in her confusion and pumped it up and down too long. Later, she hoped Earl Mingo didn't think she meant anything by that because she could see in one glance that he was the kind of man who thinks a woman is only good for one thing, and Stella was not that kind of woman by a long shot.

Earl Mingo stood over six feet tall, with black hair, too long, brushed straight back from his high dark forehead and black eyes that looked right through you. He had a big nose, straight thick eyebrows, a hard chin and a thin crooked mouth that turned up at the corners, sometimes, in the wildest grin. When Earl Mingo grinned, he showed the prettiest, whitest teeth you can imagine on a man. He grinned at Stella like he was just delighted to meet her after all. "Have a cup of coffee," he said.

"Why don't you take off your hat and sit down," Florrie said, which is what she and Earl proceeded to do themselves, only this time Florrie sat in a separate chair. "That's a pretty hat," Florrie said. "I like that little veil."

"I'd just love to stay but I can't." Stella was lying through her teeth. "Claude is watching Dawn Elizabeth and I have to get right back. I just wanted to run in and say I'm real happy about the baby, Florrie, and I never have said congratulations either, so congratulations." Stella's eyes filled up with tears then—she had been having those crying spells ever since Dawn Elizabeth was born—and Florrie jumped right up and hugged her on the spot. Stella remembered holding her little sister by the hand when she started first grade, walking Florrie to school.

"Well, I've got to go," Stella said finally, and then for no reason at all she said, backing out that bright blue kitchen door, "You all be careful, now," and Earl Mingo threw back his head and laughed.

There comes a time in a woman's life when the children take over, and what you do is what you have to, and it seems like the days go by so slow then while you're home with them, and nothing ever really gets done around the house before you have to go off and do something else that doesn't ever get done either, and it can take you all day long to hem a skirt. Every day lasts a long, long time. But then before you know it, it's all over, those days gone like a fog on the mountain, and the kids are all in school and there you are with this awful light empty feeling in your stomach like the beginning of cramps, when you sit in the chair where you used to nurse the baby and listen to the radio news.

Not that Stella ever nursed Dawn Elizabeth or Robert either one, but Florrie had two babies in a row and nursed them all over town. Anyway, with Robert in school at last, Stella had her hair frosted, bought some new shoes, took a part-time job in the accounting department at Belk's, and started working her way up into her present job in the cosmetics department. It was like she just woke up from a long, long sleep. She had done her duty and stayed home with those babies, and then she went back to the real world where she belonged. Not that Stella ever neglected those kids while she worked: she had them organized like the army, the whole family. Everybody had a chore, and she and Claude gave them every advantage in the world—piano lessons, dancing lessons, braces, you name it. Claude advanced steadily in his job at the electric company, a promotion every six years, and they built a nice brick ranch-style house with wall-to-wall carpeting and a flagstone patio. Claude was elected president of the Kiwanis Club, and Stella went on buying trips to New York City, where she stayed in hotels by herself.

And Florrie? Florrie never could seem to understand that those baby days were over. She had Earlene—six months after she got married—and then she had Earl Junior and then she had Paul who was born too soon and died, and anybody else would have left it at that. But nine years later, along came Bobby Joe, and then Floyd, and Florrie seemed tickled pink. She raised her children in the scatterbrained way she did everything else, and they ran loose like wild Indians and stayed up as late as they pleased on a school night, and spent all their money on gum. Then when they got to be older, they used to have all the other kids in town over there in that big house, too, dancing to the radio in the parlor and who knows what all, smoking cigarettes out in the yard. Florrie was always right there in the middle of it, making a cake as often as not.

Because her business had grown and grown—she never gave it up even when she had two of them in diapers at one time. And she never switched to cake mixes either, although she would have saved herself hours if she had. Florrie still made plenty of birthday cakes with roses on them, and happy anniversary cakes with bells, and seasonal cakes such as a green tree cake for Christmas with candy ornaments on it, or a chocolate Yule log, or an orange pumpkin cake for Halloween, and she had four different sizes of heart molds she used for Valentine's Day. But the town was growing and changing all the time, and you could tell it by Florrie's cakes. After the new country club opened up, she made a cake for Dolph Tillotson's birthday that was just like a nine-hole golf course, a huge green sheet cake with hills and valleys and little dime store mirrors for the water hazards, flags on all the greens, and a tiny sugar golf ball near the cup on the seventh hole. When the country club team won the state swim meet, they ordered an Olympic pool cake with a chocolate board and twelve different lap lanes. Once she worked for two solid days on a retirement cake for the head of the secretarial pool out at the aluminum plant. This cake involved a lot of oblong layers assembled just so to form a giant typewriter with Necco wafers as keys. The sheet of paper in the blue typewriter was smooth white icing, and on it Florrie had put "We'll Miss You, Miss Hugh" in black letters that looked like typing. When the new Chevrolet agency opened, she filled an order for a chocolate convertible; and after the community college started up, she made cakes and cakes for the students, featuring anything they told her to write, such as "Give 'Em Hell, Michelle" on a spice cake for a roommate's birthday.

The cake business and the children kept Florrie happy then, or seemed to, a good thing since Earl Mingo did not amount to a hill of beans, which surprised nobody. He painted houses for a while, and then he put in insulation, and then he went away working on a pipeline. In between jobs he would go off hunting by himself, or so he said, and stay gone for as long as a month. Then he'd show up again, broke and grinning, and Florrie would be so happy to see him and all the children would be too, and things would go on like that for a while before Earl Mingo went off again.

It was a marriage that caused a lot of talk in the beginning, talk that started up again every time Earl Mingo went away and then died back every time he came home, but since he kept on doing it, the talk slacked off and finally stopped altogether and everybody just accepted the way it was with them, the way he came and went. Since it didn't seem to bother Florrie, it stopped bothering everybody else too—except Stella, who felt that Florrie had stepped off the upper crust straight into scum. Into *lowlife*, which is where in her opinion Florrie had been heading all along.

For years Miss Bett had her own rooms upstairs, with her pressed flowers and her pictures from Europe in silver frames, her little brocade settee and her Oriental rug and her gold-tasseled bed. So many of the other fine things in the rest of the house had been broken by Florrie's children. Which wasn't their *fault*, exactly, since nobody ever taught them any better or ever told them "no" in all their lives.

"It's just a madhouse over here!" Stella said, not for the first time, one day after work when she was sitting with her mama in what used to be called the east parlor, looking out on the front yard where Earl Junior and a whole gang of boys were playing football in spite of the boxwood hedges on either side of the walk. Stella and Miss Bett watched through the wavy French doors as Earl Junior and his friends caught the ball, and ran, and fell down in a pile and then got up. They watched as Earl Junior and his friends waved their arms frantically and shouted at one another, the breath of their words hanging white in the cold fall air. Sometimes they had a fight, but nobody stepped in to stop it, and after a while they would get tired of fighting it seemed, and roll over on their backs and start laughing. Stella was glad that her own son, Robert, was not out in that pile of boys. In the west parlor, Earlene was playing the piano—practically the only stick of furniture in that room that was left in one piece—practicing for a talent show at school. Her fingers ran over the same thing again and again, a tinkly little melody that got on Stella's nerves. Floyd and Bobby Joe were wrestling in the hall. Every now and then they rolled past the east parlor door, for all the world like two little monkeys. Back in the kitchen the TV set was on, Florrie watching her stories and smoking cigarettes, no doubt, while she cooked. Earl Mingo was gone.

Cold sunlight came in through those high French doors and fell across the worn blue carpet, pale fine golden sunlight that reminded Stella suddenly of their childhood in such a way that it caused her to suck in her breath so hard it hurt her chest, and blurt out something she didn't even know she'd been thinking about until she said it out loud.

"Mama," she said, "you don't have to stay here, you know. You could come to live with Claude and me, we'd be glad to have you."

Miss Bett looked so pitiful and small, her eyes like puddles in her little white face. She's *shrunk*! Stella noticed. She's shrinking up like a little old blow-up doll, and no one has noticed but me. *"Mama,"* Stella said. "We could build you a little apartment over the garage."

"I had a bad day yesterday," Miss Bett said, looking past Stella out the French doors where Earl Junior was catching a pass. "Everything went through me like a sieve."

"Wouldn't you like to have your own apartment, Mama?" Stella went on. "Wouldn't you like to have some peace?"

"I'd like a little peace." Miss Bett said this like she was in a dream.

"Well then!" Stella stood up. "I'll just talk to Florrie about it, and we'll—"

"No!" Miss Bett got all excited suddenly and twisted her hands around and around in her lap. She said it with such force that Stella stopped, halfway out the door.

"We'd love to have you," Stella said.

"I—" Miss Bett said. "I—" She moved her little blue hand in a circle through the sunlight, then let it drop back in her lap. She looked straight at Stella. "I'll try to stand it a little longer," she said.

"We'll buy you a new TV."

Miss Bett lifted her head the way she used to, and touched a white wisp of her hair.

"I'll just have to bear it," she said.

But Stella sailed right past her into the kitchen where, sure enough, Florrie was sitting at the kitchen table reading a magazine and smoking a cigarette. The table was half covered up with newspapers and Popsicle sticks and glue.

"What's all that?" Stella pointed at the mess.

"Earl Junior is making this little old theater, like Shakespeare had, for school. It's the cutest thing," Florrie said.

"Listen." Stella sat down and started right in. "Listen here, I'm worried about Mother."

"Mother?" Florrie said it like she was surprised.

"I think she needs a change." Stella was going to be tactful, but then she just burst into tears. "Poor little thing. She's *shrinking,* Florrie. I swear she's just shrinking away."

Florrie put her cigarette out and giggled. "She's not shrinking, Stella," she said.

"But what do you think about her *health*, Florrie? Now really—I wouldn't be surprised if it turned out to be all mental myself, if you want to know. I hope you won't take this wrong, but I just don't think it's good for her to live under such a strain. I don't think there's a thing wrong with her stomach, if you want to know what I think. I think if she could get a little peace and quiet, and if she had some *hobbies* or something— "

Florrie threw back her head and laughed. "I can just see Mama with a hobby!" she said. "Lord! Mama's already got a hobby, if you ask me."

"No, *really*, Florrie," Stella said. "Wouldn't it be a whole lot easier for you and Earl if she came and lived over our garage?" Floyd came in the kitchen crying then, and Florrie got him a Coke, and Stella went on. "Just think about it. Think about how much easier your life would be. What do you think about her health, anyway? I've been meaning to ask you."

Florrie looked at Stella. "Well, she has her good days and she has her bad days," Florrie said. "Sometimes everything goes through her like a sieve."

"Oh!" Stella was furious. "I can't talk to you. You're as bad as she is!" Stella picked up her pocketbook and flounced out of there, right past Earlene playing the piano and Floyd

and Bobby wrestling in the hall and her mother all shrunk up to nothing in the sunlight on the sofa in the east parlor; Stella sailed straight out the front door just as Earl Junior hollered "Hike!"

So Miss Bett lived with Florrie and Earl until she died of heart failure, and when she did, it was all Stella could do to persuade Florrie to let them bury her mama decently. Florrie wanted Miss Bett put in a pine box, of all things, where the worms could get in. Then Florrie revealed that in fact this was the way she and Earl Mingo had buried Paul, the baby who had died so long ago. Stella and Florrie had a big argument about all of this in front of everybody, right there in the funeral home, but since Earl Mingo was out of town and Earlene had gone off to college, Florrie had no one to take her side and finally Claude just gave Mr. Morrow a check and that settled it, or seemed to, since Florrie did not mention the pine box or the worms again though she cried for three solid weeks, despite the fact that Miss Bett had left her the whole house out of pity.

Lord knows where Florrie got such ideas in the first place, although you can be sure she passed them along to Earlene, who turned into a hippie beatnik and won a full scholarship to the North Carolina School of the Arts while she was still in high school and went there, too, came home for vacations wearing purple tights and turtleneck sweaters and necklaces made out of string. Turned into a vegetarian and went away to college up North, where she majored in drama. Now that was Earlene.

Earl Junior was a horse of a different color. No brains to speak of, a big wide grin like his daddy, always wrecking a car or getting a girl in trouble. Earl Junior got a football scholarship to N.C. State where he played second string until his knee gave out, and then he quit school and got a job as some kind of salesman, nothing you would be proud of. But Earl Junior liked to travel, just like Earl. You would have thought Earl Junior owned all of North Carolina, South Carolina, Virginia, and Tennessee, the way he called it his "territory."

Bobby Joe and Floyd were boys that anybody would be proud of, though, in the Boy Scouts and on the Junior High basketball team for instance, boys with brushed-back sandy hair and steady gray eyes, who mowed everybody's grass on Saturdays. Stella was glad to see that those two were turning out so well in spite of the way they were raised with no advantages to speak of, and as years drew into years and it became perfectly clear who had succeeded and who had not, she pitied Florrie, and tried to be extra nice to her sometimes—bringing them a country ham just before Christmas, for instance, or having oranges sent—things that Florrie often failed to notice, scatterbrained as she was. Because there is a kind of flyaway manner that might be fetching in a young girl, but goes sour when the years mount up, and Florrie was pushing forty. She should have known how to say "thank you" by then. Bobby Joe and Floyd were almost through with high school the year that the worst thing that *could* happen, *did.*

Earlene had always been Florrie's favorite, in a way, her being the only girl, and this made it that much worse all the way around: Earlene was the *last* one, the very last person you would pick to be the agent of her mother's doom. But you know how Earlene changed when she went off to school, so you can imagine what her friends would be like: tall skinny girls with wild curly hair or long drooping hair and big eyes, like those pictures of foreign children you see in the drugstore, and of course Earlene was exactly like the rest of Florrie's children—sooner or later, she brought every one of them home.

Elizabeth Blackwell was the daughter of two Duke professors, Dr. Blackwell and Dr. Blackwell, of the History Department. You would never have guessed what was going to happen if you had ever seen her or heard her name, which sounded so well-bred and nice. But Elizabeth Blackwell wore blue jeans day in and day out when she was visiting Earlene, and she had light red hair so long she could sit on it if it hadn't been braided in one long thick plait down the back of her lumberjack shirt. Whenever Elizabeth came to visit Earlene, all she wanted to do was go hiking up on the mountain with Earlene and Floyd and Bobby Joe, and sometimes Earl went too, if he was home. Elizabeth Blackwell wore big square boots from the army-navy store, boots exactly like a man's, and no makeup at all on her pale freckled face, which would have been pretty if she had known what to do with it, especially those big eyes that were such an unusual color, no color really, something in between green and gray. She was not feminine at all, so when she and Earl Mingo ran away together it was the biggest shock in the world to everybody.

Except Earlene, who urged everybody not to feel harsh toward her friend because, she said, Elizabeth Blackwell was pregnant, and furthermore it was Earl Mingo's child. Earl Mingo must have been almost fifty by then, and Elizabeth Blackwell was nineteen years old. Now who can understand a thing like that? Not Bobby Joe, who shot out the new streetlight on the corner of Lambert and Pine with his daddy's Remington pump shotgun and then threw the shotgun itself in the river; not Floyd, who got a twitch in one eye, clammed up in all his classes at the high school, and started studying so hard he beat out Louise Watson for valedictorian of the class; not even Earlene, who took a week off from college to come home and cry and tell everybody it was all her fault. Nobody could understand it except possibly Florrie herself, who of course had known Earl Mingo better than anyone else and did not seem all that surprised. It made you wonder what else had gone on through all those years, and exactly what other crosses Florrie had had to bear.

"I would just die if it was Claude," Stella said several days after it happened, one night when she had come over to commiserate with her sister and find out more details if she could. "But of course Claude would never do anything like that," Stella added. "It would never enter Claude's mind."

Florrie stood back from the wedding cake she was working on and looked at Stella. "You never know what's going to happen in this world," she said. Florrie sounded like she knew a secret, which made her sister mad.

"Well, I know! Claude and I have been married for twenty-six years, and I guess I ought to know by now."

Florrie smiled. Her smile was still as pretty as ever, like there might be a giggle coming right along behind it, but she had aged a lot around the eyes, and that night her eyes were all red. Her hair had a lot of gray mixed in with the blond by that time, and she wore it chopped off just any old way. Florrie had six different-sized layers of white cake already baked, and she was building them up, pink icing between each layer. Floyd sat in the corner in his daddy's chair, reading a library book.

"Who's that cake for?" Stella asked.

"Jennifer Alley and Mark Priest," Florrie said. "Look here what they got in Raleigh for me to put on the top." She showed Stella the bride and groom in cellophane wrapping, a little couple so lifelike they might have been real, the bride in a satin dress.

"Lord, I wish you'd look at that," Stella said. "Look at that little old veil."

Florrie smiled. "Real seed pearls," she said.

"But Florrie—" Stella looked at her watch. "Isn't the wedding tomorrow?" Stella *knew* it was, actually, because she and Claude had been invited, but of course Florrie had not.

"Noon," Florrie said. She rubbed her hand across her forehead, leaving a white streak of flour.

"Are you going to get it done in time?" Stella asked as Florrie spread the smooth white icing over the whole thing and then mixed up more pink and put it in her pastry tube.

"Sure," Florrie said.

"If I were you, I'd just go to bed and get up in the morning and finish it," Stella said.

"I like to make my wedding cakes at night," Florrie said. "You know I always do it this way."

"That's going to take you all night, though."

"Well." Florrie started on the tiny top layer, making pink bows all around the edge. "Light me a cigarette, honey, will you?" she said to Floyd, who did.

Stella sat up straight in the kitchen chair and put her mouth together in a line, but she kept it shut until Bobby Joe came in the kitchen for a Coke and told her hello, and then she said, "Listen, that's another reason I came over here tonight. Claude said for me to tell you that if you want to go off to school next year, Bobby Joe, you just let us know and we'll take care of it." Stella had been against this when Claude first brought it up, but now she was glad she had it to say, since everything was so pathetic over here at Florrie's. Floyd had a scholarship, of course, already. Floyd was a brain. "If you want to go to college, that is," Stella said for emphasis, since Bobby Joe was just standing there in the middle of the kitchen like he hadn't heard her right.

Bobby Joe stared at his aunt and then he popped off his pop top real loud. "Thanks but no thanks," he said.

Well! Bobby Joe took a long drink out of the can and Stella stood up. "If that's how you feel about it," she said, "*all right.*"

Florrie was crying again without seeming to notice it, the tears leaking out as slow as Christmas, her blue eyes filling while she shaped three little red roses above each pink bow on the cake, crying right in front of her sons without a bit of shame.

Stella, who knew when she wasn't wanted, left. But the next day at Jennifer and Mark Priest's wedding reception, Stella couldn't eat *one bite* of that cake; it stuck fast in her throat, and thinking about Florrie gave her indigestion anyway, Florrie bent hunchbacked over that great huge cake the night before, making those tiny red roses.

And Lord knows whatever happened to Earl Mingo, or to Elizabeth Blackwell, or to that baby she either did or did not have. Nobody ever saw or heard from them again except for four postcards that Earl sent back over the next couple of years, from Disney World, from Mammoth Cave, from Death Valley, from Las Vegas—like that. He didn't write a thing on any of them except "Love, Earl Mingo." Florrie kept each one around for a while and then she threw it away, and kept on with her business, living hand-to-mouth some way, nobody knew quite how except that she had made some money when she sold off most of the backyard to Allstate Insurance, which tore up the gazebo and the fish pond and built a three-story brick office building on it right jam-up against that fine old house, and then Claude dropped by and did little odd jobs around the house that needed doing, and that was a savings, too. Other people came by all the time to see her. It seemed like there was always somebody in that kitchen having coffee with Florrie if it was winter, or Coke if it was summer, but then of course she had Earlene's children, Dolly and Bill, to take care of too, while Earlene was having a nervous breakdown after her divorce. Florrie took them in without a word and they lived with her for three years, which is how long it took Earlene to get her feet back on the ground, give up art, and get her license in real estate. Floyd is gone for good: he teaches at the college in Greensboro. Bobby Joe has never amounted to much, like Earl Junior who runs a Midget Golf in Myrtle Beach now. Bobby Joe is still in town. He lives in an apartment near the country club and works in a men's store at the mall, all dressed up like a swinging single in open-neck shirts and gold neck chains, still coming over to see his mama every day or so, breezing in through the screen porch door. Earl Junior's ex-wife, Johnnie Sue, came to visit about two years ago and brought their little boy, Chip, and she has stayed with Florrie ever since, leaving Chip with his grandmother while she teaches tap dancing at Arthur Murray's studio in Raleigh.

Johnnie Sue is not even related to Florrie, so who ever heard of such an arrangement? Stella shakes her head, thinking about it, and smokes a Silva Thin in the car as she drives across town from Belk's to Florrie's house through the fine October day, the leaves all red and golden, swirling down with the wind against the windshield of Stella's new car. Florrie's house is almost the only one left standing on Lambert Street since it has been zoned commercial, and it looks so funny now with the Allstate Building rising up behind it and the Rexall Drugstore next door.

"It's real convenient," Florrie says when Stella mentions the Rexall, again, as tactfully as possible. "I just send Chip right over whenever there's something we need."

Stella sighs. This will be harder than she thought. She had hoped to find Florrie by herself, for one thing, but Chip is home with a cold and she can hear him upstairs right now, banging things around and singing in his high, thin voice. Chip is a hyperactive child who has to take pills every day of his life. Not a thing like Stella's own well-behaved grandchildren, who unfortunately live so far away. Well. At least nobody else is here, even though the table is littered with coffee cups and there's a strong smell of smoke, like pipe smoke, in the air. Florrie, who doesn't keep up with a thing, probably doesn't even know about room deodorizer sprays. Or no-wax wax, obviously, since the floor has clearly not been touched in ages. Stella sighs, taking a kitchen chair, at the memory of how this floor used to shine and how the sun coming in that kitchen window through the starched white curtains just gleamed on the white windowsill. Now the windowsill is blue and you can't even see it for the mess of

African violets up there, and the windows have no curtains at all. It gives Stella a start. It's funny how you can be in a place for years and stop really noticing anything, and then one day suddenly you see it all, plain as day, before your face: things you haven't thought to see for years. She looks around Florrie's kitchen and notices Chip's Lego blocks all piled up in the corner, a pile of laundry in Earl's chair, the sink full of dirty dishes, a crack in the pane of the door—and then Stella's eyes travel back to the kitchen table and she sees what she must have seen when she first came in, or what she saw and didn't notice: smack in the middle of the table, on an ironstone platter, sits Florrie's weirdest cake yet.

This cake is shaped like a giant autumn leaf and it looks like a real leaf exactly, with icing that starts off red in the center and changes from flame to orange, to yellow, to gold. It's hard to tell where one color leaves off and turns into another, the way they flow together in the icing, and the icing itself seems to crinkle up, like a real leaf does, at all the edges of the cake.

"Mercy!" Stella says.

"I just made that this morning," Florrie remarks. She pushed the ironstone platter across the table so Stella can get a better look, but Stella scoots farther back in her chair. She can hear Chip coming down the stairs now, making a terrible racket, dragging something along behind him on his way.

"You want to know how I did it?" Florrie says. "I just thought it up today. What I did was, I made one big square cake, that's the middle of the leaf only you can't tell under all the icing, and a couple of little square cakes, and then I cut those all up to get the angles, see, for all the points of the leaves. Come here, honey," she says to Chip. "Let me blow your nose in this napkin. Now blow."

Stella looks away from them but there is no place for her to look in this kitchen, nothing her eye can light on without pain.

"Pretty!" Chip points at the cake. Chip is skinny, too small for his age, with thin light brown hair that sticks up on his head like straw.

"You should have seen what I made for his class," Florrie says to Stella. "It was back when they were doing their science projects about volcanos, and I made them a cake like Mount St. Helen's and took it over there and you should have seen them, they got the biggest kick out of it! Didn't you, Chip?"

"Va-ROOM!" Chip acts like a volcano. Then he falls down on the floor.

Florrie smiles down at him, then up at Stella. "Aren't you off early?" she asks.

"Well, yes, I am," Stella begins. "I certainly am. But as a matter of fact I came over here for a special reason, Florrie, there's something I wanted to talk to you about. If you could maybe—" Stella raises her eyebrows and looks hard at Chip.

"Why don't you go over there and play some Legos?" Florrie asks him, pointing.

"No," Chip says. He starts singing again in his high little voice.

"I bet you could make a submarine," Florrie says, "like you were telling me about."

"No," Chip says, kicking the floor, but then he looks up and says he might like to go outside.

"I thought he had a cold," Stella says.

"He does. But I guess one little bike ride wouldn't make it any worse than it is already. OK," Florrie tells Chip. "Go on. But I want you back here in fifteen minutes."

Chip gives a whoop and runs out the door without a jacket; it will be a wonder if he lives to grow up at all.

"Now then." Florrie folds her hands in her lap and yawns and looks at Stella. "What is it?"

"Well, I've been thinking," Stella says, "about you living over here in this big old house with not even any real relatives to speak of, living with strangers, and how this property is zoned commercial now and we could make a pretty penny if we went ahead and sold it while the real estate market is so high—"

"This is my house," Florrie interrupts.

"Well, I know it is," Stella says, "but it's just so much for you to try to keep up, and if you sold it and moved in with Claude and me, why we could pool all our resources so to speak and none of us would ever have to worry about a thing."

"*Moved in with Claude and you?*" For some reason Florrie is grinning and then she's laughing out loud. It gives Stella a chill to see her; she knows that her suspicions are all true and Florrie's gone mental at last.

"*Moved in with Claude and you?*" Florrie keeps saying this over and over, and laughing.

"Now this is serious," Stella tells her. "I don't see anything funny here at all. When I think of you over here with strangers—"

"They're not strangers," Florrie says. "Chip is my very own grandson as you very well know, and Johnnie Sue is Earl Junior's ex-wife."

"You might as well be running a boardinghouse!"

"Now there's an idea," Florrie says, and it's hard to tell from her face whether she's serious or not, the way her eyes are shining so blue and crinkling up like that at the corners. "I hadn't thought of a boardinghouse." She smiles.

"Oh Florrie!" Stella bursts out. "Don't you see? If you came to live with us you wouldn't have to make these ridiculous cakes and drag them all over town . . ."

"I like making cakes," Florrie says.

"Well, I know you do, but that's neither here nor there. The fact is, Florrie, and I might as well just tell you, the fact is you are going around here acting like a crazy old woman, whether you know it or not, and it's just real embarrassing for everybody in this family, and I'm telling you how you can stop. We can sell this house, you can come to live with us. You're just a spectacle of yourself, Florrie, whether you know it or not."

"Does Claude know you came over here to tell me this?"

"Claude!" Stella bristles. "What does Claude have to do with anything?" Then Stella squints through her frosted eyelids, and drums her long red nails on the kitchen table. "Oh! I get it!" she said. "You're still jealous, aren't you? And I came over here prepared to let bygones by bygones."

"What bygones?" Florrie's eyes are bright, bright blue, and she has a deep spot of color, like rouge, on each cheek. "What bygones?" she repeats.

"Well," Stella says, "I guess the dog is out of the bag now! I mean I know exactly how you feel. Don't you think for one minute I don't know. I know you are jealous of me and always have been. You are jealous of my position at

Belk's and my house and you resent our place in the community, mine and Claude's, and don't try to deny it. You always have. Don't try to tell me. I know you resent how Robert and Dawn Elizabeth have turned out so well, and all of that, but mainly I know you're still mad that you never got Claude in the first place, that Claude picked me over you."

"What?" Florrie says. "That Claude what?"

"You know what," Stella says.

Florrie sits looking at Stella for one long minute as the wind picks up again outside and rattles the kitchen window. Florrie looks at Stella with her mouth open, and then her mouth curves up and she's laughing, laughing to beat the band. "Lord, Stella!" Florrie is wiping her eyes.

Stella stands up and puts on her coat. "If that's how you feel about it," she says.

"I can't move over there," Florrie finally manages to say. "It would never work out, Stella, believe me." Then she's laughing again—it's clear just how mental she is.

Some people are beyond help. So Stella says, "Well," almost to herself. "Nobody can say I didn't try." This ought to give her some satisfaction, but it does not. She stands on one side of the table and Florrie stands on the other, with that crazy cake between them.

"Who'd you make *that* for, anyway?" Stella asks, jerking her head toward it.

"Why, nobody," Florrie tells her. "Just nobody at all."

Stella shakes her head.

"But you can have it if you want it," Florrie says. "Go on, take it, you and Claude can have it for dinner."

"What kind is it?"

"Carrot cake." Florrie picks up the ironstone platter like she's fixing to wrap it up.

"You know I can't touch roughage." Stella sighs, leaving, but Florrie follows her out to the car still holding that cake while Chip rides by on a bike that used to be Floyd's, trailing his high wordless song out behind him in the wind, and real leaves fall all around them. Stella doesn't doubt for one minute that if Johnny Sue and Chip don't cut a piece of that cake within the next few hours, Florrie will go right out in the street and give it to the very next person who happens along. Chip puts his feet up on the handlebars, and waves both hands in the air. Stella turns her collar up against the wind: the first signs of a woman's age may be found around her eyes, on her hands, and at her throat.

Stella gets in her car and decides to drive back over to Belk's for a little while, to put out her new Venetian Court Colors display beneath the twinkling lights of her beautiful chandelier; while Claude, out driving his boat around and around in big slow circles at Kerr Lake, doesn't even pretend to fish but stares back at the long smooth trail of the wake on the cold blue water, with a little smile on his face as he thinks of Florrie; and Florrie stands out in the patchy grass of her front yard with the leaf cake still cradled in her bare arms, admiring the way the sunlight shines off the icing, thinking about Earl Mingo and thinking too about Earl's child off someplace in this world, that child related to her by more than blood it seems to Florrie, that child maybe squinting out at the sky right now like Earl did, through God knows what color of eyes.

ALICE WALKER was born in 1944 in Eatonton, Georgia, the youngest of the eight children of a sharecropper father and a mother who would later become the radiant and powerful center of her daughter's story "Everyday Use" and the meditation-essay "In Search of Our Mothers' Gardens." As Walker has reminisced, "We were really not allowed to be discouraged. Discouragement couldn't hold out against her faith." During the sixties, Alice Walker attended Spelman College in Georgia, was graduated from Sarah Lawrence College in New York, and worked in the voter-registration and welfare-reform movements in Mississippi and New York.

Walker's published work includes the novel *The Color Purple*, which won the American Book Award and the Pulitzer Prize (1982) and two other novels, *The Third Life of Grange Copeland* and *Meridian*; two collections of short stories, *In Love & Trouble* and *You Can't Keep a Good Woman Down*; four volumes of poetry, *Once; Revolutionary Petunias; Good Night, Willie Lee, I'll See You in the Morning*; and *Horses Make a Landscape Look More Beautiful*; an earlier volume of essays, *In Search of Our Mothers' Gardens: Womanist Prose*; and a biography of Langston Hughes. She has also edited a Zora Neale Hurston reader. Her latest volume, *Living by the Word*, which includes excerpts from her journal during the years 1973–1987, takes its title from counsel she once received in a dream; it underscores her feeling that "I have come to understand my work as prayer."

The story that follows, "Kindred Spirits," a moving evocation of the solidarity that unites two sisters as well as different generations, received first prize in the annual O. Henry short story competition of 1986. It recalls Walker's thoughts about the black family, expressed to an interviewer when she published her first novel in 1970. "Family relationships are sacred. No amount of outside pressure and injustice must make us lose sight of that fact. . . . In the black family, love, cohesion, support, and concern are crucial since the racist society constantly acts to destroy the black individual, the black family unit, the black child. In America black people have only themselves and each other."

Kindred Spirits

by
Alice Walker

Rosa could not tell her sister how scared she was or how glad she was that she had consented to come with her. Instead they made small talk on the plane, and Rosa looked out of the window at the clouds.

It was a kind of sentimental journey for Rosa, months too late, going to visit the aunt in whose house their grandfather had died. She did not even know why she must do it: she had spent the earlier part of the summer in such far-flung places as Cyprus and Greece. Jamaica. She was at a place in her life where she seemed to have no place. She'd left the brownstone in Park Slope, given up the car and cat. Her child was at camp. She was in pain. That, at least, she knew. She hardly slept. If she did sleep, her dreams were cold, desolate, and full of static. She ate spaghetti, mostly, with shrimp, from a recipe cut out from the *Times*. She listened to the jazz radio station all the time, her heart in her mouth.

"So how is Ivan?" her sister, Barbara, asked.

Barbara was still fond of her brother-in-law, and hurt that after his divorce from Rosa he'd sunk back into the white world so completely that even a Christmas card was too much trouble to send people who had come to love him.

"Oh, fine," Rosa said. "Living with a nice Jewish girl, at last." Which might have explained the absence of a Christmas card, Rosa thought, but she knew it really didn't.

"Really? What's she like?"

"Warm. Attractive. Loves him."

This was mostly guesswork on Rosa's part; she'd met Sheila only once. She hoped she had these attributes, for his sake. A week after she'd moved out of the brownstone, Sheila had moved in, and all her in-laws, especially Ivan's mother, seemed very happy. Once Rosa had "borrowed" the car (her own, which she'd left with him), and when she returned it, mother and girlfriend met her at her own front gate, barring her way into her own house, their faces flushed with the victory of finally seeing her outside where she belonged. Music and laughter of many guests came from inside.

But did she care? No. She was free. She took to the sidewalk, the heels of her burgundy suede boots clicking, free. Her heart making itself still by force. *Ah*, but then at night when she slept, it awoke, and the clicking of her heels was nothing to the rattling and crackling of her heart.

"Mama misses him," said Barbara.

Rosa knew she did. How could she even begin to understand that this son-in-law she doted on was incapable, after divorcing her daughter, of even calling on the phone to ask how she felt, as she suffered stroke after frightening and debilitating stroke? It must have seemed totally unnatural to her, a woman who had rushed to comfort the sick and shut-in all her life. It seemed unnatural even to Rosa, who about most other things was able to take a somewhat more modern view.

At last they were in sight of the Miami airport. Before they could be prevented by the stewardess, Barbara and Rosa managed to exchange seats. Barbara sat by the window because she flew very rarely and it was a treat for her to "see herself" landing. Rosa no longer cared to look down. She had traveled so much that summer. The trip to Cyprus in particular had been so long it had made her want to scream. And then, in Nicosia, the weather was abominable. One hundred twenty degrees. It hurt to breathe. And there had been days of visiting Greeks in refugee camps and listening to socialists and visiting the home of a family in which an only son—standing next to a socialist leader at a rally—was assassinated by mistake. Though it had happened over a year earlier his father still wept as he told of it, and looked with great regret at his surviving daughter and *her* small daughter. "A man must have many sons," he said over and over, never seeming to realize that under conditions of war even a dozen sons could be killed. And not under war alone.

And then Rosa had flown to Greece, and Athens had been like New York City in late July and the Parthenon tiny. . . .

When they arrived at the Miami airport they looked about with the slightly anxious interest of travelers who still remembered segregated travel facilities. If a white person had materialized beside them and pointed out a colored section they would have attacked him or her on principle, but have been only somewhat surprised. Their formative years had been lived under racist restrictions so pervasive that wherever they traveled in the world they expected, on some level, in themselves and in whatever physical circumstances they found themselves, to encounter some, if only symbolic, racial barrier.

And there it was now: on a poster across from them a blond white woman and her dark-haired male partner danced under the stars while a black band played and a black waiter and a black chef beamed from the kitchen.

A striking woman, black as midnight, in a blue pastel cotton dress, tall, straight of bearing, with a firm bun of silver-white hair, bore down upon them.

It's me, thought Rosa. My old self.

"Aunt Lily!" said Barbara, smiling and throwing her arms around her.

When it was her turn to be hugged, Rosa gave herself up to it, enjoying the smells of baby shampoo, Jergens lotion, and Evening in Paris remembered from childhood embraces, which, on second sniff, she decided was all Charlie. That was this aunt, full of change and contradictions, as she had known her.

Not that she ever had, really. Aunt Lily had come to visit summers, when Rosa was a child. She had been straight and black and as vibrant as fire. She was always with her husband, whose tan face seemed weak next to hers. He drove the car, but she steered it; the same seemed true of their lives.

They had moved to Florida years ago, looking for a better life "somewhere else in the South that wasn't so full of southerners." Looking at her aunt now—with her imperial bearing, directness of speech, and great height—Rosa could not imagine anyone having the nerve to condescend to her, or worse, attempt to cheat her. Once again Rosa was amazed at the white man's arrogance and racist laws. Ten years earlier this sweet-smelling, squeaky-clean aunt of hers would not have been permitted to try on a dress in local department stores. She could not have drunk at certain fountains. The main restaurants of the city would have been closed to her. The public library. The vast majority of the city's toilets.

Aunt Lily had an enormous brown station wagon, into which Rosa and Barbara flung their light travel bags. Barbara, older than Rosa and closer to Aunt Lily, sat beside her on the front seat. Rosa sat behind them, looking out the window at the passing scenery, admiring the numerous canals—she was passionately fond of water—and yet wondering about the city's sewerage problems, of which she had heard.

How like them, really, she thought, to build canals around their pretty segregated houses—canals so polluted that to fall into one was to risk disease.

When they arrived at Aunt Lily's squat, green house, with its orange and lemon trees in the yard, far from canals and even streetlights, they were met in the narrow hall by five of her aunt's seven foster children and a young woman who had been a foster child herself but was now sharing the house and helping to look after the children with Aunt Lily. Her name was Raymyna Ann.

Aunt Lily had, a long time ago, a baby son who died. For years she had not seemed to care for children. Rosa had never felt particularly valued by her whenever Aunt Lily had come to visit. Aunt Lily acknowledged her brother's children by bringing them oranges and grapefruit packed in orange net bags, but she rarely hugged or kissed them. Well, she rarely touched these foster children, either, Rosa noticed. There were so many of them, so dark (all as black, precisely, as her aunt) and so woundedly silent. But at dinner the table was piled high with food, the little ones were encouraged to have seconds, and when they all trooped off to bed they did so in a cloud of soapy smells and dazzling linen.

Rosa lay in the tiny guest room, which had been her grandfather's room, and smoked a cigarette. Aunt Lily's face appeared at the door.

"Now, Rosa, I don't allow smoking or drinking in my house."

Rosa rose from the bed to put her cigarette out, her aunt watching her as if she were a child.

"*You* used to smoke and drink," Rosa said, piqued at her aunt's self-righteous tone.

"Your mama told you that lie," said Aunt Lily, unsmiling. "She was always trying to say I was fast. But I never did drink. I tried to, and it made me sick. Every time she said she didn't want me laying on her freshly made-up bed drunk, I wasn't drunk, I was sick."

"Oh," said Rosa. She had the unfortunate tendency of studying people very closely when they spoke. It occurred to her for the first time that Aunt Lily didn't like her mother.

But *why* didn't Aunt Lily like her mother? The question nagged at her that night as she tried to sleep, then became lost in the many other questions that presented themselves well into the dawn.

Why, for instance, did Ivan no longer like her? And how could you live with someone for over a decade and "love" them, and then, as soon as you were no longer married, you didn't even like them?

Her marriage had been wonderful, she felt. Only the divorce was horrible.

The most horrible thing of all was losing Ivan's friendship and comradely support, which he yanked out of her reach with a vengeance that sent her reeling. Two weeks after the divorce became final, when she was in the hospital for surgery that only after the fact proved to have been minor, he neither called nor sent a note. Sheila, now his wife, wouldn't have liked it, he later (years later) explained.

The next day all the children were in school, and Barbara stood behind Aunt Lily's chair combing and braiding her long silver hair. Rosa sat on the couch looking at them. Raymyna busily vacuumed the bedroom floors, popping in occasionally to bring the mail or a glass of water. She was getting married in a couple of weeks and would be moving out to start her own family. Rosa had of course not said anything when she heard this, but her inner response was surprise. She could not easily comprehend anyone getting married, now that she no longer was, but it was impossible for her to feel happy at the prospect of yet another poor black woman marrying God knows who and starting a family. She would have thought Raymyna would have already had enough.

But who was she to talk. Miss Cynical. She had married. And enjoyed it. She had had a child, and adored it.

In the afternoon her aunt and Raymyna took them sightseeing. As she understood matters from the local newspapers, all the water she saw—whether canal, river, or ocean—was polluted beyond recall, so that it was hard even to look at it, much less to look at it admiringly. She could only gaze at it in sympathy. The beach she also found pitiable. In their attempt to hog it away from the poor, the black, and the local in general, the beachfront "developers" had erected massive box-like hotels that blocked the view of the water for all except those rich enough to pay for rooms on the beach side of the hotels. Through the cracks between hotels Rosa saw the mostly elderly sun worshipers walking along what seemed to be a pebbly, eroded beach, stretching out their poor white necks to the sun.

Of course they cruised through Little Havana, which stretched for miles. Rosa looked at the new Cuban immigrants with interest. *Gusanos*, Fidel called them, "worms." She was startled to see that already they seemed as a group to live better and to have more material goods than the black people. Like many Americans who supported the Cuban revolution, she found the Cubans who left Cuba somewhat less noble than the ones who stayed. Clearly the ones who left were the ones with money. Hardly anyone in Cuba could afford the houses, the cars, the clothes, the television sets, and the lawn mowers she saw.

At dinner she tried to explain why and how she had missed her grandfather's funeral. The telegram had come the evening before she left for Cyprus. As she had left her stoop the next morning she had felt herself heading in the wrong direction. But she could not stop herself. It had taken all her meager energy to plan the trip to Cyprus, with a friend who claimed it was beautiful, and she simply could not think to change her plans. Nor could she, still bearing the wounds of her separation from Ivan, face her family.

Barbara and Aunt Lily listened to her patiently. It didn't surprise her that neither knew where Cyprus was, or what its politics and history were. She told them about the man whose son was killed and how he seemed to hate his "worthless" daughter for being alive.

"Women are not valued in their culture," she explained. "In fact, the Greeks, the Turks, and the Cypriots have this one thing in common, though they fight over everything else. The father kept saying, 'A man should have many sons.' His wife flinched guiltily when he said it."

"After Ma died, I went and got my father," Aunt Lily was saying. "And I told him, 'No smoking and drinking in my house.' "

But her grandfather had always smoked. He smoked a pipe. Rosa had liked the smell of it.

"And no card playing and no noise and no complaining, because I don't want to hear it."

Others of Rosa's brothers and sister had come to see him. She had been afraid to. In the pictures she saw, he always looked happy. When he was not dead-tired or drunk, happy was how he'd looked. A deeply silent man, with those odd peaceful eyes. She did not know, and she was confident her aunt didn't, what he really thought about anything. So he had stopped smoking, her aunt thought, but Rosa's brothers had always slipped him tobacco. He had stopped drinking. That was possible. Even before his wife, Rosa's grandmother, had died, he had given up liquor. Or, as he said, it had given him up. So, no noise. Little company. No complaining. But he wasn't the complaining type, was he? He liked best of all, Rosa thought, to be left alone. And he liked baseball. She felt he had liked her too. She hoped he did. But never did he say so. And he was so stingy! In her whole life he'd only given her fifteen cents. On the other hand, he'd financed her sister Barbara's trade-school education, which her father, his son, had refused to do.

Was that what she had held against him on the flight toward the Middle East? There was no excuse, she'd known it all the time. She needed to be back there, to say goodbye to the spiritcase. For wasn't she beginning to understand the appearance of his spiritcase as her own spirit struggled and suffered?

That night, massaging Barbara's thin shoulders before turning in, she looked into her own face reflected in the bureau mirror. She was beginning to have the look her grandfather had when he was very, very tired. The look he got just before something broke in him and he went on a mind-killing drunk. It was there in her eyes. So clearly. The look of abandonment. Of having no support. Of loneliness so severe every minute was a chant against self-destruction.

She massaged Barbara, but she knew her touch was that of a stranger. At what point, she wondered, did you lose connection with the people you loved? And she remembered going to visit Barbara when she was in college and Barbara lived a short bus ride away. And she was present when Barbara's husband beat her and called her names and once he had locked both of them out of the house overnight. And her sister called the police and they seemed nice to Rosa, so recently up from the South, but in fact they were bored and cynical as they listened to Barbara's familiar complaint. Rosa was embarrassed and couldn't believe anything so sordid could be happening to them, so respected was their family in the small town they were from. But, in any event, Barbara continued to live with her husband many more years. Rosa was so hurt and angry she wanted to kill, but most of all, she was disappointed in Barbara, who threw herself into the inevitable weekend battles with passionately vulgar language Rosa had never heard any woman, not to mention her gentle sister, use before. Her sister's spirit seemed polluted to her, so much so that the sister she had known as a child seemed gone altogether.

Was disappointment, then, the hardest thing to bear? Or was it the consciousness of being powerless to change things, to help? And certainly she had been very conscious of that. As her brother-in-law punched out her sister, Rosa had almost felt the blows on her body. But she had not flung herself between them wielding a butcher knife, as she had done once when Barbara was being attacked by their father, another raving madman.

Barbara had wanted to go to their brother's grammar-school graduation. Their father had insisted that she go to the funeral of an elderly church mother instead. Barbara had tried to refuse. But *crack*, he had slapped her across the face. She was sixteen, plump, and lovely. Rosa adored her. She ran immediately to get the knife, but she was so small no one seemed to notice her, wedging herself between them. But had she been larger and stronger she might have killed him, for even as a child she was serious in all she did—and then what would her life, the life of a murderer, have been like?

Thinking of that day now, she wept. At her love, at her sister's anguish.

Barbara had been forced to go to the funeral, the print of her father's fingers hidden by powder and rouge. Rosa had been little and weak, and she did not understand what was going on anyway between her father and her sister. To her, her father acted like he was jealous. And in college later, after such a long struggle to get there, how could she stab her brother-in-law to death without killing her future, herself? And so she had lain on her narrow foldaway cot in the tiny kitchen in the stuffy apartment over the Laundromat and had listened to the cries and whispers, the pummelings, the screams and pleas. And then, still awake, she listened to the sibilant sounds of "making up," harder to bear and to understand than the fights.

She had not killed for her sister. (And one would have had to kill the mindless drunken brutalizing husband; a blow to the head might only have made him more angry.) Her guilt had soon clouded over the love, and around Barbara she retreated into a silence that she now realized was very like her grandfather's. The sign in him of disappointment hinged to powerlessness. A thoughtful black man in the racist early-twentieth-century South, he probably could have told her a thing or two about the squeaking of the hinge. But had he? No. He'd only complained about his wife, and so convincingly that for a time Rosa, like everyone else in the family, lost respect for her grandmother. It seemed her problem was that she was not mentally quick; and because she stayed with him even as he said this, Rosa and her relatives were quick to agree. Yet there was nowhere else she could have gone. Perhaps her grandfather had found the house in which they lived, but she, her grandmother, had made it a home. Once the grandmother died, the house seemed empty, though he remained behind until Aunt Lily had moved him into her house in Miami.

The day before Rosa and Barbara were to fly back north, Aunt Lily was handing out the remaining odds and ends of their grandfather's things. Barbara got the trunk, that magic repository of tobacco and candy when they were children.

Rosa received a small shaving mirror with a gilt lion on its back. There were several of the large, white "twenty-five-cent hanskers" her grandfather had used. The grand-daughters received half a dozen each. That left only her grandfather's hats. One brown and one gray: old, worn, none-too-clean fedoras. Rosa knew Barbara was far too fastidious to want them. She placed one on her head. She loved how she looked—she looked like him—in it.

It was killing her, how much she loved him. And he'd been so mean to her grandmother, and so stingy too. Once he had locked her grandmother out of the house because she had bought herself a penny stick of candy from the grocery money. But this was a story her parents told her, from a time before Rosa was born.

By the time she knew him he was mostly beautiful. Peaceful, mystical almost, in his silences and calm, and she realized he was imprinted on her heart just that way. It really did not seem fair.

To check her tears, she turned to Aunt Lily.

"Tell me what my father was like as a boy," she said.

Her aunt looked at her, she felt, with hatred.

"You should have asked him when he was alive."

Rosa looked about for Barbara, who had disappeared into the bathroom. By now she was weeping openly. Her aunt looking at her impassively.

"I don't want to find myself in anything you write. And you can just leave your daddy alone, too."

She could not remember whether she'd ever asked her father about his life. But surely she had, since she knew quite a lot. She turned and walked into the bathroom, forgetful that she was thirty-five, her sister forty-one, and that you can only walk in on your sister in the toilet if you are both children. But it didn't matter. Barbara had always been accessible, always protective. Rosa remembered one afternoon when she was five or six, she and Barbara and a cousin of theirs about Barbara's age set out on an errand. They were walking silently down the dusty road when a large car driven by a white man nearly ran them down. His car sent up billows of dust from the dirt road that stung their eyes and stained their clothes. Instinctively Rosa had picked up a fistful of sand from the road and thrown it after him. He stopped the car, backed it up furiously, and slammed on the brakes, getting out next to them, three black, barefoot girls who looked at him as only they could. Was he a human being? Or a devil? At any rate, he had seen Rosa throw the sand, he said, and he wanted the older girls to warn her against doing such things, "for the little nigger's own good."

Rosa would have admitted throwing the sand. After all, the man had seen her.

But "she didn't throw no sand," said Barbara, quietly, striking a heavy, womanish pose with both hands on her hips.

"She did so," said the man, his face red from heat and anger.

"She didn't," said Barbara.

The cousin simply stared at the man. After all, what was a small handful of sand compared to the billows of sand with which he'd covered them?

Cursing, the man stomped into his car, and drove off.

For a long time it had seemed to Rosa that only black people were always in danger. But there was also the sense that her big sister would know how to help them out of it.

But now, as her sister sat on the commode, Rosa saw a look on her face that she had never seen before, and she realized her sister had heard what Aunt Lily said. It was a look that said she'd got the reply she deserved. For wasn't she always snooping about the family's business and turning things about in her writing in ways that made the family shudder? There was no talking to her as you talked to regular people. The minute you opened your mouth a meter went on. Rosa could read all this on her sister's face. She didn't need to speak. And it was a lonely feeling that she had. For Barbara was right. Aunt Lily, too. And she could no more stop the meter running than she could stop her breath. An odd look across the room fifteen years ago still held the power to make her wonder about it, try to "decipher" or at least understand it. This was her curse: never to be able to forget, truly, but only to appear to forget. And then to record what she could not forget.

Suddenly, in her loneliness, she laughed.

"He was a recorder with his eyes," she said, under her breath. For it seemed to her she'd penetrated her grandfather's serenity, his frequent silences. The meter had ticked in him, too; he, too, was all attentiveness. But for him that had had to be enough. She'd rarely seen him with a pencil in his hand; she thought he'd only had one or two years of school. She imagined him "writing" stories during his long silences merely by thinking them, not embarrassing other people with them, as she did.

She had been obsessed by this old man whom she so definitely resembled. And now, perhaps, she knew why.

We were kindred spirits, she thought, as she sat, one old dusty fedora on her head, the other in her lap, on the plane home. But in a lot of ways, before I knew him, he was a jerk.

She thought of Ivan. For it was something both of them had said often about their relationship: that though he was white and she was black, they were in fact kindred spirits. And she had thought so, until the divorce, after which his spirit became as unfathomable to her as her grandfather's would have been before she knew him. But perhaps Ivan, too, was simply acting like a jerk?

She felt, as she munched the dry crackers and cheese the pert stewardess brought, in the very wreckage of her life. She had not really looked at Barbara since that moment in the toilet, when it became clear to her how her sister really perceived her. She knew she would not see Aunt Lily again and that if Aunt Lily died before she herself did, she would not go to her funeral. Nor would she ever, ever write about her. She took a huge swallow of ginger ale and tried to drown out the incessant ticking of the meter.

She stroked the soft felt of her grandfather's hat, thought of how peculiarly the human brain grows, from an almost invisible seed, and how, in this respect, it was rather similar to understanding, a process it engendered. She looked into her grandfather's shaving mirror and her eyes told her she could bear very little more. She felt herself begin to slide into the long silence in which such thoughts would be her sole companions. Maybe she would even find happiness there.

But then, just when she was almost gone, Barbara put on their grandfather's other hat and reached for her hand.

JOY WILLIAMS was born in Chelmsford, Massachusetts, in 1944. She was educated at Marietta College and the State University of Iowa and has received a number of academic and writing awards including membership in Phi Beta Kappa, a National Endowment for the Arts grant, a Wallace Stegner fellowship at Stanford University, and a Guggenheim fellowship. She has published three novels, *State of Grace, The Changeling*, and *Breaking and Entering*. Her short fiction has been included in the *1966 O. Henry Prize Stories,* in *Secret Lives of Our Time,* edited by Gordon Lish, and in *The Best American Short Stories of 1978,* edited by Theodore Solotaroff. Her volume of short stories, *Taking Care* (1982), in which "Traveling to Pridesup" appears, was praised as a work of consistent percipience and wit. James Salter wrote of this collection that the "stories are like no one else's . . . They gallop over the foolish surface of a world that cannot be made right. . . . Like Eudora Welty, like Margaret Atwood, like Flannery O'Connor, she makes you long to be a writer." "She catches, better than anyone writing today, the ominous vision at the corner of the eye, and makes it inevitable," observed Mary Lee Settle. And, finally, in the words of Ann Beattie: "She is one of our most remarkable storytellers, and this is a first-rate collection."

Traveling to Pridesup

by

Joy Williams

Otilla cooked up the water for her morning tea and opened a carton of ricotta cheese. She ate standing up, dipping cookies in and out of the cheese, walking around the enormous kitchen in tight figure eights as though she were in a gymkhana. She was eighty-one years old and childishly ravenous and hopeful with a long pigtail and a friendly unreasonable nature.

She lived with her sisters in a big house in the middle of the state of Florida. There were three of them, all older and wiser. They were educated in Northern schools and came back with queer ideas. Lavinia, the eldest, returned after four years, with a rock, off of a mountain, out of some forest. It was covered with lichen and green like a plum. Lavinia put it to the north of the seedlings on the shadowy side of the house. She tore up the grass and burnt out the salamanders and the ants and raked the sand out all around the rock in a pattern like a machine would make. The sisters watched the rock on and off for forty years until one morning when they were all out in their Mercedes automobile, taking the air, a sinkhole opened up and took the rock and half the garage down thirty-seven feet. It didn't seem to matter to Lavinia, who had cared for the thing. Growing rocks, she said, was supposed to bring one serenity and put one on terms with oneself and she had become serene so she didn't care. Otilla believed that such an idea could only come from a foreign religion, but she could only guess at this as no one ever told her anything except her father, and he had died long ago from drink. He was handsome and rich, having made his money in railways and grapefruit. Otilla was his darling. She still had the tumbler he was drinking rum from when he died. None of father's girls had ever married, and Otilla, who was thought to be a little slow, had not even gone off to school.

Otilla ate a deviled egg and some ice cream and drank another cup of tea. She wore sneakers and a brand new dress that still had the cardboard pinned beneath the collar. The dress had come in the mail the day before along with a plastic soap dish and three rubber pedal pads for the Mercedes. The sisters ordered everything through catalogs and seldom went to town. Upstairs, Otilla could hear them moving about.

"Louisa," Marjorie said, "this soap dish works beautifully."

Otilla moved to a wicker chair by the window and sat on her long pigtail. She turned off the light and turned on the fan. It was just after sunrise, the lakes all along the Ridge were smoking with heat. She could see bass shaking the surface of the water and she felt a brief and eager joy at the sight—at the morning and the mist running off the lakes and the birds rising up from the shaggy orange trees. The joy didn't come often any more and it didn't last long and when it passed it seemed more a part of dying than delight. She didn't dwell on this however. For the most part, she found that as long as one commenced to get up in the morning and move one's bowels, everything else moved along without confusing variation.

From the window, she could also see the mailbox. The flag was up and there was a package swinging from it. She couldn't understand why the mailman hadn't put the package inside. It was a large sturdy mailbox and would hold anything.

She got up and walked quickly outside, hoping that Lavinia wouldn't see her, as Lavinia preferred picking up the mail herself. She passed the black Mercedes. The garage had never been rebuilt and the car had been parked for years between two oak trees. There was a quilt over the hood. Every night, Lavinia would pull a wire out of the distributor and bring it into the house. The next morning she would put the wire back in again, warm up the Mercedes and drive it twice around the circular driveway and then down a slope one hundred yards to the mailbox. They only received things that they ordered. The Mercedes was fifteen years old and had eleven thousand miles on it. Lavinia kept the car up. She was clever at it.

"This vehicle will run forever because I've taken good care of it," she'd say.

Otilla stood beside the mailbox looking north up the road and then south. She had good eyesight but there wasn't a thing to be seen. Hanging in a feed bag off the mailbox was a sleeping baby. It wore a little yellow T-shirt with a rabbit on it. The rabbit appeared to be playing a fiddle. The baby had black hair and big ears and was making small grunts and whistles in its sleep. Otilla wiped her hands on the bodice of her dress and picked the baby out of the sack. It smelled faintly of ashes and fruit.

Inside the house, the three sisters, Lavinia, Louisa and Marjorie were setting out the breakfast things. They were ninety-two, ninety and eighty-seven respectively. They were in excellent color and health and didn't look much over seventy. Each morning they'd set up the table as though they were expecting the Governor himself—good silver, best china, egg cups and bun cozy.

They settled themselves. The fan was painted with blue rustproof paint and turned right on around itself like an owl. The soft-boiled eggs wobbled when the breeze ran by them.

"Going to be a hot one," Lavinia said.

The young sisters nodded yes, chewing on their toast.

"The summer's just begun and it appears it's never going to end," Lavinia said.

The sisters shook their heads yes. The sky was getting brighter and brighter. The three of them, along with Otilla, had lived together forever. They weren't looking at the sky or the empty groves which they had seen before. The light was changing very fast, progressing visibly over the table top. It fell on the butter.

"They've been tampering with the atmosphere," Lavinia said. "They don't have the sense to leave things alone." Lavinia was a strong-willed, impatient woman. She thought about what she had just said and threw her spoon down irritably at the truth of it. Lavinia was no longer serene about anything. That presumption had been for her youth, when she had time. Now everything was pesky to her and a hindrance.

"Good morning," Otilla said. She walked to the wicker chair and sat down. The baby lay in her arms, short and squat like a loaf of bread.

Lavinia's eyes didn't change, nor her mouth nor the set of her jaw. Outside some mockingbirds were ranting. The day had gotten so bright it was as if someone had just shot it off in her face.

"Put it back where you got it," she said slowly.

"I can't imagine where this baby's from," Otilla said.

The baby's eyes were open now and were locked on the old woman's face. Lavinia spoke in a low, furious voice. "Go on out with it, Otilla." She raised her fingers distractedly, waving at the baby as though greeting an old friend.

Otilla picked the baby up and held it out away from her and looked cheerfully at it. "You're wetting."

"My God," Marjorie said, noticing the affair for the first time.

Otilla shook the baby up and down. Her arms were skinny and pale and they trembled a bit with the weight. The baby opened its mouth and smiled noiselessly. "You're hollow inside," Otilla said. "Hollow as a bamboo. Bam Boo To You Kangaroo." She joggled the baby whose face was static and distant with delight. "Bamboo shampoo. Bamboo cockatoo stew."

"My God," Marjorie said. She and Louisa got up and scraped off their plates and rinsed them in the sink. They went into the front room and sat on the sofa.

Otilla held the baby a little awkwardly. Its head flopped back like a flower in the wind when she got up. She had never touched a baby before and she had never thought about them either. She went to the drainboard and laid the baby down and unpinned its diaper. "Isn't that cute, Lavinia, it's a little boy."

"You are becoming senile," Lavinia said. Her fingers were still twitching in the air. She wrapped them in her napkin.

"I didn't make him up. Someone left him here, hanging off the postbox."

"Senile," Lavinia repeated. "Who knows where this baby has been? You shouldn't even be touching him. Perhaps you are just being 'set up' and we will all be arrested by the sheriff."

Otilla folded a clean dishtowel beneath the baby and pinned it together. She took the dirty diaper and scrubbed it out in the sink with a bar of almond soap and then took it outside and hung it on the clothesline. When she came back into the kitchen, she picked the baby off the drainboard and went back to her chair by the window. "Now isn't that nice, Lavinia?" She didn't want to talk but she was so nervous that she couldn't help herself. "I think they should make diapers in bright colors. Orange and blue and green. . . . Deep bright colors for a little boy. Wouldn't that be nice, Lavinia?"

"The dye would seep into their skin and kill them," Lavinia said brusquely. "They'd suffocate like a painted Easter chick."

Otilla was shocked.

"You accept things too easily, Otilla. You have always been a dope. Even as a child, you took anything anyone chose to give you." She got up and took the distributor wire of the Mercedes out of the silverware tray. She clumped down the steps to the automobile, banging the screen door behind her. A spider dropped from the ceiling and fell with a snap on the stove. Otilla heard the engine turn over and drop into idle. The screen door banged again and Lavinia was shouting into the darkened living room.

"We are going in town to the authorities and will be back directly."

There was a pause in which Otilla couldn't hear a thing. Her arm was going to sleep. She shifted the baby about on her lap, banging his head against her knee bone. The baby opened his mouth but not his eyes and gummed on the sleeve of his shirt. "Excuse me," she whispered.

"No, no," Lavinia shouted at the living room. "I can't imagine how it happened either. Someone on their way somewhere. Long gone now. Pickers, migrants."

She came back into the kitchen, pulling on a pair of black ventilated driving gloves. Lavinia was very serious about the Mercedes. She drove slowly and steadily and not particularly well, looking at the dials and needles for signs of malfunction. The reason for riding was in the traveling, she always said, for the sisters never had the need to be anyplace. Getting there was not the object. Arrival was not the point. The car was elegant and disheartening and suited to this use.

"Where are we going?" Otilla asked meekly.

"Where are we going," Lavinia mimicked in a breathless drawl that was not at all like Otilla's voice. Then she said normally, "We are going to drop this infant off in Pridesup.

I am attempting not to become annoyed but you are very annoying and this is a very annoying situation."

"I think I would like to keep this baby," Otilla said. "I figure we might as well." The baby was warm and its heart was beating twice as fast as any heart she had ever heard as though it couldn't wait to get on with its living.

Lavinia walked over to her sister and gave her a yank.

"I could teach him to drink from a cup," Otilla said, close to tears. "They learn how to do that. When he got older he could mow the lawn and spray the midge and club-gall." She was on her feet now and was being pushed outside. She put out her free hand and jammed it against the door frame. "I have to get some things together, then, please Lavinia. It's twenty miles to Pridesup. Just let me get a few little things together so that he won't go off with nothing." Her chin was shaking. She was hanging fiercely onto the door and squinting out into the sunlight, down past the rumbling Mercedes into the pit where the rock had fallen and where the seedlings, still rooted, bloomed in the spring. She felt a little fuddled. It seemed that her head was down in the cool sinkhole while the rest of her wobbled in the heat. She jammed the baby so close to her that he squealed.

"I can't imagine what you're going to equip him with," Lavinia was saying. "He can't be more than a few months old. We don't have anything for that." She had stopped pushing her sister and was looking at the car, trying to remember the route to Pridesup, the county seat. It had been five years since she had driven there. Somewhere, on the left, she recollected a concentrate canning factory. Somewhere, also, there was a gas station in the stomach of a concrete dinosaur. She remembered stopping. Otilla had used the rest room and they had all bought cold barbeque. No one ever bought his gasoline, the owner said. They bought his snacks and bait and bedspreads. Lavinia had not bought his gasoline either. She doubted if the place was there now. It didn't look as though it had five years left in it.

"Oh just a little apple juice and a toy or something."

"Well, get it then," Lavinia snapped. She couldn't remember if she took a right or a left upon leaving the driveway; if she kept Cowpen Slough on her west side or her east side. The countryside looked oddly without depth and she had difficulty imagining herself driving off into it. She went into a small bathroom off the kitchen and took off her gloves and rinsed her face, then she went out to the Mercedes. She sat behind the wheel and removed some old state maps from the car's side pocket. They were confusing, full of blank spaces. Printed on the bottom of the first one were the words *Red And Blue Roads Are Equally Good*. She refolded them, fanned herself with them and put them on the seat.

Otilla got into the car with the baby and a paper bag. The baby's head was very large compared to the rest of him. It looked disabling and vulnerable. Lavinia couldn't understand how anything could start out being that ugly and said so. His ears looked like two Parker rolls. She moved the car down the drive and unhesitatingly off onto the blacktop. They drove in silence for a few minutes. It was hot and green out with a smell of sugar on the air.

"Well," Otilla said, "it doesn't seem as though he wants anything yet."

Lavinia wore a pair of enormous black sunglasses. She drove and didn't say anything.

"Look out the window here at that grey and black horse," Otilla said. She lifted the baby up. He clawed at her chin with his hand. "Look out thataway at those sandhill cranes. They're just like storks. Maybe they're the ones that dropped you off at our house."

"Oh shut up. You'll addle the little bit of brain he has," Lavinia yelled.

"It's just a manner of speaking, Lavinia. We both know it isn't so." She opened the bag and took out a piece of bread and began to eat it. The baby pushed his hand into the bread and Otilla broke off a piece of crust and gave it to him. He gnawed on it intently without diminishing it. In the bag, Otilla had a loaf of bread, a can of Coca-Cola and a jar of milk. "I couldn't find a single toy for him," she said.

"He'll have to do with the scenery," Lavinia said. She herself had never cared for it. It had been there too long and she had been too long in it and now it seemed like an external cataract obstructing her real vision.

"Lookit those water hyacinths," Otilla went on. "Lookit that piece of moon still up there in the sky."

Lavinia gritted her teeth. There had not been a single trip

they had taken that Otilla had not spoiled. She talked too much and squirmed too much and always brought along food that she spilled. The last time they had driven down this road, she had had a dish of ice cream that had been squashed against the dashboard when the car had gone over a bump. Lavinia braked suddenly and turned the Mercedes into a dirt side road that dropped like a tunnel through an orange grove. She backed up and reversed her direction.

"Where are we going now, Lavinia?"

"We're going to the same place," she said angrily. "This is simply a more direct route." The baby burped softly. They passed the house again, planted white and well-to-do in the sunlight. Embarrassed, neither of them looked at it or remarked upon it.

"I think," Otilla said formally, "that we are both accepting this very well and that you are handling it OK except that I think we could have kept this baby for at least a little while until we read in the paper perhaps that someone is missing him."

"No one is going to be missing him."

"You're a little darlin'," Otilla said to the baby, who was hunched over his bread crust.

"Please stop handling him. He might very well have worms or meningitis or worse." The Mercedes was rocketing down the middle of the road through hordes of colorful bugs. Lavinia had never driven this fast. She took her foot off the accelerator and the car mannerly slowed. Lavinia was hot all over. Every decision she had made so far today seemed proper but oddly irrelevant. If she had gone down to the mailbox first as she had always done, there would have been no baby to find. She was sure of that. The problem was that the day had started out being Otilla's and not hers at all. She gave a short nervous bark and looked at the baby who was swaying on her sister's lap. "I imagine he hasn't had a single shot."

"He looks fine to me, Lavinia. He has bright eyes and he seems clean and cool enough."

Lavinia tugged at the wheel as though correcting a personal injustice rather than the car's direction. "It's no concern to us what he's got anyway. It's the law's problem. It's for the orphanage to attend to."

"Orphanage? You shouldn't take him there. He's not an

orphan, he has us." She looked at the pale brown veins running off the baby's head and faintly down his cheeks.

"He doesn't have us at all," Lavinia shouted. She started to gag and gripped her throat with her left hand, giving it little pinches and tugs to keep the sickness down. There had never been a thing she'd done that hadn't agreed with her and traveling had always been a pleasure, but the baby beside her had a strong pervasive smell that seemed to be the smell of the land as well, and it made her sick. She felt as though she were falling into a pan of bright and bubbling food. She took several breaths and said more calmly, "There is no way we could keep him. You must use your head. We have not had the training and we are all getting on and what would happen is that we would die and he'd be left." She was being generous and conversational and instructive and she hoped that Otilla would appreciate this and benefit from it even though she knew her sister was weakheaded and never benefited from things in the proper way.

"But that's the way it's going to be anyway, Lavinia."

The air paddled in Lavinia's ears. The Mercedes wandered on and off the dusty shoulder. The land was empty and there wasn't anything coming toward them or going away except a bright tin can which they straddled. "Of course it is," she said. "You've missed the point."

Lavinia had never cared for Otilla. She realized that this was due mostly to preconception, as it were, for she had been present at the awful moment of birth and she knew before her sister had taken her first breath that she'd be useless. And she had been. The only thing Otilla ever had was prettiness and she had that still, lacking the sense to let it go, her girlish features still moving around indecently in her old woman's face. Sitting there now in a messy nest of bread crusts and obscure stains with the baby playing with her dress buttons, Otilla looked queerly confident and enthusiastic as though at last she were going off on her wedding day. It disgusted Lavinia. There was something unseasonal about Otilla. If she had been a man, Lavinia thought, they might very well have had a problem on their hands.

Otilla noisily shook out one of the road maps. Down one side of it was a colorful insert with tiny pictures of attractions—fish denoting streams, and women in bathing suits, and llamas representing zoos and clocks marking historical societies. All no bigger than a thumbnail. "Why this is just charming," Otilla said. "Here we have a pictorial guide." The baby looked at it grimly and something fell runny from his mouth onto a minute pink blimp. "This is the first time we have had a real destination, Lavinia. Perhaps we can see these things as well." She rested her chin on the baby's head and read aloud, " 'Route S40 through the Pine Barrens. Be sure to see the *Produce Auction, Elephant House, State Yacht Basin Marine View Old Dutch Parsonage Pacing Racing Oxford Furnace Ruins*.' Why just look at all these things," she said into the infant's hair. "This is *very* helpful."

The two regarded the map carefully. "See this," Otilla said excitedly, pointing to a tiny ancient-looking baby with a gold crown on his head. "*Baby Parade. August*. That's for us!" Then she fell silent and after a few miles she turned to Lavinia and said, "This is not for our region at all. This is for the state of New Jersey."

Lavinia was concentrating on a row of garish signs advertising a pecan shop. She'd been seeing them for the last half hour. *Free Ice Water* one said *Lettus Fill Your Jug. Neat Nuts* one said. *Ham Sandwiches Frozen Custard Live Turtles*. She thought she'd stop and discreetly ask the way to Pridesup. *Pecan Clusters Pecan Logs Pecan Pie Don't Miss Us!*

Otilla was picking through the remaining maps when the baby tipped off her lap and into Lavinia's side. Lavinia stomped on the brakes and beat at him with her hand. "Get away," she shrieked, "you'll break my hip!" She tried to pull her waist in from the weight of his head. His smell was sweet, fertile, like an anesthetic, and she felt frightened as though someone had just removed something from her in a swift neat operation. She saw the dust motes settling like balloons upon the leather dashboard and white thread tangled in the baby's fingers. *Slow Down You're Almost There Only 2000 Yds*. The baby's face was wrinkling her linen and his hand was fastened around the bottom of the steering wheel.

"Lavinia, you'll frighten him," Otilla said, pulling the baby back across the seat. She arranged him in her lap again and he instantly fell asleep. The Mercedes was almost at a standstill. Lavinia pressed on the gas and the car labored forward, out of gear, past an empty burnt-out shack. *Six*

Lbs For $1 Free Slushies For the Kiddies. The door to the place was lying in the weeds.

"That's all right, that's all right," Lavinia said. She took off her sunglasses and rubbed the bridge of her nose. The fingers of her gloves were wet. The engine was skipping, the tachometer needle fluttered on 0. She stopped the car completely, shifted into first and resumed. *You've Gone Too Far!* a sign said. She felt like spitting at it. Otilla had fallen asleep now too, her head slightly out the window, her small mouth shining in the side-view mirror. Lavinia picked up a piece of bread, folded it into an empty sandwich and ate it.

When Otilla woke, it was almost dark. The baby had his fingers jammed into his mouth and sucked on them loudly. Otilla unscrewed the top of the mason jar and pushed the lip toward him. He took it eagerly, sucking. Then he chewed, then he lapped. Enough drops went down his throat for him to think it was worthwhile to continue. He settled down to eating the milk that was slapping his cheeks and sliding down his chin back into the jar.

They were on a narrow soft road just wide enough for the car. Close on either side were rows and rows of orange trees, all different shades of darkness in the twilight.

"It's like riding through the parted waters, Lavinia."

Her sister's voice startled her and Lavinia gave a little jump. Her stylish dress was askew and her large faded eyes were watering.

"You woke up to say an asinine thing like that!" she exclaimed. All the while Otilla and the infant had been sleeping, she had driven with an empty mind and eye. She had truly not been thinking of a thing, and though she was lost and indignant and frustrated she did not feel this. She had driven, and the instructions she had received cautiously from the few people she had seen she wrote down on the back of a pocket calendar. When she left the people, they became bystanders, not to be trusted, and she drove on without reference. And the only sounds she heard were the gentle snappings somewhere in her head of small important truths that she had got along with for years—breaking.

She had not looked at the car's equipment, at its dials and numbers for a long time because when she had last done so, the odometer showed her that they had driven 157 miles.

"How long have we been traveling, Lavinia?"

"I don't know." She remembered that when she had bought the Mercedes, the engine had shone like her silver service. She remembered that there had been one mile on the odometer then. Sitting in the showroom on a green carpet, her automobile had one mile on it and she had been furious. No one could tell her why this was. No one could explain it to her satisfaction.

"Well," Otilla said, "I suppose Louisa and Marjorie have eaten by now." She looked out the window. A white bird was hurrying off through the groves. "This is an awfully good baby," she said, "waiting so long and being so patient for his meal. And this being not the way he's accustomed to getting it besides." She looked behind her. "My, they certainly make these roads straight. It seems like if we had intended to, we could be halfway to New Jersey by now, on our way to seeing all those interesting things. We could stay in a New Jersey motel, Lavinia, and give the baby a nice bath and send out for supper and I've even heard that some of those motels are connected with drive-in theaters and we could see a film directly from our room."

The soft sand tugged at the car's wheels. The stars came out and Lavinia pulled on the headlights.

"Lavinia," Otilla said softly. "I have twelve hundred dollars sitting in the teeth of my mouth alone. I am a wealthy woman though not as wealthy as you and if you want to get there, I don't understand why we just don't stop as soon as we see someone and hire us a car to Pridesup."

"I have no respect for you at all," Lavinia said.

Otilla paused. She ran her fingers over the baby's head, feeling the slight springy depression in his skull where he was still growing together. She could hear him swallowing. A big moth blundered against her face and then fell back into the night. "If you would just stop for a moment," she said brightly, "I could change the baby and freshen up the air in here a bit."

"You don't seem to realize that I know all about you, Otilla. There is nothing you could ever say to me about anything. I happen to know that you were born too early and mother had you in a chamber pot. So just shut up Otilla." She turned to her sister and smiled. Otilla's head was bowed and Lavinia poked her to make sure that she was paying attention. "I have wanted to let you know about that for a long long time so just don't say another word to me, Otilla."

The Mercedes bottomed out on the sand, swerved and dropped into the ditch, the grille half-submerged in muddy water and the left rear wheel spinning in the air. Lavinia still was steering and smiling and looking at her sister. The engine died and the lights went out and for an instant they all sat speechless and motionless as though they were parts of a profound photograph that was still in the process of being taken. Then the baby gagged and Otilla began thumping him on the back.

Lavinia had loved her car. The engine crackled and hissed as it cooled. The windshield had a long crack in it and there was a smell of gasoline. She turned off the ignition.

Lavinia had loved her car and now it was broken to bits. She didn't know what to think. She opened the door and climbed out onto the road where she lay down in the dust. In the middle of the night, she got back into the car because the mosquitoes were so bad. Otilla and the baby were stretched out in the back so Lavinia sat in the driver's seat once more, where she slept.

In the morning, they ate the rest of the bread and Otilla gave the baby the last of the milk. The milk had gone sour and he spit most of it up. Otilla waded through the ditch and set the baby in a field box beneath an orange tree. The fruit had all been picked a month ago and the groves were thick and overgrown. It was hard for Otilla to clear out a place for them to rest. She tried to fan the mosquitoes away from the baby's face but by noon the swarms had gotten so large and the bugs so fat and lazy that she had to pick them off individually with her fingers. Lavinia stayed in the Mercedes until she felt fried, then she limped across the road. The sun seemed waxed in the same position but she knew the day was going by. The baby had cried hard for an hour or so and then began a fitful wail that went on into the afternoon.

Every once in awhile, Lavinia saw Otilla rise and move feverishly through the trees. The baby's weeping mingled with the rattle of insects and with Otilla's singsong so that it seemed to Lavinia, when she closed her eyes, that there was a healthy community working out around her and including her in its life. But when she looked there was only green bareness and an armadillo plodding through the dust, swinging its outrageous head.

Lavinia went to the Mercedes and picked up the can of Coca-Cola, but she couldn't find an opener. The can burnt in her hand and she dropped it. As she was getting out of the car, she saw Otilla walk out of the grove. She stopped and watched her shuffle up the road. She was unfamiliar, a mystery, an event. There was a small soiled bundle on her shoulder. Lavinia couldn't place the circumstances. She watched and wrung her hands. Otilla swerved off into the grove again and disappeared.

Lavinia followed her giddily. She walked hunched, on tip-toe. When she came upon Otilla, she remained stealthily bent, her skirt still wadded in her hand for silence. Otilla lay on her back in the sand with the baby beside her, his bug-bitten eyelids squeezed against a patch of sky that was shining on them both. The baby's mouth was moving and his arms and legs were waving in the air to some mysterious beat but Otilla lay motionless as a stick. Lavinia was disgusted to see that the top of Otilla's dress was unbuttoned, exposing her grey stringy breasts. She picked up a handful of sand and tried to cover up her chest.

The baby's diaper was heavy with filth. She took it off and wiped it as best she could on the weeds and then pinned it around him again. She picked him up, holding him carefully away from her, and walked to the road. He was ticking from someplace deep inside himself. The noise was deafening. The noises that had seemed to be going on in her own head earlier had stopped. When she got to the car, she laid him under it, where it was cool. She herself stood up straight to get a breath, and down the road saw a yellow ball of dust rolling toward her at great speed. The ball of dust stopped alongside and a young man in faded jeans and shirt, holding a bottle of beer, got out and stared at her. Around his waist he wore a wide belt hanging with pliers and hammers and cords.

"Jeez," he said. He was a telephone lineman going home for dinner, taking a shortcut through the groves. The old lady he saw looked as though she had come out of some Arabian desert. She had cracked lips and puffy eyes and burnt skin. He walked toward her with his hand stretched out, but she turned away and to his astonishment, bent down and scrabbled a baby up from beneath the wrecked car. Then she walked past him and clambered into the cab of his truck by herself and slammed the door.

The young man jumped into the truck and smiled nervously at Lavinia. "I don't have nothing," he said excitedly, "but a chocolate bar, but there's a clinic no more'n ten miles away, if you could just hold on until then. Please," he said desperately. "Do you suppose you want this?" he asked, holding out the bottle of beer.

Lavinia nodded. She took the chocolate and put it in the baby's fist. He cried and pushed it toward his mouth and moved his mouth around it and cried. Lavinia pressed the cool bottle of beer against her face, then rolled it back and forth across her forehead.

The truck roared through the groves and in an instant, it seemed, they were out on the highway, passing a sign that said WORSHIP IN PRIDESUP, 11 MILES. Beyond the sign was a field with a carnival in it. Lavinia could hear the sweet cheap music of the midway and the shrieks of people on the Ferris wheel. Then the carnival fell behind them and there was just field, empty except for a single, immense oak, a sight that so irritated Lavinia that she shut her eyes. The oak somehow seemed to give meaning to the field, a notion she found abhorrent.

She felt a worried tapping at her shoulder. When she looked at the young man, he just nodded at her, then he said, an afterthought, "What's the baby's name? My wife just had one and his name is Larry T."

Lavinia looked down at the baby who glared blackly back at her, and the recognition that her life and her long, angry journey through it, had been wasteful and deceptive and unnecessary, hit her like a board being smacked against her heart. She had a hurried sensation of being rushed forward but it didn't give her any satisfaction, because at the same time she felt her own dying slowing down some, giving her an instant to think about it.

"It's nameless," she whispered.

MARY MORRIS was born in Chicago in 1944 and now lives in New York and teaches at Princeton University. She is the author of the novel *Crossroads* and a collection of short stories, *Vanishing Animals and Other Stories*, which won the American Academy and Institute of Arts and Letters' Rome prize. Morris has also been the recipient of a CAPS award, a Guggenheim fellowship, and a fellowship from the National Endowment for the Arts. Her most recent collection of short stories, *The Bus of Dreams* (1985)—the title story follows here—is, in the words of Ann Beattie, "a powerful collection about the stages of life, about how one life registers upon another. She illuminates the stuff of which real lives are made, the seemingly unexceptional incidents which determine our fates." "The Bus of Dreams" reveals the broken bonds and the broken heart of a sister who has been searching for her missing sister for three years. She finally sees her missing sister's picture painted on the back of a bus in Panama City and is led to the fantastic bus dream man. In all the stories in this collection Mary Morris examines our ability to dream beyond despair. Her latest book is a work of travel literature, *Nothing to Declare*, about a woman traveling alone through Latin America.

The Bus of Dreams

by

Mary Morris

Raquel had been in Panama City for five weeks when she saw the bus with her sister's picture painted on the back. At first she thought it was a mistake, but then she knew it couldn't be. So she ran after the bus. She ran until she coughed in its exhaust, but it was no mistake. Teresa had disappeared three years earlier, and Raquel had come to find her, but she didn't expect it to be on the back of a bus.

Every day as she went to and from her job in the Zona, where she worked for the colonel and his wife, Raquel rode the buses. She tried to ride a different bus each day, ever since she saw Teresa's picture. She asked people when she got on if they knew the bus she was looking for. Raquel showed the drivers Teresa's snapshot, taken when she was Queen of the Carnival. Some smiled and said she was beautiful. Some said they wanted her picture on the back of their bus.

But then one driver who had kind dark eyes looked at the picture and nodded. He'd never seen the bus with Teresa's picture painted on the back, but he told her she had to find the bus dream man. He would know. In Panama every driver owns his own bus and every bus is different. When a man buys his bus, he takes it to a bus dream man. The bus dream man is a painter and a witch. On the back of the bus, he will paint the owner's secret desire. He paints objects of love, places that will be visited. He paints hopes, but never fears. And in the windows, he will put the names of the women loved. They say that the dream man in naming the dream brings the owner closer to finding his dream. They say that when the bus driver dies, he drives his bus right into heaven, where whatever the bus dream man painted comes true.

* * *

Raquel had never crossed the Isthmus of Panama before she came to the city, and she'd never been to the city before she began looking for Teresa. Teresa had been Queen of the Carnival just before she ran away. When Teresa was Queen, she'd worn a huge plumed headdress and a long feathery robe with green wings. She was a parrot. A sequined, feathered parrot. Because Teresa was so beautiful, their father had borrowed money from friends and from his sister in Colón. He took everything he had, which was very little, and put it into the dresses for Teresa's coronation.

Their father had taken all his savings and all the money he borrowed and bought cloth and shoes from the Americans, and their mother had sewn every sequin and feather on the gown herself by hand. They had painted her deep green eyes with stripes of red and blue like a parrot's eyes, as if she were the great bird of the jungle. Raquel had been her lady-in-waiting. She'd dressed as a smaller green bird, and she sat beside Teresa on the float that carried them through the streets of their town.

One day after the Carnival was over, Teresa said she was bored and that a friend of hers had a car. So Raquel and Teresa and the friend drove to San Lorenzo, the fort that perches above the Atlantic where Henry Morgan the pirate had invaded Panama. They drove through the U.S. Army base and the jungle and they drove along the edge of the fort that sits high above the sea. They watched the parrots fly wild through the ruins. Teresa had looked into one of the dungeons. She gazed deep into it, and Raquel saw her sister tremble and turn pale.

On the way back from the fort, two soldiers, wearing camouflage gear and carrying rifles, jumped out of the bushes and waved the girls down. They spoke broken Spanish and asked for a ride. They said they were on maneuvers and had to walk all the way back to the base. They showed them their guns and told jokes that made Teresa toss her head back and laugh. The soldiers told her she was very beautiful. She should be a star. For weeks Teresa sat, doing nothing in the house. Then one day she disappeared, leaving a note. It said she was going into pictures and she'd return when she was famous.

The first time Raquel saw her sister's picture on the back

of a bus, she wondered if it was there because Teresa was already famous. She thought it should be easy to find a famous person. She showed her snapshot to everyone she met. She showed it to the bus drivers and policemen. She showed it to the colonel and his wife. Raquel had been fortunate to find work in the Zona. She had gone to hotels, looking for work as a maid, and one of the hotels had given her the name of the colonel and his wife. They hired her because she was a good cook and because she was quiet. Mrs. Randolph told Raquel when she hired her that it was important to be quiet. Raquel had been lucky to find this job, and she knew she'd be just as lucky to find Teresa.

Raquel liked her job in the Zona. She liked leaving the slums of Panama, where she lived in a small rented room. She liked the ride into the Canal Zone. The Zona was lush and green, and the American servicemen who lived in it lived in beautiful houses. They lived on the top of the hill and they had a view of the Canal and the jungles.

The house of the colonel and his wife was dark and cool and the garden was filled with trees. Pomegranates hung from the low branches and so did lemons and oranges. Raquel picked oranges from the trees and ate them for lunch. In the middle of the garden was a pond with goldfish, covered with dry leaves that fell from the trees, and the first thing Raquel did when she went to work for the Randolphs was to clear the leaves off the goldfish pond so that Mrs. Randolph could sit in her clean white blouse and poke her finger at the noses of the goldfish. Mrs. Randolph sat and stared, her finger stirring the water in endless circles that hypnotized the fish so that they seemed to have no choice but to follow the circles of Mrs. Randolph's finger.

Sometimes Mrs. Randolph talked to Raquel. Sometimes she didn't. But Raquel never talked to her unless Mrs. Randolph wanted to talk. Sometimes Mrs. Randolph just sat in the bedroom with the shades drawn, sipping long cool drinks. But sometimes Mrs. Randolph would ask Raquel to tell her about where she came from. And Raquel told the colonel's wife how she came from a village in the Interior where the buzzards clung to the trees and the men carried their machetes to bed with them. She told Mrs. Randolph how the heat was so strong it never left their house, even on a cool spring night. How the mosquitoes coated the rooms of their house like wallpaper, and how the people drank and bathed in the same river that was their sewer.

When Raquel told Mrs. Randolph these things, the colonel's wife would close her eyes and drift back into her darkened room for the rest of the day. But once Mrs. Randolph asked Raquel what she'd like to have if she could have anything. There were many things she wanted. She wanted to marry the young man she'd left behind in her town, the one whose mustache didn't grow and who wanted to be a teacher. And sometimes she thought she wanted to nurse the sick and other times she wanted to have five children. But Raquel considered Mrs. Randolph's question carefully, and finally she said, "I'd like to live in a house where the breeze blows through."

Mrs. Randolph closed her eyes and said, "There are other things in this world besides living in a house like this."

One day Raquel told Mrs. Randolph why she'd come to the city. She told Mrs. Randolph how her father had married the woman he loved when he was sixteen years old. Her mother had borne him twelve children, and eight had died of disease. Teresa was the oldest and her father's favorite. She told Mrs. Randolph how her sister had run away. Shortly after Teresa ran away, her mother died. Every morning her father went to the fruit plantation where he worked, and after Teresa left and her mother died, he walked with the hesitant walk of one trying to find something he thinks he has lost.

In the evenings he came home and sat on the front porch, drinking rum and carving small animals out of wood. He'd sit, surrounded by his battalion of small animals. He carved dogs and cats and small sheep and cows. He also carved animals he'd never seen, except in pictures. He made an animal with a long neck and another with a long nose. He made a huge, fat animal with a horn in the middle of its head. He did not believe these animals actually existed, but he told Raquel that if he were ever rich enough, he'd travel to the place where these animals lived.

One night as he sat on the porch, surrounded by his animals carved of wood, Raquel asked if there was anything she could do for him. He gazed down the empty, dusty streets of their town. Then he looked up at her with his sad gray eyes; Raquel feared the look would enter her and she would walk with his hesitant walk.

Raquel had taken a room near the old French quarter that was not unlike her room in the Interior. She had imagined when she came to the city that she'd have a room that overlooked a courtyard where the bougainvillea worked its way to her window and, when she opened her window at night, the breeze from the sea would blow in the scarlet petals of bougainvillea and the night air of her room would be filled with the scent of fresh flowers.

But she had looked for a week and in the end settled for a room with a view of the next building, where the smell of burning kerosense and frying fish entered, mingled with the groans of old people and the muffled sounds of couples making love in the tropical heat. She'd taken a room where she had to wipe the cobwebs off her face in the morning and fight the bugs that crawled across her arms as she slept in damp sheets on a damp mattress with the smell of old mold and the impression of sad bodies.

She'd stared at herself in the cracked glass when she moved in and knew that she was pretty, but not like Teresa. Teresa had silky black hair and ivory skin. Teresa didn't have a mole on her right cheek, and her face was sculpted, not flat and round like Raquel's. Raquel moved into the room and unpacked her things. She unpacked the tortoise-shell combs the boy she loved back home had given her. She unpacked her shell beads and the white dress her mother had embroidered. She unpacked the fotonovelas she liked to read at night and pictures of Clark Gable and John Travolta. She put these beside the pictures of her family and of Teresa. She unpacked the rosary her grandmother had given her and the small statue of the Virgin in a blue robe, her trouble dolls and the amulets from the fortuneteller in her town. She wiped away the cobwebs that would return each morning and she settled in.

Raquel had also brought with her a small porcelain doll with no arms. When Raquel and Teresa were little, they'd kept a secret place. It was under the porch of an abandoned house, and they kept all kinds of things in their secret place. They kept small stones and the feathers of birds, pits of fruit and bones of animals they'd eaten. They kept old forks and pieces of tin. And they kept the porcelain doll, which they dressed in scraps of cloth their mother gave them. They built the doll a house out of cardboard with large windows and a patio. But when Teresa got older, she lost interest in the secret place. So one day Raquel collected all their things and moved them in a sack into their house.

That was when Teresa introduced Raquel to the world of boys. Teresa was five years older, and sometimes when their parents were at church, Teresa would sneak boys into the house. Once Teresa had gone out back with one of the boys and had returned breathless, her skirt slightly twisted around her waist. Another time Raquel had lain in her bed and listened to her sister's soft laughter in the night.

Now, every evening, Raquel lay on her bed in the rented room. She studied the webs of spiders, the places where the beams didn't meet. The tiny footprints of mice on the walls.

At times Raquel was late for work because of her search for her sister, but Mrs. Randolph didn't seem to mind when Raquel arrived or when she left. Once Mrs. Randolph, who sat staring into the goldfish pond, looked up and startled Raquel when she said, "Why don't you find your sister and get yourself out of this dump?"

One morning Raquel boarded a bus that had a man playing a guitar painted on the back. It also had a small house with domestic animals. In the windows, as in all the buses, it had the names of the women the driver loved. Salsa music played when Raquel got on, and people were dancing. People always danced and sang on the buses of Panama. And a man she didn't know dropped coins into the bus driver's change box for her, in exchange for a dance. She showed the driver the picture and he nodded. He knew the bus and he told her where to go in the city to wait for it.

Raquel was going to be late for work, but she was sure Mrs. Randolph wouldn't care, since she was probably sitting in her darkened bedroom, sipping a cool drink. She went to the place where the driver said to go, and she waited. She waited for an hour or more, and just as she was about to give up, she saw a bus approach. It pulled up like a great beast, spewing exhaust, and on the back of it she saw her sister's picture.

For a moment Raquel stared. She felt close to Teresa for the first time in three years. She felt her sister's dark eyes, looking at her from the back of the bus. When the bus began to pull away, Raquel yelled for the driver to wait. It was an early-morning bus filled with workers on their way to the hotels, to the Canal, to construction sites. The driver was old, with tired brown eyes, and he had crucifixes and statues of the Virgin on his dashboard.

When Raquel showed him the picture, he shook his head. He said he'd never seen her before. Except on the back of his bus. But he told her where to find the bus dream man. The dream man's name was Jorge and he didn't live in a good part of the city. But the driver told her how to get there and he told her to go in the heat of the day. He told her that the bus dream men were strange and filthy and he cautioned her to take care.

In the middle of the day Raquel left Mrs. Randolph and went to the slums in the old French quarter where the bus driver had told her to go. In this part of town the houses had been condemned long ago, but the poor just moved into the empty rooms. Four or five families lived in a room that had once been occupied by one. Raquel knocked on the molding where there'd once been a door. A man with greasy hair and no teeth came to her, and Raquel said, "Excuse me, but I'm looking for my sister."

The bus dream man smiled and said, "I just paint buses. I don't know many women." Raquel held out the photograph she'd been carrying for weeks. The man named Jorge touched it with his dirty hands. He smiled again through his rotten teeth and said it had been a mere coincidence.

He told Raquel how a bus driver had come to him with his new bus and he'd described a woman to him. "He told me," Jorge said, "she had eyes like the evening skies and hair as thick and dark as the forests. Skin smooth as stones on the beach. Her mouth was a cave at the bottom of the sea and her scent like the wind through the jasmine trees. Her body was the Isthmus, wide in some places, narrow in others, winding with many curves and treacherous places. A body whose distance you travel in no time, but it is a journey like the trip through the Canal that must be undertaken with great care." He said that he painted the woman the bus driver described and it happened to come out like Raquel's sister.

Raquel stood for a moment, thinking. Then she said, "You are telling me a lie." She clenched her fists, and her small, tight mouth spoke very clearly. "You know where my sister is. You can't just paint a picture like that."

The bus dream man shrugged. "I just do what I imagine. People have their wishes and dreams, their secret longings. I reveal them. That's all I do."

Raquel moved closer to him so that her face was up against his. He stank of paint and sweat and his hair was matted on his head. But he had dark, translucent eyes and he stared straight into hers. "Tell me where she is."

He smiled again. "Living out her life's dream."

The next day and the day after that Raquel left Mrs. Randolph sitting in her darkened room or counting the goldfish in the pond. She went and sat at the door of the bus dream man. She watched him as he worked. He was painting a huge bus in his backyard and he was painting the back with a house by a lake with six children in the lake for a man whose three children had each died at the age of three months and who had had no more.

On the third day, when Raquel was going to leave, Mrs. Randolph said to her, "What are you going to do when you find your sister?"

Raquel looked at her in surprise. "I'm going to take her home."

Mrs. Randolph shook her head of hair, which she dyed different shades of red and yellow. "Now it's too late. She won't go with you," Mrs. Randolph said. "Girls, when they come to this city and stay this long, they never leave." Then Mrs. Randolph sighed. "I had a dream last night. I dreamed I saw bones walking by the sea. They were beautiful and white like porcelain and they had flowers growing out of them. But slowly veins appeared, then blood, and it was a horrible body. Then skin. And for an instant, I saw my daughter again. My little girl. I hadn't seen her in so many years. I wanted to reach out and touch her . . . If I were you, I'd go home now." Then she added as Raquel headed to the door, "That's what I'd do if I could."

But Raquel went back to the bus dream man that day and

the days that followed. She sat without speaking as he painted the children on the back of the bus. And finally he turned to her and said, "All right, you win. I'll tell you where to find her."

The Crossroads of the World Club was located at the edge of the Zona, just below the hill where Raquel worked. She walked by it every day as she headed up the hill to the Randolphs'. It was a fairly well-known club, to those who knew about such things. It was run by a man named Eddie, an ex-Marine, who'd once swum the Canal and had been charged a quarter for his cargo potential. It was a famous story about the Canal, and they say that Eddie, after he swam it, could never leave.

Jorge told Raquel to find Eddie. He'd told her that Eddie would tell her where her sister was. "Has she gone to America?" Raquel asked, and Jorge had smiled that same smile. "You might say she's gone to America."

Raquel hesitated before entering the club. She looked up at the Zona, so green and beautiful. Parakeets flew overhead. She heard them screeching, but she couldn't see them. She looked at the American flag she passed every day and at the Marine who guarded the entrance to the Zona. He smiled at her, the way he did every day, but he looked at her strangely when he saw her hesitating at the club.

It had no windows. There were no windows on any of the floors above it, either. Raquel had never known a building that had no windows. Even in her town in the poor houses where no breeze blew there were windows. On the outside there were pictures of dark-skinned girls and a sign that read AMERICAN SERVICEMEN WELCOME.

As her eyes adjusted to the darkness, Raquel noticed the smells of the bar. It smelled of stale flowers and darkness and of the bodies of men. Raquel didn't know the bodies of men, but when she entered the bar, she knew. It wasn't a smell like her father's or brothers' or the boy with the mustache who waited for her at home. This was a bitter smell, strong, but not entirely unappealing. At night back in the Interior, Raquel had sometimes wondered about the bodies of men, wondered how she'd know them in the dark, but now she thought she'd just know.

When she could see in the darkness, she saw a bar with

several men at it and a few women in the back. At the bar she asked for Eddie, and the bartender looked her over. "You want work?"

She shook her head. "I'm working," she replied. "I want to find somebody."

The bartender shrugged and gave a call. A large burly man appeared from the back and he held out his hand to her. "I'm Eddie," he said. "What can I do for you?" She held out the photo and told him how the bus dream man had sent her here.

Eddie looked at the picture and smiled. Then he paused and stared at her. "I can see the resemblance." Raquel looked away. She'd never been the pretty one. "She'll be here tomorrow," he told her. "Come back then."

But the next day was a holiday and Raquel didn't know it. She was on her way to the club and to her job in the Zona when she got caught up in a procession. It was the day the people were carrying the bones of their leader who had died in a helicopter crash into the Canal Zone. They'd dug up his grave and they were marching, thousands of them, with his bones into the Zona. They carried banners with his words: "I don't want to go into history. I want to go into the Canal Zone." As Raquel walked, she got caught up in the crowds and they carried her along. She followed them as they wound their way up the green hill where the servicemen lived. She followed them as they proceeded past Colonel Randolph's house, where she saw the colonel and his wife, sitting on the porch, staring at the procession with the leader's bones.

At the Randolphs' house, Raquel left the procession, but neither the colonel nor his wife greeted her. When she went inside to begin her work, the colonel followed her in. He said to her, "We built it. We should keep it." And Raquel nodded and said, yes, they should keep it. But he went on. He said, "But we're going to give it back to you. We're going to give it back and watch the whole country go down the tubes." The colonel was a very tall, strong man, with his hair clipped short against his head. He reminded Raquel of a cartoon she'd once seen of Popeye the Sailor Man. Now he looked ridiculous, all puffed up and red.

Mrs. Randolph came in and sat by the pond. She glanced at Raquel and her husband, then looked at the goldfish. Her husband said something to her in English and Mrs. Randolph shrugged. She replied in Spanish, "Do what you want."

When Raquel finished her day's work, Mrs. Randolph thrust a fistful of money, all in dollars, into Raquel's hands. "Go home," Mrs. Randolph said. "Or I'll see your bones walking by the sea." And she gave her a white blouse that Raquel had admired and she told her, "Now find Teresa and promise me you'll go home."

It was late afternoon when Raquel waved to the Marine who guarded the Zona, and she felt his eyes on her as she walked into the Crossroads of the World. It was dark inside and it took Raquel's eyes a few moments to adjust to the dark. The bar was filled with servicemen in uniform and sailors on shore leave, waiting for their ships to make the journey through the Canal.

And there were women. She saw many women sitting in the rear. They all had thick black hair and high-pitched laughs. They wore tight dresses and, from the back, they all looked the same. From the back Raquel couldn't tell one from the other. But as she approached, she heard one laugh that seemed to rise above the others.

A head turned slightly in her direction. Raquel saw a woman with eyes painted like parrot eyes and lips red as a sun rising on the Atlantic and setting on the Pacific. Her skin was smooth as stones on the shore, and the scent of jasmine rose from her body. Her body was winding and treacherous as the Isthmus. It was just as the bus dream man had said. It was what Raquel expected and what she knew she'd find. For an instant, their eyes met. Then that was all.

When Raquel left the bar, the procession was gone, and it was quiet. It was very quiet. The Marine smiled at her, and she waved faintly at him. She looked up at the hill and over to the Canal. A flock of parakeets circled overhead, screeching, flying through the palm fronds of the Zona. Raquel watched them dip and swirl and shriek as they traveled back and forth across the Canal. She decided she would go home and tell her father he should be proud. She would tell him that Teresa had made it into pictures.

CANDACE FLYNT was born in Greensboro, North Carolina in 1947 where she grew up, went to college, and now lives with her husband and stepchildren. Her hometown of Greensboro is the setting of all her books. "I am trying to write about the modern South," she has written, and in three novels (*Chasing Dad, Sins of Omission,* and *Mother Love*) and a number of short stories cited in *Best American Short Stories* of 1975 and 1977 she has realized that world in a rich and well-balanced prose, with a cast of characters that seems as close to living, breathing, actual people as it is possible for literary creations to be.

The selection that follows here is the opening episode of her latest novel *Mother Love* (1987), "a work of enormous beauty and psychological insight," in the words of one reviewer, having, to quote another, "three sisters who are as believable and engaging, as full of human strengths (and shortcomings) as any characters I've encountered in recent fiction." When the three sisters, Katherine, Jude, and Louise, get together, they tell "mother stories." At the beginning of the novel, they are grown up, but not at perfect peace with their memories, of either themselves as children and adolescents, or their dazzling and infuriating mother. Throughout the narrative, the dissonances and harmonies of real sisterly bonding resonate, a counterpoint that runs through the following selection, making it an utterly satisfying and unified whole.

from Mother Love
by *Candace Flynt*

CHAPTER 1

"Whose turn?" asks Jude, the sister who is driving.

She makes a sharp cut with her station wagon through the white brick columns that mark the entrance to the graveyard and speeds up the hill. The instantaneous change from daylight to dusk is just now occurring. In the front seat with her are her two sisters. In the back are the empty car seats of her two babies, who are presently being watched over by their grandfather. They are running late. A sign warns that the gate will be locked at sundown, but no one worries: in these two years they have never seen a gatekeeper.

Neither sister answers her question. Instead, they keep talking about whether Louise, who has naturally curly hair, would benefit from a permanent. Neither may remember whose turn it is, but it is not Jude's. Last time they were together, she told the story about Mother reading her palm at her rehearsal dinner and predicting that she and Cap would get a divorce. They had all laughed, she most of all. The story has become less horrible than it once was. And, after all, Mother was right.

She edges over to the curb and kills the motor, which knocks for many long seconds before it finally dies. Her station wagon, bought pre-divorce, is a battered, untended car which lately has been looking as if it's about to collapse. She could buy a new car with her inheritance, but she doesn't want to spend her mother's money like that. Even when she started thinking of it as her own money—about a year ago—she knew she would spend it for something glorious.

Louise opens her door and, as if she never heard Jude's question, says, "It's my turn to tell a story about Mother."

The cold Christmas air quickly fills the car. Louise turns up her palm, testing for snow.

"You sound like you've prepared," Jude says, leaning forward to see past Katherine.

"Not really. I didn't think of it until today."

Jude opens her door. "A Christmas story? Those are always good. Those are always the *best*."

"No. I thought of it when I saw Max's pool."

"A swimming story . . . ?" Jude tries.

They are all out of the car. "Shut up," Louise says, starting across the grass ahead of them.

Max is their stepfather. Before they set off for the graveyard, they stopped by his house to wish him a Merry Christmas. He'd been alone, partially drunk, and had turned down their invitation to accompany them. But he kept finding ways to make them stay with him, which is why it is almost dark now. Several times a year the sisters drive forty-five minutes to get here: on Christmas Day—ostensibly their mother's favorite day; on her death day, and on Mother's Day. They don't observe her birthday because she did not. Pretending it didn't exist made her feel she wasn't aging, she explained to them. Made her feel that although time in general went on—anniversaries, Christmases, their birthdays—her time did not.

"Aren't you going to wear your coat, Weezie?" Katherine calls before shutting the door. When she doesn't answer, Katherine and Jude follow her in the direction of the grave site. After a few steps, they catch up.

"No, 'Mother,' " Louise mutters.

Katherine does not respond, though inwardly she wishes she could utter the enormous loud irritated sigh she feels.

The graveyard has no tombstones, only flat bronze markers. Two of the sisters' grandparents, one of whom died in 1948, the other in 1970, are also buried here. At the top of the hill is a bell tower almost obscured by overgrown holly trees. Otherwise, the graveyard is well-tended. Down the hill lies a natural pond, where many years ago the sisters brought Fleedlefoot—the only Easter duck which survived them—to live. Several weeping willows stand motionless in the cold air. Fleedlefoot's descendants and the descendants of other pet ducks sit huddled for warmth at the water's edge.

"I forgot the flowers," Katherine says. The other two wait while she returns to the car for the three yellow roses that she always brings. They are live roses, hard to find this time of year, these ordered from a nursery in South Carolina. The yellow rose was their mother's favorite flower; now it's the flower that all of them like best, too. Katherine hands one to each sister. Both say to remind them to pay her for it. She has never reminded them; they have never paid. It's her contribution. The flowers will be frozen in an hour, but they would never put anything artificial on their mother's grave.

By the time they reach her plot, the graveyard is dark, which makes them pay more attention to each other's face. Each sister is always intent on what the others are thinking, although Katherine and Jude pay less attention to Louise because she is still so young. They are both approaching thirty, Katherine just ahead of Jude. The two older sisters are tall, chesty, slim-hipped, and leggy, built like the women on their mother's side of the family. Any exercise they do is devoted to flattening their stomachs. Any exercise Louise does is aimed at slimming her thighs. She is built like the women on their father's side of the family: narrow shoulders, small breasts, and thick hips. Katherine and Jude have squarish faces which they each soften by wearing their hair to their shoulders. Louise's face is round, innocent, and open, her naturally curly hair full around her face. All three sisters agree with their mother's long-ago assessment that Louise is cute, Jude is beautiful, and Katherine is striking. But both Jude and Katherine believe that Louise will eventually outgrow her cuteness and become pretty. She's only twenty-one.

"Wouldn't Mother give her eyeteeth to still be here?" Katherine asks.

"Hell, yes," Jude answers.

"Don't talk like that," Louise says.

Katherine frowns. "Jesus Christ, Weezie."

"*Stop* it," Louise says shrilly. "We're in a graveyard. You ought to have a little respect. For God, if not for Mother."

"We're at our very own mother's grave," Jude says. "We're just being natural. We're talking exactly the way she would talk. You ought to try it sometime, Weezie. Stop always thinking about what you're *supposed* to do. Do what you *want* to do." She pauses. "God *isn't* here."

"You both make me sick," Louise says. Her cheeks are flushed; her eyes accusatory. Accusing them of being too much like their mother, Katherine thinks. Which, perhaps, they are, Jude especially. "I don't want to argue," Louise continues. "We're standing on her grave."

"Not *on* it," Katherine says.

"Yes, we are. Where do you think the casket is? Under that postage stamp? She's here. Under our feet." With the growing dark, the sense of graveyard has become stronger. Louise thinks that if there were tombstones here her sisters might be more reverent.

Katherine's face suddenly brightens. She stretches informally, ending the gesture by placing a hand on each sister's shoulder. Neither of them relaxes under her touch. "She's not under our feet. She's right here with us," she says, looking pointedly at both expectant faces. "No, she isn't." She grins with the knowledge that they all share. "If she were here, nobody would be having any fun."

Louise steps away so that Katherine's hand drops off her shoulder. "Why do you always cut her like that?"

"I'm not cutting her. Look, Weezie, this is what we decided. We aren't going to rosy her up. We're going to remember her as she was. No purple haze. We agreed to that two years ago. It's not disloyal." Katherine's voice becomes husky. "We're her daughters. If we're going to spend time remembering, we should remember her for how she was. She was a pain in the ass."

"She was also wonderful," Jude says.

"She was horrible," Louise suddenly blurts. She is half laughing and half crying. "At least she was horrible in this story I'm about to tell." She giggles and her cheeks perk up. "Does anybody know about the cheese toast?"

Giving a little curtsy, Louise lays her rose on the bronze grave marker. Katherine and Jude do the same. There is a sudden tender moment among them.

"I'm getting cold," Louise says, vigorously rubbing her arms.

"Want to share coats?" Katherine asks. The three sisters draw together again, two coats for three—each a little cold, each a little warm. Katherine thinks of the ducks.

"Why weren't we ever like this when she was alive?" Jude asks in a rare soft voice.

"She wouldn't let us be," Katherine murmurs.

"We *were* like this when she was alive," Louise says. She moves out from under their coats until she is standing behind the grave. "Sometimes we were friends; sometimes we weren't. You can't make everything her fault."

"Tell us about the cheese toast, Weezie," Katherine says in a soothing voice which is also intended to warn Jude off. But then, to make sure the truth is stated, she says, "Of course we were friends. But none of us was happy. She kept us from being happy." They weren't really friends, Katherine thinks. Being sisters is not the same. But she can't deny *everything* Louise says.

For several long moments Louise does not speak. Finally she says, "I was happy. I've always been happy. Almost." She looks at Katherine, who lowers her eyes to avoid comment. "I guess I loved her more than you two did."

"That does it," Jude says. She kneels, picks up one of the roses, and walks quickly away from the grave. All Katherine and Louise can see is the bobbing white fur collar of her coat. They wait to hear the car door open and slam, but the sound doesn't come. Suddenly Jude is back with them.

"I don't know why I did that," she says to Katherine. In the dusk, her expression is indiscernible, but both sisters hear the trembling in her voice. "I don't know why I took away the rose." She kneels again at the marker. She begins peeling away the petals of the flower. She scatters them around the grave.

"That's pretty," Katherine murmurs.

Jude says, "Some of the time, Louise, Mother made us unhappy. Don't you remember?"

"Yes, I remember," Louise says quietly.

Cars that are passing on the street beyond the gate have by now turned on their headlights. Across the valley hundreds of empty apartments begin to light up, suddenly changing character. The air is growing distinctly colder. Each sister feels fine pricks of ice begin to hit her face, but no one comments. Even if it were snow, which they all love, no one would comment, Katherine thinks. No one is happy enough to mention something pleasurable.

In a dutiful voice, Louise begins: "I was having a back-to-school swimming party. It was when I was about nine, I think." Her tone picks up. "The twins—ugh! how I hated them—came, and Marylou and Carla—all my growing-up friends. This is so typically Mother . . ." She gives a slight shivery giggle. Jude continues to squat by the grave. Katherine considers offering to share her coat again but decides against it.

"Mother was in a mood, of course. She'd dressed up for my party in her Greek Isles caftan and gold high heels. That morning I had gone with her to the grocery store to buy Cokes and potato chips, but all of a sudden she yelled out the Dutch door, 'How many pieces of cheese toast should I fix?' Carla Covington looked at me like Mother was crazy. In a very nice voice I called back that no one was hungry, although we'd all just gotten out of the pool to eat. I didn't know what to do. My friends didn't want *cheese toast!* What I suggested was that everyone lie down on their towels to sun-dry for a while and then we'd all go in and get our refreshments. I hoped maybe Mother would go upstairs or something.

"I remember wanting to explain to them but not knowing what to say. But at the same time I also believed that whatever Mother did was going to turn out right. And that when it didn't, it wasn't because she was mean or out of control or just nuts. It was because *I* didn't know the whole story. I still sort of feel that way. That I've never known the whole story about Mother."

There is a long concentrated pause, something like a silent prayer at church, Katherine thinks. Weezie always poses a question like this. It used to be that she wanted Jude or Katherine, Katherine in particular, to try to answer it, but she seems to have realized that they have no final explanations, only more stories than she has because they're older.

"Then out she came," Louise says in a fresh, amused voice. "For effect, I suppose, she slammed the Dutch door behind her. She marched toward us, carrying a platter in one hand, her other hand on her hip. I stood up. She was so tall—"

"You were just short," Jude says.

"No, she always seemed tall to me."

"She was tall and she carried herself beautifully," Katherine says.

"But she didn't scare men," Jude adds.

"Men couldn't be scared then the way they can be today," Katherine says.

"I mean, she was proud but also very vulnerable."

"I know exactly what you mean."

Louise looks from one of them to the other, pouting. So often, her sisters mutually remark about things she never even noticed about Mother. Mother had always seemed big and fearsome to her. But she didn't scare men. What does that mean? Suddenly she notices the quiet. They're waiting for her to continue.

"She was so tall," Louise says. "She towered over me. She shoved the platter under my chin. She said, 'Here's your goddamn cheese toast.' "

"As if you'd asked for it," Jude says, chuckling.

"And that it had been a pain in the ass to fix," adds Katherine. " 'Here's your goddamn cheese toast,' " she repeats, hooting.

"Watch your language," Jude says, cutting her eyes at her younger sister. This time, Louise is able to laugh.

"What did you do?" Katherine asks. She is struck once again by the original ways their mother found to pain them.

"I ran up to my room, crying."

"You should have said, 'Thank you, Mother,' " Jude says.

"I know that now. Then I was nine."

"What happened to the party?"

"It went on," Louise says simply. "A few minutes later I heard Mother come upstairs and lock her bedroom door, and I went back down. She'd sent someone in to get the Cokes." Louise pauses before adding softly, "Everyone ate the cheese toast."

"They did?"

"They liked it better than potato chips."

"At that age, did you realize Mother was loaded?" Jude asks.

"Of course not."

"What did you think was wrong?"

"I didn't know. I guess I thought I'd done something to make her mad, but I didn't know what. Or maybe I thought . . . How do I know what I thought when I was nine? Besides, how do we know what had to do with drinking and what didn't?" Louise rubs her arms again.

"It *all* had to do with drinking," Jude says.

"I think you're wrong," Katherine says. "It was more complex than that."

"Bye, Mom. Bye, you two," Louise says, starting toward the car. "Although I want to hear what you're saying, I don't want to catch pneumonia."

Jude blows a kiss in the direction of the grave. Katherine tilts her head and then begins to follow. She had almost started to *explain* the complexity. They catch up with Louise to share coats.

"Did you swim the rest of the afternoon without a lifeguard?" Jude asks, which is something she would think of now that she has children.

Katherine answers for Louise: "I don't think they had a lifeguard before *or* after the cheese toast."

"I wonder what the other mothers thought," Jude muses.

"They probably didn't know."

"Someone could have *drowned*," Louise says in a suddenly angry voice. Although it was her story, she hadn't considered the implication of five nine-year-olds swimming unsupervised.

"But no one *did*," Katherine says.

They crowd back into the front seat, where Katherine always insists they all sit so that no one will miss anything. This time, Louise is in the middle. Jude starts the car and turns the heat on high.

"One of my friends could have drowned and it would have ruined my life," Louise repeats heatedly.

"You didn't even think about it until I mentioned it," Jude says. "Save your tears for something that *happened*."

"Of course, the possibility's horrible," Katherine says. "But nobody ever drowned in our pool."

"How do you feel about Carla Covington now, anyway?" Jude asks.

"I'm glad she's not *dead*," Louise says. She giggles. "I guess I'm glad. Carla wasn't exactly my favorite person. She told the whole fourth grade that we had spiders in our pool. Everybody who *has* a pool has spiders in it. And she pulled up my dress one day when we were standing in the lunch line. That was in second grade." Louise's voice grows more faraway. "And then in high school she sneaked and dated Billy." Billy was Louise's boyfriend from the ninth grade through her sophomore year in college. "I drove by her house one night, innocently, and his car was parked there. He always said he was visiting her brother. Maybe he was," she adds softly. "If somebody had drowned, though," she says, returning to her indignant tone, "it would have probably been Marylou, which I really couldn't have endured."

"No one *drowned*," Jude says in a thoroughly irritated voice. "Aren't you warm enough yet? I'm suffocating. How is Marylou, by the way?"

"Turn it down," Louise says. "I'm having lunch with her on Thursday. Do you remember when the professional baseball team came to town? You and Katherine had already gone away to college. Marylou married the first baseman."

"Are they happy?" asks Jude.

"Yes, they're happy," Louise says, her voice growing defensive again. It's a question her sisters always ask. *All* her married friends are happy. She's sorry, mildly sorry, that they can't say the same about theirs.

"I don't know a single person now that I knew in high school," Katherine says.

"I was always closer to my college friends," says Jude.

Louise wonders if they are criticizing her again.

"The first friends I ever made, I made in college," Katherine says. "But my *best* friends I've made since." The truth is, Katherine is not close to anyone right now. Secrets she might confide to potential friends she never does, thinking that the people she really wants to tell things to are her sisters. But she doesn't. "I never trusted anyone until after college," she continues. "Until after Frank, really. There's no set pattern, is there?"

They are not criticizing her, Louise decides. She hardly has any friends, anyway—from high school *or* college. Even Marylou is just someone from her past. They haven't talked to each other since Mother's funeral.

Traffic on Interstate Highway 85 is slow, partly because of the sleet, which is coming down steadily but not sticking, but mostly because of the Christmas travelers. Beginning with their parents' divorce fifteen years ago, they've each traveled this road hundreds of times, sometimes together, sometimes in pairs, sometimes separately. When their mother was ill those last seven weeks of her life, at least one of them traveled the road every day. Now they are on this road maybe five times a year.

The sisters are quiet. They can be comfortable together in long periods of silence, as long as no one begins to think that one of the others is being quiet for a reason. If that happens, then the possibility of an argument exists.

Of the time she spends with her sisters, Louise likes it best when they are like this. She can feel close to them now and not have to listen to their ideas, which are almost always identical, and try to reconcile them with her own. Between them, her sisters have persuaded her not to quit college, to go abroad for a year, and to dump Billy, who because he didn't go to college had become less and less suitable for her. "You've outgrown him, or you soon will," they'd said, although she could never have outgrown his sureness in the face of all her uncertainty. And now in less than six months she will have a degree in history from college, which is supposed to be important, as no doubt she will someday realize. Her sisters have lengthened her skirts, forced her to let the blond grow out of her hair, wiped off her blue eye shadow. But they *do* know so much, and it seems silly not to take advantage of their experience. And she hasn't had someone better—a mother—since she was nineteen, and, really, she may never have had a mother at all. The story most recently acknowledged by her sisters is that their mother fell in love with Max just after she married their father—when she was twenty-one and walked past him on the post-office steps. So what real mothering, except perhaps from Katherine and Jude, had she ever had? Three kids and seventeen years of marriage later for Mother, five kids and twenty-seven years of marriage later for Max—they found a way to be together. They'd waited all that time. True love, forever love, someday love was what she'd felt for Billy, so, to an extent, she's always understood what Mother went through. But it hadn't helped *her*. Motherless, she, too, now believes that Billy might not have been right for her.

She had a sort-of boyfriend, Gérard, the year she spent in Paris on Hollins College Abroad. Even though she was still taking birth-control pills, and she knew that Katherine and

Jude would have said to go ahead and go to bed with him, she'd decided not to. It wasn't that Gérard wasn't handsome or that his English wasn't the sexiest English she'd ever heard. It was that she knew her sisters would have thought she should have the experience. How long will it take her, she wonders, to choose to act even if they agree? On the other hand, how long will it take her to stop doing what they say? She'll always regret not going to bed with Gérard. And she'll always remember that her sisters never knew he existed.

Of the time Katherine spends with her sisters, she likes it best when the conversation is honest and careful. She loves her sisters as she would love different children, each for different reasons. As perhaps their mother loved each of them. Katherine knows she was their mother's favorite. It was Mother's talent that Jude and Louise probably thought the same thing. But Mother also hated her the most. And that was the difference. What Katherine loves about Louise is her solidness, which she used to regard as Louise's naïveté. Louise will not make many mistakes, because she won't take many risks. There's virtue in that, Katherine is beginning to realize. Jude, on the other hand, will do anything, which Katherine admires, too. While neither sister is totally her favorite, Jude is the only one who can truly upset her.

She knows so much about these two sisters of hers, and though they don't realize it, they know so little about her. When she assumed the position of surrogate mother so many years ago, she encouraged them to believe she was invincible, but she's surprised that they still think her so. They're all grown up now. How can they accept without question what she offers about herself? More than other daughters, they should realize that those bulwarks of strength—mothers—are not what they seem. Last October, at a dinner party she and Frank gave, Jude, drunk and behaving obnoxiously to the date they'd gotten her, announced that Katherine was the sanest person she has ever known. The tone of the remark brought it close to an insult, but Katherine knew Jude meant what she said. Being so sane, she can't tell them the dangerous thing that is going on in her life. For one reason, she fears they'd never recover from losing their belief that she has everything under control. It gives them hope that one day they will, too. For another, it would do *her* no good. They aren't old enough or experienced enough to give her advice. They're her sisters, though. Why don't they sense that something's wrong?

Of the time Jude spends with her sisters, she likes the sparring best. Not that she likes to fight—well, maybe she does—but mostly she likes the mental exercise. She's so much nicer to her kids, she's noticed, when she's spent some time with her sisters. She's more persuasive than either Katherine or Louise, and she feels a certain power over them when she's able to make more sense.

She knows more than they do, because, through no fault of her own, she's endured more. She lost the world that she always expected to possess—the secure world of marriage and family—and survived. Her sisters are scared. Scared that something might happen to them, too. But she's no longer scared. There's nothing left to be scared of when everything you thought you had is gone.

What happened was she finished high school and went straight to the same college as Cap, where they got married, and with family help she finished her education, because no one wanted him to grow away from her. Instead, she grew away from him because—though hardly anyone knew it (she'd taken pains to keep it concealed)—she was smarter and more ambitious than he and she wanted to be somebody. Except that she doesn't want those things anymore. It's all right that Cap's gone. What's been hard is no longer living where all her friends live, not having any money, not going to the country club every Friday happy hour, not doing all the things she'd grown up planning to do. But, thank God, she doesn't care about those things anymore. She's in the process of looking around to find out what she does care about.

Talking to her sisters, especially to Katherine, helps her define what she wants and she's discovered she doesn't want the same things her sister does. For years she would accede to Katherine's wisdom. But Katherine is no longer wise. She's become like every other married person: complacent, self-righteous, and boring. Safe, too. But she's also the sister that Jude at one time would have died for. Katherine is one of them, yet not quite. She's intense, too intense, when she ought to be so relaxed. Jude tries to fit her into the married slot—angrily, on account of how happy Katherine acts—but deep down she knows that Katherine doesn't completely fit. Katherine is octagonal, and the married slot, everyone knows, is round.

Sometimes Jude believes that the whole six years—hell, the whole twenty-six years—she lived in the manner of her parents—was a huge mistake, her trying to be someone she's not. It's hard for her to remember being ordinary or being happy being ordinary, but she knows that for all those years she was both those things. She's now as flamboyant as she was dull before. But was she really dull? She remembers trying to be dull. She remembers never saying about half the things she felt like saying. She remembers wondering if she really belonged, although what she and Cap had had was everything she knew she'd ever wanted. She is finally herself now: wild, free, open, exciting. Smart, independent, available. She hopes someone will notice.

"Are you doing anything tonight, Weezie?" she asks.

"Why?" Louise answers groggily. The sway of the car has made her doze.

"Never mind."

"I didn't even hear what you said," Louise says. "I was asleep."

"Lucky you," Jude mutters. She put both hands on the steering wheel, instead of the casual hand she normally steers with. "I wanted to know if you'd come home with me and help me put the kids to bed."

Louise waits too long to answer, so Katherine says, "I will."

"I don't want to keep you away from Frank," Jude says. The comment is made without rancor, but Katherine knows her happy marriage has made Jude feel abandoned. She forgets how alone Katherine was those years Jude was married and she wasn't.

"You won't be keeping me from Frank. He can take care of himself for another hour."

The exit to Greensboro, North Carolina, their home, looms ahead. Jude takes it without slowing. She is a fast, purposefully reckless driver. Katherine, who is a fast, accidentally reckless driver, does not mind riding with her. Louise, who is a slow, careful driver, does. It's a two-mile long exit ramp because of some politically motivated highway construction, and Jude travels it faster than she did the highway. Louise's body stiffens. She puts her knees together and folds her hands in her lap. Katherine considers intervening on her behalf but decides not to.

"I really don't feel I got to see enough of them today anyway," Katherine continues. Their earlier schedule was hectic: celebrating at their own homes (except Louise), celebrating with their father, sending Jude's children to ex-spouse and ex-in-laws, getting them back, leaving them with Daddy to go see Max, visiting Mother's grave. She's hardly seen her niece and nephew. "What's Christmas for?"

"Christmas is for families," Jude says sarcastically.

Louise draws herself up to say something, but Katherine discreetly elbows her. "Has it stopped sleeting?" she asks.

"Yeah, Katherine, it's stopped sleeting," Jude says. "I don't want you to come home with me," she adds curtly.

"Whatever," Katherine says. If she insists, Jude will resist more firmly.

"I'll be happy to help you put the children to bed," Louise says. "I haven't seen enough of them, either."

Jude doesn't answer. Katherine leans forward slightly to catch a glimpse of her face. She is squinting because of the headlights of an approaching car.

"All right?" Louise asks.

"Sure. Whatever suits you."

The next thing Louise is going to say is that if Jude doesn't want her to come, then to forget it. That she's doing the favor, and Jude should be appreciative. With all her powers of concentration, Katherine silently begs Louise not to say those things. She touches Louise's arm with her fingertips.

Louise turns angrily, but when she sees Katherine's imploring expression, dramatized by the passing headlights, she withholds the comment she was going to make. She feels the way she's always felt: that she just doesn't know the whole story. Maybe it's wrong to be so acquiescent. Maybe it means she has no center, which is how she so often feels. But maybe she's not old enough to have a center yet.

Jude has curled both arms around the steering wheel. She looks so tired. Almost involuntarily, Louise puts her arm lightly around her. Katherine, sensing the gesture, puts her arm around Louise. Tears that she is proud of fill Louise's eyes. Katherine is flooded with relief and gratitude and, once again, hope. Jude says gruffly, "What's all this?" But she feels that someone has wrapped her in the red velvet comforter Mother used to tuck around them when they were sick. The feeling is reflected in her voice.

ANN BEATTIE was born in Washington, D.C., in 1947. She was educated at American University and the University of Connecticut. She has been a recipient of a Guggenheim fellowship (1978) and has been a frequent contributor to *The New Yorker*, and her fiction has been included in many prize-winning collections of short stories. She is the author of three novels, *Chilly Scenes of Winter, Falling in Place,* and *Love Always*; and two volumes of short stories, *Distortions* and *Secrets and Surprises*. In her fiction Beattie tells the stories of disaffected young people who felt defeated after the sixties and depressed in the seventies. The flat tone of nihilism, of a dead-end shopping-mall consumerism, is easy to catch in her work. What has escaped some readers and reviewers, however, is her quirky and freshly deadpan humor and her sympathy for her characters, which comes across in the writer's passion for the particulars of her characters' worlds. The suburban focus of her writing as well as her exposure of the hollowness behind American plenty has contributed to her work being compared with that of John Cheever, J. D. Salinger, and John Updike. Updike, in turn, has compared her to Muriel Spark; he seems to understand Beattie's creative temperament and style better than any other critic: "The accretion of plain lived moments, Miss Beattie has discovered, like Virginia Woolf and Nathalie Sarraute before her, is sentiment's very method; grain by grain the hours and days of fictional lives invest themselves with weight." The novelist Mary Lee Settle has acclaimed Beattie's stories as "the most perceptive since Salinger's. They are not just good writing, not just true to life; they have wonder in them and vision. She shows us haunted images of ordinary days, seen with the clarity of the child's eye in 'The Emperor's New Clothes,' " Settle's insight is an apt introduction to the haunting clarity and memory of the story that follows, "Happiness." No matter how separate the adult lives of two sisters may turn out to be, they are never separated from their mutually haunting and emotional spheres of influence and memory.

Happy

by
Ann Beattie

"Your brother called," I say to my husband on the telephone. "He called to find out if he left his jumpsuit here. As though another weekend guest might have left a jumpsuit."

"As it happens, he did. I mailed it to him. He should have gotten it days ago."

"You never said anything about it. I told him . . ."

"I didn't say anything because I know you find great *significance* in what he leaves behind."

"Pictures of the two of you with your mother, and you were such unhappy little boys . . ."

"Anything you want me to bring home?" he says.

"I think I'd like some roses. Ones the color of peaches."

He clears his throat. All winter, he has little coughs and colds and irritations. The irritations are irritating. At night, he hemms over *Forbes* and I read Blake, in silence.

"I meant that could be found in Grand Central," he says.

"An éclair."

"All right," he says. He sighs.

"One banana, two banana, three banana, four . . ."

"I think you have the wrong number," I say.

"*Fifteen years*, and you still don't know my voice on the phone."

"Oh," I say. "Hi, Andy."

Andy let his secretary use his apartment during her lunch hour to have an affair with the Xerox repairman. Andy was on a diet, drinking pre-digested protein, and he had thrown everything out in his kitchen, so he wouldn't be tempted. He was allowed banana extract to flavor his formula. The secretary and the repairman got hungry and rummaged through the kitchen cabinets, and all they could find was a gallon jug of banana extract.

"I got the Coors account," Andy says. "I'm having a wall of my office painted yellow and silver."

The dog and I go to the dump. The dump permit is displayed on the back window: a drawing of a pile of rubbish, with a number underneath. The dog breathes against the back window and the sticker gets bright with moisture. The dog likes the rear-view mirror and the back window equally well, and since his riding with his nose to the rear-view mirror is a clear danger, I have put three shoe boxes between the front seats as a barrier. One of the boxes has shoes inside that never fit right.

Bob Dylan is singing on the tape deck: "May God bless and keep you always, May your wishes all come true . . ."

"Back her up!" the dump man hollers. Smoke rises behind him, from something smoldering out of a pyramid into flatness. The man who runs the dump fans the smoke away, gesturing with the other hand to show me the position he wants my car to be in. The dog barks madly, baring his teeth.

"Come on, she'll get up that little incline," the dump man hollers.

The wheels whir. The dog is going crazy. When the car stops, I open my door, call "Thank you!" and tiptoe through the mush. I take the plastic bag filled with garbage and another pair of shoes that didn't work out and throw it feebly, aiming for the top of the heap. It misses by a mile, but the dump man has lost interest. Only the dog cares. He is wildly agitated.

"Please," I say to the dog when I get in the car.

"May you always be courageous," Dylan sings.

It is a bright fall day; the way the sun shines makes the edges of things radiate. When we get home, I put the dog on his lead and open the door, go into the mud room, walk into the house. When I'm away for a weekend or longer, things always look the way I expect they will when I come back. When I'm gone on a short errand, the ashtray seems to have moved forward a few inches, the plants look a little sickly, the second hand on the clock seems to be going very fast . . . I don't remember the clock having a second hand.

The third phone call of the day. "Will you trust me?" a voice says. "I need to know how to get to your house from the Whitebird Diner. My directions say go left at the fork for two miles, but I did, and I didn't pass an elementary school. I think I should have gone right at the fork. A lot of people mix up left and right; it's a form of dyslexia." Heavy breathing. "Whew," the voice says. Then: "Trust me. I can't tell you what's going on because it's a surprise."

When I don't say anything, the voice says: "Trust me. I wouldn't be some nut out in the middle of nowhere, asking whether I go right or left at the fork."

I go to the medicine cabinet and take out a brandy snifter of pills. My husband's bottle of Excedrin looks pristine. My brandy snifter is cut glass, and belonged to my grandfather. It's easy to tell my pills apart because they're all different colors: yellow Valium, blue Valium, green Donnatal. I never have to take those unless I go a whole week without eating Kellogg's All-Bran.

A bear is ringing the front doorbell. There are no shades on the front windows, and the bear can see that I see it. I shake my head no, as if someone has come to sell me a raffle ticket. Could this be a bear wanting to sell me something? It does not seem to have anything with it. I shake my head no again, trying to look pleasant. I back up. The bear has left its car with the hazard light flashing, and two tires barely off Black Rock Turnpike. The bear points its paws, claws up, praying. It stands there.

I put a chain on the door and open it. The bear spreads its arms wide. It is a brown bear, with fur that looks like whatever material it is they make bathroom rugs out of. The bear sings, consulting a notebook it has pulled out from somewhere in its side:

Happy birthday to you
I know it's not the day
This song's being sung early
In case you run away

Twenty-nine was good
But thirty's better yet
Face the day with a big smile
There's nothing to regret

I wish that I could be there
But it's a question of money
A bear's appropriate instead
To say you're still my honey

The bear steps back, grandly, quite pleased with itself. It has pink rubber lips.

"From your sister," the bear says. I see the lips behind the lips. "I could really use some water," the bear says. "I came from New York. There isn't any singing message service out here. As it is, I guess this was cheaper than your sister flying in from the coast, but I didn't come cheap."

I step aside. "Perrier or tap water?" I say.

"Just regular water," the bear says.

In the kitchen, the bear removes its head and puts it on the kitchen table. The head collapses slowly, like a popover cooling. The bear has a long drink of water.

"You don't look thirty," the bear says.

The bear seems to be in its early twenties.

"Thank you," the bear says. "I hope that didn't spoil the illusion."

"Not at all," I say. "It's fine. Do you know how to get back?"

"I took the train," the bear says. "I overshot you on purpose—got my aunt's car from New Haven. I'm going back there to have dinner with her, then it doesn't take any more smarts than getting on the train to get back to the city. Thank you."

"Could I have the piece of paper?" I say.

The bear reaches in its side, through a flap. It takes out a notebook marked "American Lit. from 1850." It rips a page out and hands it to me.

I tack it on the bulletin board. The oil bill is there, as yet unpaid. My gynecologist's card, telling me that I have a 10 A.M. appointment the next day.

"Well, you don't look thirty," the bear says.

"Not only that, but be glad you were never a rabbit. I think I'm pregnant."

"Is that good news?" the bear says.

"I guess so. I wasn't trying not to get pregnant."

I hold open the front door, and the bear walks out to the porch.

"Who are you?" I say.

"Ned Brown," the bear says. "Fitting, huh? Brown? I used to work for an escort service, but I guess you know what that turned into." The bear adjusts its head. "I'm part-time at Princeton," it says. "Well," it says.

"Thank you very much," I say, and close the door.

I call the gynecologist's office, to find out if Valium has an adverse effect on the fetus.

"Mister Doctor's the one to talk to about prescription medicine," the nurse says. "Your number?"

Those photographs in *Life*, taken inside the womb. It has ears at one week, or something. If they put in a needle to do amniocentesis, it moves to the side. The horror story about the abortionist putting his finger inside, and feeling the finger grabbed. I think that it is four weeks old. It probably has an opinion on Bob Dylan, pro or con.

I have some vermouth over ice. Stand out in the back yard, wearing one of my husband's big woolly jackets. His clothes are so much more comfortable than mine. The dog has dragged down the clothesline and is biting up and down the cord. He noses, bites, ignores me. His involvement is quite erotic.

There is a pale moon in the sky. Early in the day for that. I see what they mean about the moon having a face—the eyes, at least.

From the other side of the trees, I hear the roar of the neighbors' TV. They are both deaf and have a Betamax with their favorite *Hollywood Squares* programs recorded. My husband pulled a prank and put a cassette of *Alien* in one of the boxes. He said that he found the cassette on the street. He excused himself from dinner to do it. He threw away a cassette of *Hollywood Squares* when we got home. It seemed wasteful, but I couldn't think what else to do with it, either.

Some squash are still lying on the ground. I smash one and scatter the seeds. I lose my balance when I'm bent over. That's a sign of pregnancy, I've heard: being off-kilter. I'll buy flat shoes.

"Do you know who I really love?" I say to the dog.

He turns his head. When spoken to, he always pays attention for a polite amount of time.

"I love you, and you're my dog," I say, bending to pat him.

He sniffs the squash seeds on my hand, noses my fingers but doesn't lick them.

I go in the house and get him a Hershey bar.

"What do you think about everything?" I say to the dog.

He stops eating the clothesline and devours the candy. He beats his tail. Next I'll let him off the lead, right? Wrong. I scratch behind his ears and go into the house and look for the book I keep phone numbers in. A card falls out. I see that I have missed a dentist's appointment. Another card: a man who tried to pick me up at the market.

I dial my sister. The housekeeper answers.

"Madame Villery," I say. "Her sister."

"Who?" she says, with her heavy Spanish accent.

"Which part?"

"Pardon me?"

"Madame Villery, or her sister?" I say.

"Her sister!" the housekeeper says. "One moment!"

"Madame!" I hear her calling. My sister's poor excuse for a dog, a little white yapper, starts in.

"Hello," my sister says.

"That was *some* surprise."

"What did he do?" my sister says. "Tell me about it."

It takes me back to when we were teenagers. My sister is three years younger than I am. For years, she said "Tell me about it."

"The bear rang my doorbell," I say, leaving out the part about the phone call from the diner.

"Oh, God," she says. "What were you doing? Tell me the truth."

For years she asked me to tell her the truth.

"I wasn't doing anything."

"Oh, you were—what? Just cleaning or something?"

Years in which I let her imagination work.

"Yes," I say, softening my voice.

"And then the bear was just standing there? What did you think?"

"I was amazed."

I never gave her too much. Probably not enough. She married a Frenchman that I found, and find, imperious. I probably could have told her there was no mystery there.

"Listen," I say, "it was great. How are you. How's life in L.A.?"

"They're not to be equated," she says. "I'm fine, the pool is sick. It has cracked pool."

"The cement? On the bottom or—"

"Don't you love it?" she whispers. "She says, 'It has cracked pool.' "

"Am I ever going to see you?"

"He put me on a budget. I don't have the money to fly back right now. You're not on any budget. You could come out here."

"You know," I say. "Things."

"Are you holding out on me?" she says.

"What would I hold out?"

"Are you really depressed about being thirty? People get so upset—"

"It's O.K.," I say, making my voice lighter. "Hey," I say. "*Thank* you."

She blows a kiss into the phone. "Wait a minute," she says. "Remember when we played grown-up? We thought they were *twenty*! And the pillows under our nightgowns to make us pregnant? How I got pregnant after you put your finger in my stream of urine?"

"Are you?" I say, suddenly curious.

"No," she says, and doesn't ask if I am.

We blow each other a kiss. I hang up and go outside. The day is graying over. There's no difference between the way the air looks and the non-color of my drink. I pour it on the grass. The dog gets up and sniffs it, walks away, resumes his chewing of the clothesline.

I've taken out one of the lawn chairs and am sitting in it, facing the driveway, waiting for my husband. When the car turns into the drive, I take the clothesline and toss it around the side of the house, so he won't see. The dog doesn't know what to do: be angry, or bark his usual excited greeting.

"And now," my husband says, one arm extended, car door still open, "heeeere's hubby." He thinks Ed McMahon is hilarious. He watches only the first minute of the *Tonight* show, to see Ed. He reaches behind him and takes out a cone of flowers. Inside are roses, not exactly peach-colored, but orange. Two dozen? And a white bag, smudged with something that looks like dirt; that must be the chocolate frosting of my éclair seeping through. I throw my arms around my husband. Our hipbones touch. Nothing about my body has started to change. For a second, I wonder if it might be a tumor—if that might be why I missed my period.

"Say it," he whispers, the hand holding the flowers against my left ear, the hand with the bag covering my right.

Isn't this the stereotype of the maniac in the asylum—hands clamped to both ears to . . . what? Shut out voices? Hear them more clearly? The drink has made me woozy, and all I hear is a hum. He moves his hands up and down, rubbing the sides of my head.

"Say it," he's whispering through the constant roar. "Say 'I have a nice life.' "

MARY ROBISON was born in Washington, D.C. in 1949 and grew up in Ohio, the setting for her novel *Oh*! Her short stories, which appear regularly in *The New Yorker* and *Esquire*, have been collected in three volumes: *Days* (1979), *An Amateur's Guide to the Night* (1983), and *Believe Them* (1988). Robison's fiction has received unanimous high praise from some of our most eminent reviewers and writers. James Wolcott has written, "Mary Robison isn't afraid to light a few hotfoots, tweak a few noses. [Her] flair for brittle talk and catastrophe could result in a comic novel one wouldn't be ashamed to place on the shelf next to the best of Evelyn Waugh." Frances Taliaferro has said that "the temptation is to hear in Mrs. Robison and her colleagues the voice of a generation, the near nihilists in blue jeans who survived the heyday of the counterculture and now sit passively by while the iron enters their souls. Such identifications are convenient . . . but Mrs. Robison's work will not fit cozily into 'the New York sensibility' or the pigeonholes of social history. At her best, [she] is both wise and entertaining, a technician with a sense of humor, a minimalist with a good eye for what can be salvaged from lives of quiet desperation." Finally, Richard Yates believes she writes "like an avenging angel, and I think she may be a genius." The mother of two children, she was a Guggenheim Fellow in 1980 and the Briggs-Copeland Lecturer in English at Harvard. "Sisters," the story that follows here, is a fine example of her absolutely original sensibility, and of the sureness with which she renders the odd discontinuities of our everyday lives. The stories in her latest collection, *Believe Them,* are, in the words of the novelist and short-story writer Bobbie Ann Mason, "terrific—full and resonant and packed with feeling. Her verbal energy is just astonishing."

Sisters

by
Mary Robison

Ray snapped a tomato from a plant and chewed into its side. His niece, Melissa, was sitting in a swing that hung on chains from the arm of a walnut tree. She wore gauzy cotton pants and a twisted scarf across her breasts. Her hair was cropped and pleat-curled.

"Hey," said Penny, Ray's wife. She came up the grass in rubber thongs, carrying a rolled-up news magazine. "If you're weeding, Ray, I can see milkweed and thistle and a dandelion and chickweed from here. I can see sumac."

"You see good," said Ray.

"I just had the nicest call from Sister Mary Clare," Penny said. "She'll be out to visit this evening."

"Oh, boy," Ray said. He spat a seed from the end of his tongue.

"Her name's Lily," Melissa said. "She's my sister and she's your niece, and we don't have to call her Mary Clare. We can call her Lily."

Penny stood in front of Melissa, obscuring Ray's view of the girl's top half—as if Ray hadn't been seeing it all morning.

"What time is Lily coming?" Melissa asked.

"Don't tell her," Ray said to Penny. "She'll disappear."

"Give me that!" Melissa said. She grabbed Penny's magazine and swatted at her uncle.

"Do you know a Dr. Streich?" Penny said, putting a hand on Melissa's bare shoulder to settle her down. "He was a professor at your university, and there's an article in that magazine about him."

"No," Melissa said. She righted herself in the swing.

"Well, I guess you might *not* know him," Penny said. "He hasn't been at your university for years, according to the article. He's a geologist."

"I don't know him," Melissa said.

Penny pulled a thread from a seam at her hip. "He's pictured above the article," she said.

"Blessed be Mary Clare," Ray said. "Blessed be her holy name."

Penny said, "I thought we'd all go out tonight."

"You thought we'd go to the Wednesday Spaghetti Dinner at St. Anne's," Ray said, "and show Lily to Father Mulby."

Penny kneeled and brushed back some leaves on a head of white cabbage.

"I'd like to meet Father Mulby," Melissa said.

"You wouldn't," said Ray. "Frank Mulby was a penitentiary warden before he was a priest. He was a club boxer before that. Years ago."

Ray stuck the remainder of the tomato in his mouth and wiped the juice from his chin with the heel of his hand. "Ride over to the fire station with me," he said to Melissa.

"Unh-unh, I don't feel like it." She got off the board seat and patted her bottom. "I don't see what Mulby's old jobs have to do with my wanting to meet him."

"Why do you want to meet him?" Penny said. She was looking up at Melissa, shading her eyes with her hand.

"To ask him something," Melissa said. "To clear something up."

At the firehouse, two men in uniforms were playing pinochle and listening to Julie London on the radio.

"Gene. Dennis," said Ray.

"What are you here for, Ray?" Dennis said. "You aren't on today. Gene's on, I'm on, those three spades waxing the ladder truck are on." Dennis made a fan with his cards and pressed them on the tabletop.

"I'm supposed to be buying a bag of peat," Ray said. "Only I don't want to." He went around Dennis and yanked open a refrigerator. Under the egg shelf there was taped a picture of a girl in cherry-colored panty hose. "I'm avoiding something," he said. He pulled a Coca-Cola from a six-pack and shut the door. He sat down. "My niece is on the way. I'm avoiding her arrival."

"The good one?" Gene said.

"The good one's here already. I pushed her in the swing

this morning until she got dizzy. This is the other one. The nun." Ray held the can off and pulled the aluminum tab.

"Don't bring her here," Gene said. "I do not need that."

"What*ever* you do," Dennis said.

"No, I wouldn't," said Ray.

"You can bring that Melissa again," Dennis said.

"I wouldn't do that, either. You all bored her." Ray drank from the can.

A short black man came up the steps, holding a chamois cloth. His shirt and pants were drenched.

"Charlie," Ray said, tucking his chin to swallow a belch. "Looking nice."

"They got me with the sprinklers," Charlie said. "They waited all morning to get me."

"Well, they'll do that," Dennis said.

"I know it," the black man said.

"Because they're bored," Ray said. He sat forward. "I ought to go set a fire and give them something to think about."

"I wish you would," Charlie said. He pulled off his shirt.

"Why the hell is he at the lead?" Melissa said. She was looking at Father Mulby, who wore an ankle cast. They were in the big basement hall at St. Anne's, and the priest was carrying a cafeteria tray. Fifty or sixty people waited in line behind him to collect plates of spaghetti and bowls of salad.

"Lookit," Ray said. "You and Sister Mary Clare find a seat and have a talk. Penny and I'll fill some trays and bring them over."

"No, no," the nun said. "It feels good to stand. I've been sitting in a car all day."

"Besides, we couldn't think of anything to tell each other," Melissa said.

"Melissa, there's a lot I want to talk about with you."

"I'm sure."

"There is," Sister said.

"Hey," Ray said to Melissa, "just go grab us a good table if you want to sit down."

"I do," Melissa said. She left her place in line and followed Father Mulby, who had limped to the front of the room and was sitting down at one of the long tables. She introduced herself and asked if she could join him.

"It's reserved," he said. "That seat's reserved for Father Phaeton. Just move over to that side, please." The priest indicated a chair across the table.

"Okay, okay," Melissa said. "When he gets here, I'll jump up." She sat down anyway. Her long hair lifted from around her throat and waved in the cool exhaust of a window fan.

Father Mulby glanced across the room and lit a Camel over his spaghetti. "I guess I can't start until everyone's in place," he said.

"That'll be an hour," Melissa said.

"Here's Father Phaeton," Mulby said.

Melissa changed sides. Ray and Sister Mary Clare joined them and sat down, with Melissa in between. Penny came last. She looked embarrassed to be carrying two trays, one loaded with silverware, napkins, and water glasses.

Ray passed the food and utensils around. "Someone will be bringing soft drinks," he said to Melissa.

"Coffee?" she asked.

"No," Father Mulby said. "We don't serve coffee anymore. The urns and all."

"I'd like to be excommunicated," Melissa told him. "I want the thirteen candles dashed to the ground, or whatever, and I want a letter from Rome."

"I don't know," the old priest said. He forked some salad lettuce into his mouth. "If you kick your sister or push me out of this chair onto the floor, I can excommunicate you."

"What's this about, Father?" said Sister Mary Clare.

"Nothing," Ray said. "Just your sister."

Melissa leaned toward him and said, "Blah, blah, blah." She pushed her plate to one side. "I just have to hit Lily?" she asked Mulby.

"That would be plenty for me," he said.

Ray said, "Eat something, Melissa. Act your age."

"Don't mind me," she said, leaning over the table. She batted the priest's eating hand. "Is that good enough?"

"I'm afraid not," Mulby said.

Father Phaeton, a man with red hair and bad skin, asked Melissa to pass the Parmesan cheese.

"Ignore her, if you can, Father Mulby," Ray said. "I'm sure it's her blood week."

"And the saltcellar, too," Father Phaeton added.

Mulby jerked forward. His large hand closed down on Melissa's wrist. "It's not that," he said to Ray. "I can tell that about a woman by holding her hand, and it's not that."

Penny was lying on the sofa at home. She had a folded washcloth across her forehead. Her eyes were pressed shut against the pain in her head, and tears ran over her cheekbones.

"It's not necessarily a migraine," Ray told her. He had drawn a wing chair up beside the sofa. "My head's pounding, too. Could've been the food."

"I don't think church food could hurt anybody, Ray," said Penny.

The nieces were sitting cross-legged on the rug. "Why not?" Sister Mary Clare said. "It's not blessed or anything. Myself, I've been woozy ever since we ate."

"I just meant they're so clean at St. Anne's," Penny said. "And none of you are sick like I am. Don't try to convince yourselves you are."

"I'm not sick," Melissa said.

"You didn't eat a mouthful," Sister Mary Clare said. She exhaled and stood up.

"I wonder why you visit us every year, Melissa," Penny said.

"Do you mind it?" Melissa asked. "If you do—"

"She doesn't," Ray said.

"No," Penny said, "I don't mind. I just wonder if you girls could find something to do outside for a bit."

"Lily can push me in the swing," Melissa said. "Okay, Lily?"

Penny said, "You should have talked to Father Phaeton, Melissa. They say he's dissatisfied with the life."

"That would have been the thing," Ray said. He told the nieces, "Maybe I'll go out back with you, so Penny can get better."

Penny took his hand and squeezed it.

"Maybe I won't," he said. He turned the washcloth on his wife's brow.

* * *

Sister Mary Clare stood in the moonlight by a tomato stake. She was fingering her rosary beads.

"Don't be doing that," Melissa said. She moved down to the end of the lawn, where it was bordered by a shallow stream. She bent over the water. In the moonlight, she saw a school of minnows swerve over a fold in the mud next to an old bike tire.

Sister Mary Clare followed Melissa and said, behind her, "I won't be seeing you again. I'm going into cloister."

Melissa leaned against a tall tree. She dug her thumbnail into a bead of sweet gum on the bark.

"And I'm taking a vow of silence," the nun said. "Do you think it's a bad idea?"

"I think it's a good idea, and probably what you want. I'm glad."

"If you care, I'm not very happy," Sister said.

"You were never happy," Melissa said. "The last time I saw you laughing was the day that swing broke. Remember that day?"

"Yes. Ray was in it when it went."

Melissa smiled. "He used to pay me a quarter to sit on his lap and comb his hair."

"I know," Sister said. "He still would."

Melissa hugged herself with her bare arms. "It won't matter before long. I'm getting old."

"So is Ray," Sister said. "But he's why you come here, I think."

"So what? There aren't many people I like, Lily."

"Me neither."

"Well, there you are," Melissa said. "The miracle is, I keep having such a good time. It almost seems wrong."

"You still do?"

"Every day," Melissa said, heading back for the stream. "Such a wonderful time."

IVY GOODMAN was born in Harrisburg, Pennsylvania, in 1953. Her stories have appeared in *Fiction, The Ark River Review*, and *Ploughshares*. One story was included in *Prize Stories 1981* and another in *Prize Stories 1982*. She has studied at the University of Pennsylvania and Stanford University, where she was a Mirrielees Fellow. "Revenge," the story that follows, was included in her first published collection of short stories, *Heart Failure* (1983).

Revenge
by
Ivy Goodman

We don't know why she disappeared or why she mailed back Mother's checks before she walked off to who knows where, or perhaps someone drove her. She doesn't have a car herself, and the police say she sold her bicycle. Anyone in her right mind would have cashed those checks before vanishing. "I can't accept these checks," she wrote. "But I want you to know that I greatly appreciate everything. I have decided to change my name and default on my education loans. Don't try to look for me."

She has always tended toward melodrama. When she was thirteen she strode bleary-eyed into a drugstore to buy a bottle of aspirin to kill herself with. She thought you could kill yourself with aspirin. Once inside, distracted by the magazine rack on the main aisle, she forgot about pain killers and wasted her dollar on something called "Teen" or "Sixteen" or "Fifteen." You know the kind of periodical: the numerically descriptive name always appeals to a younger set, the audience toward whom it's aimed anyway.

"I don't buy magazines now," she said the last time she visited. We were standing in a grocery, in line at the check-out. "I look at them while waiting in places like this." Casually, she chose that week's "Notorious" from a stack near the chewing gum. "Or else I go to the library. You'd be surprised at all the junk they have in the library."

No, her terrible tastes haven't changed, but that day even she mocked them. "You have to laugh at yourself," she said later, tossing a throw-pillow in my living room.

"Put that pillow down," I told her. It was one of many I've needlepointed. But she doesn't approve of crafts. She doesn't approve of needlepoint.

"Look." She prodded my block initials, stitched in red at the tip of a bargelloed conch shell. "It's like signing your name to follow-the-dots. Why don't you stop buying kits and make up your own patterns?"

"I don't have to defend myself to you. So you've read more books than I have. Does that make you a better secretary?" After eighteen years in the classroom, she types for a living. "And it's not even a living. Mother told me about the checks she sends you. In California." Paradise burst with a needlepoint. See, I can be as clever as she thinks she is. "I know what you really are. At twenty-five, an aging, depressed camper in black tee shirt and khakis, riding a bicycle." I smiled. That always has bothered her.

"Witch," she said. "Everyone knows you're uglier."

"Would you like my magnifying mirror? I have one that will triple the size of your laugh lines. Before you know it, you'll have a definite muzzle. You should take better care of your skin. If only you weren't still battling acne."

"You . . . ."

She wanted to hit me, I could tell. I decided to let her pound me like a pillow for old times' sake. Then I would strike once, hard, and make her crumple before telling Mother, who was visiting, too, and dozing in the family room. But over the years, my sister has learned to sublimate. Instead of me, she turned on my seashell puff, which is backed with velveteen, and bit into a corner of it. She gritted. She wrenched. But the piping defeated her.

"Do your gums ache?" I took the pillow, damp with saliva and dashed with teeth marks, away from her. "You're worse than a dog. Why don't you rest your head in your paws? Go lie down somewhere."

I left her crying in the dining room, Mother still asleep on one of the downstairs loungers. "See you later," I called. It was two-thirty, time to pick up Stefan, my son, at his nursery school.

When I came back with Steffy, who was plucking at a necklace he'd strung that afternoon, I found both Mother and Anna slouched on the family room sofa and glaring at the fish tank. "Hello," I said from the top of the stairs. "The life's gone out of Anna, I see. Mother, you're awake again."

Steffy scrambled down the steps, one at a time but quickly, and shouted, "Hi, everybody."

"Hi," Anna said, turning away her face, sallower than ever above her favorite dreary crew neck.

Stefan rushed to Mother and tugged at the knitting in her lap. Mother said, "Oh, I forgot I was working on this. Betsy, I know you two were fighting. Make up."

I shook my head. "I don't want to aggravate you with the details, Mother."

"Aggravate," Stefan murmured.

"I'm sorry." Anna barely moved her lips. "I'm oh so."

"I'll bet you are." I smiled. "Zombie."

"Stop it," Mother said. "When you two fight, it's a knife in my side."

"And Betsy twists it," Anna said.

"Who dug it in in the first place?" I asked. "Who carries a bowie in her pants pocket?"

"Stop it! Stop it! If you don't, I'll bang your heads together." Instead, Mother gripped Stefan's head, he cried, and then she hugged him. "See how you confuse me?"

"It's a game, Steffy," I said. He nestled his face in Mother's bosom and giggled there. "That's right, make nice. Nana's sorry. Aren't we all."

"Yes," Anna sobbed, "that I'm alive."

"Well." I hesitated. "Only most of the time."

"You girls take my heart and tear it. *I* could die." Mother dropped her cheek onto Anna's black cotton shoulder and wept out loud. "My own flesh and blood. Both."

Startled, Stefan lifted his head with a wail.

"Mommy's coming, Steff." I stumbled downstairs and onto the sofa with tears in my own eyes.

"Girls," Mother said.

"Betsy," Anna said.

"Anna," I said.

Mother clutched my neck, Stefan, sighing, curled on my hip, wiped his nose with a hank of my hair, and I stretched some fingers to my sister, who squeezed them hard. For five minutes at least, we hugged and whispered ("I'm sorry," "No, *I'm* sorry," "Forgive me," "Why do we?" and "Never again") while Stefan parroted us and hummed. That's how we settle things in our family, although nothing stays settled for long.

But happiness hovered for a while. Uncharacteristically generous, Anna began cooking dinner, manicotti from scratch, dough, filling, and sauce. She puttered in the kitchen until six. (Quite therapeutic. That's why I encouraged her, even though my husband, Solomon, is not a pasta eater.) Only one crisis arose. Unobserved, Stefan patted his baby hands in the bowl of grated Parmesan, licked his fingers and patted again, scratched his scalp, picked his nose and wiped his hands on his jersey and jodhpurs (in whatever order). When the bowl overturned, we finally discovered him, fuzzy all over with pale cheese dust. "No," Anna said, "oh no."

"Don't worry, he's fine. Mother," I called, my palm raised to keep my laughing son at arm's length, "would you wash Steff?"

Squirming, he whined, "Leave me alone, go, go," while Mother buffed him all over with a damp dish towel. Not satisfied, she carried him upstairs for an early bath.

Anna squeezed a sponge into the sink and said, "I guess I'll wipe up the floor." She bent down and brushed cheese and shards into a pile near my chair. "After I'd grated all that. And the bowl."

"Don't worry about the bowl."

Still squatting, she looked up. "Betsy?"

"What?"

"I can't please any of you anymore."

"You can if you try."

"Oh?" On all fours, she edged closer, open mouthed, a large depressed pet. She had no idea who she was. I could have told her anything then. ("Oh?" "Yes?" "I am?")

Through the evening she stayed tame, at the table speaking softly, after dinner gladly rinsing all those sauce-stained plates and stocking the dishwasher alone. Then, a night of broken sleep (in a sleeping bag on the living room floor—she could have joined Mother on the sofa bed, but she adamantly shook her head no), and she was Miserable Anna, snarling at her leash again.

But withdrawal is nothing new for her, and as usual, within twenty-four hours, she warmed. At the end of the week, when we hugged goodby at the airport, she said, "Betsy, I don't want to leave you. I'll try to come back soon."

Every few days the police call for information, but what more can I say? I would quote from old letters if I could, but when one arrived, annually, my custom was to tear open the envelope, skim the note, scrawled on a card with buds blooming in the margins, and then destroy everything before the mailman reached my next door neighbor's box. Still, let's see how good my memory is: "Thanks so much for remembering my birthday." "The blouse is beautiful and fits perfectly." "I love the orchid sweater." "Candles burn in the candlesticks this second, even though it is mid-morning, sunny and bright, here." "Kiss each other for me. Love, Anna."

We "remembered" her birthday because she remembered ours, along with wedding anniversaries, and for the strange things she sent us (painted papier mâché boxes, four rag rugs the size of place mats, a string game, several unassembled kites, and books, books, and more books, probably because they can be sent fourth-class special rate), we had to repay her somehow. Actually, I enjoyed wasting time once a year, jamming plastic hangers down sportswear racks, picking through piles on display tables, occasionally asking for something out of reach that struck me as particularly hideous. It was fun to go after what I'd never want for myself (thank God), what I hoped I'd never have to see again. I bought it, asked for a box, and shipped it parcel post to insure that it would reach her days, if not weeks, after she celebrated. Of course, I spent a fair amount for these things and gave the price tags to Mother, who could be depended on to do her part unwittingly by telephone. "Anna, did you get the package from Betsy yet? Oh, I'm sure you will, any day now. I hope you like it. Don't tell her I told you, but you better like it, she spent thirty dollars for that peignoir set."

When the battered box, which had travelled by land across the continent, finally arrived on Anna's doorstep, I imagine she cut the scratchy twine with scissors she'd had handy for days, in anticipation. The brown paper, already torn, would peel off easily; the pink gift wrap, if I bothered with it that year, would be next; and then there'd be the box itself, from Teenland, Artifactory, Cuddle Up, or any of the worse stores, and dented probably. The lid would shake in her hands. She would be breathing hard enough to blow the inner tissue sheets apart. And after lifting out that cheap-looking expensive robe and nightgown, dripping lace and embroidered LONELY; after trying on the mis-sized plaid blouse (the tag said six but twelve was more accurate) with the flapped yellow breast pockets; after stepping back and realizing that the frosted glass candlesticks still looked like frozen slush, even from a distance; after sniffing and dabbing for twenty minutes before concluding that the very orchid mohair pullover on her back was making her nostrils twitch so; she would scream the way she screamed when she turned ten and hated the necklace our Aunt Ella gave her. That's right, another birthday down the drain, Anna.

Her optimism crushed again, my sister wouldn't merely give up, shelve the gift in her closet, and sit down to pen a thank you. She would ball the sweater, hurl it toward a wall, and shriek in frustration when it unfolded midway there. She would poke her fingers through the loosest neckline stitches, wind excess yarn around her pinkie, and tug until her fingertip swelled red. But no runs, no ravels; that mohair was sturdy stuff, and she wouldn't have the nerve to lift her scissors to it. She would stomp on the shirt, spit in its pockets, and then cram it into her laundry bag, to be drowned in a hot wash at the end of the work week. Not until she held it up, fresh from the dryer and still billowy, would she read the tag that said, "100% Polyester Fibers. Unshrinkable." In due time, after failing to smash them, she probably donated the candlesticks to a thrift shop. Only one year was she bold enough to send something (that peignoir set) back to me. "Lovely, but too small across the bodice, Betsy." Bodice? After I threatened Mother and Mother threatened her, she never tried that again. The past few years she must have calmed down over honey-lemon tea and iced cookies before composing the sweetest notes to us. "Kiss each other for me. Love, Anna." Kiss each other where, Anna?

We are really alike, my sister and I. I am just waiting for her to become herself. On paper she was powdered sugar; in person, gloom, doom, and superiority. Don't you think we saw the contradictions, Annie? She struggled to keep her distance from me (after all, until she disappeared she lived thousands of miles from here), but sometimes, in adolescent desperation (though she should have outgrown *that* years ago), she telephoned. "Dates," I always summarized after she stopped crying. "Boys. Things between people never go perfectly. Why don't you get married already?"

After she's found, before long, she will marry. And after that, she will have children. She will do what I've done.

Except I did it first, Anna. Remember that when you need advice about colic, drapes, finances, and the drudgery of a sixth anniversary.

Enough. I must get the salads ready. Solomon just turned into the driveway, and Stefan, smearing the window with his fingers and tongue, gurgles, "Daddy, Daddy," from the living room. I glance out the back door, and for just a moment I think I see my sister, her dark eyes peering out from inside Stefan's log cabin playhouse. I shudder, decide it's nothing, and towel the lettuce dry.

"Bitsy-Betsy," Solomon calls.

"Coming, Solo."

I move to close the door and catch her eyes again. No, it can't be.